FRAGMENTED DESIRES

M.K. Jensen

Contents

HI,

Thank you so much for taking a chance on my baby debut! If you are reading this, just know that I am already filled from the tips of my toes to the top of my head with gratitude for this actually happening. My goal is to always write stories about characters that will make my readers feel seen, heard, and loved. That you see the struggles that they face and the actual hardship of overcoming them. The "too much" that we all tend to feel about our personalities and how we can find our home outside of blood relations. I want to make sure that all my readers feel important and cared for. If you are not here for spice, then feel free to skip chapters:

And I implore you to check the content warnings. Your mental health is always the most important. Thank you again and I hope you find a home at West Haven.

Off page overdose

Explicit sexual content

Off page recount of rape (very brief and non descriptive)

Retelling of physical abuse

Grief

Panic attacks

Physical Violence

Anxiety rep

Insomnia

"This is life, and imperfection is beautiful.
And don't be afraid of that."
-Dylan O'Brien

Playlist

BAD DAY – CHARLOTTE SANDS
DAYDREAM – WE THREE
TRIBULATION – MATT MAESON
BITE MARKS – ARI ABDUL
LOVE ME – EX HABIT
NOTICE ME – ROLE MODEL, BENEE
HOLD ME STEADY – BOUNDARY RUN BREATH
AWAY – ARTEMAS
FEEL SOMETHING – JAYMES YOUNG
SMELLS LIKE TEEN SPIRIT – STEVIE HOWIE
WANT ME – STEPHEN DAWES
LOVE BITES (STRIPPED) – JADE LEMAC
FEELS LIKE – GRACIE ABRAMS
I'LL BE DAMNED – GAVN!
SWEET DREAMS (ARE MADE OF THIS) – WEEZER
FALLING APART – MICHAEL SCHULTE
SUGAR – ROBIN SCHULZ, FRANCESCO YATES
(LEAVE ME) WITH MY MIND – BENNIE
SHIVERS – DISTRICT 78, MIKAYLA LYNN
YOU'RE LIKE – JAMIE FINE
SWEET DREAMS – RAVENS ROCK
TWIN FLAME -MGK
END CREDITS – EDEN, LEAD KELLY
ROUTINES IN THE NIGHT – TWENTY ONE PILOTS
KEEPER – MACKENZY MACKAY
CONTROL – ZOE WEES

One

"You taught me my language."

AJ

T he heart is such a fickle bitch. She takes and gives when she feels necessary and without any regard for how it will affect anyone or anything.

His heart is just weak. Sometimes this just happens. He needs to have less stress in his life. Healthier meals. Light exercise but not excessive exertion. He needs to live like he is retired, because he is. His body has taken so much impact.

That's what the doctors said to me. Like I could somehow control what he chooses to do with his life. Eddie chooses to live his life the same way he raised us all, with impulsive decisions and a *-I'll handle it-* attitude towards everything. He's not a man of planning and processing. He is barely a man who plans what he is going to eat for dinner.

"I played 'ward'." Eddie's voice breaks through my thoughts, bringing back to the game we are playing. He's annoyed and I can hear it in the shortness of his words, but when our eyes meet over the Scrabble board, his expression can be mistaken for emotionless. But I know him well enough to know that he is trying to keep me from becoming emotional. "It's your go, or you can continue to sit and think about how you plan to keep me a prisoner in my own home." He's testing my ability to stay unaffected by what happened to him. To pretend like I didn't just wait for hours in a hospital waiting room while they ran test after test on him and we had to wait for answers. But I don't answer him, and instead I play 'coward' off his word, watching his head dip a bit.

His voice is low with apprehension, "you're taking it easy on me… How long are you going to be mad at me?" He lays down a few more letters to spell out a word that I'm pretty sure isn't even real, but I'm not going to correct him this time. I'm not intentionally taking it easy on him. I just don't have the energy to think about Scrabble at the moment and pretend we are having a normal Sunday night dinner.

"It was a message. I'm not taking it easy on you. I was calling you a coward." I play my next word as he leans forward and rests his arms on the table. I glance up and catch him watching me through narrowed eyes. Whatever seems to be resting in his mind, he lets it go as he sighs and drops his arms back down from the table.

He clears his throat before saying, "Avery, they shouldn't have called you." His words are a momentary apology. His jaw sets as he continues, "I told them I would handle it because I knew that it would just upset you. I'm alive. I'm not dead." His words seem aggressive but he delivers them with reassurance. He starts rearranging his letters, clearly trying to move the conversation on.

I wasn't having it though, "a heart attack is fucking serious, Eddie." He chuckles at me as I get up to get a bottle of water, grabbing him one too, and placing it down in front of him.

"Language, Av." He scolds me softly as he tilts his head back to where my chair still sits vacant, inviting me to sit back down. I make a show of staying back and leaning against his island counter instead.

"You taught me my language." I open my bottle of water, stare down at it in my hands, and watch as the sweat droplets race down the side. I try to swallow but then I think about what heart attacks usually result in, and my throat gets tighter. I think about how lucky I am to be in the same room as him. "Heart attacks are serious." My voice is no louder than a whisper of a breath. I feel my eyes start to burn, but I fucking hate crying, and will myself to hold in the tears.

I don't even hear him get out of the chair before he is standing in front of me and taking the bottle of water out of my hands. He sets it down on the counter next to me before he wraps me up in a hug. His arms swallow me whole and the second he tucks my head under his with the back of his hands, the tears I'm fighting so hard to keep locked in free fall.

"I know, kid. I'm so sorry." His voice is softer than it had been earlier. For such a big bear of a man, he's always able to comfort me with the steadiness of his voice. Less than thirty seconds. That's how long I allow myself to feel helpless before I pull away from his hug and wipe the residual tears from under my eyes. I turn back around to where I have all his meds lined up on the counter and start sorting them into a daily organizer. They are mainly just supplements and aspirin, but I've convinced him that they were prescribed by the doctor mixed with his blood pressure medicine and new anxiety medication to help regulate his stress levels.

I can tell he's cleaning up the Scrabble board and letters from the noise and find myself thankful for the type of man Eddie is. He's always been this way with me. Ever since he met me when I was fifteen years old. He never pushes me, but he always gives me space to feel what I need to feel and react the way I need to react. He's the closest thing I have to a parent, and I nearly lost him.

Eight years he has been taking care of me. Now I have to make sure I take care of him because the thought of losing him paralyzes me. I sat in that waiting room for over two hours waiting to just see him. Then I sat in the room by his hospital bed for five more waiting for him to wake up. And when he finally did wake up, he was only awake long enough to squeeze my hand and tell me he was okay before sleep took him away again.

Oliver had sat next to me and just held my hand. We sat in silence for a long time together just listening to the consistent and haunting beeps of the hospital machines until Eli and Maxwell came back to the room. The triplets are all the best personalities split into three people. Oliver is my best friend. Eli and Max are like little brothers, even though they are two years older than me.

They all took me in when I lost everything. A shadow that they plucked off the streets. Eddie brought me in to clean the gym floors and sanitize equipment at the end of the classes every day when he first met me. The boys didn't even know I existed for a couple of years. I came in when everyone left, and worked hard to make sure I left no trace of me being there. That's the way I liked it and Eddie never questioned me. He just left the key on the counter to lock up with a note to leave it in the mailbox when I left.

I did that for two years, until he offered me the apartment above the gym when he realized I didn't have anywhere to stay. He paid me to clean, but that was just enough to buy food and a few clothes when I absolutely needed them. It was too cold to stay on the streets and I knew Eddie wouldn't ask questions. That was our agreement. I mark off the checklist, he allows me to stay in the apartment, and he asks no questions. He had groceries dropped at the apartment door every Sunday though. Always accompanied with a note to join him and his sons for dinner.

I threw that stupid blue post-it note away every Sunday for eight months. Who used blue post-it notes? Eddie never brought it up when he did see me. He never asked me any questions. He would always just smile and wave as he walked out the door, the key always on the counter waiting for me to lock up the gym after I cleaned. Still it was the most that anyone had ever given me. Consistency.

Then one day, there was a knock on my door. When I peeped through the hole fully expecting Eddie to be standing there, it was a younger version of him. I don't know why I opened the door that day, but I did.

Oliver was standing there holding a pair of worn out gloves. He extended them to me, and just walked down the stairs with no hesitation that I would just follow him. And I did. We've trained every day since then.

"The boys will be here in about an hour. Eli and Maxwell said that they would cook dinner." The sound of the box sliding across the bookshelf pulls me from my thoughts. The same bookshelf that I have because I love his so much that the boys searched every thrift store until they found an exact replica for my birthday last year.

"Does that mean we should go ahead and order a few pizzas? Just in case?" The laugh that leaves him makes my heart feel a little less constricted. I know he is alive and standing before me, but it feels impossible to shake the feeling that flooded my body when I got that phone call that he was lying in a hospital bed.

"They'll just pout." He pulls out his phone and waives it at me. "I'll place the order about thirty minutes after they get here." I'm finishing putting his pill bottles back in the medicine cabinet when he comes to stand beside me.

I hand him the medicine schedule I meticulously wrote out and straighten my shoulders to imitate him when he wants to be serious. "You have to follow this. Down to every little detail." I tap the paper before he takes a magnet and puts it on the fridge next to us.

"I promise." He opens the fridge and there is no stopping the grin I'm wearing when he hangs his head in defeat. I know he's looking at the empty shelf where he always keeps his beer. "What the fuck did you do with it?" I'm fully smiling at how *he* is the one pouting now.

I walk over and pat him on the shoulder before I open up the freezer to show him that I also got rid of all the overly processed frozen meals and frozen mozzarella cheese sticks he has a slight addiction to. "Your diet also has to change, Eddie." He has a tendency to eat girl dinners most nights. That's probably what led to an unhealthy heart.

"Avery." He warns as he shuts the fridge and pivots to me. A normal person would find his menacing stare intimidating. But this man taught me to not be fearful of anyone else in my life ever again, especially not him. So, I hold my ground.

"Eddie." I match his stance by crossing my arms over my chest and we have a staring contest that I know I will win. Eddie needs glasses and his eyes have been bothering him a lot more lately, but he refuses to go to the eye doctor. After less than a minute, sure enough, his eyes start to twitch.

"Damn it." He admits defeat and I smirk as I walk over to sit in the living room. He follows me and folds his body in his chair and sulks like Max does when we all gang up on him.

"Doctor's orders. Clean diet. No exertion, no stress, relaxing activities only." I remind him and turn the tv on, putting on Love is Blind. We have just enough time to watch one episode before the guys get here. He loves the show but will never allow them to know he watches it. It's been our little secret since season one.

"I have to coach classes, Av. I don't have a choice. Oliver has his rehab and can't take on any more classes. Max and Eli already have a full schedule." He runs his hand through his hair, which is still full and thick even in his old age. Must be good genes because all the West men have the same hair. Slightly fluffy, the lightest shade of brown, and with a slight curl.

"You actually don't have to coach at all. I already sent out an email to the rosters that I'll be filling in for you. And I'll take over striking with fighters. You can write up the workouts and I'll just execute them." I turn the volume up on the show to really drive home the point that I am not going to allow room for discussion or argument. He's too important to too many people. If the doctors want him all but on bed rest, I'll make sure that happens.

"Of course you did. For someone who does not like people... you sure are offering to take on a lot of interaction with people." He raises an eyebrow at me and I just shrug my shoulders.

"I owe you everything, Eddie." My throat tightens again as I pick at the loose thread on his worn out couch. It's my favorite couch, it always provides the perfect nap. Or the safe space to figure out what I'm struggling with.

"You don't owe me shit. You deserve everything you have, Avery. You've fought hard for it." He reminds me with full authority. He's been with me every step of the way as I taught myself how to live a full life, free of fear and hardship. Silence blankets the room for a few long moments before he clears his throat. "When you decided to become the boss of my gym did you also see that I have a new fighter coming to train in a few days?"

Well, that steals all my attention. He gets up and grabs some paper-work from the kitchen table, walking back into the living room. Then he drops a folder in my lap. "His name is Rory. He and Oliver used to train together a bit when they were younger. Competed against each other a few times. He has quick hands and fantastic ground work. He's a solid fighter. He just entered a new circuit to try and make his way through one final time for the UFC. Has a fight set to secure a sponsorship for the big leagues." Eddie goes through his breakdown like he does any other time we have a new fighter that wants to train with him.

"What is his footwork like?" I question as I grip the folder a little tighter in excitement and anticipation. It's always exciting to get to train someone new, but I will be training this guy on my own. Eddie full on laughs at my question, as I expect him to. I've always been such a fan of good footwork. Makes a fighter look like a poet. It's the foundation for every fighter that makes an impression on the sport. Footwork will separate you from skill and luck. Discipline is found in the footwork.

"I'll let you be the judge. He'll be at the gym on Monday morning. Since you want to put me on house arrest, you can take over his training." He thinks he's giving me the order to train him, but I wasn't going to give him the option. He needs to take it easy, and if I have to fight him to make him do it, I will. He nods to the folder I'm holding one last time before giving the show playing on the tv his full attention.

I open the folder and memorize all his fight card stats, training history, and pull out my phone to pull up some of his recent fights. I always love watching fighting. I grew up around it and learned to appreciate the dedication of it. It's an art. I've never trained a fighter solo, but I'm excited. Eddie has taught me everything he knows. I've trained every day for roughly the past six years. I never fought professionally, but I could have. Eddie made sure of it. I genuinely just enjoy training. It's my therapy and honestly without it, I probably wouldn't be here. That's how Eddie met me. I passed by his gym every day on my walk home. Eventually, I would stop and just watch his classes until they were over from the sidewalk. One day he came out and introduced himself and asked if I would be interested in making some extra money. I don't know what Eddie saw in me that day, but I am so thankful that he did. Eddie saved my life before he even knew what my life entailed.

Two

*"I don't trust people
who actually sleep."*

AJ

The air is different when I'm in the gym before the sun breaks the sky and creeps through the front doors. It's eerie and peaceful, wrapped up in a space that always allows me to spill my thoughts without uttering a word. It's just my playlist, my heartbeat, and the darkness. I've had the same routine since I was seventeen. I wake up, I work jump rope, I lift, I take a few laps around the building, and then I hit the bag until my arms can no longer hold a form.

Eddie used to tell me that the sound of hitting a bag was like listening to classical music for him. I always returned his sentiment with a look that clearly showed he was full of shit. I hate classical music. I respect that it has its place and is a part of history. Personally, I am desperate for music that has the ability to interrupt my thoughts instead of pulling a blanket over them. When I first started my morning workouts at the gym, I was always accompanied by Oliver or Eddie. Oliver usually was my workout partner six days out of the week. Occasionally though, Eddie would want to step in. I think he missed the one on one time we used to have when he first brought me in. Eddie would teach me proper order of everything and the best way to take care of my body afterwards. For a man in his forties, he makes it a point to keep his body in the best shape I have ever seen. I guess when you've trained martial arts nearly your whole life it becomes as natural as breathing. Still wasn't enough to protect his heart from nearly failing.

When Oliver showed up at my doorstep with those gloves that day I would have never thought that training would be something that was as vital as breathing in my life. Some days I thought it was what saved my life. Then I realized it was the way Eddie intertwined training with the way he stepped in as a parent and gave me a purpose more than idly walking the streets. Steady is the only word that comes to mind when I think about describing Eddie. And he took his own steadiness and built a foundation here at the gym to help others find theirs. I admire that.

I'm finishing up stretching the tightness out of my muscles when I hear footsteps across the floor. I don't remember the door opening but I didn't have to look up to know it was Oliver. He perpetually smells like cinnamon and mint from all the muscle rub he uses, and he's been using more of it lately since his rehab with his injured left leg after having surgery. He always complains of the way his muscles won't relax. His shoes stop a few inches from where I am bent over stretching my hamstrings.

"You sleep any?" The accusation is drenching his voice. I silently curse the fact that he knows me so well. I even used a little bit of concealer this morning to hide the shadows under my eyes. I straighten back to regular height, which is still about half a foot shorter than he is with my five foot four inch frame.

I narrow my eyes at him as I open my mouth, "I don't trust people who actually sleep." I turn to grab a jump rope, also grabbing an extra one for him. If he's going to come here and berate me for my sleeping habits then he can work out with me too.

"You need to sleep, AJ..." He grabs the jump rope, but his hand closes over mine for a moment making me look back up at him. He opens his mouth and closes it and then opens it again. He is clearly weighing his words. "You have to sleep. I know you don't want my help anymore, but you have to sleep." His lips smash together in a hard line. He hates confronting me. We don't do that to each other. We never push, we just allow the other to take up part of our space with the comfort of always knowing we have that space to be in. It's a safety net for us both.

I give him a small smile before pulling my hand away. "My body will give out like it always does and then I will sleep." I dismiss his worry. I walk over and grab my phone to put on some music. I pull up my go-to playlist and scroll to connect to the sound system when Sweet Dreams starts playing loudly. I swing my head to find Oliver holding up his phone as he winks. This song has always been one of my favorites and I have it on every playlist because I'm only slightly obsessed. I even have it in every covered version released. It just scratches my brain in all the right ways.

Roughly an hour later, we reach the gym breathless and our muscles feeling more than loose from our morning run. I saved my bag work for last this morning. Which may have been a bad decision considering the two guys who have now set up their equipment on the open floor. Max and Eli both perk up with the biggest smiles on their faces when they hear the door open.

They drop the bags they are pulling equipment out of softly and rush over to us. "AJ… please be in our video…" Max's voice is an octave higher with the way he is begging through a whine. Maxwell is the youngest of the triplets and it's moments like this when it truly shows. He is used to getting his way just by flashing his cute dimple and a soft smile. I don't blame him though, it works nearly every time.

"Leave her alone, Maxie. She was in one last week, which means she's reached her limit." Eli says as he pulls me in for a hug. He quickly pulls away in mock disgust. Probably because he can feel the sweat residing on my skin. "You smell. Maybe you should go shower and take a nap." He lightly pushes me and scrunches up his nose, but he's smiling.

I slap his chest and push him back a few steps while he laughs. "How dare you. I do not smell!" I say, pulling my hair out of my ponytail to start braiding it down my back. When I hit my bag I always prefer a braid so my hair doesn't swing so violently back and forth. Then it dawns on me the second part of what he said. I turn around to face all three of them at the same time. I look each one directly in the eye as the feeling of being targeted burns my chest. The heat travels up my neck and I take a breath to keep the angry tears from stinging my eyes. I hate when they do this.

"I absolutely will not allow you to gang up on me. It has just been a few stressful days getting everything lined out to take over Eddie's classes. Making sure he has what he needs and doesn't leave his house. He is the one that you all should be bullying." I scold them. At least I try to. The bottom line is, they have been like this for a few years now. If one thought that I needed something the other two banded together to try and make it happen. I love them, but the thought of putting them in a chokehold always seems so pleasing when they team up against me like this.

Max puts his hands up before reaching behind me and grabbing a small hand towel off the clean rack. He hands it to me and lightly squeezes my shoulder before saying, "We hear you. Dad just wants to make sure you are taken care of too. You worry about him enough for all of us. It's our job to worry about you." I can feel a groan bubbling up from the depth of my throat. Before I am able to release it, he continues talking. "Time to film. I want to finish before Rory gets here." He turns around to make his way back to where they left their equipment and Eli follows after him. Max is the sweetest out of the brothers. He's always cracking jokes and emanating warmth in whatever room he walks into.

I hear what I think is meant to be words, but sounds like an irritated mumble coming out of Oliver's mouth as his brothers go back to filming their content. Honestly, I'm impressed with how serious they are with it. I face Oliver, his face all scrunched up and jaw tight, and ask him, "Why does your face look like that?"

He motions for me to sit on the bench in the space in front of where he is now sitting. His whole body taking on a new kind of stiffness. Oliver and I are best friends. A few times, that had become questionable and messy but he is still someone I can read almost better than my favorite worn out book. Then I remember that Eddie told me Oliver and the new fighter that is coming in to start training, Rory, used to train together and compete when they were younger. Eddie did not mention any bad blood between the two guys though. I have a feeling that's what Oliver is about to educate me on though since he clearly got agitated at just the mention of Rory's name.

He grabs my wraps and holds his palm out for me to place my hand in his. He is so focused in this moment, his eyes following every motion of the wrap as it circles my hand and wrist. His thoughts are lost in the motions. He has my wrist intricately wrapped now and he tests how tight he has it by pulling it before wrapping around again. Normally, I enjoy watching him wrap my hands up. It's therapeutic in a way. Watching something come to completion with such care to detail and determination. I wait for him to tell me what is bothering him, but it becomes clear when he is almost finished wrapping my other hand that he has no plans to let me inside his thoughts today. So I don't push. That isn't how we function with each other. I let him finish my wraps, and then I wrap his hands in silence as well.

"Pad work or bag work?" He asks me as we rise from the bench. I raise my eyebrows at him because he actually hates holding pads and with my height difference... holding them for him was hard. Not to mention that he has to hold back so much power when I am the one holding the pads for him. I look up at him and take in the slump of his shoulders and the barely there tick of his jaw that hasn't gone away. He isn't angry, he's anxious. Over Rory? I bet he could easily work him over in the ring. That is what Oliver is best at. He can put pressure on you in the ring to the point where it feels like you are suffocating. I want to ask again what is bothering him but I really want to get some bag work in, it silences the chaos in my mind. And I need the chaos to go away with all the extra stress I've been putting on myself. But I relent to give Oliver what he clearly needs at this moment.

I start walking towards the ring and smile at him over my shoulder as I tell him, "Grab my favorite set. Lucky for you the run has loosened up my legs. And I've been dying to work on some kicks." I catch a glimpse of a grin on his face before I reach up to pull myself up on the ropes to enter our ring. I remember when Eddie had the new ring brought in. The gym was a mess for a week afterwards while we rearranged and found everything a new home.

Oliver steps into the ring with me and slips his hands through the handles of the pads. He glances up at the giant clock we have on the wall by the front doors and nods before saying, "We have about thirty minutes before your new project walks through those doors. Let's get started." He tilts his head at my gloves on the ground. I could hear the teasing in his voice as I wrapped the velcro around my wrists. "I expect you to not hold back at all. I know how hard you can hit, A." He slaps the pads together and I get into position.

Three

RORY

"**A**J should be at the gym already when you get there. Go through the front doors and I'm sure you'll find them all in the ring or by the bags," Eddie instructs from the other end of the call. Initially, I was supposed to start my training a week ago with him. Then he called me and let me know that he had suffered from a heart attack and would have a replacement set up soon. I assumed it would be Oliver taking over since I know he is the closest to Eddie out of his three sons.

Whoever this AJ is has to be a good replacement because I know Eddie wouldn't allow anyone less than near perfect to take over for him. I used to come to Eddie's gym, West Haven, when I was younger and train with the triplets. I even competed against Oliver a couple of times. Oliver's a good guy. From what I remember, he was always helping his dad out. I know it couldn't have been easy on Eddie raising three boys without their mom. I remember when my mom told me about how she died bringing them into the world, and I could never fully understand that until I was a bit older. Even now I can't fathom having to take on that burden of such grief and despair, while pouring everything good you have into your kids. Eddie is one of the few men I have met that gives everything he has, all the time, and never requires anything in return. That's why my mom respects him so much.

That's one of the reasons I moved back to South Carolina from California to train with him. I love my coaches on the West Coast, but I miss being here. This was where I discovered my passion for the sport. This was where training changed my life. Plus my mom is here, and I know she spends way too much time working and not enough taking care of herself. Being back closer to her will ease so much worry I have for her. The excited squeal she let out when I told her that I was thinking about moving back only helped seal the decision. She immediately offered for me to stay with her, but also started searching for apartments for me as well. She is always doing the best, and the most, for people at the same time.

I pull up to the gym parking lot and take the next five minutes after putting my car in park to look at the building. Lots of new upgrades since the last time I was here ten years ago. There is even an outside gym that looks serene while no one is in it. But working out in this heat? I know that would be killer. The humidity in the South is a different type of element. Eddie runs his gym like a home. If you had the opportunity to be here, and train here, then you would be taken care of.

I'm here because I have been missing something vital. The feeling that I used to get when I would step into the ring, my heart pounding in time with the anticipation of the fight. My fights have all been solid. In fact, I have a great record. But it all feels too much like a job now. Just something I show up and get done. The last time I remember truly loving this sport, and the dedication it takes to do well, was here. This is my last shot at trying to make this into a career. I have circulated through circuits and have come within a breath of getting signed, and would always get told that I didn't have what they were looking for. That's it. No critique about how I needed to work on anything, just that I didn't have *something*. Mom was actually the one that suggested I come back and train with Eddie. So here I am, searching for whatever it is that I'm missing. If anyone can help me find it, it's Eddie. Or hopefully whoever he has replacing him.

I walk to the front doors of what will hopefully be the start of a breakthrough for me. I was told to arrive around six this morning so I don't expect there to be a lot going on this early. If Eddie still follows the same routine as before, I know that they will have classes rotating this afternoon. But when I open the doors, the therapeutic sounds of gloves hitting pads reverberate through the room. I quickly clock two of the triplets to my side working with jump ropes, but my eyes only graze their presence for maybe a second before they are solely focused on the girl in the ring.

She probably wouldn't notice if half the building was crumbling with the immense focus that she has on the drills she's running. I'm fairly certain Oliver is holding pads for. She is fast. She's hitting her target before I can see that she even moved. Oliver has her working through a combo full of jabs and a few hooks. But when she fakes him out with a question mark kick, I feel my eyebrows stretch higher. That isn't an easy kick to throw, let alone land. She did it effortlessly. She breaks out this tiny smirk as she goes right back into position to start striking again.

"One more time." Oliver instructs her as she gets set back into her fighting stance.

I watch her work her drill with grace and a surprising amount of power. She has to be barely over five feet tall. How does she have so much power in such a tiny body? Who is she? I know Eddie doesn't have a daughter. Maybe she is Oliver's girlfriend. I don't recognize her as a fighter. She could be though. She moves with a purpose, with direction and passion, like it is her own version of an art medium.

I move next to the ring and drop my bag down as she throws her last hook. With the distance between us now closed I can see the tattoo of a snake wrapping around her thigh. The head travels down while the tail moves towards her hip and hides behind the shorts she wore. She isn't covered in tattoos though. Just that one. Unless she had some hidden somewhere very small that I can't see. I could tell, even from here, that every ounce of her is solid muscle though. Her matching sports bra and shorts fit her like a second skin and her skin has just a light glow, not a tan exactly. I glance back up to her face and see that she still hasn't noticed me standing right here. She's fully locked in to only what was happening inside the ring. They both stop after a few more strikes. She walks to the corner while trying to catch her breath. I watch as she uses her teeth to undo the velcro and take off her gloves. That shouldn't be attractive, but for some reason I find myself wanting her to rewind and do it over again.

"Hey man, it's been a while." Oliver's voice sounds so close, like it is right in my ear. I turn to my left and sure enough he is out of the ring and now standing next to me. He's smirking at catching me ogle the girl that is still in her own little world in the ring behind him. He leans back against the platform of the ring and crosses his arms. He appears happy to see me, but something is a little off about the way he's talking to me. Like he is having to work at showing that happiness.

"I know. I missed this place," I say, smiling at him. Then I remember what happened with Eddie and make sure he can hear my genuine concern when I speak my next words. "I hated hearing about your dad. He told me AJ would be training me until he was good to come back. Just know that I'm also here if I can help with anything else." And I mean it. It takes a lot to keep a gym running and Eddie does a lot of it himself. I don't mind helping out if I can.

Oliver nods, always a guy of very few words. He looks back up at where I'm standing and meets my eyes when he says, "He will bounce back. The man is a tank. I've never seen anything take him down."

I can't help the chuckle that leaves me. That is such a true statement.

"Rory, my guy!" I feel an arm drape over my shoulders, and then Maxwell appears to my right grinning ear to ear.

"Hey Maxie." I turn to give him a small hug, calling him by his childhood nickname. Maxwell has always been the happiest of the triplets, never without a joke at the ready, and always wearing the biggest smile.

Eli walks up to me right behind Maxwell and shakes my hand as I let go of his brother's. I nod at him and say, "Happy to be back guys."

The triplets grew up looking exactly the same. They always had the same type of clothes and hair styles and shoes. I have to take a double look at all of them to make sure that I did know who was who. Oliver still has the same hairstyle, shaggy and kind of in his face. He wore an upgrade from the cheap chain he got when we were at the mall as kids. Eli was full of sharp edges now. His ears are pierced in multiple places, he has a full leg sleeve, glasses that I don't remember him wearing before. His hair has the West signature shaggy look but shaved on the edges. Maxwell's is a lot like Oliver's just shorter and curlier. Maxwell has always been all boyish charm and unseriousness.

I straighten back out and look at all three of them before addressing the most obvious question left to be answered. I look around to see if I missed anyone else in the gym with the obvious distraction of the girl in the ring. "Who's this AJ guy? I came prepared to get my ass handed to me repeatedly by Oliver, but Eddie said that AJ would be taking his place while he's recovering." All three of them just stare at me, but just like when we were kids, they all have a mischievous glint to their eyes. They all have the same eyes, and when they look at you like this, it's fucking creepy. "What? Is he an asshole or something?" I am suddenly a bit less confident meeting my new trainer.

A chill runs down my back and I know that I have messed up before I have even met the guy.

They all dip their heads at the same time and then look up at the ceiling. "Fucking triplets," I mutter as low as possible. I did not miss this part about them.

"Hey, A?" Oliver calls out to literally the blank space around us. He looks at me expectantly. I just have no idea what he is expecting.

"Yeah, Avery, you here?" Maxwell cups the side of his mouth and speaks a little louder. He even makes a show of searching around dramatically.

"Avery Jude, get your cute ass down here." Eli holds his hand out behind him, and *she* makes her way through the ropes and steps down from the platform. They all make eye contact with me and I know that however I handle these next few seconds are going to be vital.

She is going to be my new trainer. Don't focus on how pretty she is. Don't focus on how pretty she is.

But I can't get my thoughts prioritized like I need to. Because while I was impressed by her before, I am fully fucking captivated by her now. She walks up to me with all the confidence in the world and I feel my throat get a little tighter. Her eyes look like crystalized smoke, or like a raging storm approaching. Stormy gray eyes. I thought that was something people made up. I've never seen gray eyes before. She is so close I can see the sweat trickling down her neck and can smell something like flowers sprinkled in spice. She doesn't look like the same girl that was in that ring earlier. There is no trace of a smile or cleverness that was there when she was working with Oliver earlier. *A, Avery, Avery Jude....*fuck. AJ. I'm an idiot.

I clear my throat in an attempt to organize my faltering thoughts. I go to introduce myself, but she speaks first. "I'm AJ. Pretty sure Eddie has already caught you up to speed, but I'll be running your training for him." She is standing defensively now, probably used to dealing with guys who didn't take her seriously. It took me all of five seconds watching her earlier to know that she has skill.

My head is still trying to catch up though. Eddie only has sons. Now that she is standing with the guys, I don't get the vibe that she is dating any of them. It's more like she *is* one of them. Like she belongs here just as much as they do. Who was she?

I put my hand out to shake hers and attempt to introduce myself. "Hi, I'm Rory." She doesn't break eye contact, makes no attempt to shake my hand, doesn't even smile.

"I know." She starts to walk away and I follow her. She didn't tell me to follow her, but I feel like that is what I need to do. When she starts talking again, I know I made the right choice. "I'm not going to start your training today. You can watch today and do a little free workout if you'd like. Eli will be leading your jiu jitsu training still. I'll just be taking over your striking." She reaches a bench that has a bag on top that I assume is hers. She pulls out an oversized zip up jacket and throws it on over her body, covering the majority of all of her exposed skin.

I see another open bench area with open lockers and make my way over there. I lay my bag down on the bench and start pulling off my own hoodie.

"What are you doing?" Her voice is softer now, full of apprehension. I look back up to her and give her a friendly smile.

"Unpacking my stuff?" I say as I gesture to the empty locker in front of me. I watch her face scrunch as she clearly weighs a thought in her head.

"You don't have a comment about me training you?" Ah. She was prepped for a fight and when I didn't give her one, she's lost now. Most guys in this industry are assholes. It comes with the territory. We all train long and hard and when we win, it validates us. Sometimes that validation is recycled into training harder. Sometimes it results in cocky assholes thinking that they don't have to keep getting better.

I turn to face her as I speak. "Do you need me to make a comment about it?" I take a step closer and tilt my head towards the ring. "About how clean you were with your hands? Maybe how you were so focused that you didn't even notice me coming into the gym? How mesmerizing watching you was?" I take another step towards her. "Or maybe you want me to make a baseless comment about you being a girl?" I raise an eyebrow as I take the final step without overcrowding her but close enough that I can feel her exhale reach my own skin. I glance down only for a second before I meet her eyes again. Being this close to her, I am surrounded by the same scent as earlier, only it's more intense. Wildflowers and spice.

I make sure I speak my next words very clearly and with no room for her to doubt that they are true. "I'm not a thoughtless man, AJ. I'm sorry to disappoint you with not behaving the way that most men do when they are intimidated by your skillset and gender, but rest assured I have plenty of thoughts about you in my head right now. None of them are that you are somehow incapable of running my training." I step back just an inch and reach for the collar of my shirt, pulling it off before tossing it to the bench. I give myself a generous moment of watching her try and fail to not stare at my tattoos, and fight the urge to smile at her clearly being frustrated with herself for wanting to look. I grab my water bottle from my bag and motion to the back door that I am pretty sure leads to the outside gym area. This time I give her the smallest grin and say, "I am however a very good listener. I'll go get a free workout in before classes start so I'm not in your way." I start to walk away but can't help myself from throwing over my shoulder, "I'm really looking forward to training with you, AJ."

I watch Eli and Maxwell laughing at the entire interaction as I walk past them as well. Oliver however was calculating something in his head. He holds my stare for a few moments before making his way behind me. I can only assume he is walking to her. Maybe they are together.

Four

*"I know what it feels like
to be in that void."*

RORY

Two days. That's how long she has spent just watching me. And it'll be the whole day. She will be coaching or teaching but somehow she's aware of every move I make. How do I know this? Because I'm equally aware of every move she makes. The difference is that I'm watching her because my eyes gravitate to her ever since I first walked through the doors. She is sizing me up though. She's watching to pick me apart. But I let her watch all the same because I like her eyes on me. There's just something about her that is alluring.

The last class just left for the day. I'm pretty sure it's her favorite one. It's the women's empowerment class Eddie offers at the gym and she was vibrating with passion the whole time she led it. I stayed over on the mats and did free weights and stretches and just watched her. I still haven't figured out her connection to Eddie and the guys yet, but it was clear she belonged here.

I watch as she refills her water bottle from the water jug in the corner of the gym. Her hair is in a braid again. She only wears it two ways, up in a ponytail or in a loose braid. And it fully depends on what she is doing or teaching. It's also clear she has a favorite student. Watching her these past few days has taught me a lot about her. She only has a few people she actually likes being around and it's easy to tell because Avery Jude is very selective with whom she gives her genuine smiles. I am not on that list, yet. But this young girl is one of the few that is always on the receiving end of those smiles. It's almost like AJ is her big sister. It's endearing. Completely different from the girl I met a few days ago.

"She is going to call you out for being a creep." The words come from somewhere on my left and when I turn I see Eli lowering to sit next to me. I've also noticed that he is the most calm of all the brothers. He's always just kind of here, observing.

I give him a sheepish smile at being caught before shaking out my hair. The sweat is making it stick to my skin a little. "I am trying to not stare like a creep, promise." Eli full on laughs. "She doesn't really talk to anyone though. Is it because she is shy? I didn't get that vibe." Closed off was more of the vibe that I got. I can't go to Oliver for any information regarding her. He had his guard dog bite bared for me the minute AJ stepped in front of me. Maxwell, if I remember correctly, is a huge open book and would absolutely go tell her I was asking about her. I can't have that. But Eli? Eli was the one that I connected the most with when we were all younger and hopefully he can be the one to let me know more about her without me having to ask. He's so up front with his thoughts, but not in your face. Even when he was younger he knew how to read a room and be involved in just the right ways. He is my in.

"She's definitely not shy." He confirms my thoughts, "she calls me on my shit daily." He speaks in a hushed tone and I know that it's so she doesn't overhear us but also not so soft that she suspects something. I look up to see if she has moved from the water jug, only to see her staring right back at me. She glares at me driving home that she knows I've been watching. I throw her a wink, letting her know that I like being caught. Staring is a reflex at this point. I love making sure she knows that I'm aware of her. Her chest always gets a soft shade of pink when I wink at her. Which makes me want to do it more often. Flirting with her is easy. But if she is going to be my trainer, I need to trust her. And for that to happen then I need to know more about her. That doesn't seem like it's going to be easy but I love a challenge.

"She just doesn't like people." Eli breaks mine and Avery's stare down. "It took us all months to get her to even talk to us when Dad first brought her around." Eli's voice carries such care in it that it's easy to see how much they all care about her.

"Eddie brought her here?" I question him but I know by the tilt of his head he isn't going to be giving me answers. She is protected by all of them. To them, I am here to train, not get to know her more. But to me, it's one in the same. Relationships between fighter and coach are intimate in a sense. You have to be able to be vulnerable and create a team.

"Dad didn't tell you anything about AJ?"Eli asks with slight confusion. I shake my head no before standing up. Eli also stands and then leans in a little closer. "She might be dad's favorite. So just be careful. Don't treat her like she is just another girl at the gym. She has a bite and she will eat you alive." Eli reaches down to pick up his bag and throw it over his shoulder. "Not to mention, she can probably kick your ass. She trains more than any of us." He warns. Then his face breaks out in a shit eating grin over my shoulder and I know she is now behind me.

Eli steps around me and gives her a quick kiss to her temple as he walks by her. They are all so tender with her. Like she is breakable but they don't let her know. "See you tomorrow, A. Try to get some rest!" He calls over his shoulder before he reaches the side door leaving us standing alone together.

I bring my eyes back to look at her. Impossibly stormy and somehow still bright gray eyes hold my attention hostage. "Why are you here?" She barks. No nonsense.

I pull my head back a little with how her question caught me off guard. "To train?" I ask it as a question because I feel like that is the obvious answer.

"You could train anywhere. It's not like we are full of first class athletes here," she motions around the empty gym. Ah, she means literally here in this gym.

"Are you discrediting Eddie's talent with training fighters?" I try to add a little playfulness to my tone to lighten her mood but she stays on target with her question.

The flinch of her eyes shows me the respect she has for Eddie and the instant regret that her words might have not reflected that. "Of course not. I'm just pointing out that you are training for a fight in a promotion that could be your ticket to the professional circuit." She takes a small step forward after she is done speaking, regaining her defensive stance.

She just doesn't like people.

I don't think it is as simple as her not liking people. I think this girl just has trust issues that could fill a sinkhole the size of Russia. Which could cause problems if she is supposed to train me to win. I need to rectify that.

"I need to feel something again when I am fighting." I speak with every ounce of honesty dripping from my tongue. She wants a serious answer, I can be serious. AJ is a good trainer. I can't deny that, even after just two days of watching her do it. She notices everything. And she pays attention to what others feel confident in, builds that up, and then works on the weaknesses in between. She does it in a way that they don't even know she is correcting them, she's intuitive of every thought and action. She leads through her coaching.

I take a step back to give her space and to try less her need to feel defensive. She likes having space. I think it helps her feel more in control.

"When I trained with Eddie when I was younger I loved every part of fighting. I loved waking up and sweating before the sun even came up. I loved laughing so hard I felt like I was going to hyperventilate on the mats after we had a super hard session and were just joking around. I loved that Eddie made sure I never questioned if what I was doing mattered.

He made sure I knew that I mattered. I had a purpose. He taught me that dedication wasn't something that came easily. But he also never made me feel like I would be nothing without the fighting and training. That life was worth so much more." I lose my voice momentarily. I need her to know I was here for a real reason. I run my hand over my face before I continue, "My whole body used to vibrate with anticipation and excitement when I fought. The adrenaline never goes away but it feels different now. I could feel every heartbeat of the people in the crowd. And I was excited to keep pushing forward. Now I'm just good at it, and the crowd cheers, but I can't feel the vibrations." I let the words fall sincerely because that is what we need. She needs to know that I have heart for this sport because that's what matters to her. I can tell by the way she puts every ounce of her body into every motion. The way she focuses so intently that everything else falls away.

She stands still for a few heartbeats, considering my words, before she allows herself to look me over and nods quietly before speaking again. "I know what it feels like to be in that void." Her voice was just a whisper but fully understanding. The fact that what I said resonated with her only makes me more curious about her.

She starts walking to the mats and like my body is tethered to hers, I follow easily. She stops in the middle of the mats and motions for me to stand in front of her.

"Let's shadow box a little today." Her voice is full of all the confidence of the girl that had been leading training and classes today and I fight a smile. We are having a moment and I don't want to ruin that. I successfully broke into those fortress level walls of self preservation if only for this moment.

I got my stance ready and brought my hands up, awaiting her instruction. Then I realize something and drop my hands before looking at her and asking, "No guard dog today?"

The look of confusion flashes on her face before her eyes turn into a soft rage. This is why her eyes remind me of a storm. And I really have to fight with a smile now. Riling her up does something to me. Her voice is full of anger when she speaks again, "Oliver isn't my guard dog." Good to know she knows who I was referring to. "I don't need guarding." She clips before waiving at my hands by my side, "you will if you don't get those hands back up though." She motions for me to bring my fists back up.

I could push Oliver not being here some more, but I choose not to. If she feels comfortable with it just being us, I will do whatever I can to keep her living in that level of comfort. I obediently bring my hands back up. We start working through some simple combos. I shift my focus from her to our training. Our bodies just move back and forth easily.

After about two or three rounds of shadowboxing, I look up at her for criticism. She has yet to give any feedback to me. I open my mouth to ask her a question, but she holds up a hand before walking to the equipment shelf and grabbing a pair of pads. She walks back over to me and holds them up.

"I'll partner with you now, just work the same combos. I want to show you something this time though." Her voice holds a shred of amusement and I don't think that she means to give that away.

With every hook and jab, I find myself anticipating what she wants to show me but her face gives away nothing that she has planned. I pivot my back foot to move to cut my angle and create more space. But what I find instead is a lack of space between my body and the mat. She just fucking swept me. *Motherfucker.*

I am staring at the ceiling as her body comes into view. I can see a very obvious gleam to her eyes, no longer stormy but an almost translucent gray now. She tosses the mitts to the floor as her voice carries down to where I was laying on my back. *Because she fucking swept me....*

"Your base could use a little work." Her shoulders shrug with the nonchalance of her voice. Like she didn't just get the better of me. "You were right though. You are very good. Took me some time to figure out what was causing your footwork to occasionally get sloppy." That's why she has been watching me. I've been watching her because she intrigued the fuck out of me. Meanwhile, she has been watching me because she was doing her job as my trainer. She is still standing over me, but her body has relaxed a little more. She is enjoying every second of knowing she landed that leg sweep. And I found myself with a matching sentiment. Her pride was a sight to see.

"I think that you just like the look of having me below you, Avery Jude." She does the thing I like most about her when she gets flustered. She opens and closes her mouth and then opens it again only to have her lips rest in a line. I throw a wink up at her at the obvious lack of words rushing to her brain.

"Stop winking at me."

"I like winking at you." I speak from where I am still lying flat on the mat.

"I don't care what you like, Rory." Her voice has lost its amusement, but her eyes are still on me. Her walls obviously put carefully back in place. She reaches down, grabs the pads and tosses them onto my stomach. "You can sanitize the equipment and the mats since you decided to take a nap down there. I'll see you tomorrow." She doesn't even give me a chance to respond before she walks out the doors and ascends the stairs to the upstairs apartment. I only know there is an apartment up there because Eddie gave me hours that I could be in the gym because AJ lives above in the apartment. And if I needed anything I could risk knocking on the apartment door but no guarantee I would get an answer. Now I know why. Avery Jude might appear cold to most people but she has passion running in her veins.

Five

"Don't tell me what to do."

AJ

I unlock Eddie's door while barely holding on to all of my groceries I bought to restock his fridge. As the door starts to open up, Eddie appears on the other side with his fatherly scowl. "You're going to hurt yourself, Avery." He scolds but still reaches out to grab some of the bags from me. Eddie is really just a big softy. He looks burly but he cares more about me than anyone else ever has.

"I lift heavier and you know it." I remind him as I kick the door closed behind me.

"I can also do my own grocery shopping." I hear him grumble behind me from where he is following me into his kitchen. He's just mad because he knows I have healthier options in these bags than his normal groceries.

I don't even give him a response. Instead, I open up his cabinets and fridge to prepare to put the groceries away. And sure enough... His cabinets are still barren and all that is available in the fridge is a fruit tray and some stray broccoli. I simply turn around, raising my eyebrows at him before laughing at the obvious lack of grocery shopping he has done. He needs me and he knows it.

After realizing I wasn't going to allow him to help me, he takes up residence on his favorite bar stool at the island counter across from me. I pause putting everything away when he asks, "What are you doing for dinner tonight? The boys won't be here. Apparently, they have a friend visiting and they are going with him to that bar they like." There is an annoyingly suggestive tone to his voice. I know he's asking without using words why I didn't go with them. But he should know by now that I don't like going out with them like that except on certain occasions. People make me uncomfortable. The lack of control of a situation that could occur keeps me from truly enjoying myself. I'm fine as long as I'm with the guys, but I hate holding them back just to make me feel secure.

"Oliver invited me, but I want to have dinner with you instead." I pull ingredients out onto the counter for dinner then I smile over my shoulder at him, ignoring the judgement he's currently giving me. Eddie likes to think that I should be out with friends more. I disagree.

I hear him clear his throat, "well, it will be dinner with me and a guest tonight." The feeling that he is warning me lingers in the quiet between us. Eddie never has guests. He also doesn't like people much like me. It's one of the reasons I think he understands me so well. I go through the small list of people he would invite over. All the boys are going out tonight. I'm here. Which leaves one person that he would invite over.

"Who's coming?" I ask, but I already know the answer. Because of course he would invite him. Why wouldn't he? I know that they are still close after talking to the guys about Rory's connection to Eddie.

"He wants to come and visit since he hasn't had a chance since he got back in town. And since you're here, it could be a good way to kind of warm you up to him a bit more." He thinks this little parent trap moment is cute, it's not. I see right through him.

When I turn to face him, I brace myself with my hands on the counter and take a deep breath. I open my mouth to explain to him that I am handling the training just fine. And I don't need him to play mediator. But he beats me to my own words.

"This isn't about you." He corrects my spiraling thoughts. Eddie never fails to read the thoughts that drown me out. His tone switches from correction to a steady and strong one. "He needs to *know* you are in his corner. He has every skill to be successful and I know you know see that. But we have roughly six months to wake back up that part of him that makes him unstoppable. He deserves this chance. He's fought nearly his whole life for it and I know he has what it takes to make it." He's settled in his words. He leaves zero room for discussion and I know he's right. I've watched Rory work for nearly a week now. And his movements are tight, nearly perfect. He's technically more sound than most people I've seen. But it's like he's all motion, no heart. Rory is an incredible talent. I can admit that. I'll never do it openly to him but he does. And he has followed every tiny instruction I've given him this past week without hesitation.

I'm a good listener...

His voice creeps into the crevices of my thoughts. He's always kind to any of the kids that come in, even if they aren't. He's switched out the water jugs for me while I'm teaching. He gives me every ounce of respect without making me earn it. That's something that still unsettles me more than anything. More importantly, he doesn't make my skin crawl and he gives me space. He's always creating more space for me like it is a lingering thought in his head and he knows I need it. I don't know what to do with that.

He makes me *nervous.*

I finally look back up and meet Eddie's eyes. "I hear you." I know that is all I need to say because Eddie's shoulders drop a little and his eyes scan over my body. He's always checking my state of being. He's been doing that since I was a teenager. He sighs and I know I don't pass the check. "You have to sleep, Avery. You push too hard to not take care of your body." His voice is gentle, "and your mind." This isn't the first time we have had this conversation. It's an ongoing battle. It's not my fault that my mind doesn't stop long enough for me to rest.

If it was as simple as just closing my eyes and falling victim to sweet dreams, then I would gladly surrender to that. It never is though. My reservoir of energy is always stretched to the brink of collapse until eventually my body finally gives up the fight. Until that happens, I survive.

I do try to wear myself down though. I run... a lot. I work out more than I need to, more than my body should be enduring. I take those gummies that decorate every shelf to help aid my sleep routine. I've tried other ways to tire out my body but I decided that isn't a healthy outlet anymore. And with the added stress of making sure Eddie is okay and taking on more than my usual share of responsibility at the gym, I am exhausted. I know my eyes have deep shadows at this point. I have aches in my neck from the lack of sleep. But my mind never willingly goes silent.

A knock at the door pulls me out of my self pity, and I watch Eddie get up from where he is sitting to go and let Rory in. I grab the vegetables and start rinsing them. I can hear Eddie and Rory talking at the door. I place the vegetables on the counter and sit the cutting board down expecting them to round the corner from the front hallway.

When I look up though, all I am met with is green eyes and a surprised man staring back at me. No Eddie, just him. Why does he have to be so tall? I'm such a slut for tall men.

"Avery Jude... I didn't know you were going to be here." His eyes search mine and his voice is now full of a quiet wonder. He recovers quickly from his shock of seeing me in Eddie's apartment as he leans on the counter next to me and hooks his thumb over his shoulder with a soft smile, "Eddie told me to tell you that he was going to go and check his mailbox real quick." Of course he is. Sneaky bastard.

I'm still staring at him when I notice his eyebrows draw in a little like he is concerned with something. Then I watch his eyes rake over where my tank top shows off my bare stomach, his eyes moving to my shoulder, and then my neck before finally landing back on my own eyes. His lips part slightly and I can feel the unsteady breath leave them. I hate this part of meeting new people. This is why I generally avoid meeting new people. They never know how to respond when they see the raised and scarred flesh decorating my stomach. They want to give pity or pretend they didn't see it. Sometimes they just stare openly, too caught off guard to process the cuts. Most think they are self-inflicted and their eyes reflect the understanding that they think they have over a situation that they know nothing about.

The feeling of ice chills the back of my neck and I'm only aware that my hands are shaking because I hear the knife rattle ever so lightly against the cutting board. I drop it so the sound stops. I didn't even think about the scars being visible because it's just Eddie and the guys that are ever here. And they all know. If I am teaching the kids, I always wear layers. I feel my chest fall victim to the weight that makes my breathing thin and strained. My skin is now crawling and I grip the edge of the counter with the hand that was holding the knife a little tighter to keep my knees from buckling. And for whatever reason, I'm able to maintain eye contact with him.

Something shifts in his eyes in the time it takes me to take another faltering breath. I watch him make the decision to not ask questions even though I am pretty sure he is dying to do so. I would be. *Who is this girl with scars like that? Why did she do that to herself?* I never have the energy to correct assumptions when I'm fighting my own body for control.

"I can cut veggies while you prep the meat?" He proposes, his voice decisive but gentle. He tips his head to the back counter where I have the steak tips resting in a bowl ready to be seasoned. I feel him step behind me, close enough that I can smell the laundry detergent mixed with his cologne. I don't know if it is the mixture of those scents or his tone of voice, but I don't want to immediately pull away. I take a steadying breath and relax before stepping to the side where he can take the knife and start cutting.

"I've never seen your hair down before." I hear his words, but my body is still unwilling to bring words out of my mouth. "It always surprises me how different a girl's hair looks when it isn't in a braid or pulled up. My mom used to work at one of those high end salons and is always able to transform her hair into anything she wants. It's wild." He is absently talking as he cuts the vegetables as I am just standing behind him trying to gather back control. It's a technique a therapist used to use with me for my panic attacks. The vibrations of the room are a little softer as I listen to the knife slice and make contact with the board. My nails dig into the meatiest part of my hands and I exhale a full breath.

"Are we making a stir fry?" When I look up at him in confusion he points to the counter next to me. "I saw the rice on the counter too. I love a good stir fry." He groans and throws his head back where it falls between his shoulder blades. He still has his back turned to me and I notice his tattoos move as his arm flexes from holding the knife. Another deep exhale and an even steadier inhale. The pressure is slowly vacating my chest.

I feel my knees again and notice my hands relax by my sides. Another exhale. I can feel the sweat on the back of my neck and the heat inside my ears still, but my breathing is steadier than before. I feel my lungs expand and my feet turn me around to face the back counter. Following suit with getting dinner prepped.

I pick up the seasoning and start getting to work. A bottle of water is placed down in front of me with the top already screwed off. His voice is laced with so much kindness that it makes tears prick my eyes when he breathes out, "atta girl, Avery Jude." Then as if the words were never even spoken, he pulls his phone out and starts playing music. I don't know where he learned to do that, to calm someone down from a panic attack, but I am grateful.

The front door opens at the same moment the music starts to pick up and Eddie walks in with a very hesitant smile on his face. He left us alone to keep me from hiding from talking to Rory while he was here to carry the conversation. He's always known me so well. I don't look up at where

I know he is standing at the end of the counter. The same spot Rory was standing when he saw the scars.

"You guys look like you have this under control. I'm going to start up the Blackstone." We bought him that damn grill two years ago for a Father's day present and he used it every single chance he got. He loves it.

"I'm..." I start but he cuts me off.

"Don't you dare apologize to me." Rory's voice is full of something much stronger than how I feel at this moment. It has been a long time since I allowed someone seeing my scars to put me into such a state of panic. Thankfully it didn't get out of control. It's hard to not be pulled back into the memories of what happened years ago. But I have spent years training my head to fight the triggers. And if Rory had asked me what the scars were from, I know I would have broken.

But he didn't. He gave me space. He seems to always be doing that.

"Don't tell me what to do." I hope the words land with the confidence I try so hard to fill them with.

I hear him chuckle before responding with, "There she is." And then he was back to prepping the vegetables and I was back to prepping the meat.

We spent the rest of the evening in a charged quiet. Eddie and Rory reminisced about when Rory was younger. And every so often, Rory's eyes would find mine and they were full of reassurance. This guy had no idea what my story was. He isn't put off from me not being bubbly and full of life. It is like he knew I just needed space to be in the moment.. And that makes me really fucking nervous.

Six

"No more sad boy shit."

AJ

Walking into Eddie's office the next Saturday morning I am quickly reminded of all the work I have put off since I took over his regular workload plus my own at the gym. Our social media is practically nonexistent, since I'm the one that normally posts on it and keeps it on schedule. I have memberships to input and file away. Payroll needs to be finalized. And the office is a disaster zone with all the things left unfinished. I take a steady inhale before I sit down in the office chair that always seems to swallow me because it was bought for a man more than twice my size.

I turn to the computer and feel my body go slightly limp. A blue post-it steals my focus. I pull it from where it is barely hanging on to the screen.

I'm still in your corner, even from my apartment.

Eddie. It's been a little while since he has left me one of these notes, but they never fail to make my heart feel like it's being wrapped in a warm hug. I pull out my phone to text him thank you.

AJ

If I pull the cameras and see you working out. I'm not cooking you dinner this week.

Eddie

Love you too. Take care of our boy.

AJ

> **Not my boy.**

Eddie

> **Give him a chance, Avery.**

I switch over to my Spotify app and put on my favorite playlist, not even giving Eddie a reply before I flip my phone face down. It isn't that I don't want to give Rory a chance. I'm just doing it the best way I can, with distance. I've been following the training program and executing it without a single complaint from him. But I don't have to be his friend. I just need to be his trainer.

He has history with Eddie, with the triplets. But that was before me and I don't owe him the same kind of camaraderie that they already have established. My job is to make sure he is prepared for this fight in six months. And he will be. Eli told me that his jujitsu training is going strong. His striking is phenomenal. Honestly, he's making my job very easy. He just has to stay consistent and I have no doubts he will win. I've even been doing research on his opponent, Jason Radford. I've watched every fight he has had, in every promotion, for the past two years. Jason is strong, but he always seemed to get ahead of himself by a second. He comes out with aggression and major offense, but he doesn't pay attention to who he is fighting. You can tell he just mirrors any training he had. There's no intuition.

That could work against most fighters. It will be difficult against Rory though. Moving in the ring is as second nature as breathing for him. I've been using Eli and Maxwell as training partners so I can watch Rory with sparring rounds. Watching him is...enthralling. He makes you appreciate the art of the sport. The way you train the body to move.

He told me he just wants to feel something when fighting again. And I know what he means, but I don't know how to coach that. I'm not

Eddie. He would know exactly how to connect in the way that Rory is searching for. But when I asked Eddie for guidance on how to get Rory back to where he is desperate to be, Eddie just told me that I would figure it out. I know that he is going out of his mind not to be in the gym every day, but I feel like he's also enjoying this form of torturing me a little too much.

Two hours later, my best friend walks through the office door carrying what I know is a double shot caramel latte. And if Mia made it, it will have some kind of random flavor shot in for me to try. She is our usual barista at the coffee shop around the corner and is like walking sunshine, literally. She has super curly blonde hair and always models the brightest smile. She's someone that makes my day a little brighter every time I go there. I think she makes everyone's days brighter.

Oliver sits down across from me on the other side of the desk and gives me a smug smile. He slides the coffee cup my way and sits back comfortably in the chair. I can't help the glare I shoot his way before picking up my cup. I take a sip and it is definitely a flower flavor but not lavender. Maybe rose? I would have to ask Mia when I saw her next.

His grin turns into a full smile now. "Mia let me pick the extra flavor this time. How did I do?" He asks, obviously proud of his decision of flavor.

I take another small sip and let the flavor rest on my tongue for a minute longer to try and figure it out. Then I pick up the cup and take off the lid to smell it. "Rose?" I ask him. By the way his eyes get bigger and brighter, I know I'm right.

He leans forward resting his elbows on his knees before saying, "How many hours of sleep did you get last night?" I knew he would bring that up today. Oliver is never afraid to call me out on anything and everything.

"I'm happy to report I got a whole four hours last night." I inform him with a bright smile.

I watch him contemplate if he wants to fight with me on something that I have no control over or just move on. After a few long moments, he decides to move on. "Are you going to come out with us tonight?"

The guys always like to go to one of the local bars on Saturdays. It's just a local dive bar but it's had some upgrades done to it. I only go with them occasionally and when I do, it is one of the few times I will let myself let go and the guys always take care of me. It just isn't something I personally like to do all the time.

I give him a slight shake of my head and he gives me a sad smile. "We miss you, A." His voice is tender.

"I just have a lot going on. You know how it is trying to run this place." He chuckles and stands to look out over the glass windows. The office is on the same level as my apartment, above the gym. But the office has an inside entrance and is on the opposite side from where the apartment is. He pulls at the back of his neck a little. His tell for when he's uncomfortable.

He doesn't even look in my direction when he asks, "How is the training going with Rory?" I can tell there is something he still isn't telling me. A hard feeling towards our new fighter that he keeps held close to his chest. I didn't ask about it the first day that Rory got here, but he's been here nearly two weeks now and honestly, I need Oliver to step up Rory's training. Eli and Maxwell have been great, but Oliver can push harder. He just always seems to be "caught up with something" when I ask him to come and help. He's evading and I just haven't had the time to figure out why.

"He's incredibly talented." I answer him. I can hear his snort from across the room. "You ready to talk about it?" I ask him in the same tender tone he used with me earlier.

He turns around to face me now, and rests his back against where the glass window meets the wall. "About what?"

"We don't do this, Ollie." I remind him. "Why are you avoiding working with him?" I ask him. His eyes meet mine and I see the vulnerability there. I don't want to push, but I also know he needs to work through this. Whatever this is.

He glues his eyes back to the carpeted floor and speaks softly, "When we were younger, everyone would always talk about how Rory was going to go pro one day. How he was just destined for that shit. And I would train side by side with him every day, A. Every day I would do the same workouts and eat the same meals, and put in the same time. Go and compete in the same promotions. And I was good." His voice breaks a little bit on that last word. And he sounds so sad in this one moment that I stand up to make my way in front of him.

"You are also incredibly talented." I make sure I put every ounce of reassurance I can into my words.

He looks back up at me, or back down to me since I was about half a foot shorter than him. He clears his throat before speaking this time. "I'm hurt and talented. It's not the same. I was never going to go as far as him anyway." He stands up a little straighter before continuing, "It's just hard being in the same training gym as him again. My sponsor let me go with this leg injury. He is training for a shot at the dream, A. And he deserves it. Truly. It's just hard. I'll get over myself." He plasters a fake grin back on his stupidly handsome face and reaches out to envelope me in a hug.

I squeeze my arms extra tight around him. "I need your help to push him in sparring. You're the only one that can keep up with him. Eli and Max try but they aren't you." My words are slightly muffled against his chest.

"I'll be there Monday." He promises when I pull back from our hug.

"Good. *You* are my favorite fighter. No more sad boy shit." I lightly slap him and he laughs with his whole body.

He kisses my forehead before giving me a genuine smile this time. "Thanks for being you, A."

"Always in your corner." I remind him. I turn and look at the clock. I raise an eyebrow at him before asking, "You want to go for a run with me?"

"Did you already go for a run this morning?" Of course I did. He knows I have a routine that I rarely deviate from. He tosses his head back staring at the ceiling for a second before glancing back over to me. "Of course you did." He says deflatedly before reaching into the cabinet next to him and tossing something at me.

I catch it and read the label. His favorite protein bar.

"Please eat that before going back out for another run. And keep your location on." He's being protective and it makes me roll my eyes. He's acting like I haven't been running like this for years.

"You always have my location." I assure him. He reaches in to give me one more quick hug before heading towards the door.

"If you change your mind, just text me and I'll come pick you up and bring you to the bar." He spoke the words over his shoulder as he was leaving. I will not be changing my mind and we both know this.

Running by the ocean has always been one of my favorite things to do. Living near the beach can sometimes be super chaotic, but being in a smaller town keeps things pretty minimal for the most part. Sunset runs are incomparable though. With every gust of salty wind, it's like a kiss to my skin. It reminds me that I'm alive.

I make my way down my favorite stretch of my route, where I often find the couples that have lived here their whole lives going for a walk.

It always makes my chest expand in a different way seeing them. Some recognize me from my routine runs and give me a smile and a wave.

I turn my head to take in the fullness of the view and my breath catches in my throat. Sitting on the bench to my right was a tall guy with dark hair and broad shoulders who I wasn't expecting to see. I come to a halt and take in the new view of him hunched over what looks like a notepad.

I dare to walk a little closer before he inevitably notices I am in his space. He always notices me and I hate how aware of that I am.

His hands move over the notepad laying across his lap. His hair looks a little messier than usual. Like maybe he's been running his hands through it. Or maybe that is just how it looks outside of the gym. I didn't pay too much attention to it the other night when he had dinner with me and Eddie. I was too distracted fighting myself to not break down fully.

I lean a little closer to try and see what he is drawing while hoping I don't give away that I'm here. I can see his head slightly move as he glances up and back down a few times. Going from something in front of him back to his notebook.

He's drawing the couple walking on the beach. It's not complete yet but that's clearly who it is.

"The benches are public property. Which means you can come and sit next to me and not be a creep…" He teases. I feel my cheeks warm with his words and bite my lip to keep from laughing. I knew he would notice me without me having to announce I was here.

I make my way around the bench and sit on the end opposite of him. He reaches into the bag by his feet and pulls out a bottle of water. He looks up at me and grins as he offers it to me. I don't know why I expect him to shy away from the notepad now that I am sitting next to him but he doesn't. He simply goes back to sketching completely unfazed that I am here.

It's not an uncomfortable silence, but neither of us speak. I bring my feet up to the bench so I can hug my knees close to my chest and just watch the waves lap at the sand.

"Thanks for not making a big deal out of what happened at dinner the other night." The words tumble out of my mouth before I realize I am even saying them. He pauses his hand from moving across the page and looks back up to meet my eyes, always searching for something. I don't know for sure I would give him what he was searching for even if I knew what it was. But something about him always searching moved something in my soul.

"Do they happen often?" His voice is calm as he speaks and goes back to sketching, our comfortable silence settling into comfortable conversation.

"Not so much anymore." I admit because I feel like he is someone who appreciates honesty. "I think I didn't want you to see me weak. Most everyone I'm around a lot has seen my scars. When you noticed them, I didn't want to have to answer questions and then I just... couldn't breathe." God, what was happening? I want to be honest but not *that* fucking honest.

"You don't have to tell me anything you don't want to, Avery Jude." He says without looking up again.

"Why do you call me that? You can just call me AJ like everyone else. It's weird." I speak, but my focus is now on watching him draw. The way his hands move is surprisingly elegant. Can a guy have elegant hands when his day job is using those same hands to fight?

I watch him shrug his shoulders and his lips tip up a little, "I don't like AJ, everyone calls you that." He tilts his head at me. "Eddie calls you Avery. And I kind of like how your full name sounds together." He says as he looks back up at the couple.

"Okay." I don't know what else to say to that. It's just a name, and if he wants to use my full name then I don't think I have a problem with it.

"I have an idea." I blurt, deciding to try something new. Eddie's text from earlier reverberated in my head.

-Give him a chance, Avery-

I turn and cross my legs so I am now facing him on the bench. I hold my hand out towards the notepad. "Can I see?" His green eyes meet mine again and I can see the amusement in them making the green a lighter shade than normal. He hands the sketch over easily and moves so his arm is draping over the back on the bench creating a little more space and giving me more of his attention at the same time.

"What is your idea?" He prompts me to continue.

I can't tear my eyes away from the beauty of what his hands created. This is how he sees what is right in front him. It's stunning and real and beautiful.

"You need to trust me more. I need to figure out how to train you to feel again when you fight." I state. I barely catch the nod he gives me because my eyes are still tracing every delicate line. "I hate twenty questions. It's too long and annoying. And people ask the dumbest things." His laugh fills my ears. I raise my head and let my gaze trace over the lines of his face like I did his drawing. He has kind eyes but sharp features.

"How about one question per day? We each get one." I suggest. I can handle one question a day.

He reaches back down into his bag again, and this time he pulls out his phone and starts typing. I give him a few moments. Maybe he thinks my idea is dumb? I'm just trying to do exactly what Eddie suggested...

He hands me his phone a few seconds later. I glance down at the screen. It's open to the screen for adding a new contact and my name is typed as "Jude". I immediately look back up at him in confusion and shock.

"What if my question comes to my head and I'm not around you? And honestly, you're my trainer. I should have your number." He speaks so nonchalantly when I know damn well he knows I am confused about what he used as my contact name not me giving him my number. He smiles, shrugs, and then fucking winks. "Changed my mind. I think I like Jude the most." And for whatever reason, I don't feel like it is that big of a deal. I put my number in and then hand it back over to him. He types out something. I feel my phone vibrate in the side pocket of my leggings and know he texted me.

Rory waives for his notepad back. Neither of us make an effort to get up and leave. We just let the quiet rest between us, him sketching the couple and me letting the sound of the waves calm me.

Seven

RORY

Jude

> **Meet me at the gym at 5:30 am. Eddie just upgraded you to my new running partner.**

That text came through at five am and I can hear her reluctant obedience to Eddie through the screen. I figured for sure I would have to be the first one to text her after I made her put her number into my phone. But that was just last night and here I am staring at her name on my screen. Something about the fact that she not only knew I would be awake, but I would also show up without question, made me smile a little too brightly this morning. I have no idea why I like having her bossing me around this much, but I'm always in a better mood when she is. Maybe it's the fact that she is actually giving me some of her attention she refrains from giving so much.

It takes me an embarrassingly short time to get ready. I'm dressed and downstairs within ten minutes and it only takes me another ten to get to the gym. I pull in and notice she is already standing in front of the gym stretching. She has her headphones over her head and her eyes closed, so she doesn't notice me walking up to her. It gives me a minute to actually appreciate how beautiful she is. Every part of her body is toned to perfection and I've seen first hand how hard she works every day to keep it that way. Her nearly black hair always has a shine to it. That's the only way I know it's actually brown. Because when the sun hits in, it glimmers with the different shades.

As always, my eyes are drawn to her tattoo. She rarely wears sweatpants, she's always in those tiny shorts that really show off the intricate viper that wraps around her upper thigh. Every time she moves, the tattoo moves, making it look alive. I've sketched it more times than I would ever admit to her. It's striking, alluring, stunning. Just like her.

"It's just a tattoo, Rory. You have like fifty." Her words are accusatory as she catches me staring.

I wet my bottom lip, bringing my eyes up her body until they land on hers. I attempt to deflect from my obvious perusal of her body, "have you been staring at me, Avery Jude?" The words leave my mouth with a trickle of hesitation because I realize I really want her answer to be yes.

Her face gives nothing away as she asks, "is that your question for the day?" *That isn't a no...*

"Give me more credit than that. I wouldn't waste my one question on something I already know the answer to." The straight face I'm trying so hard to keep in place falters when she scowls at me. A small chuckle leaves my throat at how flustered she looks even if she is quick to hide it. I motion to where her headphones are hanging around her neck, "what are we listening to?" She loves her music. She's always losing herself in her workouts when she has her headphones on.

"It's my running playlist." She states like I should already know that too. She wraps her hands around each side of her headphones and pauses, looking back up at me. "You can listen to whatever you want to listen to." She offers.

"I want to listen to what you are listening to."

"You probably won't like it." She's dismissive but I push anyway.

I tip my head to the side and raise my eyebrows at her. "I can decide what I like." I stay standing in front of her. I'm willing to wait until she lets me see the playlist.

I watch as she debates with her own thoughts while I wait patiently in front of her. After a few seconds she looks back up at me and exhales slowly. She pulls her phone out from her shorts and starts typing out something. My phone vibrates and I grin knowing she just sent me the playlist. Small victories are how I'm going to break through her defenses.

"I assume you brought headphones." She's exasperated with the whole interaction but I am just happy that she's sharing her playlist with me. I pull my phone out of my pocket and confirm I'm right. I'm now staring at a playlist that I know holds songs to let me see a real side of her. I'm scrolling through when her voice comes from far away, "keep up or go home!" She shouts over her shoulder already setting pace down the sidewalk. I pull my own headphones out of my pocket and push play as I make my way to catch up with her.

I run alot. It's been a regular addition to my routine since I was a teenager. But I have never run like this. Avery Jude is on a mission but I catch up to her and manage to keep pace, stealing glances her way every chance I can. Her playlist is fast paced and emotional. It seems to be driving her forward. She's completely disassociated to everything else around her, immersed in the way the songs ripple through her body. It's like the first day I saw her in the gym. Nothing else around her matters but the thoughts that are clearly being thrown around in her head.

I am half a second behind her now, wondering if other people in her life are as intrigued with figuring out Avery Jude as I am. Or if they just accept the way she keeps everyone at a distance. It's like she has them all in the exact role she wants them to be in. Eddie is the man that stepped in and gave her the hope that not all parents are nightmares. Eli and Maxwell are the brothers I assume she has never had. Oliver? I haven't quite figured out what the full history is between them. Their dynamic just feels a bit more tethered than the others.

I follow close behind her as we take another turn. My heart stops beating as I round the corner and she steps to cross the road at the exact moment a car is turning. Half a second. That's all it takes for my hand to reach out with desperation to pull her back to safety. My arm snakes around her waist and I stumble backwards until my back hits the brick wall behind us. She rips her headphones off and they quickly fall to the ground, both of our heads snapping to where the horn is blaring from the car that nearly took her out.

I can feel her breathing turn erratic as she realizes what just happened. Her hand lifts to cover mine which is still lightly wrapped around her hip. I don't want to scare her further but I absolutely am not ready to let her go yet. She doesn't feel like she is steady enough to stand on her own. Her hands shake and they grip lightly to whatever piece of skin she can find.

"Breathe through your nose, Jude. Steady breaths." I keep my voice calm and low so it doesn't startle her. I squeeze her to me reassuringly and take a deep breath, moving her body in sync with my own. I feel her chest expand, but the exhale from her lungs causes her body to shake with the release of the adrenaline from her body. I take another deep breath and feel her breathing start to even out. "Atta girl." I whisper kindly as she exhales a little more steady this time. We stand here, her full weight being braced by my body, for a few moments just breathing.

When she finally comes down from the shock of what just happened she turns around to face me. My hand is still resting lightly on her bare skin and I feel it pebble under my fingertips. Her shoulders slightly shake as she looks up and our eyes meet. Exhaling slowly, her eyes dart back and forth between mine.

"Thank you…" she breathes out. Her voice is hoarse and barely audible but I watch her lips move to form the words.

I don't think as my other hand reaches up to rest against her cheek. I keep my touch light, afraid of shaking her up more than she already is. "You kind of scared the shit out of me." She more than scared me. I thought for sure she was about to be hit by that car. I let my eyes take inventory of her body making sure that nothing is actually hurt. And I watch her shiver again. This time from the wind chilling the sweat on her body. Instinctively, I pull off my hoodie and help her into it.

"Thank you..." She repeats with her voice still small, but she seems to be more herself as she reaches down to grab her headphones from where she dropped them in her haste to take them off earlier. I watch her gather herself and notice that my hoodie swallows her small frame. She puts her hands on her hips and it cinches the material. I watch her move her hands to take the tie out of the bottom of her braid and run her hands through her hair as she softly paces back and forth for a minute. I step back closer to the wall to give her space to collect herself.

When she finally stills and looks at me, time pauses. Her hair is wild from the waves left behind from the braid and wind blown strands from running. Her cheeks still a warm pink from having to catch her breath. Her perfect legs and that snake peek out from the hem of my hoodie. And storm gray eyes stare back at me. This is Avery Jude. In her purest and simplest form.

It's a good look for her.

"Thanks for not letting me die. We can finish our run now." She is definitely back to normal now. She starts to put her headphones on but I grab them from her grip before she can.

I hold them out of her range and shake my head. "Absolutely not. We are going to go into this cute coffee place and you are going to get a warm drink." I nod to the coffee shop across the street. I can feel the argument boiling up from her core and the way her lips pinch together. "Please don't." I beg her. " You are cold and probably still in a little shock." I hold my hand out for her to take, my fingers itching to feel her skin again. *Let me take care of you...*

I watch her stare at my hand but make no movement to actually take it. She tilts her head to glance up at the coffee shop and then nods her head slightly as she steps around me to walk across the crosswalk. Agreeing with me without being vocal about it. Brat.

I step in line behind her easily. "I don't know if you can be trusted to walk across." I tease her as she starts to walk over the crosswalk. She flips me off as I reach her side.

She rolls her eyes. "I said thank you. Don't make it a thing,"she huffs. Clearly deciding that she isn't going to make a big deal out of what happened. I can't help the grin that spreads across my lips at her words. I love that every ounce of her is full of fight. She nearly just got run over by a car, clawed her way through another panic attack, and is just dismissing it like it's just another day in her life. She's the definition of grit.

When we get to the counter in the shop I let her order because I have no idea what to even begin with, but when the barista gives the total I gently push Avery out of the way and pay. She leads us to a table outside on the sidewalk. The sun is fully set in the sky and the air is more awake than before we came into the coffee shop.

Avery sits across from me peeling the label off her coffee cup. She brings her legs up and crosses them over each other in the seat. Her lips cover the small opening at the top of the lid and the faintest smile ghosts across her face. She leans forward, letting her cheek fall in the palm of her hand as her elbow rests on the table. "Why do you draw?" She asks as she brings the cup back to her lips to take a fuller drink. There's so many answers to that question.

I play with the edge of the lid before responding, "is this your question for today?" I feel my eyebrow raise a little bit. When she suggested this game to get to know each other better I knew that she would come with hard questions. Questions that will make me reveal something she can't figure out by simply watching me. Because she has tried that already. She thinks in the details that lay under the surface of people. But I'm not hiding anything and I think that's what throws her off. She doesn't have to search hard to know anything about me, she just has to ask. And asking puts her more at risk of being seen.

"You're really good at it for someone who throws punches as a career." She continues her search for an answer when I don't give her one.

"I do so much more than throw punches. You know that." I remind her. Then pull myself forward by gripping the end of the table. "Wait, was that a compliment, Avery Jude?" Her eyes roll but her lips curve into a smile. I love making her smile.

"Did you teach yourself?"

"That's two... the deal was only one per day, yeah?" I remind her. I watch her cute nose scrunch up as she shoots me a mild glare that holds no real weight.

"Fine. Who taught you?" She ignores the one question a day rule by asking her third. She takes another drink of her coffee and I notice she hasn't shivered since she has been drinking the warm drink. A part of me is unreasonably happy that I was able to take care of her in that way.

This was an easy question to answer. I love talking about the woman who gave me my love of art. "My mom did." I smile warmly thinking of my mom teaching me the basics of drawing. "And when I outgrew what she could teach me, she made sure that I took classes when they were available and kept me stocked on supplies. Youtube did wonders as well." That causes a laugh to tumble from her lips and I know at this moment that I am going to make this girl laugh as much as I possibly can. It's a sound that deserves to be heard more.

I take a big gulp of my now lukewarm coffee before asking my question. "Why are the guys always telling you to get more sleep?" She avoids my question by drinking the rest of hers. But if she can push for an answer, then I can too. "Come on, it's basically an everyday conversation with you all." I've heard them request that she sleep more in nearly every conversation that I've been around for. I also haven't been oblivious to the darker circles under her eyes, or the way that she seems more exhausted than is socially acceptable. However, I know she's taking on a lot. She's teaching twice as much. Add in the extra one on one training with some of the athletes and the office aspect of running the gym. I would be more concerned if she wasn't running on fumes. I just wish that she wasn't.

She chuckles, but it lacks lightness this time. It has more annoyance than humor. "The guys worry over if I stub my toe getting out of bed in the morning. I'm just a little more tired than usual. It'll even out once I get used to the schedule of covering more." Her voice holds an almost too steady tone. She's lying.

"We promised honesty." I remind her.

She puts the coffee cup down and folds her hands on the table. She takes a deep breath before harshly letting it go. I don't care if she is aggravated. We need trust and trust is strengthened through honesty. Honesty can be scary but I'll earn it from her.

I can see her cheeks and jaw tense in sync from her grinding her jaw. She swallows hard, fighting against the want to drop the conversation but knowing I won't let that happen. "I don't sleep." She finally barks out. "I've never really slept well anyway but sometimes it gets pretty bad. They worry. Eventually, I find ways to wear my body down or it just gives out entirely and I sleep. It's really not a big deal." Her words are rushed and she is making too much of an effort to make it sound like it wasn't a big deal. Which is a dead giveaway that it is. I wonder what her definition of bad is.

"What do you do to wear your body down? Maybe I can help. Extra workouts? Yoga? Meditation?"

She brings her eyes to meet mine and holds them. I can see them turn playful as her lips tip up slightly. I sip my own drink, even though it is cold and gross now, waiting for whatever answer she is deliberating on giving me.

"Sex." She says sweetly. And now I am choking on my drink. *Fuck*. I glance up and she just shrugs before standing.

"Can we walk back to the gym now?" She asks, grabbing my drink and her empty cup to toss in the garbage can and starts walking down the sidewalk back to West Haven like she didn't just casually let me know that she uses sex to wear her down enough to sleep. Like leaving me watching her walk away in my clothes isn't going to affect me at all. Like my thoughts aren't now lingering on Avery Jude and sex. Or who she uses to wear herself down. But I get no answers because she is already getting far away from me and like always, I find myself following her.

Eight

*"I was a bit preoccupied
learning other things as a kid."*

AJ

"**T**his one seems good!" Eddie turns the computer around to show me yet another applicant that I already know I won't like.

He called me a few days ago and suggested that we get a media assistant. Someone to help run some of the stuff that I run for the gym, but even I have to admit my failure in keeping it all consistent since I've been filling in for Eddie. We always have a decent turn over with the beginners classes. People get this proactive thought in their head that they want to do something new and learn to defend themselves or blow off steam. Then the problem that originally brought them into the gym subsides, and so does their attendance. Having consistent social media appearance is what keeps the rotation going for those classes. It also helps with all of our nonprofits that we do with foster care kids and domestic violence and SA. Programs that I built from the ground up with Eddie's unwavering support. Programs that are the beat of my heart, keeping me moving forward in life. A small impact is still an impact.

Kids need a safe space to challenge and express themselves. Not everyone is a singer, or an artist, or can just create things. The majority of kids have fluctuating emotions and need a space to process them and channel them. Some kids genuinely need to learn how to defend themselves because the system is forever broken and you never know what you will face. I know that first hand.

One day I asked Eddie if I could sponsor a girl from a foster program I was also once a part of. And he never even made eye contact with me as he handed me the packet of forms to fill out. The next Scrabble Sunday, we sat down and fleshed out a program. He had a friend walk us through the grant process. It took a few months, but the program is now large enough to host ten kids every month. Ten kids I am able to support through the suffocating feeling of either being abandoned, unwanted, unloved, unworthy, or cast aside.

"Avery, did you hear me?" Eddie's voice echoes through my lingering thoughts. I look to where he is pointing back to his screen. He has moved on from the previous girl and I'm now staring at Mia. Mine and Oliver's favorite barista from the coffee shop we love.

I motion for Eddie to bring his laptop closer. Mia Cassidy, her name reads at the top of her resume. Her resume is filled with four current part time jobs and an entire page of recent positions. She also attached a portfolio of photos and links to several social media accounts that she manages. Mia always made me feel a little bit warmer. Her smile alone would make any person that walked through the doors want to smile back at her and feel welcome. I think she could be a really good presence at the gym. The kids would all adore her.

"I know how protective you are of the programs and the culture we've built. But she seems super qualified. And she listed Oliver as a reference." Of course she did. I'm pretty sure Mia has had a crush on Oliver for a few months now. One time we were at the coffee shop and there were no other customers and she tried to coerce him into learning how to make his own latte. He declined, of course. But her smile never drops when she is in the presence of others. Her confidence seems to never falter from what little bit of time I've spent around her.

"I think we should interview her." I click on the link to look closer at some of the social media accounts she manages. Scrolling through her work made one thing very clear, she brings life to it all. She's passionate. And she knows how to build something.

"Just like that?" I could hear the skepticism in Eddie's voice. I'm never this agreeable. Normally he would have to placate my need to question it all and then I would relent anyway. But not now. I need help and I'm not too proud to accept it.

"She's an incredibly sweet girl, doesn't let her emotions control her, and I think the kids will love her. Plus she's super cute and fun. So maybe the guys won't give her such a hard time when she tries to get photos and videos of them." I watch Eddie wear a full smile on his face and tap the table. He loves when he wins so easily.

"I'm not even going to question why you are being so uncombative about this. I'm just happy you're willing to interview her! If I'm honest, I was getting scared," he releases a breath before he walks over to the bookshelf to grab our favorite game. I forgot it was Sunday. It's been a long few days. Training with Rory is going super smooth. The guys have all been helping out as much as possible, but keeping up with everything is getting a little hard. Not even taking into consideration my lack of sleep. So deciding to move forward with Mia will hopefully help alleviate some of it.

Scrabble with Eddie always helps me organize the chaos in my head. It feels like home in a sense. It's a consistent moment in time that keeps me grounded despite the chaos that populates my mind. Just a way to allow my mind to work without consequence.

"I forgot it was Sunday. I don't have a dinner planned..." He turns around with the scrabble box in his hands and his smile easily transforms into a grin. I hate when he has that look on his face. It's the look of being two steps ahead of me and it means that I'm going to have a harder time than usual beating him at the game tonight. I never lose though and it drives him mad. Eddie's confidence is always a scary thing, it's experienced confidence and it makes me feel like a child and unprepared in a way.

"I have guests coming, and they are bringing dinner with them." He announces like having people over is now going to be a common thing. Wait. Guests? As in more than one? I know it's not the boys. They went out again last night. Eli said that Max got super drunk and has a massive hangover. Eddie doesn't really care that the boys go out, nor does he care that they drink. They always tend to keep it away from him anyway. And Eddie prefers it that way, otherwise he would want to lecture them. Eddie hates having to lecture anyone.

I swallow the impending feeling of knowing who is on the guest list tonight. "Who's coming, Eddie?" The pressure under my sternum leads me to believe it will be Rory again. Ever since he saved me from possibly decorating a car with my blood type, I might be actively avoiding him. I might have been letting Eli do more floor work with him instead of focusing on his striking. Which is why he is here at the gym to begin with. I *might* be a tiny bit frustrated with how easily I let facts about me slip out when he asks. He makes it so easy to talk to him though. He doesn't expect anything, but he is always interested in what I choose to tell him. And he remembers it all like it's his job. The fact that he pays that much attention is unsettling.

I've stayed committed to answering one question a day. It isn't a bad way of giving him just enough while still maintaining a safe distance from him. Rory is infuriatingly charming though. I never thought I would use that word to describe a guy before, but here I am, caught up on a guy who makes me smile through texts. He will never know that though.

"I think it will be more fun if we leave it a surprise." He's amused by this whole situation. Eddie is now setting up the scrabble board at our table by the window. We both like this particular window. It was host to the plant that he got from his wife's funeral 25 years ago. The plant that the boys have replaced three times without him knowing. The plant that I now meticulously keep alive because it makes me feel more whole. I never got to meet his wife. It is tragic that none of her sons got to know her either. But Eddie keeps her love alive where he can.

"I hate surprises." My voice is deadpan. I really did. I like knowing what is coming. It helps me stay prepared, and if I'm prepared then I can keep a safe distance from things.

"I know." He chuckles. He actually chuckles. Why is he in such a good mood? I like grumpy Eddie so much more. He's more my speed.

I try to keep from whining as I plop into the chair across from him. "This isn't funny, Eddie." He hands me the bag so I can grab my random letters as he sets up two other letter holders. For the two unwanted guests. "Scrabble Sunday is our thing." I try to emphasize my lack of desire for these guests to show up. "You said each kid gets a thing, I chose this." The pout in my voice is annoying even to me, but I don't care. I don't like letting new people into my safe spaces. Eddie is my biggest safe space. It's a very uneasy feeling having to open that space up. Even for people he trusts.

"Get over it. Sharing is something you should have learned as a kid." He's antagonizing me. Finding joy in my discomfort. This is further proof that it had to be Rory. Eddie is always fawning over the guy. Why? I know why. Rory is ridiculously talented at what he does. Even I get inspired just by watching him. And Eddie has such a soft spot for him.

"I was a bit preoccupied learning other things as a kid." Like how to hide bruises and not offend narcissistic teenage boys with a hunger for blood. I don't have to say that out loud because he knows that. Out of everyone, he is the only one that knows the full depth of what is held in my past.

His eyes harden, "don't joke like that tonight. You will scare Melinda." Who the fuck is Melinda? *Two guests.* I've been so focused on them being Rory that I haven't even thought about who the other guest is.

"It's not joking if it's factual, Eddie."I roll my eyes. I know what he is saying though. Not everyone is able to understand trauma in the same way as those of us who have experienced it. It makes people uncomfortable.

The knock on the door came as Eddie opened his mouth to probably say something to remind me again to behave. I hate behaving.

"Don't be a brat." He barks as he points his finger at me as he stands up. I have to hold my tongue from giving a less than favorable response. He's happy about tonight and I don't plan on taking away from that. He deserves a good night.

"I'm always a brat. It's a state of mind." I mutter while his laughter travels through the kitchen as he goes to answer the door. I prepare myself. I didn't know I needed to be prepared to face Rory outside of our trainer and fighter relationship.

Sure enough, Rory's voice accompanies Eddie's, which is followed by a much softer one. I stand and turn to see them walking into the room. Rory's eyes immediately find mine and he gives me a kind smile. The woman, who I assume is attached to the softer voice, is standing right beside Eddie. She is practically radiating with brightness, and I can't miss the way that Eddie also lights up now that she is in the room. They clearly know each other well. This must be Melinda.

Melinda, who seems to look a lot like Rory. Melinda, who has the same smile as Rory. Melinda, who has the same green eyes as Rory. *Oh shit.* Melinda is Rory's mom. If this isn't bad enough with just Rory being here, now I have to meet his mom? This is why he told me to not be a brat.

Her voice is just as bright as she looks, "wow, you are stunning!" She exclaims as steps in front of me holding out her hand to shake mine. "I'm Melinda. Rory's mom." She motions to where Rory is standing. I already figured that out, but thanks. "He hasn't stopped talking about you by the way. He says you are very impressive with your coaching skills. Smart and strong." She winks at me as she shakes my hand gently. Then her other hand envelopes the other side of my hand, sandwiching it between both of hers. She gives me the kindest smile. It's genuine and warm and I immediately want to pull away. She doesn't even know me and she is treating me like I've done something right just by training her son. She's just as unsettling as her son. Why is he even talking about me? "Thank you for taking care of him." She adds. I can't fight the urge to glance over to where Rory was standing. I also can't help but notice that he has a wave of pink traveling from his neck to his cheeks. He clearly didn't expect his mom to lack boundaries by revealing what he shares with her. He doesn't seem upset though. Which irks me.

Melinda lets go of my hands and I quickly face Rory. He squares his shoulders with a small smirk on his face, anticipating whatever I'm going to say.

"Talking about me to your mom? How cute." I clip. I don't even care that I'm calling him out in front of his mom. I probably should reign it in a bit before Eddie actually gets upset with me, but considering the blush that is intensifying on Rory's cheeks, maybe I will keep it up. It's a cute look on him. This is Eddie's fault. He should stop bringing him over for Scrabble Sunday.

His mom lights up even more, if that's possible, and smiles brilliantly at Eddie. "Oh she is fun! I love her." She pats Rory's shoulder as she passes him and says something softly that I can't quite make out. She takes a bowl that I missed Eddie holding and motions for Rory to follow her fully into the kitchen. The space feels more breathable without them in here.

"I literally just got done saying don't be a brat." Eddie is on me the second they are out of ear shot. I stand my ground in front of him. He should have known how this would play out when he invited them. This is on him.

"You brought his mother?" I hiss at him. "You could have at least warned me. I would have probably put on real clothes, Eddie." I whisper harshly, keeping my voice low considering they are still only a few feet away. I don't think they can hear us though and if they can, they aren't acting like it.

"Stop being so dramatic, Avery. You have on real clothes." He waves his hand up and down motioning to my very unimpressive outfit. I had thrown on a pair of sweatpants that I am positive I stole from one of the boys, and a black tank top with fuzzy socks that I always keep here. The floors in this apartment were always like walking on a sheet of ice. We weren't supposed to be having a dinner party so I dressed for a night in and scrabble.

"Clothes that make me look like a homeless person!" I throw my hands up and immediately tuck them under each other to try and not bring attention to our little whisper argument. I also am trying to not think too hard about why I didn't want his mom to think I don't care enough to dress like a normal person. Parents and I don't get along too well. Eddie has been the only consistent parental figure in my life that I didn't have to leave too soon or that I had to hide from.

"She said you looked stunning. And Melinda doesn't lie." He leans in closer to me, voice low and deep.

I take a step closer to him and stare directly up into his eyes, holding it for about twenty seconds before I notice his eye start to twitch. "You seem to know an awful lot about Melinda." I accuse. His eyes widen the tiniest bit, but it is enough to throw off his concentration and he blinks. I win.

"Damn it." He wipes his hand down his face and lets out a rough hum. "We're old friends. She is basically an angel in human form and you will be on your best behavior for her tonight. She's been looking forward to meeting you and you won't beat her too bad at Scrabble either." Oh, he is using his serious voice. Eddie rarely uses that voice anymore. Little did he know that I have zero intentions of being anything but kind to her. Rory on the other hand? I'll act accordingly with him.

I salute him like the brat he raised and walk backwards to join them by the counter. Leaving Eddie looking after me with an apprehensive expression.

Nine

"I'm a good listener."

AJ

Melinda is pulling out some kind of casserole that smells like it has been cooking in someone's great grandmother's kitchen for six hours. And Rory's taking out a different container.

"Is that pie?" I feel my heart kick up a beat. I love pie.

"Chocolate. Your favorite right?" Rory's no longer blushing. No, instead he is grinning like he won something.

"How do you know that?" Now my heart is beating faster for an entirely different reason now. He just shrugs his shoulders. He clearly has no plans of letting me know how he found out chocolate pie is my favorite.

"Oh I hope you love it! He worked really hard on it this afternoon. Didn't like the consistency of the first one, so he made a second one." Melinda beams behind where Rory is standing and not making eye contact with me. It shouldn't be a comical image, but with the height difference it made me want to giggle. I hold it in though. I'm actively working on Eddie's request for me to not be a brat tonight. Then my brain catches up with the words that left her mouth. Rory *made the pie.*

"There's no fucking way you bake and draw." I blurt out. I hear the groan that leaves Eddie's body from the other room from my language. I mouth an apology to Melinda and she waives me off.

"I can do a lot of things, Jude." He brings his eyes up to rake over me. I'm suddenly more aware of my outfit of choice. "You just never ask.

Maybe you should utilize your question of the day better." He throws me one of his infuriating winks. I let out a frustrated sound which just causes him to grin wider.

"Oh, are we playing Scrabble? I love that game!" Melinda rushes over to the table and I glance over my shoulder to see Eddie joining her. I like her even more now.

"She is actually really terrible at it. But she likes to play 'cute' words and it makes her happy," Rory explains as I watch his mom and Eddie get started on a game. Rory moves to stand beside me as we watch Eddie and Melinda talk animatedly while organizing letters. I realize I've never seen Eddie with a friend like this. It makes my chest fill with warmth.

I feel Rory leaning in closer to me but I don't bring attention to it. He has a tendency to throw me off balance. It's easy to tell that he's attracted to me and clearly he is attractive in general. But his presence shakes me up sometimes. His intoxicating scent wraps around me. His breath kisses my neck and he speaks so gently, "you look adorable, Avery Jude." I inwardly groan over my outfit again. I truly do look homeless, not adorable and for some reason he is being nice about it.

I turn my head only to realize he is much closer than I thought. Our noses are practically touching with the way he is making his body smaller to be more level with me. I flick my eyes to his and take a deep breath to calm my nerves and work to steady my voice. I have no plans of letting him know how he affects me. "Do you always flirt this much?" I don't let my voice waiver, even in his close proximity. He might flirt a lot with me, but he still always gives me the most respect anyone has ever given me outside of the guys and Eddie when we are in the gym. He listens to every direction I give and executes it without doubt or hesitation.

His green eyes don't waiver. My favorite color has always been the lighter shades of green. And his eyes hold every light shade of green with flecks of dark. It grows harder to swallow the longer he keeps eye contact.

He licks his bottom lip as he tucks a hair behind my ear, his finger light as a feather falling down my neck as he drops his hand back to his side.

He raises one eyebrow and when he speaks, his voice is barely audible and it leaves goosebumps crawling over my skin. "Flirt with my trainer? I feel like that wouldn't be incredibly smart." He pauses and I watch his throat move as he swallows. "And we both know you don't like dumb guys, Jude." He lets his stare linger for a moment longer before changing his entire demeanor and clasping his hands together. He speaks louder for Eddie and Melinda to hear as he asks, "Who's hungry?"

Eddie and Melinda make their way back over and start making a plate. I, on the other hand, am still trying to figure out how to breathe properly. What the fuck was that? And why was I so into it?

The pie is unfortunately perfect. I have always loved chocolate pie. I had this one foster mom who would make one for dinner every Friday night. I wasn't able to stay with her for long, but she was one of the kind ones. I was maybe eight when I lived with her, and she would sing and dance as she cleaned up after dinner while I sat at the table and ate pie. She was a little eccentric now that I recount my time with her, but she was fun. And her kindness is still imprinted on my heart.

"It's the best pie you've ever had, right?" Rory is sitting across from me. The Scrabble board nearly full, only a fourth of the bag still full with letters to be drawn. Melinda and Eddie decided that they would rather watch tv in the living room. I bet he even let her pick what they're watching. Eddie is a gentleman like that.

"That's presumptuous." I keep my focus on the game in front of me. I'm only beating him by a few points, which I find slightly enraging. I don't lose.

"Question of the day time." He clears his throat and I oblige his unsubtle queue for my attention. He motions over the board before asking, "why do you love this game so much?" Sometimes his questions are so simple they throw me off.

"I love words," I say simply. Words have so much meaning and I love anything that allows me to get lost in that. It's one of the reasons I love music so much. I wait for him to ask me to elaborate, but the request never comes.

He plays the word -axis- and I know he feels proud of himself because it moves him five points above me, but I am prepared for the letter x and he left an opening on the board. I play -xerus- and keep my lead.

"What kind of word is that?" He points wildly to where the letters are lined up on the board. "That's not real. Eddie! Google this word!" Rory calls into the living room, spelling out my word I just played. It didn't give me a lot of points, but I knew he would cause a scene about it. And that alone is worth it. Rory always finds a way to unsettle me but I never seem to have the same affect on him. It's nice finally watching it happen, even if it is just because of a scrabble word.

"It's an African squirrel, dear!" Melinda calls back from where she is sitting crossed legged with a bowl of popcorn watching some kind of scary movie. An angel who loves blood. I feel like we could actually get along so well. In fact, she hasn't made me uncomfortable in the slightest the whole evening. It's so foreign to me. Feeling comfortable with another person so fast. But she approaches every question with care and tenderness. I never feel like she is asking for any alternative purposes. She just simply wants to know more. Her honesty makes it easy to give her answers.

"Who even knows something like that!" His voice is full of shock and maybe awe? Rory ran his hand through his hair, roughing it up. I decide, at this exact moment, I like this look on him. Slightly sleepy, fully invested, and clearly fluxed.

I shrug my shoulders and motion for him to play his next word. He smiles as he shakes his head and gathers his next word to play. Not at all upset that I'm beating him, just still perplexed at my vocabulary.

"So, you bake?" I attempt small talk. It feels pathetic but he smirks at me asking the same question from earlier as he lays down the letter tiles.

"I'm a good listener." I wait for him to explain what that has to do with baking. When I don't respond right away, he looks up at me and tilts his head. "Remember?" His words from our first time meeting each other wash over me. "Being a good listener means I'm also good at following instructions. I found a recipe and tried it out." Of course he did. Rory is probably one of those annoying as fuck people that are good at anything they try. It's unnatural for people to not be bad at things.

A cold chill shakes my shoulders and Rory is quick to notice. "You want my hoodie?" I know he doesn't mean anything by the offer. He's just a person that takes care of other people. He always helps the kids out in class when he sees one is struggling. He offers to help me carry any boxes that get delivered to the gym. He is just a helpful guy. But the fact that his other hoodie is still laying on my bed doesn't escape me. I don't need two of his hoodies in my possession. One is too much.

I shake my head to gently decline but he's already stripping his hoodie off. He passes it over to me and because I am, in fact, freezing and have been for the past hour I put it on over my head. I let the residual warmth from his body cover my own.

"Thanks. I'll bring it back to you in the morning along with your other one." There's amusement in his eyes at my obvious attempt to act unaffected.

I play my last word for the game and take the win. I don't know how I would survive if I lost to him at my favorite game. But it was the closest game I have played in a long time. Not even Eli came this close to beating me, and he reads more than I do.

"I really like your mom." We both start to clean up the game. And there is just a quiet peace that surrounds the end of the night.

"She's the best." His words are full of a tender type of love. I really love the smile that he wears when he talks about his mom. It's sweet. "She has always had this carefree nature about her. It's infectious. Makes everyone around her feel lighter." That's exactly what it is. She makes the air lighter. What a perfect way to describe her.

"I'm glad Eddie invited her. I think he needed someone besides me and the guys to visit him." I nod to where his mom and Eddie are laughing in the living room. It's nice to see him like this. He spends all his time taking care of us and the gym. He deserves to have moments of pure enjoyment.

"Maybe we can do it again?" He pours the last of the letters back in the bag as he asks the question. I don't miss the hesitation in his voice. Is he asking for me and him to do this again? Or all of us to do this again?

"You asking me out, Rory?" I fail at keeping the interest from bleeding out in my voice. He makes a sort of snorting sound like my question is ridiculous.

"On a date with my mom and Eddie? Not likely." Melinda and Eddie must have noticed us cleaning up, because they are now making their way to where we are. "Ready to go?" He asks his mom and she nods through a yawn. The poor woman is sleepy.

While Melinda hugs Eddie, Rory leans in closer, invading the space around me. "You'll know when I ask you out, Jude. I promise." He speaks softly, but there is intention laced through every word. Does he actually plan to ask me out? I don't know how I feel about that. I don't date. For good reason. I'm not a fan of letting anyone close. I have too much baggage for anyone to have to sort through to get to the good parts.

But the prospect of having Rory ask me out definitely scares the shit out of me, and exhilarates me.

Ten

"Did you say I scare the
shit out of you?"

AJ

Eddie gave me full control with the interview for the media manager position. Something about him trusting me with so much settles a part of my soul. Eddie has always been like that. He is always there to catch me when I falter but he gives me space to try accomplishing whatever it is I'm trying to do. Well, with the exception of last Sunday night. There was no space given to me that night.

Watching him with Melinda, you would never guess he had a heart attack just a few weeks prior. He was so full of life and contentment at the same time, oblivious to any of the moments between me and Rory. I don't think he would have particularly cared if he did witness them, but those moments have thrown me off since that night. Rory has the ability to always make me feel like I'm experiencing emotions for the first time. It makes me feel a bit unstable. At the same time, he never made me feel unsafe. He gives me a safe space to feel and that is what shakes me up.

He's always looking at me like he's trying to decipher the thoughts that aren't spoken and reside only in my head. I don't hate it. I don't hate having him always steal glances my way. I don't hate that he gives me physical space but is still able to gently make sure I am aware of his presence.

Two knocks on the office door pull me back to what I'm supposed to be focusing on, the interview. Mia walks in with her sunshine smile and hair to match. She has on a pair of overalls that have probably seen better days and a cute baby pink tank top underneath. I always admire that she seems to only wear the bare minimum makeup, mascara and always the same red lipstick. Her skin keeps a warm glow but not overly tan. Softly beautiful, that's how I would describe her. She makes something as casual as overalls look like they belong in a magazine and that's a skill.

"Hey Mia, thanks for coming in before your shift. I know it's super early." Fridays are some of the busiest days at the gym, and I really want to get this interview out of the way. Mia doesn't know it, but she already has the job. I didn't even really want to interview her after talking to Eddie more about it. Something in my soul tells me she will be the perfect fit here, belongs here. Eddie told me that I should still go through the process of interviewing her anyways. So here we are.

"I actually stopped by the shop and made us coffee before coming here. I figured you have a busy day today, and Fridays are always a bitch. Might as well have coffee to make it tolerable." And just like that, I'm already more confident that she is our girl for the job. She hands me a coffee cup and I know it's probably what I always order. She likes to experiment with Oliver. I personally find keeping the same order comforting. Creature of habit.

I pull up her portfolio she has attached to her resume and get my pen ready for the questions I have prepped to ask her.

"Can I just say that I really want this position and I know that I probably didn't wear the right outfit for an interview but I'm really good at what I do and I have better outfits. Truth is this is my first real interview. I kind of bullied my way into the coffee shop. And everything else I listed on the resume. But this job intrigues me. So many opportunities. And I love what you do. I mean, you kind of scare the shit out of me. But you're also a badass. I already have so many ideas that I think you would love. I also volunteer for two of the programs you started here. I have my own equipment and a marketing strategy planned out for all social media." I don't think she takes one breath the entire time she talks. She only stops to pull out her phone. She slides it across to me and I look down to see that it's opened to the notes app. "I know that isn't very professional either, but my brain is weird and I love that app. I can mock it up and email it to you? I should have done that before."

I let her continue her rambling as I reach over to gather a full hire packet that we give every new employee. Mia resembles a box of crayons that tumbled out and then a toddler shoved them all back in. She's clearly living life by the moment, but she is right. She's very good at what she does. And she doesn't make my head hurt. In fact, I think I haven't stopped smiling since she came into the room. We need more of that energy here. Energy that brings life.

She's still rambling about something but I'm not fully paying attention. I write in big letters HIRED on the page of questions I printed out and never even asked her. I place that paper on top of the new hire packet and slide them and her phone back to her.

Only then does she stop talking. I watch as the whole thing unfolds in front of me. She stops speaking, glances down at the paper, her eyes widen and then she looks up at me, back down at the packet and then back up at me. Her eyes are slightly watery now but she smiles that brilliant smile. "You're hiring me?" Her voice is so soft, as if she can't believe it.

"I'm hiring you." I stand up and grab my coffee cup to take a sip. Then I remember something she said in the midst of her jumbled ramble. "Did you say I scare the shit out of you?"

"I also said you are a badass. That part is important." Her grin is infectious. I feel myself mirroring it unintentionally.

"Mia, I think you are going to be perfect here." She picks up the folder and her phone, cradling everything as she winks at me. The vulnerability in her voice from a moment ago is already gone. She is wearing her full confidence again.

"I'll fill this all out and have it returned on Monday?" I nod my head and she beams.

"I'll walk you through the little things I always do, but I would like to hear more about this marketing strategy you have. Can you hang out for a few hours on Monday?" She shakes her head yes with so much enthusiasm that her wild curls come untucked from behind her ears.

"See you Monday, boss," She winks and prances, literally, out of my office.

In less than twenty seconds, barely enough time for my office door to close, it's opening again. Rory comes through in nothing but a pair of shorts and it takes great effort to meet his eyes and not let them linger on all his tattoos on display.

"Was that Mia?" He wears that carefree smile of his and for whatever reason, him noticing Mia makes my chest seize up a little.

"You know her?" I raise my eyebrows at him. How does he know her?

"She teaches a kids art class at the youth center on Tuesdays and Thursdays." He acts like that should make all the sense in the world to me. And when he clearly understands that I am missing the connection, he continues explaining. "My mom is the new director of the youth center. I go to help do some heavy lifting sometimes or just to hang out with the kids." Of course he did. Because why wouldn't he be a super hot guy, who is nice, and has a heart for kids. For fucks sake.

"I just hired her to help manage our social media. Eddie thinks I'm spreading myself too thin." Just like always, I let more information tumble out of my lips than necessary when he is around.

"The kids adore her at the center, everyone does actually. I'm sure she'll do an incredible job." He takes the seat that Mia was just sitting in earlier, not caring if I was busy and didn't have time to talk to him right now.

"Shouldn't you be training with Eli right now?"

"Shouldn't you stop avoiding me and actually show up to training at least once this week? I miss you." *I miss you.* He doesn't know me well enough to miss me. He is probably just tired of training ground work so much. Watching Rory's fight videos, it's clear he loves striking the most. Just like me.

"I'm not avoiding you." I find myself trying to stand a little taller as if that will keep this conversation from going where he seems committed to trying to make it go. I am, in fact, kind of avoiding him.

"You are." He crosses his arms and gives me that boyish smirk that he knows works on everyone. "If this is because you don't want to give my hoodies back, you can keep them. It won't hurt my feelings." Damn him. I don't know how he keeps such a non-caring attitude but trains with all the seriousness that makes my own heart flutter.

I can feel the uncomfortable heat creep up my chest and neck. It actually has nothing to do with the hoodies. Although, they are ridiculously comfortable. The perfect amount of soft and worn. Maybe he can tell me how he makes them feel like that.

"You can come over after the gym closes and pick them up actually. I just keep forgetting them." Something about what I said brings his entire body to attention. He leans forward and rests his elbows on the top of his thighs.

"I'll absolutely come over." Fuck. *Did I really just invite him over to my apartment?* It took me forever to invite the guys into my private space. I didn't even realize those words had left my mouth. It's clear he isn't going to let me take them back now though.

"And I'll meet you for training this afternoon. I have a lot of paperwork to do today." Hopefully he leaves now.

"Deal." He stands back up, and this time I allow myself the guilty pleasure of taking in his body and the art that covered it. Normally, shirtless guys don't distract me this much. But I love tattoos. They are so intricate and beautiful and tell you so much about a person. And the thought that maybe he designed some of them himself enters my mind. I won't ask him that though. I wouldn't dare give him the satisfaction of knowing I was looking.

He turns back around when he reaches the office door and looks at where I have my coffee in my hand. "I also ordered us some breakfast. Coffee isn't substantial enough. And I need my trainer at full energy." He leaves immediately, giving me no room to even try and argue with him.

I let a sweaty, shirtless, annoyingly chipper Rory coerce me into *lightly* sparring with him. Lightly meaning that I can go nearly my full strength and he is just tapping me. Literally. Every time he finds a slight opening, he just takes his glove and barely taps me on the side of the head. My very locked down control is dwindling by the second.

We are three rounds into a five round session and he looks like he is having the time of his life. We were supposed to just work on footwork drills and light bag work today. But Rory tag teamed me with Eli to get me into the ring and show him first hand how to 'implement' the footwork drills. It really didn't take much convincing though. I actually enjoy sparring a lot. It lets me focus all my thoughts and anxious vibrations into spurts of moments. It's freeing.

The bell sounds for the fourth round to begin. We are only working five two minute rounds. So we won't tire out too easily and to ensure we can implement fundamentals more. Normally, I would have Oliver in the ring working with Rory but he said that he had to take care of something tonight and needed to go prepare for it. I try to not let that bother me too much because he doesn't always tell me everything. But he texted me instead of showing up at the gym or apartment to tell me and that was unusual for him.

I pivot quickly out of reach for Rory to land a leg kick and use the moment to execute a switch kick to his abdomen. Eddie taught me that move a few years ago and I love having the opportunity to land it. I'm small and quick, which gives me the mobility needed to land closer strikes.

"Damn you're fast."He blows out a breath as he shakes his head as he gets back into base. He's not pushing hard at all. He's mainly just letting me put in work.

"She runs enough, she should be. She has better cardio than all of us." Eli speaks up from where he is balancing on the ropes in the corner.

"Cardio doesn't make me faster, dumbass. It just means I don't get winded like you babies." I call out, never taking my eyes off Rory. I go to throw a simple round house kick and he catches my leg. I know I'm about to hit the ring's floor and prepare myself for the fall.

However the fall never comes. Rory pulls me closer instead of letting me fall, and now I find myself balancing on one leg and trying to remember to breathe properly. Rory's chest is flush against my own and I can see every detail of his tattoos this close. They shine a little brighter with the sweat rolling down his body and I feel his hand wrap around the space where my snake tattoo bends around my thigh.

"Cardio is about making sure you have *endurance,* Eli. Making sure you can last." His voice is low when he speaks like his words are for me even though it's Eli he is talking to. His hand squeezes my thigh, just once, before releasing it. My legs feel too unstable to stand on and my entire body burns like it's being ignited.

The end of the round bell sounds and I use that as the perfect excuse to collapse to the ground. Rory starts to take his gloves off as he stands over me.

"Yep. Don't know what that was." Eli waives his hand between where Rory is standing and I'm dead weight on the ground. "But I'm going to leave now. Love you, A!" I can hear his voice get further away but I barely register him leaving because I am still caught up in whatever that moment was with Rory. I seem to stay caught up in these moments. Which is problematic to say the least. His training is some of the easiest training I've ever been a part of. He listens to every little detailed part of what I'm asking him to do, and just sees it through.

"Let's rest the last round." I tap the spot next to me, still gloved up. I remember him saying that this was part of what he loved about the gym and training when he was younger. Laying on the mats after class and just talking. Eddie taught me that what makes a trainer and fighter relationship strongest is the small things. The things that help us communicate without having to. The things that our brains recognize with the other just because we know the small things about each other. Oliver and I have that. It's why he wants me in his corner for each of his fights. I need to cultivate that with Rory more. Because Eddie is right. Rory has what it takes to actually make it, his passion just needs to be revived. And I want to be in the corner when he makes it happen.

"Let's get these gloves off of you." He opens his palm for me to give him my hand. I watch him take the glove off and then start unwrapping my hand as well. Silence blankets around us as he takes my other hand and does the same routine.

He drops his body down next to mine and the only noise in the air is our mixed breathing slowly becoming steadier as our heart rates lower. I close my eyes and let my body sink further into the floor beneath me. I'm a big fan of these moments as well. After a long day of the gym being alive and loud, this is like a deep breath before it rests for the night.

"Is it a viper?" His voice softly interrupts my meditating thoughts. Clearly seeing the confusion on my face, he clarifies his question by pointing to my thigh. "Your tattoo. Is it a viper?" My body goes from relaxed to feeling like I'm backed in a corner in the time span of me taking a breath in. I hate that about myself. The instinctive need to be self preserved.

"Yeah, it's a viper." I let the words fall into the empty space. I can't stop my mind from nose diving into the memory of when I got this tattoo and the girl I got it for. Chloe was the strongest person I have ever known and it's been a really long time since I gave myself space to think about her with someone new.

"I'm man enough to admit that I might have gone through a giant rabbit hole of snake tattoos to figure that out." And without him even trying, he pulls me from falling over the edge of my spiraling thoughts. A small laugh escapes my chest and releases all the pressure that was trying to take up residence there.

My phone starts ringing from where I left it on the bench. I contemplate whether I want to actually move or stay and my body chooses to stay. Then it rings again. And my thoughts immediately go to Eddie. I quickly make my way over to pick it up when I see Maxwell's name and face light up my screen.

"Don't be mad," he pleads and I feel the goosebumps rain over my skin at his apprehensive tone.

"What happened?" I rush out of the ring and stand facing away from Rory.

"Ollie is going to need you tonight." Max's voice is hushed but the background is loud enough that I have a feeling I know where he is.

"What do you mean? Is he okay?" The noise in the background gets quieter and I know he is moving away from the crowd.

"Remember I asked you not to be mad?" His voice is thankfully clearer now.

"I swear to God if you don't tell me what the fuck is happening I'm going to smash all your recording equipment and hack into your dumbass tiktok account." I hear him gasp on the other end.

"He's going to need you in his corner." He pauses for a moment before continuing. "Literally. He's fighting tonight." I fucking knew it. Dirty little liar.

I tilt my head upwards and grit my teeth. "I'll be there in an hour." I hang up the phone and start towards my apartment, not even taking a minute to gather my stuff first.

Eleven

"I'm with her."

RORY

A very Jude is breathtaking when she lets herself feel. When she lets herself just be in an unfiltered moment of emotion. I watched nearly every emotion flicker over her face during that phone call. The one she ended on though? It made the hair on the back of my neck stand up. Something was wrong. There is no doubt it was one of Eddie's boys with the way she was talking on the phone.

I scramble to get on my feet and out of the ring to follow her. She's moving so fast that I have to jog to catch up with her. She pulls open the front door with so much aggression that her tiny frame stumbles right back into me. My hand wraps around to catch her from tripping over my shoe as she loses her balance.

"Making this a regular occurrence, Jude? I'm okay with that." Whatever sound that just escaped her chest is the most comical and slightly terrifying noise I've ever heard her make. A growl mixed with exertion from pushing herself off of me.

No jokes when she is mad. Got it.

Although, I'm not really joking. I am more than okay with being her body colliding into mine.

"I need to close up, and get changed, and grab a fight bag, and make it to The Poolhouse in an hour. And I need-"

"Let me help." She pauses at my offer, her pretty gray eyes looking up at me. I grab the door and put my foot in place to keep it held open for her. "I can lock up. I can grab the fight bag. I don't know what The Poolhouse is, but I can drive you there." I offer to do it all, just hanging on the hope she will let me help her. No one ever helps her.

"I can do it myself. I don't need your help. Thanks though." Her eyes are like steel as she stares me down. She walks through the door trying to slam it closed behind her but my foot is still in place, keeping the door wide open. Which seems to only frustrate her more and I'd be lying if seeing her all worked up doesn't crack something in my chest wide open. Watching Avery Jude *feel* is my new favorite thing to witness. I haven't realized before now how much she keeps hidden behind those gray eyes and practiced smiles.

"I didn't ask if you needed my help, Jude. I told you to let me help." I open my palm for her to give me the keys to the gym so I can lock up for her. She glares at me hard. I can see the brewing rebellion at my offer to help, and I can't help but deliver a smile until she relents. She hands over the keys though.

"The bag is in the office lockers. Grab the green bag, not the blue one. I hate the blue one."

"Is the bag mint green like your favorite color or regular green?" I fight the smile at her obvious interest in how I know her favorite color.. I've had that one figured out since the end of the second week when she wore four different workout sets in the same mint green color. It always seems to make her skin glow a little more and her eyes a little brighter than usual.

Her voice is fragile when she asks, "how do you know that's my favorite color?"

I tip my head to the side slightly and grin at her. "Are you going to waste your question of the day like that?" I feel like it should be obvious to her that I pay attention by now.

I watch her chest rise and fall twice as she tries to make up her mind. So I push a little harder to help assure her that I'm serious about my offer to help. "Go get ready, I'll get your bag and take care of things here." We stand still, just resting in each other's space a few moments longer. I know she's warring with herself to trust me or not. And if I was just a regular attendee of the gym, she absolutely wouldn't. But we have been circling each other for nearly a month now and I feel certain that the want to trust me will win out in her head.

"I'll meet you back down here in fifteen minutes," she decides. I watch her head up the stairs to her apartment. As soon as she is safely inside, I make quick work with getting everything taken care of for her.

Fifteen minutes later I am waiting by my car for her to come out of her apartment. The time spent waiting gives me a minute to really consider why I have such an incessant need to not let her do things on her own. If she went for a run, I was already out front of the gym, ready and waiting. If she was teaching a class, I found myself gravitating to whatever area she is teaching near. I have no set workout plan anymore, I just stay in orbit around her. And now I'm following her to whatever the fuck The Poolhouse is. Unprepared but ready for whatever I'm following her into.

The sound of her footsteps coming down the stairs breaks my thoughts and brings my entire focus on her. The outfit she's wearing makes my entire body come to attention. And the dark lipstick painting her lips makes all of my thoughts form into the singular need to kiss her. She doesn't notice me watching her right away, which allots me time to really take her in. She has on a pair of jeans that seem to be worn in. AJ strikes me as the type of person to have a favorite pair of jeans. The top she's wearing? It wasn't until this moment that I realized that Avery Jude is a menace to society. She's wearing a corset top that has me choking on air. It's painted on skin, seamlessly following the curve of her breasts and cinching in tight around her waist. Her hair is down, in soft waves. The exact way that I complimented her on that first night I visited Eddie and she was there.

She closes the distance left between us and smiles up at me. In a rare moment for us, she is giving me a genuine smile. "I know how to not look like a gym rat, you know." She clearly caught me ogling her. But jokes on her, I like her any way she looks.

I savor one last look at her, words falling from my lips with conviction. "The way you look is criminal, Jude. Completely unfair." A sweet shade of pink makes an appearance on her cheeks but she doesn't shy away from me this time. I like that I can make her blush. Her phone buzzes in her hand and we both glance down at the screen. The moment is now broken. Maxwell's face lights up the screen for only a second before she ignores the call. Her fingers fly across the screen as I open the passenger door for her. I get in the driver's seat and drive, hoping she gives me directions as needed since I still don't know where we are going. "Which one is in trouble?" I have a good feeling which one could make her react this way. Pissed off but jumping at the call of being needed. She would baby Maxwell and Eli would never worry her like this. But Oliver? One thing that has become abundantly clear since I've been back is that they are connected on a molecular level. The type of connection that makes me second guess if I should really be having so many indecent thoughts about my trainer.

"Ollie." Her voice seems far away and I don't have to look over to know she is staring out the window. She puts on a playlist and we let it fill the space. It's her way of shutting down the conversation. I know her well enough to know that if she wanted to talk about whatever Oliver has gotten himself into, she would. I'm just thankful she let me come with her. The amount of weight she allows to sit on her shoulders is enough to make anyone crumble. But she spends every day not allowing a single person to doubt her ability to handle it all.

I follow the map and it leads us into the next town over. We pull up to an abandoned rec center and the parking lot is full. She motions for me to go around the back where a smaller gravel parking lot was marked off. I know exactly what we are walking into now. Me and the guys used to sneak into these when we were younger. It was a free for all, non sanctioned fight. It was rare that anyone actually made it pro in this sport. And for those that didn't, they end up here. Fighting isn't something that you just stop doing. It becomes a part of your DNA, the way you breathe. And the nature of it never really leaves you. That's why this place exists. It's a community for everyone who shares the same hunger for the sport.

They called her and expected for her to come here alone? What the fuck.

Getting out of the car, I notice the graffiti painted on the back of the building: THE *POOLHOUSE*. She is getting the fight bag out of the back seat of the car. Oliver is going to fight tonight and that's why he needs Avery to be here. She's going to corner him. I wonder how often this happens. I imagine she probably hates places like this. Avery likes to be as in control of a room as she can be. It's less unpredictable. My mom is the same way. Avery didn't hesitate to put herself in a situation that made her uncomfortable for Oliver though. He called, she showed up. That type of loyalty is forged.

"So are you and Oliver together?" The question leaves my mouth before I even realize that the words are real. I don't regret it though. You have to ask questions to get answers. And if she is in some kind of complicated situation with Oliver, then I need to recalibrate my thoughts and take a step back from inserting myself into her life like this.

"That's your question of the day?" She swings around to where I stop following her. She looks at me suspiciously. She has a harshness in her eyes that I recognize as defensiveness.

"It's an important question." I swallow hard. I need to know. Before we go into this building and I am overcome with the need to keep her close and protected, I need to know if I even have a chance at earning the right to feel that way.

"Oliver is my best friend," she says, like it's obvious. Like I should not have asked such a dumb question. I wait for her to elaborate but she clearly is not going to. At least she didn't say yes. I plan on hanging on to that small fact.

We enter the building and my entire body moves to frame the back of hers. This place is disorienting with how packed it is and the way the music is shaking the air around us. My reflex to keep my eyes on her at all times is at war with trying to make sure nobody is a threat around us. She weaves through the crowd with precision. Eyes follow her through the path she carves out of the waves of people. We end up at a back door. The giant bear of a man says nothing even though his eyes widen in surprise at seeing her walk up. He opens the door quickly for her then he tries to close it directly behind her but I leave no space between us to give him that option.

"He's with me, Rob." She announces as she keeps walking forward past us both and *Rob* gives me a death glare. He's big but I could take him. If I need to.

"I'm with her." I give him a wink as I pass him and keep close as she marches down a long hallway.

She opens a door to our left and there sits Oliver, shirtless and hands wrapped. Fight ready.

She marches right up to him and I can't feel the rage she leaves behind her as she goes. "You're a dumbass. Your dad literally just had a heart attack. Thankfully he doesn't know about your side hobbies or this would probably cause him to have another. And you want to risk hurting yourself, again, for what?" She doesn't even stop to take a breath before she starts in on him. I'm also pretty sure Eddie definitely knows about the side hobbies, nothing gets past that man. Nothing ever did.

He stands up and I watch the guilt wash over his face. "I told them to not call you, A." Sighing, his eyes seek out his brothers who must have shrunk themselves into the corner the second she entered the room because I didn't notice them when we came in. I don't blame them. She is beautifully terrifying.

Avery hangs her head before calmly saying, "can we get a minute? I need to prep him." She makes it sound like she's asking, but it is absolutely a demand. We are all obedient and leave the room. I don't think any of us are brave enough to argue with her right now.

"He came with you?" I hear Oliver ask her as we exit the room and I have never been so desperate to know what the words would be that came out of her mouth next. The door shuts as she starts to speak and it's too muffled for me to make sense of.

"Thanks for coming with her." Eli says as soon as I turn away from the closed door and face them both.

"You expected her to come alone? To these kinds of fights?" I take a step towards them, faltering the containment of irritation of them making her come down here like this. Shouldn't they be trying to look out for her?

The blank expression coming from both their faces is identical. I'm clearly missing something but I can't figure it out just yet. I look at Eli, silently willing him to fill me in.

"You know she is a crowd favorite here, right?" Maxwell is the one to give me the information I was missing. And then it all makes so much sense. The way she didn't have to make eye contact with anyone since the minute we entered the building. The way she was able to just move with authority. She isn't out of place here.

"She hasn't fought in a while though." Eli corrects, looking quickly over at Max before looking at me. "Oliver needs her. She's never not been in his corner since she started coming to any of the fights. He didn't want us to call her, but he hasn't fought since his injury." Eli is trying to ease my worry, and while I am thankful for that, I still don't like that they all just expected her to show up when asked. "And he needs this fight. He's been struggling with losing his sponsorship and everything else lately."

Everything else means me being back. I know that he has been avoiding training with me, but I couldn't figure out why. But it makes sense now. I can't imagine losing the one thing I've worked my whole life for.

"What are the stats on his opponent?" Instead of allowing my worry about them overworking her to take over, I pivot my focus to helping Oliver win this fight.

I see them both relax a little more. "This isn't like fights you are used to, Rory. They don't have stats but his name is Andie. He has less experience than Ollie, but he's aggressive. Likes to come in strong and hard."Eli lists off what he knows.

"Does he know about the leg injury?" They both nod their heads.

"That's why we called her. She will be able to read Andie's movements faster than the rest of us." Of course she will. She's impressive.

The door creaks back open and Oliver walks out ignoring the rest of us standing in the hall. Avery follows him and hands me her jacket and phone, also not making eye contact. She's pissed at Oliver's selfishness, but she isn't going to let him go into that ring alone and I respect her ability to do that. To separate what is needed and what is still going to come.

We follow Avery and Oliver out of the hallway to the door we came in at. As the door opens, the noise is eruptive. A vastly different atmosphere than when we first came here. I watch Oliver push through the large crowd, the rest of us right behind him. We enter into a giant opening and it becomes abundantly clear why they call this place The Poolhouse.

The crowd is surrounding the most worn down, underground pool I've ever seen. All water was long gone and the paint appears to have been chipping away for years. Surrounding the pool are two levels of crowd filled space. Oliver descends a ladder and I watch him assist Avery down as well. We follow. I immediately clock his opponent across the abandoned pool. He is slightly taller and maybe an inch broader in the shoulders, but Ollie has always been leaner in his fight weight. He likes the ability to move faster and endure longer. And it works well for him. He's mastered being smaller by using it to his advantage. He lets his opponent underestimate him and then strikes harder than they could possibly anticipate.

The ref checks their wrapped hands. Even though this is clearly not a sanctioned fight, I guess they want to make sure no one got seriously injured or it's just for show. My eyes, as usual, easily find Avery. She is every bit the collected trainer that I saw and experienced on the first day meeting her. Watching her in this environment is a thrill. She has confidence and strength vibrating off of her. She's hungry for what's to come.

There is no ring. It's just the worn down floor of the pool. Before I know it, the fight has started. Avery's eyes never leave Oliver's opponents' feet the whole first round. This girl is obsessed with footwork. Oliver lets this guy move around a lot, dodging anything he attempts to throw. I can see the slight favoritism on his injured leg as he moves but I don't think Andie is picking up on it. After a few seconds of Oliver baiting the guy to move in closer, Oliver pivots his back foot quickly and drives his whole body into a right hook. He keeps the range close as he lands a few body shots and finishes with a knee into the guy's ribs. Round one easily goes to Oliver. Andie is too eager and that's exactly what Oliver wants.

"How many rounds?" I throw the question out for either of them to answer.

"Three." Thank fuck. Less time in that cement pit means less stress on her and less chance of Oliver getting injured again. Eli doesn't leave my side while Maxwell wanders off to a different group. Round two starts and Oliver takes a nasty right hook. Blood pours from his bottom lip but he doesn't look too shaken. His hands weren't up. He wouldn't have taken that hard of an impact if they were.

"You own hands! Use them." I can hear Avery's voice slice through the abundance of voices in the building. Oliver's hands retract back to his head and tuck in. He digs his heel in and moves to the right to avoid a kick to his injured leg. And immediately takes more control of his space. Only a few jabs are exchanged in this round. Oliver is a bit more hesitant now but still aggressively controlling the movements. He retreats into the corner where she's waiting. I watch Avery talk and cool down Ollie. She's so zoned in on their conversation that I'm sure she hears and sees nothing else. Oliver is nodding at whatever she is saying. I believed his brothers when they said he didn't want to bring her here tonight but it's also clear how much he is depending on her to help get him through this. He needs this win. Mentally. And she helps lock that win in. I get it. Fighting is almost more mental than physical. Losing such a giant opportunity like a sponsorship on your last round of trying to actually make it? That had to be the most crippling attack on his life. Add in the physical therapy from his injury, and all that has happened with his dad. I feel for the guy.

Round three starts and Oliver comes out even more focused than when he initially came into the fight. The air all around is charged and filled with hunger for a winner. Everyone waits with baited breath over what is about to happen.Oliver lands a beautiful combo and I can tell it really hurts the guy by the way he folds over. Andie stumbles back as he tries to straighten out and Oliver takes that split second as an opportunity to kick him straight in the abdomen and comes back in with a left hook to end the round early. Andie crashes to the ground with a cracking sound that reverberates in the hollowness of the pool before the crowd's cheering eclipses it.

Oliver is swarmed by the crowd but Avery doesn't stay with him. I watch her climb up the ladder and walk up to us, stopping in front of Eli. "Get him cleaned up." Her eyes are all stormy with her demand.

"AJ." Eli softly attempts to talk to her but she stops him before he can say anything else.

"No. He could have been seriously hurt. He is barely back to being able to train fully. He's lucky he's talented and Andie has a lousy leading leg or he would have lost tonight." Eli opens his mouth to defend his brother and then closes it. She's pissed and he can see that he isn't going to help take her anger away right now.

"I can take you home." He offers instead. It sounds more like an apology.

"I have a ride." Her eyes cut to me, silently communicating that I'm her ride and I better go along with it. As if she even needs to confirm that I was her ride. I give her a soft wink and she turns her stare back on Eli. "Get him cleaned up. Ice the leg. I left the bag in the room. Don't leave it a mess, and bring it back to the gym when you are done. " Eli nods and accepts his fate as his brother's babysitter for the rest of the night.

I can't stop myself from looking back up at Oliver to find that he is already watching the entire exchange. His eyes on the back of Avery's head. I tip my head to him to try and convey that I will take care of her. She might be mad at him now, but they would be fine probably by tomorrow. And I don't want him to worry about her while she storms off. Selfishly, I'm fine if he takes a back seat from worrying about her at all.

Twelve

*"Trusting people makes
me want to vomit."*

AJ

I slept maybe two hours last night, collectively. And around three the night before. The fact that Oliver was so selfish made me want to fight him myself. Luckily I caught Michael's slight rhythm step before he would advance and found the opening for him to land the right shots to win that fight. It could have definitely gone south much faster. Oliver must have been training in his garage to keep me from knowing he had a new match. Maybe that is what upset me more, the fact that he trained for this and didn't tell me. That he didn't think that I could be trusted? If it wasn't for Maxwell and Eli, then he would have gone into that fight fucked in the head, and lost. We all knew it.

I stare at my five missed texts and two missed facetime calls from Ollie.

Missed facetime

Oliver

> **I really am sorry, A.**

Oliver

> **I didn't get hurt and I won.**

Missed facetime

Oliver

> **Thanks for being in my corner.**

Oliver

> **We both know you aren't asleep. I'll meet you for a run in an hour. I'll run until I puke so you can stop being mad at me.**

I consider his offer. Making him run until he pukes sounds pleasing enough. But I also know that making him stress a little longer will be more satisfying. Running has been one of the outlets I use to exhaust my brain for the longest time. And normally Oliver is my favorite running partner. We just keep pace with one another and let our feet hit the ground. No secondary thoughts flooding my brain. No stolen glances to my left to make sure he was still there. No lasting burning sensation from him saving me from nearly being hit by a car. No sharing playlists. No sharing details about our lives. Just running.

I reach for my phone again and back out of my thread with Oliver. My fingers hover over a different thread that I've found myself lingering on more than once lately. Always stopping myself from texting him though. A thread that leads to the guy that keeps showing up when I need him. A guy who gives me space while simultaneously keeping me in his. A guy who is supposed to just be the fighter I'm training.

Rory's name blurs the longer I stare at it. I know that if I ask him to hold mitts for me this morning, he will. My mind gravitates towards him before I even have a chance to back out of the thought. Then my phone vibrates with a text from him.

Rory

> **I have an idea.**

AJ

> **Most people have ideas.**

Rory

You can't say no.

I mean, you can. Obviously.

But please don't.

AJ

Are you a serial texter? That's not attractive.

Rory

You already think I'm attractive.

This guy. The fact that a smile appears on my face without permission only slightly makes me concerned.

AJ

What's your idea?

Rory

Let's not go for a run this morning. I know you're really into cardio. But I think we should try different cardio.

AJ

I'm not having sex with you.

Rory

I wasn't offering. Meet me at the gym at the same time as usual.

AJ

You're bossy this morning.

Rory

> **Please.**

If a girl could deny Rory Davis when he said please... Well, that girl wouldn't be me.

AJ

> **I'll be there.**

I dig out my favorite mint green set for the gym today and grab both his hoodies. It actually makes me sad to have to give them back to him because one of them is the most comfortable thing I've ever worn. He doesn't seem too pressed about getting them back. I invited him to come up and grab them when he dropped me back at my apartment Friday night. But he just sat in the driver's seat of his car and did that staring at me thing he does where he tries to wait for me to tell him something without him asking. Sometimes I think he is too afraid to ask but then I'm always reminded that Rory is the type of guy that if he wants to do something he does it. He would ask. He's letting me meet him. Creating space and giving space.

I find myself more comfortable than I'm willing to admit. I like being around him. Rory is so steady and unwavering in who he is. Everyone knows this. He's intentional with everything he does. He has to be. He has every part of his life set. He knows what it's going to take to get to where he wants to be. He enters a room and everyone feels his assuredness. His tattoos only add to his whole strong and steady persona. Tattoos that I absolutely spend far too much time cataloging. They have no organization or theme. He's covered in flowers and landmarks and abstract art. I have a feeling that he probably designed some of them himself. He keeps that sketchpad with him every day. Always using his rest times drawing in it.

The other day, it was out on top of his bag while he was in the showers and it took every ounce of strength I had to not steal a glance at it. I don't even think he would tell me no if I asked to look at it. Now that I think about it, he never tells me no.

When I reach the front doors of the gym, Rory is there to greet me with a cut off shirt and sweatpants. It's ridiculous how attractive he is. His hair is still wet like he had just taken a shower and his bangs are falling in front of his face. Bangs shouldn't be so hot on a man. When he notices me getting closer, his smile grows wider.

"You finally brought me my clothes back?" He nods towards where I have his hoodies resting between my arm and my side.

"I offered for you to come up and get them Friday and you refused." I remind him as I toss the hoodies at him. He catches them both effortlessly with one hand. Damn him and his big hands.

"You were tired and I figured you wanted to just probably stay inside once you were there." I did just that actually. After the fight, I didn't want to be around anyone.

"Don't pretend to know me, Rory." I know I sound harsh but it doesn't seem to affect him.

"I wouldn't have to pretend if you would actually let me." His words should sound like an accusation but they bleed with a plea. A plea I'm going to do my best to ignore.

"What are we doing today?" I change the subject as he walks us through the door and we make our way over to the benches by the hanging bags.

I watch him sit down on the bench and unzip his bag. He glances up at me and then to the space that is open in front of him on the bench in invitation. When I take the seat, he unpackages new wraps and holds out his hand, palm up, and wiggles his fingers for me to place my hand in his.

"I get sent wraps like once a month from different brands." He takes out the gray colored set of wraps and begins wrapping my hand. We are sitting so close that I can feel the heat from his body and his smell infiltrates every molecule of air around me. "My mom used to do this thing she would call change of habit days. Days that she would wake up and do everything new. We would go buy breakfast instead of making it and order something we hadn't tried before. Or we would walk a lap around the neighborhood before getting into the car. She would play a new band instead of the playlist she always wanted to play." The mixture between the way his voice is soothing and the way he is wrapping my hand makes goosebumps pebble all over my body. The deep vibrations of his voice lulls me in a way. "She told me she really struggled with anxiety and panic attacks when I was old enough to understand it." I nod for him to continue when he glances up at me to make sure I'm paying attention. "She would always say that sometimes our brain needs to be reminded that there's more." He finishes the one hand and I'm already giving him my other hand before he has the next wrap ready to go. I'm desperate to hear more about Melinda. "She said that if she could find that feeling of finding something new that she loved, it made everything else feel less suffocating. I want to try that today. That's the idea I was talking about. A change of habit day." I watch as he circles the wrap around my wrist and feel the tips of his fingertips hold my body captive from the smallest touch. "You're still struggling with getting an ample amount of rest. I assume you aren't using your normal fix..." His eyes hold a pinch of unease as he brings that back up. I had told him I normally use sex to wear me down enough to sleep. When I said it, I obviously meant to just throw him off a little. I didn't expect him to hold onto what I said. Or for it be brought back up between us.

"No." I have to clear my throat of the hard bubble that won't go away. "Not for a while anyway." He finishes the second wrap and pulls his phone out of his bag. He types for a few moments and I feel my phone vibrate from the side pocket of my shorts.

"I made a new playlist. You have new wraps. And we can do some of my favorite bag warm ups as a new workout instead of your usual run." *Change of habit.* It's sweet he thinks that this will help me. That he is trying to help me. It makes me a little uncomfortable, but it is sweet.

"I like my playlist." I mumble.

"Listen, I love your playlist. I promise you will like this one too. Trust me." He picks up my headphones and hands them over to me.

"Trusting people makes me want to vomit." That earns me a full laugh. I wasn't joking. I hate trusting people. The thought of giving them that type of availability to me makes my skin crawl.

"I put your favorite song on it." He bribes. I quickly scroll through the playlist and sure enough Sweet Dreams is listed somewhere in the middle of it. When I look back up at him, he gives me a wink before turning and walking back to the bench. "You can get started and I'll be there in a minute!" He tosses the words over his shoulder as I head to the bags.

Fifteen minutes into the warm up and I can admit that this playlist is actually really good. Would I admit that to him? Not a chance. Rory moves to the bag two down from me and I try to not delve too much into why it bothers me that he is choosing to be so far away from me. Then I realize he needs the space, physically. He is over there throwing spinning kicks to the bag. I've seen quite a few guys come through the gym with a huge Tae-Kwon-Do background, but we are mainly a striking and jiu jitsu gym. The guys picked up a passion for jiu jitsu and convinced Eddie it would bring a bigger training base to the gym and they weren't wrong. They are some of our largest classes.

I pull the headphones off my ears and walk over to him. "Teach me." I request as I point to the bag.

"Teach you?" I must have caught him off guard because his annoying smirk isn't plastered to his face like usual.

"The kick." I nod again to the spot where he had just landed the last kick. "Teach me." I take my headphones all the way off and lay them on the ground away from us. "Change of habit, yeah?" I remind him.

He gathers himself and nods slightly. "Alright, Jude. I'll teach you." He moves over to stand parallel with me. "Take your leading leg," he taps his leg. "It's going to be your constant. It will be the one you spin on and just kind of throw a roundhouse with the back." He goes through the motions of what I should do so I can mimic him.

"That doesn't sound too hard." I shake out my body as I replay what he just did. I just need to get the angle right.

"For you, it won't be. You just have to figure it out." I don't miss the way he compliments my capability so easily. "Here, watch me a few times and I know I don't have to say it, but watch my feet." He says with a shit eating grin. He knows I love footwork. Ever since I swept him, he has been giving me hell about my obsession with it.

I watch him as he demonstrates the kick a few times. And we spend the next few minutes straightening out my spins. Which sounds counterproductive because a spin isn't straight. But Rory is showing me that my hips have to have direction so I can land on the bag where I want.

"Your mom really taught you a lot." I haven't been able to stop thinking about the fact that she took the time amidst whatever she was struggling with mentally to make sure her kid understood you can always work through something. To have a parent love you so much that they introduce that into your life so early. To be protective and still realistic. Until Eddie, I never experienced that. He spent his whole life with it.

"She taught me everything I know." He comes up closer to stand directly behind me. "Let's try it slower so you can feel how it is supposed to feel and then you can speed it up." I nod. I feel his hands lightly rest on my hips at the same time his breath kisses my ear. "Is this okay?" I think I nod again, but can't be sure. His closeness makes the air a little thinner.

"So let's try two spins. Lead leg and then you start the spin with the back…" He doesn't seem to be too affected by our closeness which makes me feel slightly embarrassed that I am. His grip tightens for a second before he lets out a slow breath.

"I brought coffee!" Our heads jolt around to see the little ball of chaos that is Mia walking to us. Rory takes a step back, but I can still feel his body heat so I know he didn't step back too far.

I glance up at the clock we keep on the wall, "I didn't realize it was already close to eight, I'm sorry. I'll just go grab a jacket and we can get your walk through started." I walk over to where I keep some spare stuff in one of the lockers to grab something to cover up. No jacket in sight though. I usually always keep a jacket close. The scars always make the kids ask questions and I can't handle new people constantly staring at them.

"Just keep mine." I turn to see Rory offering me his hoodie and something in me warms. I take the hoodie and push my arms through it easily. I unravel the wraps to give them back to him but he stops me from handing them over. "You can keep them too. They are the same shade as those storms you have for eyes. Don't girls like matching?" His smirk is back in full force and this time I'm grateful for it. The awkwardness of him taking care of me dissipates with that smirk.

I glance over his shoulder to see Mia just eating this entire interaction up. She has a tiny grin on her cute face and her nose is slightly scrunched up. She's still holding the two coffees in her hand. Oliver comes in from the back doors. He's pouring sweat and must have ditched his shirt while on his run. The run he probably assumed I was going to be joining but got distracted and never answered him this morning.

"Hey Ollie, shirtless is a good look for you." Mia's the first to greet him. Her entire demeanor turns playful. Meanwhile Oliver looks like he would rather be anywhere but right here between us all right now.

"Perfect timing!" I motion between him and Mia. "You can take Mia through a walkthrough of the gym. She's going to be our new social media manager. Put on a shirt and be nice," I warn him.

"A." He starts walking towards me but I throw a hand up stop him.

"You want to help me? This is helping me." Mia doesn't seem too upset by the change of plans. Honestly Oliver can do a walkthrough and show her the ropes in his sleep. I just don't want to talk to him yet and I've had a good morning. Rory's plan to knock around the cloudiness in my head worked and I don't want to ruin that with Oliver apologizing and me telling him that he should be more careful. He's a grown ass man. If he wants to push himself to the point of possible injury again, he can. But I can sense he is spiraling and I'm trying to hold this gym together. Monday morning is not the time for this conversation.

"You can also take the smallest kids class today." Now that, I add to his schedule because I am still slightly pissed at him and I'm petty. Teaching the smaller kids class is the most daunting. They never listen and it's similar to what I assume it would be trying to herd wet cats.

"You're joking." His whole face drops with unbelief. I'm not.

"Nope." I smile up at him sweetly and pat his chest, completely forgetting that he is disgustingly sweaty. "The kids love you and Mia needs to see all aspects of the gym so she can start working on a profile for the socials."

"I'm here for it all." She agrees instantly and in that moment I am once again thankful for hiring her.

"Okay, you can be mad. I'll take the punishment of teaching the kids class. But you can't stay mad, A. You're my best friend." My smile softens as I make eye contact with him. He isn't wrong. I can never stay mad at him. It's an annoying fact. No matter how dumb and grumpy he is, I am always here to support him.

"And you're my best friend Ol. But you're also a dumbass. Rory and I have footage to watch." I turn to Mia and she offers me the coffee she is holding. "If you need me, just come get me," I tell her.

"You got it boss." She turns on her heel and is now face to face with Oliver. "I'll wait while you go and get changed." And with that, I know that I won't have to worry about her with Oliver at all. I might actually need to worry about Oliver with her.

"Punishing him with the kid's class?" Rory is following me up the stairs to the office. We don't actually have fights to watch but I'm thankful that he just went along with it.

"Change of habit." I grin over at him and for the first time in a while, I feel a tiny bit lighter.

Mia survived the day. I felt bad at first pairing her with the grumpiest form of Oliver but her smile never dropped. The whole day she was practically vibrating with an energy that has forever been foreign to me—carefree. The kids adored her from the first second. Her first day and she already started a new end of class ritual of sitting them all down and asking their favorite part of class. The kids lit up with bright eyes and even brighter smiles. It was endearing.

I came out of the office after finishing up the last of the paperwork to bring to Eddie's this week and ran right into Mia.

"How are you so solid and still so little? You will have to give me your workout routine because damn." Her eyes are as bright as ever as she assesses me from head to toe. "No wonder they all love you. Hot and bossy. Deadly combo." I genuinely will never understand how so many words come out of her mouth at one time.

"How was your first day?" She had already made a spotlight post on the website. We got good traffic because of Eli and Maxie's jump rope videos. People love seeing them. They thought that it was extra attractive since they were twins. When they would rarely convince Oliver to do one with them, our memberships would always spike a little because then the realization that they were triplets was made. Is it unethical to let them boost membership sign ups? Probably. Did any of us actually care? No.

"Oliver was fine if that's what you are really asking." Damn. I opened my mouth to respond but in true Mia fashion she just kept talking. "He did act like he didn't want to teach the kids and something about you missing a run. So I told him to stop being a bitch and just take it." The sound that escapes my chest was meant to be a chuckle but I think I choked on air instead.

"He deserved it. I promise."

"I vote we get tacos." She winds her arm through mine and starts walking, giving me no option but to fall in line beside her. This girl even smelled like sunshine, like laying in a field of your favorite flowers and the sun hitting your face. And suddenly the air got harder to breathe and my throat lost all comprehension on how to swallow. She reminds me of Chloe. Her bright smiles and the way she fills every forgotten space of a room. Mia is a force. "Oh and margs! Obviously." I give her my best attempt at a smile. If she wasn't attached to me and holding me up, I would collapse on the floor. I don't know how I didn't realize why I was so drawn to her to begin with.

Thirteen

"Why doesn't she fight?"

RORY

I watch Eddie put his beer down on the counter between us. The label is far past the sweating stage and has begun to flake off in disgusting wet slices. Eddie has been asking me for updates weekly since the second week I got here. I know he trusts Avery with the gym and the boys to help run everything. He's just worried about burdening them too much. His love for them all is so unwavering. Especially his love for Avery.

"If she knew you were drinking right now, I don't think I could protect you." I tilt my head to where the beer is resting on the table. And then I picture the absolute war path she would be on if she were here right now and smile.

"She's so full of fight. Always has been. Like there's a wire in her that can bend but never break." Eddie's voice is full of admiration when he talks about her, always. I wonder exactly how long he's known Avery. It's evident that he raised her in a lot of ways. They share the same kind of grit in every situation. The same softness to meet people but remain guarded. "How are you two doing with the training?" He brings the conversation back to his usual questioning.

I take a second to consider my answer. Training with Avery feels more private the more time I spend with her. I told her I wanted to feel again when I was on the mat and she has made me feel every breath that's been taken in her vicinity. I've drawn those scars on her body more times than I can count. I can't help but think about what she's gone through to bear them. I've drawn the smirk she wears when she knows she's about to say something that I wouldn't expect to come out of her mouth. I've drawn her in that sin drenched outfit repeatedly since she wore it a few nights ago. My entire notebook is bordering on creepy where it's full of her. I know she's thought about looking at it too. I caught her side eyeing it when she thought I wasn't paying attention. She always has my attention though. "Training is better than it has been in a long time. I actually taught her how to do a tornado kick this morning." Mentioning it brought back the memory of my hands on her bare waist, how soft her skin was, how she smelled like wildflowers and spice. Which is perfect for her.

"Isn't she supposed to be the one training you?" He arched an eyebrow but a silent smile tilted the left side of his face. I don't think Avery could do anything wrong in his eyes.

"Why doesn't she fight?" I take a risk asking the question. I know he probably won't answer it and at the same time it reveals my obvious interest in her past.

And just like that, his smile fades. I don't mention that I'm educated on how she obviously used to fight at The Poolhouse. They clearly don't want him to know or think he doesn't know. There's no way that Eddie didn't know. He knew every time we got ourselves into trouble when we were younger. Every time we snuck out the side door, he was waiting for us when we got home. He never really yelled at us. Just told us that we should be more considerate and always careful. Eddie has always had this disposition about him where he is steady but heartfelt.

I watch him pick at the label a little more before deciding on his answer. "Whatever you want to know about Avery, you need to ask her. She's fought for her story to be her story." There's a sadness and pride that floods his eyes as he recalls something.

"I'm trying." I answer honestly.

I watch as he assesses me with creepily observant eyes. The same eyes that knew every time I lied when I was younger. I'm not lying at this moment. I've been trying with every ounce of my soul to get to know Avery Jude. And while she's been giving me small glimpses, she is still so careful with revealing too much. I've learned quickly that the more I just show up, the more willing she is to let me her. So I keep showing up.

"You like her." He realizes. It's not like I'm trying very hard to hide it though.

"Who doesn't like her?" I deflect, poorly. Eddie's laughter trickles over the table and up the back of my neck. I knew he would easily see through that.

"I've known that girl since she was fifteen years old and she's never once allowed herself the peace of knowing a relationship outside of the ones she has between me and my boys." He cautions as he finishes off his beer and tosses the bottle into the trash causing it to clatter to the bottom.

I don't why I feel the need to settle that she and I don't have a relationship but I do. "Nothing is going on between us. She's my trainer." He actually snorts. This bear of a man snorts and the disbelief it holds lingers in the space around us.

"I don't give a shit about her being your trainer. You're both adults." He clarifies, propping his hand under his chin and zeroes his eyes in on me. His stare holds the weight of years raising boys that test every limit of existence. I don't waiver under his stare though. I expected this speech when he inevitably figured out I was growing to like her a lot more than just whatever we are currently. "You're going to get hurt." His voice drops kindly and a heaviness expands in my chest. That's not what I was expecting him to say.

"I haven't even done anything." I defend.

"You will. You can't help it. It's why you are on the brink of making your dream you've had since you were a kid a reality. You aren't afraid of putting in the work for what you want. You've always been one of my kids, Rory." He assures me before leaning forward, "but that girl knows nothing but hurt and it's taken her a really long time to realize she doesn't have to be chased by her ghosts. She's made a haven with this gym. And if she feels like that is threatened, she'll remove the threat." He doesn't have to tell me how guarded she is. I've spent weeks just trying to get her to give me slivers of who she is. And his words make me even more desperate to know more about her.

"I don't really know what you want me to say here, Eddie." I blow out a breath. I'm not afraid of getting hurt by her and like he said I'm willing to put in the work. I just don't know how to show him that.

"Don't go after her unless you can handle it. That's all I'm saying." He's definitely saying more but I respect his ability to be protective of her without being an asshole.

Knocking comes from his front door and we both exhale the tension of this conversation at the same time, resetting the air around us.

"I know she is worth it all." I promise him before I stand to answer his door.

I didn't come to his apartment to talk about my heavy crush on the girl that eclipses my days like a storm cloud. If Eddie can tell that I'm drawn to Avery, it is only a matter of time until the guys take notice. Those conversations won't be nearly as tame as this one was. Oliver will probably threaten to murder me. I open the door and my thoughts become a reality as Oliver stands on the other side. His eyes widen for a fraction of a second before he turns ready to fight.

"What are you doing here?" Oliver has such an edge to him since I've been back in town and I haven't quite figured out what I did to trigger that.

"Visiting your dad." As much as I think that's obvious, I still answer him.

He steps through the door as I exit through it, our shoulder brushing. Then he stops.

"You smell like her." His voice is low. Avery. He is talking about Avery. I noticed it as soon as I put my hoodie on. Wildflowers and spice.

"She borrowed it." I lift the material up from my chest. I don't tell him that I have no plans on washing it out. I turn to leave.

"She doesn't need you messing with her head." His voice comes at my back. I was just about to head down the stairs to get back to my car. But something about his tone has me turning around and closing that distance between us.

He gently shut the door, probably to not alert Eddie of the conversation.

"I don't think she would really appreciate you telling me what she needs," I point out to him although I'm sure he already knows she would be ripping him apart if she were here right now.

"You don't even know her." He barks as he rolls his shoulders.

"You do." I say simply. "And you still put her in a place of having to come and rescue your ass because you didn't want to lose and are too dependent on her." I'm careful to not raise my voice because if Eddie knew we were out here having this conversation he would just be annoyed.

"Did she say that?" His features pinch with hurt.

"She didn't have to, Ol." I clear my throat and loosen my stance. "Listen, I get that you two have a messy history. And it's clear you have a different relationship with her than your brothers do. But she's strong. She doesn't do things unless she wants to. And you all could be doing a lot more to help her out right now." He leans back into my space and his eyes hold so much confusion and anger right now. Probably because he knows I'm right and he feels guilty. I definitely stuck a nerve with him.

I feel my phone vibrate in my pocket and notice it's the two vibrations back to back. I set that to her contact because I wanted to know when it was her. Is that weird? Probably. I pull my phone out and can't help the smile that overtakes my face.

Jude

> **Question of the day: Will you come pick me and Mia up?**

Rory

> **Send me your location. On my way.**

I pocket my phone and take a step back from Oliver. The air is getting a little too charged and even I know that if I start an actual fight with her best friend, all my work with her will be lost. That isn't something I'm willing to risk.

"Your history with her doesn't give you the authority to say who is deserving of her time." I put every ounce of authority behind my voice. Because whether he realizes it or not, I'm not here to hurt her. I'm here to fight. Finding her is a gift. "Apologize to your best friend and maybe listen to her. Fighting right now isn't worth a lifetime injury." I take notice of how his balled up fists are slowly unclenching as he loses his anger.

I turn back around to make my way back to wherever she needs me to go when he calls back out to me.

"Don't hurt her." His voice free of all aggression and now replaced with wariness.

"Don't think I have it in me to do that." The contrast to the warning that Eddie had just given me is prevalent in my thoughts. I realize that he is absolutely right. If anyone was at risk of getting hurt, it's me. But I live my life by taking risks. I'm a pro at it.

Fourteen

*"Are you going to get us
more salsa?"*

RORY

I find the girls sitting on a curb outside of a Mexican restaurant drunk and giggling. Avery is still in my hoodie, folded over in laughter, and hugging what looks like a white paper bag close to her chest. Mia is sitting so close to her that she's practically sitting in her lap. It's almost like an out of body experience to see Avery lit up like she is. Even her cheeks are flushed from how hard she is laughing. I should probably be more concerned that the first day Mia starts working with Avery she has her drunk on a sidewalk on a Monday night. But seeing her without the heaviness that always follows her around makes my chest feel a certain way.

"Oh shit!" Mia screams as something plummets to the ground and splatters red everywhere. "The great salsa demise! I now know what heartbreak feels like." She cries out and is almost in tears. Chips and salsa. These girls are eating chips and salsa on the curb, all but sitting in the road, and having the time of their lives.

"I'll get us more." Avery stands up and immediately starts stumbling backwards, but I'm close enough to step up behind her to keep her from falling completely backwards.

"I got you, Jude." I ease her back into standing steadily. She turns so fast that she nearly falls again. I expect to see an annoyed look on her face at my closeness, one that I am accustomed to and have even started to find endearing, but that's not what I find. Her eyes are big and glassy, a soft smile teasing her lips.

"I knew she texted you!" Mia is clapping now that she has her hands free of the salsa bowl she was cradling. Her excitement is palpable.

"Did you steal the whole ass salsa bowl from the restaurant?" I ask now that I can make out that the bowl on the ground is not in a to-go container, but in fact, the actual black bowls that they serve to you at the table. I shake my head as both of their expressions turn sheepish and their lips remain tight with them trying to hold in laughter. "Deliequents. Both of you." I waive between them.

"Omg! That should be our group chat name!! West Haven Delinquents." Mia's excitement only makes her voice get more high pitched. She has her phone out and is typing furiously. This girl's brain always runs at hyper speed.

West Haven Delinquents

Mia

> New group chat bitches! Someone will have to add Mr. I Hate My Life.

Maxwell

> Hey sunshine! How did we not already have a fun group chat?

Eli

> We do, it's the family group chat, idiot. Are you girls good?

Eli added Oliver to the chat

AJ

> All safe. Rory is here too.

AJ added Rory to the chat

Rory

> I have them. But I'm taking their phones now. So I can get them into the car.

Oliver

> Who created this?

I close out of the chat and start my attempt at rounding the girls up. Mia stands shakily but her smile is full of mischief. "Look at you playing good boy and coming when she calls." Mia winks at me. Well, she tries really fucking hard to wink, but her nose scrunches and both her eyes close. Then she starts giggling furiously. "When we were talking about which of you would be the best call, she said you." She sings the last part. My heart rate picks up a tiny bit when I notice the kiss of pink on Avery's cheeks. She chose me to call.

"Have you been talking about me?" I turn all my attention to her now and I don't let the fact that she hasn't stepped back escape me.

I watch her smile lazily. Her gray eyes seem so light and I can't find the strength to look away even as Mia continues on from beside us. "Oh, we talked about *all* of you. It's seriously unfair that you all are coworkers. Sexy coworkers. Even AJ thinks so." She hiccups and then giggles again.

"Talking about me and calling me sexy..." Avery punches me in the arm but I don't let my own smile falter. I keep my eyes glued on hers.

"Are you going to get us more salsa?" Mia pouts in a small voice.

I dip my head lower to get perfectly eye level with Avery, "you want more salsa?"

She nods hard enough for some of her hair to fall in her face. I gently push it out of the way. "Let's get you girls some more salsa. But only after I get you safely in the car." I gather them both on each arm and somehow gravitate them to the car without anyone falling.

They devour the whole new bag of chips plus the extra one I got them. Impressively, they only spilled a tiny bit of the salsa though. Mia demanded that Avery get in the back seat with her instead of sitting up front with me. And they play what Mia calls her "even baddies get saddies" playlist. I get Mia dropped off easily and make sure I hear the door lock before I make my way back to the car.

Avery has climbed up from the back and into the front. When I get back inside the car I notice it smells like her. She looks over at me with an expression that I've never seen on her before. Then she looks out the window. "Thanks for coming." Her words are so soft that I'm not sure she actually spoke them.

"You asked me to." I back out of the driveway of Mia's apartment and hand my phone over to Avery to put some music on because I know that it makes her feel more comfortable. "I don't think I've ever seen you laugh like that."

A small hiccup of laughter comes out of her before she smiles gently. "I like Mia. She's so free." I know exactly what she means. I've only known Mia for a short time but free is a perfect word to describe her.

"I think I went a little too hard on changing the habits today." It was hard to believe that was just this morning. A warmth spreads through my body that she took my advice that I gave her this morning.

"Sometimes it's good to go hard." I tell her. A giggle erupts from her whole body, literally. Her body is shaking with it. I'm so thankful she chose to ask me to be the one to come and get her. This is a sound that I am going to try my hardest to make happen over and over again.

"Do you like to go hard?" There's a residual giggle left in her as she asks. Ah. Something about Avery Jude thinking dirty things make my dick twitch.

"Do you?"

"Avoidance. Solid tactic." She folds her arms over her chest and draws her legs up before shrugging, "maybe you can't go hard. It's okay, not every girl is into it. Everyone is meant for someone. Maybe you'll meet a girl and she can teach you." *This girl.*

"She's brave with a little alcohol." I grin at her and pull back into the parking lot of the gym and put the car in park. Her smile drops and she draws her sad eyes up to meet mine.

She is playing with the strings of my hoodie as she asks, "do you think we could actually drive a little longer?" My hand readily finds the gear shift, putting this car back on the road is the easiest choice I've ever made. More time with her? I'll take that.

We have been driving for maybe ten minutes when I feel her turn in the seat to face me. "Why don't you have a neck tattoo?" That question only slightly catches me off guard. I don't take my eyes off the road even though I can feel hers on me.

"You already used your question of the day, Jude." I remind her.

"That was a dumb rule. Answer the question." She dismisses the very thing that was her idea. I don't argue because it was a dumb rule. I've been dying to ask her all the questions.

"No specific reason, just haven't." I make another turn, no idea where I'm really going but just keeping the car on the road like she asked me to do.

"Would you?" I swear that is interest in her voice.

"Do you like neck tattoos, Avery Jude?" I know I have a giant grin on my face but I can't help it. I also know she has been indexing my tattoos since she first saw them. I bet she's wanted to ask me about them too.

"Neck tattoos are hot." I wish I could be facing her now, but I have to drive. I want to see the look in her eyes knowing she is probably picturing me with a neck tattoo.

"I'll remember that." I do turn this time to look at her, the road is straight and there isn't a car in sight. "You know, for whatever girl I meet that teaches me how to *go hard*." I wink before I bring my eyes back to the road, letting her sit there with her mouth slightly open.

"Why haven't you asked me about my scars?" Her voice loses all amusement and is so small that I have to turn down the music to be sure she actually said them. Suddenly the air is thinner. I didn't think she would bring them up again since that night at Eddie's. Of course I want to know about them. I just didn't want to make her feel like she had to tell me if she didn't want to.

"You will tell me about them when you are ready." I decide to still leave it fully in her control to tell me about them or not.

I feel her hum vibrate through the silence of the car. She settles deeper in the seat.

"Why did you ask me to come tonight? Why not ask Oliver or Eli?" I ask a different question because I'm not ready for our conversation to be over. Honestly, that's the question that has been on my mind since the second I read her text standing in front of Oliver.

Like she knows how desperate I am to know her reason for choosing me, she makes me wait for her answer longer than necessary. The longer the question rests between us, the harder it is to breathe because I don't know what her reason is going to be. But I know what I want her reason to be. "I don't know. My fingers just went to your name first." The vacuum that was stealing all my air is now gone. I was her first choice, at least for tonight. I know that means something more than just being asked to pick her up. The trust we both need is growing.

"So..." My hand flexes around the steering wheel. I'm still not ready for us to stop talking. "You and Mia talked about us guys?" I feel her foot nudge my thigh as I chuckle. She is turned completely sideways in the seat now.

"We talked about a lot of things." She picks up her phone and changes the song to something soft but still moody acting like my question was no big deal. "Chloe would have loved Mia." Her body is still facing mine, but her face is resting against the window and her eyes are closed.

"Who's Chloe?" I keep my voice soft to match hers because whatever she is about to say feels fragile.

"She was my foster sister." I pick up on the past tense and I expect her to leave it at that. Any time I get close to her revealing anything about her life outside of who she is today, she gives me nothing. "She had wild hair like Mia's but it was more strawberry blonde instead of golden blonde. And she was so full of life, Rory. Every day she would do whatever she wanted, with whoever she wanted, whenever she wanted. She always said she wanted my gray eyes because guys loved a girl with gray eyes." Her eyes are a storm just like her and I do love them. "But I loved her green eyes. Green eyes have always been my favorite." I work hard to not look at her because she just said that her favorite color is the exact color of my eyes. I only let myself live in that realization for a moment before I give her my full focus again. Clearly she lost Chloe at some point in her life and I'm afraid if I speak right now she will stop talking.

"Chloe would probably make taco and margaritas a thing every Monday." I take the risk of finally glancing over at her. She wore a sad smile and her eyes seemed tired. "I miss her."

I want to reach over and hold her hand but the fear of breaking this delicate trust that is tethering her at this moment stops me. I keep driving for a while longer, just letting her music play and her rest. When I eventually pull back up to the gym I let the car idle until she is ready to go up to her apartment. I want to give her space to come back out of the memories she had escaped to by talking about Chloe.

"I'm not giving you your hoodie back." She chirps. Clearly she didn't need the time that I thought she did. The tiny smirk she was wearing when she asked me to get her more salsa is back.

"I have more hoodies. Keep it." I nod.

She reaches for the handle but glances over her shoulder before actually opening the door. "Help me up to my door?"

"Always." I open my door and get out to open her door. Squatting down, I give her my back, "hop on. I don't want to face a firing squad of Eddie and the guys if I let you get hurt." I really just want to take care of her.

There's that giggle again. "I have a feeling you wouldn't let me get hurt anyways. You're kind of a closeted sweetheart." I was prepared for when her arms wrapped around the top of my shoulders. I was in no way prepared for her legs to wrap around my waist. The legs I have spent an immeasurable amount of time memorizing. I allow my finger tips to dig into her thighs just deep enough to hold her to me. My whole body buzzes with how her body is embracing mine and her smell surrounding me.

This piggyback ride is going to fuck me up.

I make it to the top of the stairs and sit her down as gently as I can. I move to the right to allow her to unlock her door. Instead of going inside, she spins to face me. Her beautiful face tilts up at me.

"Rory?" Her eyes are still lighter than they normally are and so full of life right now. I inch closer to her and she doesn't shy away. She nudges her chin up a little more to bring her lips even closer to mine, stealing my breath.

"Yes, Jude?"

"Do you want to kiss me?" I swallow the groan that climbs up my throat. I want to kiss her so fucking badly. But not while she is clearly upset by whatever wreaked havoc in her head earlier in the car and she still has alcohol in her system.

"More than you possibly can imagine." I admit. We are so close that I can feel her breath on my own lips. And I make sure to fill each word I say next with absolute conviction. "And I will." I drop my voice to a steady whisper and allow our noses to barely graze as I lift her chin a little so she can see the sincerity in my eyes. "But not tonight."

The softest and sweetest smile tilts her lips and she closes her eyes for a breath. She knew I wouldn't kiss her. She just wanted to be a brat. "You never answered my one question." She whispers, eyes still closed, and lets her chin rest heavier in my hand.

"What question?" Honestly, she could ask anything of me at this moment and I would give it to her.

"Do you like it hard?" *This fucking girl.*

I let the tips of my fingers travel lightly over her neck until I have my four fingers on the back of her neck and my thumb presses on her pulse point at the base. I pull her closer to me to the point where there is now no space between us. I bring the same hand up to brush the bits of wavy hair behind her ear. And take my time moving my hand to trace her cheekbone before cupping it completely. She must like that because she presses her cheek into my palm. My thumb follows the line of her bottom lip before I move it to rest on her chin again and lean down until my lips are barely touching the shell of her ear.

"I like sex that leaves you trembling." I reach behind her with my other hand and open her door for her. I notice the goosebumps inching up the side of her neck and I want so badly to see if they travel everywhere else.

I kiss her cheek tenderly before taking a step back before I really lose control of this situation.

"Get some sleep." I swallow thickly. It takes every ounce of strength to walk away from her, but one thing is for certain. I am going to do everything I can to make Avery Jude mine.

Fifteen

*"Then just don't give up.
And don't fuck up."*

Rory

The girls are definitely feeling the after effects of their Margarita Monday. Mom called me in for assistance because Mia has a raging headache and my mom has the biggest soft spot for that girl. She took one look at her and sent her home to take a hot shower and rest. Tuesday is one of Mia's volunteer days at my mom's youth center, and luckily for that little menace, I have already completed my training for the day and am able to cover for her.

As soon as I enter moms office she beams at me. She jumps from her chair and wraps her arms around my waist and squeezes extra tight. She's had to hug me at waist level since I was seventeen years old.

"Thanks for coming. That poor girl looked so sick." I'm sure she did. Mom pulls back and starts walking out of her office. She leads me down the hallway while she continues speaking. "She planned to teach sunset painting today. So it's actually perfect that you are filling in!" I volunteer at her center a lot. Lately my focus has been shifted to Avery but I will always have a love for the kids here.

"The girls had a great night last night. I'm sure Mia needs rest. Avery lagged all day today too but she doesn't have it in her to not show up and take care of things. I wish someone would have told her to go home and rest." Mom turns right into her open classroom full of easels that had been donated by one of the schools when they upgraded. I admire her for how much she puts into making sure the kids get what they need.

She's created a home here for each one of them and I always love coming here and helping her.

"Avery is old enough that if she wants to go home instead of working, she can make that decision." I know she's right but it still upsets me. No one seems to want to take care of her the same way she takes care of all of them, except Eddie. But she's sidelined him. Didn't stop him from making sure I knew the score where his pseudo-daughter is concerned.

You're going to get hurt.

Eddie's warning has been on repeat in my head. I'm not afraid of Avery Jude. Her ability to keep everyone where she wants them and not close to her only makes me want to fight my way past her walls.

"Rory." My head snaps to where mom is holding out paint brushes to me.

I grab the brushes and place a few in each empty jar already placed at each station. "Sorry, Mom."

"You worry about her." She hums as she brings the pitcher of water to fill up the glasses at each station.

"She's my trainer. I need her to be healthy and not so exhausted that she can barely function." I avoid her probing.

"Can she barely function?" She's standing across the tables from me now, her eyebrows raised. She's met Avery. She already knows that girl is capable of doing whatever she needs to do.

"No." I give her the answer she needs me to say outloud.

My mom motions for me to sit down as she takes her own seat. "Avery is a strong girl. We have a few kids that take her classes as part of the scholarships she and Eddie set up, and they always come in and talk about how cool she is. I think every one of our teenage boys has a crush on her and our young girls want to be her when they grow up." I bite the inside of my cheek to keep from interrupting her. I know that Avery is amazing. But that's not her point. "If you push your way into her safe space, she will only guard herself more. You know that." I do know that.

I watched my mother for years get over the abuse my father gave her. Abuse I was never privy to because it happened before I was born. But it was like she had to rewire her brain periodically to regain the peace she built for herself.

I've continued to watch her teach young people how to create that same peace in their own lives. My mom is a light.

"Eddie told me that I would get hurt." I know I don't have to explain the rest of the conversation between me and Eddie. Mom knows that I like Avery. She clocked it the second we walked into Eddie's apartment and I couldn't stop staring at her. She gave me hell over having a crush the minute we left that night.

"You probably will. Relationships are hard. People get hurt all the time." She leans forward and smiles warmly.

"We're not in a relationship, Mom." I run my hand through my hair. Her smile doesn't drop and her eyes are even lit up now. "I like her." I didn't admit that to Eddie yesterday, but it feels good to say it out loud now.

"I know." Her smile is smug now.

"She won't even look at me as an option." And I don't know how to change that.

"She makes sense, you know. You two make sense." She ignores my grumbling entirely. "She fits your life and you fit hers. You are both so hyper focused on training and paving your own way."

"I've never met anyone that can really understand the amount of time and dedication this takes. My schedule makes it impossible. My diet is restrictive and makes going out on dates hard. I have to stay regimented in everything." I let out a breath and let my thoughts linger on my training with Avery this morning and how easy it was. How she falls in sync with every part of my day and I don't have to ask her to. Because our lives are in the same orbit.

"She fits," mom says softly, like she can hear all my thoughts wildly running through my head right now. "And she is beautiful." She's hauntingly beautiful.

"Very much so." I agree.

"And smart." She points at me, still wearing the same smile. Her knowing smile.

"She kicked my ass at scrabble. I had to use all of my concentration to just keep up with her." I loved watching her play that board game. It was like she was sucked into a different reality and all that she noticed was the words.

"Just keep being patient with her. It's hard wading through parts of yourself that you keep in the dark because you don't want that darkness to contaminate people. It takes time to realize you are more." I reach out and envelope her hand in both of mine. My mom is the strongest person I've ever known. She's taught me so much about healing and how it's new every day.

I don't know what Avery is healing from. I think about the scars on her body daily and what caused them. The history behind them. How I can erase the pain that she still stores in them. When she started to have a panic attack the first night I saw them, my blood weighed my body down like it was being filled with steel. I wanted to take it away. Whatever was causing her to feel like she couldn't breathe. But I did what my mom always taught me. Just stay calm and talk. And I let her wait it out as she regained control over it.

"She's my trainer. And she's incredible. She notices the things that even the most seasoned trainers I've worked with can't pick up. Her brain functions on a different frequency when she trains." I have to change the subject because I can see my mom swallow thickly. I hate when she feels like she has to revisit everything she's healed from too.

"Oh, you *really* like her." She pulls her hand out of mine and stands to go back to prepping the stations again.

"She makes me feel something every time I'm near her." Avery asked me why I came back to West Haven to train again. And I told her it was because I wanted to feel again when I am in the ring. And now I'm having to sort through feelings outside of the ring as well.

"Then just don't give up. And don't fuck up." She tosses a roll of paper towels at me.

"Language. Your kids will be coming in any second. You're supposed to be a role model." The room fills with laughter as she walks towards the door.

She lingers in the doorway as she looks at me. "She will see that you are also worth it." And I'm reminded why my mom is one of my favorite people. She always knows exactly what to say to make me feel like life isn't suffocating me.

"I love you." She blows me a quick kiss before actually leaving this time and leaving me alone in this art room.

Keep creating space for her.

That will be easy enough. I love having her near me. It makes me feel like I'm doing more than just breathing. Avery gives so much every day to the ones she loves most. She fails at giving herself the same love and energy. Mia is doing so much for bringing that freedom into her life but I can do it too. I can be patient. I can show her that I fit too.

Sixteen

"Oh the guys should be terrified."

AJ

Monday Margaritas have become a habitual thing now. This is week three, and honestly it feels so good to just have a conversation with someone that isn't a man. I didn't realize how different it is to just sit and talk about everything and nothing all at once. Mia makes it easy too. I watch her drink from her second cherry margarita, still wearing that same brilliant smile she always adorns. Her lips are practically stained cherry.

I'm taking careful sips of my first drink though. After having to ask Rory to pick us last time, I made it my one mission to not have to need him to do it again. The way he left my body vibrating is not a feeling that I think is safe to make happen again. In fact, I've made the guys take over a lot of his training these past two weeks. I told them I needed more time to work with Mia and get her up to speed. She has a lot of ideas to really push the charity aspect of the gym. I don't need the extra time to work with her though. I could easily just use my downtime between morning and afternoon classes.

I need space from Rory. No matter where I am in the gym, I can feel his eyes on me. He hasn't brought up that night again, but the space between us stays charged. I don't know what gave me the delusional confidence to ask him so much in his car that night, or to tell him about Chloe, but it felt nice. To just talk without the shadowing weight of someone demanding to know more. And then what happened outside my apartment door. My body is acutely aware of his any time we are in the same vicinity.

"I set the goal for ten new sponsored memberships to give out for next year. That gives you almost a whole new class to add to the schedule. And…" Her hesitation pulls me out of my unbalanced focus to give her my full attention.

"And?" I prompt her to continue.

"I was hoping if I can pull off raising the funds for these sponsorships that we can use them for a women's only class for anyone who needs to recapture their strength. No specific wound or circumstance to be eligible. Or for kids that can come over from Melinda's center and have extra time in classes. " I have a women's self defense class already but we could merge some sponsorships into that class and still open up a new class for kids from Melinda's center.

"I would need help running a new class," I contemplate out loud.

"I can do it." She's always so eager.

"You would have to learn the basics to be able to teach the class."

"I'll work hard to learn. The guys can teach me. You have so much on your plate. But I can do this." She has a special pleading in her eyes that lets me know this is important to her.

"Okay."

"Okay?!" Her tiny little body trembles with so much excitement that she nearly spills her cherry margarita. She's the sweetest and most chaotic person I know.

"How are you planning on raising the money for the sponsorships?" Mia's look shifts to the one that only took me a few days to easily decipher as her diabolical brain functioning in the highest gear. I appreciate brains that never seem to rest.

"I left the list in your office. I'm tired of work talk. I have far more important questions." Mia can play off that she doesn't place the sponsorships on a high level of importance but I know they are. She gets the same look on her face that I do when I talk about helping the kids and young women in our community. Passion laces her words when she speaks about it. Maybe that's what my gut was telling me when I hired her. Our souls yearn for the same change in the world.

"What important questions?" I say with careful anticipation. I already know what she's going to ask me. I would have girls that come into the gym all the time and ask me about guys. And when I wouldn't huddle up with them and participate in a gossip circle, they eventually stopped taking class. Which is more than okay with me. Eddie's gym is a serious gym for fighters and a safe haven for any youth that need it. It's a duality that shouldn't work but does. That is the goal, always.

"What's the story between Oliver and Rory? Sometimes they are like normal and then other times the whole gym gets colder." She fakes a shiver for dramatic effect, causing me to smile. I sit my drink down to accommodate me moving closer to the table.

"I actually don't know what their deal is." I wasn't going to out Oliver for feeling insecure with Rory being there. He and I are back to normal after I spent a few days giving him a rough time, but he's been more distant than normal. Which is a little bothersome.

"I just assumed it was over you." She starts in on the chips again while my appetite diminishes with her words.

"Why would it be over me?" I feel my body get a little smaller in the chair.

"Why would it not be about you?"

A small smile forms on her lips. I should feel cornered by this new direction of conversation but I actually feel like I can talk to Mia because while she is full of energy she doesn't make a big deal of things. Which is a foreign feeling for me to have someone other than the guys make me feel like I can speak freely.

Fuck it. Might as well let it out to someone. At least with talking to Mia about it, her reactions will be entertaining. And I know she won't go and tell the whole gym or make it awkward.

"Ask whatever you want to ask me." I nod to her, giving her permission to not hold back.

"Fuck, Marry, Kiss. It would be a disservice to society to kill one of them off." She explains her reasoning for changing the normal options of the game. My lips twist as I think about my answers. When she realizes I wasn't going to back out of her questioning she gets giddy. "Oliver, Eli, and Rory. I feel like Maxwell is just too precious and deserves all the hugs."

"Well, that boy will fuck anyone that laughs at his jokes and thinks his dimples are cute. Don't underestimate him." Maxie used to really struggle with who he is and then one day he just blurted out over Sunday dinner that he might bring home a boyfriend one day and we better all be nice about it. Eli and Oliver were already well aware of Maxwell's sexuality even without him telling them. So they weren't surprised. Eddie just sat his drink down and looked at Maxwell and said, *"That's rude. We're always nice."* And nothing else was said about it.

"Oh I love that for him. A healthy sex life makes everyone happier." She nods once and then waivers her chip frantically at me to answer her question.

"Marry Eli. He's the best cook out of them all and always buys my favorite snacks for the gym." I take a deep breath before giving my next answer. "Kiss Rory." I shut down my mind from going back to the memory of me asking him if he wanted to kiss me. I look up at Mia and shrug before saying, "And I've already fucked Oliver, so..."

"I fucking knew it!" She squeals as she throws the chip she just bit off of at me, thankfully before she dipped it in the salsa.

I catch the chip before it goes over my shoulder because she is a lousy aim. "It lasted only a few months. And it got a little messy, so we ended it." It really was as simple as that. It was fun but it wasn't what either of us really needed.

"And you're still friends? That's impressive." She leans in over the table and drops her voice a little lower. "Was it good?" Her eyes dance as they shift between looking at each of mine.

"Have you seen Oliver?" I ask her. Of course it was good. But just because something feels good doesn't mean it is something that is good for you.

"So you all just chose friendship instead?" She asks another question. I can't blame her for being curious. She works with us both and sh's very persistent in making this friendship happen.

"I have a hard time sleeping." I start, "one night we both got super drunk. And he's ridiculously attractive and I trust him." Which is probably the biggest reason behind our very short friends-with-benefits adventure. "We hooked up and I slept until noon the next day. We decided to treat it as a one time thing only. Then I was going on roughly two weeks of no sleep again and we thought, 'why not'. So, we did it again and again. And it became a necessary habit." I take a shaky breath. Eli and Maxwell obviously knew what was going on with me and Oliver. We were all pretty sure Eddie did too, we just didn't bring it up in his presence. "Then we realized it wasn't fair to each other because we love each other but we would never be in love with each other."

"Does Rory know?" Why would she ask that?

"No idea. Don't care." I mutter. Her chuckle catches me off guard and causes me to pause from dipping my chip. "Why are you laughing at me?"

"I'm laughing at the pure audacity you have to tell me that you don't care about what Rory thinks."

"You don't know me." A coldness seeps through my voice that I didn't mean to let out.

"I know that you have obviously gone through a lot of unfair shit." Her voice softens. "And that's probably why you choose to make life better for all those kids at the gym." I lean back in my chair feeling that familiar feeling of my chest suffocating under a heated weight. "Remember when I told you that you kind of scared the shit out of me?" I'm barely able to make my head move to let her know I did remember. "You still do. You're right, AJ. I don't know you. But I feel your passion for making a difference because I have it too. I know I'm a lot. Like so much. But I'm really good at what I do. And together we can make a super good team. And I like you. I don't have to quiet who I am with you. I don't know if you do that on purpose, but you are the first person outside of my grandmother that does that consistently and gives me the opportunity to just be me." She finally takes a breath. "So I don't know you. But I want to help you."

I don't know how to respond to her. When Mia talks, she gives you a lot to respond to. But words are escaping me at this moment. It's the fact that she told me she doesn't have to be quiet around me. And I felt the heartbreak crack in her voice in that one sentence. Mia is a beautiful little ball of chaotic sunshine. You can't be around Mia without her contagious laughter and smiles making you feel lighter. I've been around a lot of people that are the exact opposite of that and I hate that she feels like her personality is anything less than a gift to the world.

But I also saw the hard passion in her eyes when she talked about making a difference. You aren't that passionate about making others feel capable unless you have felt utterly hopeless in your life. I told Mia that she doesn't know me, but the reality is that I don't know Mia. I think she just pathed her own way to stand in my corner.

"I think we could be a good team too, Mia." I have the unrecognizable urge to reach over and grab her hand. Instead I choose to bring the conversation back to the topic that I know she would go crazy over. "I asked Rory to kiss me the other night."

A sharp noise, that resembles what I think is a scream, echoes off the brick wall of the restaurant from where we were sitting outside. It is a good thing she has already finished her margarita because I am certain she would have spilled it all over the table.

"And?"

"And he told me he would kiss me." Her jaw is fully unhinged now. "But not that night. And he obviously hasn't tried since then. He hasn't even brought it up." I am trying to not let that fact bother me as much but his words are digging under my skin.

"Do you want to kiss me?"

"More than you possibly can imagine."

"Oh. That man is so down bad." I find that hard to believe. I wasn't really drunk that night. I remember every word I said. I could tell he wanted to kiss me because he kept looking at my lips and he stayed close enough I could feel the warmth radiating from his skin. But the fact that he hasn't even tried to have a full conversation with me this whole week is abnormal.

"Clearly not. Which is fine. He needs to focus on his fight. All of the guys get like this when they have a fight coming up. You have to have the right mindset to step into the ring with someone else like that." I know that better than most people. I train them to be in that mindset. I've had to stay in that mindset myself. Life is a fight.

"Oh he is. He is just trying to play his game perfectly so he doesn't scare you off. You're kind of skittish, A."

"I am not skittish."

"You absolutely are. If someone even gets remotely close to you, you take three steps back. Physically and emotionally." I swallow down the argument to tell her that she is wrong.

"I don't like giving people the opportunity to be in close proximity." Except with Rory. From day one, he has been in my space.

"Fair. But we both know that you want him." She holds the last chip from the basket up and her mouth is stretched wide in a smile. "I have a plan."

"Those words coming from you actually terrify me." She smiles devilishly.

"Oh the guys should be terrified." She starts laughing and my own laughter bubbles out of my body. Whatever soul ended up with Mia will never live a boring life.

Seventeen

"Mia is a menace."

RORY

"**T**hey are definitely plotting our murders." Maxie is getting his equipment set up in his designated area for filming. I asked one time why he didn't film with more background of the whole gym and the scared look that glazed over his eyes made my own skin crawl with fear. Apparently Avery isn't a huge fan of them filming their content here. It helps the gym out with foot traffic but it absolutely brings in unserious applicants to join the gym just to hang out with the guys. I tried and failed to imagine being in the shoes of those girls that wanted to join just to hang out and 'look pretty.' Maxwell's words. Not mine.

"Not my murder. They both love me." Eli is getting the headphones and jump ropes prepped. I've watched them make their videos each week. I honestly never knew the work that went in behind creating that kind of content. They take it seriously. Everything matters. They make sure the time of the day and the amount of natural light that comes into the gym is the same. Which is nice because Eddie designed windows near the ceiling to allow a lot of natural light to come in without the glass being on the ground floor. The guys also spend a lot of time each morning engaging with their followers and making a list of what songs they are going to make a routine to. They even coordinate their outfits to be 'more aesthetically attractive'. I don't think that either of them really has a hardship of being found attractive. Being triplets always brought them a lot of attention.

Avery has spent nearly every second with Mia this week. Part of me is super happy to see her make a friend in Mia. Mom said all the kids loved her when she would come in and teach the art class. I've even joined Mia a few times when she was struggling with something to teach them. She definitely has a way of making the kids feel like they were all going to make a career out of being artists. They always leave the class dripping with pride for their work. So yeah, I'm happy Avery and Mia have found each other. But I miss her spending so much time training me.

We still go for our runs in the morning, but now we mix in bag circuits on top of that. We don't usually talk a whole lot during it. She's been really keeping herself holed up in her head lately. She looked at me expectantly, but I'm not sure what exactly she is waiting for me to say. That's a lie. I know exactly what she wants me to bring up. Truth is I didn't know how to bring up the fact that I am a dumbass and should have just kissed her when she asked. It's all I could think about for the past two weeks. Two fucking weeks. I'm twenty-eight years old and I am fumbling with this girl.

"Rory quit daydreaming about our girl and focus. You promised to be in this video." Maxwell pulls my concentration back to our little huddle.

"Your girl?" I ask them and Eli and Maxwell both fold over in laughter. I didn't think it was a funny question though.

"I'm sorry, is she your girl?" Eli raises an eyebrow at me, a clear challenge to see what my answer will be.

I want to say yes. I want there to be no ounce of doubt about who she belongs to. At the same time it's something that I feel strongly she would hate. This whole conversation. Avery Jude belongs to no man. And she would probably punch us all in the balls for even thinking for a second she did.

"Are we filming or not? Today is a rest day for me and I don't think I want to spend it here with you two idiots all day filming." I motion to the empty gym behind us.

"First off, we are professionals. Second, deflection is not a cute trait." Maxwell defends. I glare in his direction. I'm not deflecting. I just for sure will not be telling them about me almost kissing Avery. And if they keep digging then I will want to.

"She might give you a chance. I don't really know what her type is because I've only seen her with one guy and even that wasn't a relationship. It was just..." Eli pauses to find the right word, and his brother finishes his sentence. It isn't as common as you might think for them to do the creepy triplet stuff but when they do , it's still weird.

"A mess. That was a mess." Maxwell's words land and stir up even more questions for me.

"Are you talking about who she used to have sex with to help her sleep?" Both their heads snap in my direction so fast I am afraid that they pulled a muscle.

"She told you about that?" All of our heads turn to the growl of a voice that came from behind us. Oliver is walking up with an expression that is a mix of anger and disbelief all at the same time.

"She just told me that she would use sex to help her sleep." I inhale deeply. I know that I just entered uncharted water with Oliver. He doesn't like me much anymore on his best days. When Avery is brought up in conversation, he hates me. I don't know if he ever told her about the conversation we had outside his dad's apartment. I bet he didn't.

"She didn't tell you who it was with?" Eli's voice lost all the joking it was infused with earlier.

I shake my head. I don't know what is safe to say at the moment in regards to the topic of conversation.

"Good." Oliver huffs out. He turns to his brothers and holds out his arms and grins. "This is your once in a month chance to have me in one of your videos." I watch Maxwell literally jump onto his brother's back and pretend to choke him out while shouting in excitement. Looks like I won't be needed afterall.

Eli's eyes find mine and hold my stare, an apology written all over his face. It's fine. Oliver needs to feel like he has some control in the gym and I'm not going to stand in his way. I grab my sketch book from my gym bag and make my way to the outside gym.

Flipping through the book all my thoughts go back to Avery Jude. She is in every line of every drawing. She always did such a great job keeping her emotions in check but her eyes are never shy of being expressive. And they are my favorite to draw. I flip the page to my most recent portrait of her standing before me at her apartment. She had the softest look on her face that night. I could have kissed her and she would have let me. But she would have done it simply because she is attracted to me. Not because I am a regular appearance in her thoughts like she is mine. Actually that is too simple of a definition of what she is . Avery Jude haunts every thought I have.

Eddie's words also echo in my head.

You're going to get hurt.

Eli mentioning that they had never seen her in a relationship before hasn't escaped me. Avery didn't trust. That is obvious. But I know she trusts me at least a little bit. Or she wouldn't have called me that night to come and get her. She knew Oliver or either of the guys would have dropped whatever they were doing to come when she called. She chose me that night. I don't want to scare her with how much I like her. I just haven't figured out how to do that yet. Which is why I haven't brought that night back up. I don't want to give her any space or opportunity to say it was an almost mistake and we should just pretend it didn't happen.

"Hey loser." Mia's usually bright voice is a touch softer as she comes to sit next to me. I didn't even realize she was this close until she spoke. So much for spacial awareness. As a fighter, that is actually one of my best skills.

I close my book before she can see the subject and lean further into the wall, rolling my head to look at her. "I'm actually a titled champion. Furthest thing from a loser." I grin.

She knocks her shoulder into mine while mocking my words. "The guys said I'd find you out here." She tries to grab my sketchbook but I'm faster. "Secrets don't make friends, Rory." She pouts.

"Oh, are we friends Mia?" Her tiny face morphs into what I think she means to be a glare but it is too soft to be scary.

"You want me to be your friend." She states as she crosses her arms.

"Why's that?" Of course we are friends. I just like messing with her a little bit.

"Because you have a crush on my other friend and I happen to be organizing a bonfire and night swim." She reaches over and pokes me in the arm. "That she will be at. And you're only invited if we are friends."

"Avery will be there?" She looks so proud of herself in this moment. I would be proud too. I guess Avery has the same problem we all did. Saying no to Mia is like kicking a puppy, you just don't do it.

"And she will be in a hot as fuck bathing suit." She wiggles her eyebrows at me and I can't help the full blown laugh that escapes my chest at the ridiculousness that is her.

"Who's invited?" I shouldn't ask but I can't help it. I need to know what I'm walking into.

"The triplets, obviously. And I'm sure a few other people will show up. The beach isn't crazy busy at night, but the locals all like a good night swim." Even with having Oliver there, I am not going to let that deter me from trying to get some alone time with Avery. And now the other part of what Mia said is creating a beautiful mental image of Avery in a bathing suit in my mind.

"So I'll see you at the bonfire at 7:00?" She's standing now, staring down at me with a giant smirk dancing on her face.

"I will be there." I promise. Mia does a happy dance and claps and then just walks off.

I wasn't prepared.

I had gone through a catalog of what kind of bathing suit she would be wearing, like a slideshow in my head. There is no way I could have been prepared for this. We'd been sitting around the bonfire for maybe thirty minutes when Mia and Avery showed up. Their arms are bundled with blankets and snacks. Mia sends Eli back to get a cooler of drinks out of her jeep.

The girls strip down to reveal the barely there bikinis they are both wearing. I think I see a flash of pink on Mia before all of my attention is solely contained in this moment in time seeing Avery standing in front of me in a simple black bikini. The bottoms riding up high over her hips, showcasing the legs I've been obsessing over since I first saw her. Mia's hand catches Avery's, tugging her towards the ocean.

"What the fuck are they wearing?" Oliver's voice came from somewhere on my left but I can't tell you for sure because I don't think I have blinked in over a minute. I can't manage to stop staring at her. When the girls turn around, Mia is all but dragging Avery now. We all know Avery would easily be able to resist if she wanted to. But I think a part of her wants to be a little free. That's what she kept saying that night, about Mia, about whoever Chloe was. That they are both just so free.

"You have to know what a thong bikini is, Ol." One of the brothers is speaking but I still can't hear anything properly because the only sense that is functioning properly is my eyesight.

"Anyone going to join us?" Mia calls out to our group from where she is waist deep in the water. I just know she is wearing a smug smirk too.

Two guys start to move forward. They came with Eli and Maxwell. I don't even know their names. But the sight of them moving towards her sends a slight possessive rage down my spine. "Do you like the ability to walk?" The words tumble from my lips with a threatening breath. I guess my mouth is working just fine.

"Do you all know who this is?" Eli and Maxwell step up beside me. Maxwell is wearing a shit eating grin on his face. I didn't even have to look at him to know, he has been wearing it since he was five.

"Rory Davis." One of the guys says too quickly.

"We were trying to just be normal. Obviously we know who you are, man. We've watched nearly all of your fights. This is your year." Fanboying has never impressed me. What impresses me even less is the fact that up until just this moment they had their eyes glued to Avery's ass.

What I'm about to do would probably get my ass kicked by her later. But a man has limits. And a man obsessed? His limits died when another man thought he was going to have the opportunity to go for a swim with said girl he was obsessed with. Not happening. She can yell at me later.

"I suggest you pack up your stuff and leave. They don't need swimming partners." Oliver beats me to the point I was about to make. Interesting.

Both of the guys just keep standing and glancing between us and the girls. Clearly not understanding.

"You know I could easily just break your legs, right?" Would I? Probably not. Maybe. The odds get higher the longer they keep standing here in front of us and not leaving.

"Your girls. Understood." The scrawnier of the two holds his hands up before pushing his friend back to where the cars are all parked. We watch them walk away and I feel like the air is suddenly easier to breathe.

"Mia is a menace." Oliver grumbles as he runs his hand through his hair, shaking it out a bit.

"I think she's good for A. Makes her a little braver in a way I haven't seen her be." Maxwell sits back down and nods toward the girls. "I've seen her square up with grown ass men, but I have never, in the ten years I have known her, seen her wear a bikini. I think Mia is a magician." Funny, the rage I felt for the guys staring at the girls earlier doesn't exist in the slightest as Maxwell stares at them.

I squat down to go through the giant pile of stuff the girls dropped to the ground when they first got here. It only takes me five minutes, but I find two giant fluffy towels and toss one to Oliver.

"What am I supposed to do with this?" His trademark scowl is present on his face and he's still grumbling all his words. Maybe it's because of our little ball of sunshine wrapped in pink strings. This could be a fun development. Actually, the more I think about it, Mia would eat him alive.

"Let's go get the girls. That water is probably freezing by now." I start walking down the short path to where they are shivering in the water. I watch them both as they let each small wave move their bodies back and forth. Eyes closed and heads tilted up where the moonlight illuminates their faces. They look peaceful. Shivering and lips trembling, but peaceful.

Eighteen

"I thought you liked me trembling?"

AJ

"It is freezing. This was not part of the plan. I hate being cold, Mia. Hate it. I'd rather get punched in the face, repeatedly." This is honestly worse than the ice baths that Oliver would make me join him in during fight camps. I was prepared for those.

"I didn't know you had that many words, Av." We are facing each other, both kicking our feet softly just to stay afloat. The waves are barely rolling tonight. It's like the ocean is taking deep breaths.

"Shut the fuck up, Mia. I'm mad at you."

"You love me." Her cackles are choppy. Probably from the ice cold water trying to enter her lungs. When she pulled out the bikinis from her bag in my apartment earlier, I wasn't even remotely surprised. Mia doesn't live by society's expectations. She wants to do something, she does. She wants to feel a certain way, she does. She wants to wear something, she does.

She looked at me and grinned and told me that nobody would pay attention to my scars because my ass would steal the show.

"Rory couldn't even swallow when you stripped out of your clothes. My plan was executed perfectly." I watch her face morph into the same expression she always gets when her mind decides that she is going to cause chaos. "Watch."

She throws one of her hands up and screams out to where the guys are all still standing by the bonfire. "Anyone going to join us?" The two guys who showed up with Max and Eli start to walk this direction but stop only a few steps in.

"Disgustingly predictable." She turns back around to face the open water and leans back until she is floating.

"I wish people were less predictable. That's why I like you." The softest smirk covers her lips. "I used to think you hated the world."

I turn on my back and join her. The cold has subsided a little and the waves are therapeutic in the way they gently move our bodies.

"I do hate the world."

"You hate the darkness that exists in the world. But you survived it, Avery. And now you teach others that they don't have to survive it, they can fight it. And that's an unpredictable outcome for people like us. People expect us to stay broken, not grow." I keep my eyes closed but I can hear her shaky exhale. "Fuck those people. Scars don't define brokenness. They don't make us weak. They teach us how to love without causing them."

I don't know what darkness she is harboring in her, but I make the decision at this moment to fight it with her. She's never asked me about my scars. She never pushes to ask why I do any of the things I do or why I keep the same handful of people as my only company. She barreled in and claimed a spot that seems to have always been waiting for her.

"Fuck those people." All other words didn't seem large enough to fill the space between us.

I reach out to take her hand and squeeze so she knows that I understand. Rehashing what we went through doesn't make it easier to understand. Sometimes it really is just enough to sit with someone who understands. That we are still here, and we didn't lose who we are. We can make others stronger and love them the way that they deserve. We can make sure there is a space for them to feel safe and seen and heard. The gym needed Mia. She is loud and feels everything. She makes sure that no one feels obligated to be quiet. She is the one to teach them that light can exist.

"You two are going to catch hypothermia." Oliver's words come out in such a huff that we both laugh. "Get out of there." I can just picture his face all scrunched up.

"Ask nicely." Mia pulls on my hand to keep me from actually getting out.

"I didn't ask at all, pretty girl." A small pause and I swear I hear the opposition bubbling in her blood right now. "I have your towel with the cherries on it. So you can come and sit by the fire and be warm." That catches her attention. She pulls us into a position where we are now facing the guys.

Rory winks at me and holds up my own towel as well. He is obviously going to just let whatever is between them play out and I am happy to do the same. Anything that riled up Oliver is some of my favorite entertainment. Sometimes me and his brothers would make a day full of ways to piss him off.

"How'd you know that was my towel?" Whatever had allowed her to let her guard down just moments before is quickly replaced with Mia's every day energy.

"Are you kidding me right now?" Oliver says like the answer was obvious. "You are a walking cherry bomb." He isn't wrong. She even keeps cherry suckers in my office drawer now too. She said sometimes she just needed a treat and she didn't trust keeping them downstairs because the sweat would ruin the flavor. And I'm pretty sure there is a cherry lip gloss in my car that she left the last time we went to get margaritas and tacos.

"Awe. You paying attention to me, Ol?" She is having too much fun with this. I've watched men literally stumble trying to get her attention. She knows what kind of effect she has on men. And it seems Oliver isn't immune either.

"Are you getting out?"

"Are you going to ask nicely?"

I think I love her. I glance back at Oliver and I swear I can see his teeth grinding from here.

"Please." I only knew that was what he said because I could make out the way his lips moved but the words were not audible.

"Hey Rory?" I call out to him without looking at him. He would follow my lead, like he always does. It is one of the most attractive things about him.

"Yeah, Jude?"

"Did you hear Oliver say something?"

"Oliver was talking? I thought he was just trying to make the ocean go away by glaring at it." Mia's smile is brilliant as she realizes she has both of us in her corner.

"Please." Oliver never breaks eye contact with her as he speaks the one word he knew would get her out of the water.

I want to die laughing right now but I find the strength to keep it pushed down a little longer. I watch as Mia lets go of my hand and walks as slowly as she possibly can up to the shore to meet Oliver where he stands. They stare at each other for a moment before she takes the towel and wraps it around her before walking past him without saying a single word.

Unpredictable. You never know what Mia is going to do and I think it is her way of keeping control over what is happening in her life. If she was constantly moving then it didn't allow someone the time to figure out her next move.

"Are you going to stay in there and freeze or come out and join the rest of us? Your choice, but I know how much you hate being cold. I even brought an extra hoodie for you."

"Or you could join me? We have extra towels in the back of the jeep." Did I want to particularly stay in this giant ocean sized liquid freezer?

No. But did I want Rory to be a little closer? Yes. Watching Mia just go with whatever she was feeling in the moment is slightly inspiring. I will never be as free as she is. But I don't want to walk around always trapped in my own head. I want to be able to have better days and have moments that feel less suffocating.

He doesn't even hesitate to make his decision. I watch him reach behind his neck and pull his shirt off. He doesn't take his time getting into the water either. Rory moves into the water with purpose, like he does everything else. In a few short strides he is now standing in front of me.

He is so close that the heat of his body is warming my body. He glances down at my lips and I watch as he wet his bottom lip before the left side of his mouth lifts into his trademark smirk. His hands find their way to my skin, I feel his thumbs hook under the thin fabric that rests on top of my hips.

"You're trembling." His words ghost over my lips. I am having to keep balance on the very tips of my toes while he stands strong because he is roughly a foot taller than me.

"I thought you liked me trembling?" I barely get the words fully out of my mouth before his hands move to dig into my thighs. My legs wrap around his waist and his lips take ownership of mine.

My hands tangle into the waves of his hair that hang at the base of his neck. I nip at his bottom lip as he holds my body in perfect balance with his. The moonlight and salt water makes every inch of inked muscle shine. I bite down a little harder and his hands grip hard in response.

"Fuck, Jude." His voice is breathless but he doesn't allow that to stop him from moving one of his hands into my hair and angling my head to where he wants me.

His grip is punishing in the way that he wants to make his own mark on my body. One from passion instead of hate. One that I would be able to look at and want more of. His tongue sweeps over mine and he tastes like a mixture of salt water and the mints he likes.

He pulls me closer while still giving us enough space between us to catch our breath. He takes careful steps backwards until we are out of the water. He sits me down with care and grabs the towel he placed on the ground on top of his hoodie. We stay silent as he wraps the towel tightly around my body.

"I should have kissed you the other night." A hum leaves my lips and I watch as he steadies his breaths. I don't know exactly what this kiss means. I know that I don't regret it and my whole body is vibrating with wanting to do it again. But I can see questions piling up behind his stare.

"Let's go sit by the fire." I offer him. I don't want to make this moment less by hashing out the reasoning behind it. Plus I'm freezing and that fire is calling to me.

We make our way back to where everyone is sitting. Mia is sandwiched between Eli and Maxwell laughing so hard that her body is shaking. Oliver is sitting across from them lost in his own thoughts but he quickly clocks us as we get closer.

He tilts his head to the spot next to him. And I know that he wants to talk to me. So I make my way to sit next to him and Rory walks back to the cars to grab one of the towels from the back on Mia's jeep that I told him about.

"Are we good?" Oliver doesn't waste any time getting straight to the point.

"We're always good. Even when we aren't good, we're good. You know that." Oliver is someone that I don't think I can survive without and he feels the same way. Our lives are just entwined.

"Does he know that you don't do relationships?" I knew he was going to bring up Rory.

"Whatever your issue is with Rory, it's between you two. Keep me out of it. Mia will think you are jealous. And that will be messy." I catch Mia glancing over to where we are talking.

"Mia doesn't care what I do." There is something hidden beneath his words, but I don't think now is the time to hash that out. We need to get on the same page regarding whatever is happening between me and Rory. Because he isn't wrong. I don't do relationships. I don't know how. And I'm pretty sure I would fuck it up in the cruelest way. I am not going to put someone through that. It isn't fair to them for me to have to learn how to be good in a relationship. Rory is too good for that. He deserves good.

"You need to figure your shit out with Rory. He could really use you to get him ready for this fight in a few months." Truth is, I need Oliver to help me with Rory's training. Eli is doing his best. Maxwell isn't at the skill level. Oliver is fast and strong. He taught me so much. The difference is that he can actually go the rounds with Rory where I can't without getting severely hurt.

"I'm trying."

"Try harder." He nods his head before letting it hang low between his shoulders.

"Okay, A." His voice is resigned but full of promise to me. "For you." He wraps his arm around my shoulders and pulls me into a side hug before kissing my temple and whispering, "If he hurts you at all. I'll bury him."

I know he would. Oliver and his brothers would take on the world for me. That's why they are my family. And now we have Mia. It is a warm feeling watching them laugh and be happy. Rory comes back with a towel wrapped around his waist but still shirtless. I was wrong earlier. I thought that his tattoos looked perfect highlighted by the moon. But they dance with the flames of the fire and I can't look away. Even as he hands me his hoodie that isn't covered in sand.

He goes to sit on the other side of Eli, giving me time to finish my conversation with Oliver. I don't know what exactly is going to happen with the feelings growing between us but I don't want to leave this moment. This moment is full of the freedom of doing what you want with who you want and dancing with the love of having people in your corner.

Nineteen

"I give no fucks, Eddie.
I'm not a kid."

AJ

Sleep has been extra sparse lately even with Mia taking on more of the work at the gym. I even skipped Sunday dinner this week because I didn't want to worry Eddie with the way my eyes have hollowed out further. Eli dropped off enough tea to keep my shelf stocked for a year. And Maxwell had showed up the night before last with extra fuzzy blankets and a movie to watch and cuddle to try and help me relax enough to fall asleep. Oliver just offered to run with me at two in the morning every night like clock work.

I have been pushing Rory extra hard, even partaking in some of the training myself to get an extra workout in. I'm not taking in enough calories for the amount of work I've been punishing my body with but I'm trying. Oliver keeps trying to shove protein bars down my throat but as soon as I hear the wrapper rip I can feel the contents of my stomach trying to climb up my throat. The thought of taking care of new people at the gym is starting to make my skin crawl. Thank God for Mia. She has been a saving grace to me in so many ways that I can't even fathom how I was managing this without her. She was hired for social media, but I quickly talked to Eddie and asked if we could promote her to manager alongside me.

She can see how quickly I've diminished in just one week. But she never pressures me to talk about it. Talking about it does nothing. It gives no room for healing. I just have to push through it. And it will pass. It always passes. I just have to give it more time.

I can do that.

I open the door to the gym office and find a blue post-it note on the desk.

You skipped dinner last night.

That's it. That's all that is written on the note. I pull out my phone to call him and apologize. But there is a text I missed from this morning.

Ollie

> **Want to do some light ring work this morning?**

Sent fifteen minutes ago. There is still about an hour before the morning class will start and today is a rest day for Rory. Some light sparring with Oliver could be pretty fun.

AJ

> **Already at the gym. Meet me in the ring in five.**

I switch over to call Eddie as I make my way downstairs. Rang once and then straight to voicemail. He doesn't even know how to keep his phone on do not disturb and he stresses if his battery is below seventy percent because he thinks he might get stranded somewhere one day and need his full battery percentage. Which means that he just ignored my call. I didn't think that me skipping dinner would upset him so much. But the thought that I might have, makes my stomach feel heavier.

"Hey, where is your dad? He just hit the ignore button on me." I put my bag down on the bench next to where Oliver is sitting and already wrapped up.

"Here, I'll wrap you up. I'm faster at it." I find my seat in front of him and he wraps up my hands like he has done a hundred times before.

"Where's your guy?" He asks without even looking up at me. His tone holding a certain edge to it.

"He's not my guy and you know that." A huff leaves his lips but he doesn't argue. "Today is his rest day. If I could guess he is with his mom at her center." I know that Mia has been meeting with Melinda about some charity event she wants to hold to help bring more kids into the youth center and offer them member sponsorships through the gym. But I haven't made my way over to see what the center is all about.

"He always was a momma's boy." His voice holds a shadow of sadness that I've learned to recognize well with the boys. They never got the chance to have that type of relationship with their mom and I can't imagine what it must be like to know you had a wonderful and beautiful mom and never got to know her. I don't know who my parents are but I also don't care.

When I was a kid I was more haunted by the thought of who my mom was and if she regretted leaving me with strangers. She had walked into a diner one night and asked a young couple to watch me while she went to go and get something out of her car and never came back in. And the couple did what any normal person would do, called the cops. I was in the system less than a day later.

He wraps the last rotation around my wrist and velcroes the end. "Are we sparring or doing glove work?" I have no useful words regarding his comment about Rory being a momma's boy, so I do what we do best. Don't talk about it and focus on training.

"Sparring." His voice carries throughout the empty gym. The sun isn't fully up yet and the air that fills the empty space has a lighter essence.

I swing myself through the ropes and find my footing on the ring floor. I love being in the ring, surrounded by the shadowed outskirts, and knowing that in this open space I'm able to use my body as a weapon instead of hiding behind it as a shield. It took me years to feel confident enough to enter a ring with another person. The first time I fought, I grew addicted to the hunger for it. The ability to draw blood instead of counting the wounds that would need time to heal. It was a toxic healing and it scared me. Eddie taught me how to wield my strength and manipulate another's weakness. And I took what he taught me and caused destruction.

The first time I fought, I won. And the crowd adored it. I was a tiny girl and was trained by the best. Eddie has many titles under his coaching career and several fighters that are still defending titles that have worked with him at some point. Then I realized I was counting down the days until I got to step foot in that hollowed out pool again. It was harder finding girls that were willing to fight at the skill level that venue required. Bets were always made. I went undefeated for over a year, The Poolhouses first female gladiator in a sense.

Then one night I fought a girl that gave me whiplash. Her blonde hair was in braids and she had the rosiest cheeks. I didn't know her name. I still don't know her name. I saw that girl's nameless face pouring blood to the point of unrecognition and I got nauseous. I looked at her and saw Chloe with a broken nose sitting outside under the back porch between the giant trash cans. She had gotten into it with Kyle that night and she never would tell me what happened. She just told me the same answer every time I asked– *what's the dream tonight?* We sat there between the trash cans for hours talking about what we would dream that night if we could choose. It's where she taught me to smoke. It's where we were able to finally have a reprieve from suffocating inside that house. It's where we became sisters in every sense of the word besides blood.

I couldn't make the blood disappear. I grabbed a rag and immediately tried to clean up the girl's face. I didn't want to know anything about the girls that I fought in The Poolhouse. I just wanted to feel something. But everything I felt was born from a void of everything good. I just remember seeing that girl, her blonde hair tainted by her blood. Blood that I caused to spill from her body. And I ran to the back and out the door and emptied everything from my stomach and cried until Oliver found me and held me until I was coherent again.

I haven't fought since then. I've only spent time in the ring with one of the guys or Eddie. Where I am safe from my own haunting.

Oliver and I go pretty easy the first round, just getting a feel for the atmosphere for today. Some days are therapy sparring days and we go harder. Some days we just go through the motions and work our own thoughts out in our head. And some days we are just messing around. Today is clearly a work things out in our head day. Oliver's tell is always the small pinch between his eyebrows. He's trying to figure out if he wants to tell me what is bothering him or not.

I go to throw a roundhouse kick and miss. I pivot back to my base and keep good range. I am always able to break through the middle with Oliver. Staying in closer range makes it harder for him because he is so much taller than me. And I love to agitate him by staying in his pocket.

"Keep in mind the way you want to set it up. You're so good with your hands, but if you are sparring with me or Dad then you have to use your legs more. Remember that question mark kick I taught you?" It is one of my favorites to this day. It took me three months to master that kick and I nearly pulled a muscle from repetitively throwing it.

"You want me to throw the question mark?" He goes over to grab his mouthpiece he laid down on the edge of the mat. The fact that they always kept those laying literally anywhere and everywhere is disgusting.

"I want you to throw it and land it five times before the last two rounds are up. We won't go hard, just focus on the technique."

We spent the next two rounds doing exactly that. He gave me refreshers on how to set it up and find the space to do it. The whole point of this kick is for it to sneak up on you. It poses as a simple teep kick and then before you realize what is happening, if done correctly, you are taking a kick to the side of the head. And it's enough to throw your opponent off their routined focus and allow you to rally and throw in a solid combo right off it.

"Oh good. You're already here and it looks like you're ready." I nearly break my neck at the sound of Eddie's deep voice commanding the space between us.

"What are you doing here?"

"Funny you ask. Doc called and asked me how I was feeling being back at the gym. Imagine my surprise because my sweet Avery had told me that I was still on rest duty only." He's not happy. I knew he wouldn't be. I square my shoulders and make an effort to stand a little taller.

"I've been handling everything just fine." He swings his legs through the ropes and is now facing me.

"Yeah. Handling it so well that you're getting what? Two or three hours of sleep at night?"

"You know I don't sleep well." I defend.

"You're overworked, Avery." His tone sounds so much like a father's that I feel the air bubble catch in my throat.

"I'm not overworked. The gym has stayed organized. Memberships are actually up. I hired Mia and she has been incredible!" I wish Mia was here. She would help Eddie understand that I am handling things.

"That's not the point. You weren't meant to take over and stay working like this. You need rest. Your mind needs rest." He softens his tone just the smallest amount but leaves no room for argument.

"You know my mind is the problem, not the gym." My shoulders feel lifeless and my eyes burn from trying to keep the damn of tears from breaking. I've worked really hard to not be too emotional but all it takes is Eddie being disappointed in me the slightest bit and I feel the ground crumble beneath me.

"Take the day off, Avery." Once again, no room for argument. I don't care though. I don't need a day off. Working keeps my mind busy and I need it busy.

"Absolutely not. I have a class to teach."

"I have class to teach. And I'll cover yours." He motions to the door but I don't even look in the direction he is pointing.

"No."

"I don't know if you know this or not, but I own this gym."

"I don't know if you know this or not. But you're not kicking me out of the gym."

"It's just one day, Avery."

"I give no fucks, Eddie. I'm not a kid." His head drops and I see him stifle a groan from having to deal with my attitude.

"You're my kid, Avery." His jaw is tight and there was a flash of hurt in his eyes before his chest expands and I know what's about to come. "Fine. You land one point on me, and you can stay. One round. One shot." I look at Oliver and he winks at me. He's telling me, *you got this.* But his encouragement means little at this moment because he's a dirty little traitor. He knew Eddie was coming in today. And he had us spar because this is how we deal with disagreements in the family.

"Deal." The familiar charge of adrenaline starts to flood my body and my finger tips itch. My favorite thing about sparring with the West men is that I can go as hard as I want and I don't have to be professional.

Twenty

"All men belong on their knees."

RORY

W hen Mia called me and asked me for a ride to the gym this morning the very last thing I thought we would be walking in on was Avery and Eddie in the ring together. Wasn't he supposed to be on strict resting orders?

"Are you sure you want to do this? Wouldn't want to hurt your weak heart, Eddie." Her voice has a different pitch to it than it normally does. The closer we approach the ring it quickly becomes clear that Avery is fuming with frustration.

"Being mean isn't going to change my mind, Avery." He gives her such a pointed look but it only makes her body vibrate more. I don't know what is happening but my blood runs cold at the sight of her so visibly upset.

"What is punishing me and kicking me out of the gym going to help?" Her voice is shaky with an emotion that I don't think I ever imagined hearing from her. She's embarrassed.

Eddie sheds his hoodie and is now only in his shorts. There must have been a home gym in his apartment because it's clear he hasn't missed a day, even after a heart attack. Avery looks the complete opposite of how she looked the first time I entered this gym and she was putting work in the ring. She doesn't look strong and focused. She looks weathered and void and I want nothing more than to place her back in that water and let that peaceful look wash back over her face.

"You're being dramatic. Telling you to take a day off isn't punishment. Most people would consider me the best boss in the world." Eddie raises an eyebrow at her and I am pretty sure Avery is about to actually growl at him.

"Who is that?" I almost forgot that Mia was standing next to me because when Avery is near, she steals all my focus.

"Eddie." My answer is clipped, but Mia doesn't mind. She's just as confused as me by the situation in front of us. What is Eddie doing back? Why are they standing in a ring like they are about to spar? Why is she *so* upset?

"I'd get in the ring with Daddy West any day." Leave it to Mia to make all eyes go to her in a serious situation.

"Do you ever actually think before speaking?" And leave it to Oliver to say the impossibly wrong thing at every moment. These two are volatile.

"Oh my apologies. I didn't realize my thoughts needed your permission to leave my lips." I watch Mia swing her whole body and face Oliver.

"He's my dad..." Oliver throws his hand out to motion where Eddie is still talking to Avery in the middle of the ring. "He's got gray hair!" Honestly, it's hard not to laugh at the absolute bewildered look on Oliver's face. And if my nervous system wasn't going a bit haywire trying to figure out what was happening, then I would be laughing.

"Gray hair can be hot." Mia shrugs her shoulders and then her trademark- I'm going to start shit- grin spreads like wildfire across her lips. "Know why I love a salt and pepper bearded *man*, Oliver?" The emphasis she puts on the word, man, is what causes Oliver's entire body to appear larger. I can see him grinding his back teeth from where I am standing on the other side of Mia. He clearly isn't going to answer her. "It means they are well seasoned. Comes with age." She throws him a wink. "Maybe you will get there one day."

"For fucks sake." He walks over to where Eli is getting the timer set up on the edge of the ring. Maxwell comes to stand next to me and lets out a big sigh. None of the three of them seem remotely concerned for whatever is happening in front of us and that is troubling.

"What are they doing?" I finally ask since none of them are going to clue us in.

"Family disagreement." Maxwell states. "If she lands a shot, cleanly, then she wins whatever they are arguing about." His dimple is digging in deep with his anticipation of watching this.

"Eddie just wants her to take the day off. She's arguing because she's a freak and loves to work." Maxwell waves for us to move all the way up to the side of the ring.

"She's not a freak." My chest feels a wave of heat as I glare over at him. "Being at the gym every day is her routine. Her brain needs routine. And she clearly feels attacked right now." I know she doesn't need me to defend her. It just comes so natural to me now though. I can't stand the thought that she would feel, for even a second, that any of us weren't behind her.

"Kick his ass!" Mia screams over my shoulder, causing me to grin when Eddie squints in our direction. At least Mia is in her corner too.

"Great, now we have an audience." Eddie shakes his head but Avery's body is still tense. "It's not an actual fight." He clarifies to Mia and then points to Avery. "Don't be a brat, keep your base, and watch your range." He holds his gloves up for Avery to bump. "You land a point, then you can stay and keep working yourself to death. You don't land one, you take the day off. You can even take Mia with you." He offers and I can feel Mia's body quiver with excitement next to me.

"Paid!" Mia argues from the sidelines.

"Yes ma'am." Eddie nods to her and Mia's whole face lights up.

"I'm not a kid anymore. This is dumb." Avery's words are a harsh whisper.

"You're always my kid. And you're right. This is dumb... just take the day." Eddie isn't giving her an inch. I've sparred with her enough to know that she is smarter and faster than nearly every guy I've encountered. She can very well pull this off. Although, I'm already trying to figure out if I can somehow convince her to use her day off and spend it with me instead of Mia since it's my rest day.

"Now it's about landing a shot. I lose, our day is paid off and you buy us tacos." Avery's body loses its rigidity, but I can still tell that she is off. Eddie telling her that she would always be his kid softened her. Avery could use the day off though. I've been telling everyone that she works herself too hard for weeks. Every time I would bring it up to the guys they would just assure me she was fine.

"That's my girl!" Mia blows a kiss to Avery right as the bell goes off to start the round.

As expected Avery did not come out fast, she's calculating. She's giving space to gauge how Eddie is going to play this round. Eddie throws a few soft side kicks that Avery brings her shin up to protect against. She counters every time, but makes no contact. Playing defense isn't her style, she likes control. So what is she doing? They have less than a minute left in this one round and she hasn't allowed her eye contact to be anywhere but on Eddie at all times. It is clear Eddie has the control, which was to be predicted. He trained her, but I can tell that even he is slightly confused on why she isn't taking more opportunities.

Eddie sets her up to throw a kick that I knew he had every intention of catching. He keeps his middle open, and she goes for the teep right down the middle but in the time it took you to blink, her foot flicks in a half circle landing on his head in a flawless question mark kick. The way she moved her leg so fluidly made the viper on her leg look alive and slithering. It was fucking beautiful.

"That a girl, A!"

"Holy fucking shit!"

"Hell yeah!"

The triplets all react with the same energy. I think it takes Eddie a minute to realize what she did. I wish he would have seen it from my angle. It was a perfect set up. I bet she has practiced that kick a few hundred times.

"That's my girl!" Oliver shouts from the side. Apparently she is everyone's girl. I probably should be more jealous over the way Oliver explodes through the ropes and swings her in a circle. But the pure uncontained joy that is lighting up her entire face is worth sitting back and watching her enjoy this moment.

She pushes off of Oliver and throws a really hard leg kick to the mid thigh on his good leg causing him to drop down on a knee from where she just dead legged him. "Fuck, A. What was that for?" He groans while holding his leg.

"Because you knew he was going to do that." She uses her teeth to undo the velcro on her gloves and tosses them down to the ground. "Traitor."

"Why do you think I had you work that kick!" You can hear the pain coming through his words as he grits his teeth and I can't help the low laugh that leaves my mouth.

"And now we are even." She throws her wraps down where he has both legs stretched out in front of him trying to stretch the cramp out. She turns, quick on her feet, and gives Eddie a pinched stare. "I'm still taking the day off and I'm taking your card out of your wallet for the tacos."

"Good." Eddie's voice is full of pride and I know it's for more than her being able to land that kick on him. She is willingly going against what makes her feel safe. She's acting with a spark of impulsiveness and freedom. And it looks good on her.

Mia is jumping up and down holding a bottle of water. I don't even know where she got that bottle from. She holds it out to Avery and kisses her cheek.

"You're such a badass. I don't know what that was but you looked hot as hell doing it." I agree wholeheartedly. Hot as hell isn't even an appropriate enough statement for how she just looked. She looked alive. "Oh I got us shirts! We can stop by my place and get ready before we go eat." Mia is steering Avery towards the door but my hand wraps around her elbow stopping them. I glance at Mia, silently begging to let me have a moment with Avery before she steals her away. Mia grins and I know she understands my silent request. "I actually need to grab something from the office super fast. Be right back." She saunters off.

I know I won't have long because Mia has no ounce of patience in her body. "Are you okay?" I use the fragile hold I have on her elbow to guide her closer to me.

"Why wouldn't I be okay?" She can act like she isn't upset but the way her chest grew a little redder gives away that she is.

"Because that was intense." My hand falls from her elbow and is now a ghost touching her hip but she doesn't shy away from me. She looks up at me with her gray eyes and my eyes track the breath she releases from her lips.

"It's how we handle the small things. It's the West's form of flipping a coin." Her right shoulder lifts slightly and she gives me a soft smile that quickly turns downward.

"You're upset though." I push a little harder as her body leans in closer towards mine.

"Sometimes I overreact. I just needed a minute to realize he's right. I could use a day off." She takes a small sip of the water Mia gave her.

"Would it be wrong if I said that I enjoyed you putting Oliver down like that?" I expect her to be upset over me saying anything negative about her best friend but she just keeps staring at me.

"I prefer men on their knees, Rory." She taps my chest and her normally stormy eyes are now shimmering with amusement.

"All men belong on their knees." Mia's voice echoes through the gym. Per usual, I didn't even hear her walk back up to us.

I squeeze Avery's hip and pull her closer as I lean down to brush my lips at the shell of her ear and whisper. "Noted." Her hand is still on my chest and the restraint it takes to not kiss her should be studied.

She steps back but still doesn't take her eyes off of me, rewarding me with one of the smiles I feel like I fight for my life trying to always earn.

"Have fun girls." Eddie is resting his arms over the ropes with his boys all standing under him. Oliver is obviously still recovering because he has most of his weight on the opposite leg of the one that Avery kicked.

Neither of the girls even turns around to say bye. Instead they reach the door and both throw up a middle finger, laughing, and barely making it through the door.

Twenty-One

"Is that frosting?"

Today was hell. I forgot how having Eddie as a coach makes you feel like you are fighting for your life just to take a full breath. It's supposed to be my rest day. I tried to escape out of the side as Eddie was arguing with the boys, but I fell short of the evasion of Eddie's periphery. He caught me before I even made a few steps towards the door. And that's how I ended up spending my one day off from the gym teaching Avery's class and trying to take pictures and videos for Mia.

And now I'm on the other side of Avery's door just staring at the chipping paint like a creep. When she left with Mia this morning, the urge to follow her out the doors was more like starvation. I want to spend all my free time with her. I want to sit with her when she wants the world quieter. I want to be the one to see how her face transforms into pure joy when she learns a new technique. I want to convince her to spend time with me. I live for every glare she shoots my way when she is done with my shit for the day. And I want to earn all her smiles because she rarely gives them.

When Eli called me out for sulking around the gym today without her around, he told me I was just too attached. I didn't bother giving him a reasonable response. I wasn't going to deny it. Eddie has already clocked my low key obsession and now Eli was declaring I was wasting my time. Mia is the only one that gave me encouragement to pursue her.. All while she is being the best wingwoman a guy could ask for.

That's why I am still standing and staring at a closed door with the girl I adore on the other side. Mia texted me to let me know that Avery was officially home and might be open to having company because she's in a good mood when she dropped her off. That text was sent to me roughly fifteen minutes ago. It took me an embarrassingly quick amount of time to make my way over here, trusting Mia's advice.

I'm not prepared for the sight that awaits me on the other side of the damn door. Avery stands in front of me with her eyebrows slightly pulled in, a spoon dangling from her mouth, half of a shirt barely covering her breasts that read tacos, and no motherfucking pants. I normally would consider myself very respectable, unless wanted otherwise. In this moment, every ounce of restraint vacates my body. I can't stop staring at her standing there in this scrap of a shirt and the tiniest black panties that ride up her hips. She looks sinful. Especially since her hair is down and messy. My favorite way. Her tattoo on full display with her perfectly toned legs unhidden.

When she realizes that I'm just standing here, swallowing my own tongue, unable to even form a thought, a devilish smirk tilts her lips as she pulls the spoon from her mouth.

"If you are going to stare at me like that, you could at least say hello first." Her voice is sweet tonight.

"Do you always answer your door with no pants on?" I raise my eyebrows and nod to her bare legs. I need her to put pants on. *Please put pants on.*

"I hate pants." She makes a disgusted face like the idea of wearing pants is a personal offense. Dear God. What if Eddie had been the one knocking on her door? Or a complete stranger. What if someone was here to kidnap her? That's a dramatic thought, but it could also happen.

"Is that frosting?" I notice that there is a small smear of pink on the inside of the spoon.

"Don't tell Eddie." Her eyes widen slightly as I walk past her into her apartment. She shuts the door and walks towards the counter where there is a strawberry container of frosting sitting. "He will go into his lecture about fueling your body. Even though I know that man has a secret stock of beer in his fridge that he hides from me and still eats garbage when I buy all the healthy food." Avery hoists herself up on the counter and pulls the container of frosting back close to her chest to take a new bite.

Her legs dangle over the counter, causing her hips to dip inward begging for my hands to be on them. I need her to fucking put pants on so I can focus. I know she is pushing me to break and ask her to do so though. We've been playing this game for months now. She knows I am completely undone by her and she revels in it. But if I make my intention of wanting to be closer to her too apparent, she withdraws. I am in a constant state of being fed the crumbs she gives me. She doesn't even willingly give those to me. What she doesn't know is that I'm not scared of putting in the work for her to let me have more.

"Did you and Mia have a nice day off?" I somehow make words come out of my mouth like her being half naked in front of me is not terrorizing me. I lean on the counter right next to her, close enough that I can smell her perfume.

"She made us shirts." She discards the icing to show me her shirt. She pulls at the hem, which only causes the material to stretch tautly over her chest. "Hers says tequila." *Of course it does*. Tacos and tequila– the perfect accessories to every girl's friendship.

"The question mark kick you landed on Eddie today was beautiful." I pick up her spoon and dip it into the icing to take a bite myself and notice that there are small crunches in the icing. My face must have given away my surprise though because she starts laughing.

"I put mini chocolate chips in it." Her voice is light.

"Who knew 'stick to her routine Avery Jude' had a wild icing-with-toppings side?" I tease her. She reaches out to steal the spoon back from me. The same spoon that I just had my tongue all over. Is it pathetic to be turned on by that? Absolutely, but in my defense, she is still sitting on this counter, pants be damned. My eyes trail to where that viper tattoo is staring back up at me. All the muscle in her legs always make that snake look more alive than is possible since it's just ink in her skin. I can't stop my fingers from reaching out to softly trace the inked scales edged on the outside of her thigh.

Her breath hitches and I catch her gripping the handle of that spoon a little tighter. Avery has never shied away from my touch, even from the very beginning. And I wasn't unaware of how much of a privilege that was at first but now I do. I am, however, too much of a coward to ask her why she's comfortable with me in this way out of fear that she will start to pull away.

I move slowly, with more confidence than I normally show her, until I'm comfortable standing between her legs. The best part of her deciding to hoist herself up on this counter? She's more level with me. I don't have to search to find that storm in her eyes. And the scent of wildflowers and spice surrounds me.

"Are you ever going to tell me what this tattoo means?" I ask softly. One thing I know for certain is that this tattoo means something soul searing to her. She only has one tattoo. And I know it's by design.

She lets the spoon fall from her lips. Her eyes search mine and whatever she is needing to find, I hope like hell she finds it. Intimate moments like this with her are delicate. And just like when she was in my car, I fear breaking it.

"Chloe." The name is just a breath from her lips but the heartbreak fills the space between us. Whatever happened to Chloe is something that haunts her.

"I wish I could have met her." Her eyes flash between mine with too many emotions to catalog. She hasn't explicitly said that Chloe is no longer alive but I easily put those pieces together. She recovers well though. She dawns a cute half smile and her eyes turn teasing.

"She would have eaten you alive, Rory Davis." She reaches over to get another spoonful but I grab her wrist and stop her before she is able to bring the spoon to her mouth. I guide her wrist and the spoon to my own mouth. It's sickly sweet with the added chocolate chips.

I bring my thumb up to wipe away the little bit of frosting I can feel leftover on my lips, "what about you, Jude? Would you eat me alive?"

"I'd leave a mark." Pure confidence bleeds through her words. And I think that they are meant to be a warning, but I welcome them anyway.

I grab the spoon that is still lingering in her hand and toss it in the sink to our left. My hands easily wrap around the tops of her legs to dig into the back of her thighs, pulling her closer to me. I let my eyes search over every inch of her exposed skin. I feel it pebble when my hands press just a tad tighter. I watch as her abs clench over the waistline of those damn black panties. Her nipples pebble under the thin fabric of the shirt and the prettiest blush covers her neck, traveling up to her cheeks. She swallows thickly when I tilt her chin up to me.

"Hey, Jude?" I whisper and her breath stutters. "I'm going to kiss you now." *Please let me.*

Two quick breaths, that is all the time I allot her before my lips crash against hers. My hands travel up her leg until they are cupping the back of her calf and pull it up to wrap around my waist. Her hands twist in my hair at the nape of my neck, causing me to groan into her mouth as her nails dig in harder. She nips at my bottom lip and I can feel her grin when she pulls another moan from me. Kissing her burns up every nerve in my body like my blood is on fire.

My lips move to nip her jaw, letting my tongue travel down until I'm sucking at the hollow space of her neck. The sweetest whimper leaves her lips causing my dick to pulse as she uses the leverage she has with her hands wrapped around my neck to grind her hips against me. I'm pretty sure she will have marks on her skin tomorrow and that only drives me harder. Her other leg wraps around me and I feel her legs lock at the small of my back. Her thighs pull me closer into her.

I've imagined her legs wrapped around me more times than I am willing to admit and my imagination wasn't even close to what it feels like in this moment. My thumb finds her clit over the thin black material. The second I put pressure there, her back arches and a beautiful claws it's way out of her throat. She catches her balance by reaching one hand behind her, giving me better access to her.

"Tell me to stop." I pant, giving her one last chance to put that wall up she likes so much and praying that she chooses not to.

"I will actually punch you in the dick if you do." Only Avery would cause me to laugh while I have her in this position on her kitchen counter. And who am I to deny her? My hand gently reaches under the material that is separating and just the feel of her is enough to make me come undone.

But she doesn't want soft. She grabs my wrist and wraps her small hand the best she can around mine, guiding me down further until my middle finger finds her center. She pushes that finger all the way in and presses harder showing me exactly what she wants and likes. It's fucking sexy as hell. Her taking charge like this. And I plan to give her everything she wants.

"I need more." She demands, gasping when I drive a second finger in and curl. Her legs constrict tighter as she relinquishes her controlling hold on my neck to tap her neck. "Kiss here." She talks me through something else she likes and I do exactly as I'm told.

We fall into a steady rhythm of her digging her heels into my back while holding me in place for my lips and teeth to map out the slope of her neck. I really hope there are marks there tomorrow. She moves her hips in time with my hand and I feel her tighten around my fingers. I open my eyes to make sure she still has her hand behind her to stabilize her before I move my hand from her hip to circle around her throat. I let my teeth sink into the delicate skin beneath her ear before letting my lips land just on the outside to whisper in her ear. "Ride it out." I know she is close. I can feel everything get tighter and her breath is scratchy. I capture her lips again at the exact moment her release hits her. She bites down hard on my bottom lip and I know I am leaking in my shorts but I can only focus on the way that she is fighting for her life with the grip she has on me. I let up the pressure from her neck and trace her bottom lip softly with my tongue before a grin overtakes my whole face. I move my hand from her neck to rest on her thigh and feel the muscle quiver under my fingertips. "You're fucking trembling, Jude." She is so lost to the sensation overtaking her whole body that whatever words she tries to speak are only a mumble.

After a few moments, she is finally able to catch her breath. Her sleepy and sex hazed eyes open to land on mine. I pull my fingers out of her slowly to give her a minute to adjust back to a sitting position. She still seems unable to speak or she is putting too much consideration into what she should say. Either way, leaving her speechless is my new favorite thing to do. I reach over and dip the same two fingers that were just inside her into the icing and bring them to my mouth. Making sure she is watching, I lick every last bit of icing off. "This might be my new favorite treat." I lean in to give her the softest kiss before taking her hand and leading her to where she has scrabble laying out on her living room table.

"What just happened?" She asks as she takes a seat on the couch. I grab the blanket and drape it over her lap because her not wearing pants is seriously going to cause me to enter an early grave.

"You know what just happened." I clear the board and put the letters in the bag and shake them up.

"We're not going to talk about this?" She leans forward and stops my hand from grabbing our letters out of the freshly mixed up bag.

"No. We aren't."

"Why not?" I can hear the worry in her voice, and that is enough to make me stop and turn to face her.

"Because you don't want to date me. And I am pathetically obsessed with you. And what just happened doesn't have to be dissected. It can just be a moment. One of my favorite moments." Her eyes are full of all the emotions again. I know the score. I was going to take Eddie's warning seriously. I don't want to push her. But I also don't want her to question where I stand.

"You're obsessed with me?" It's cute how disheveled she is.

"You know I am." I gently take her hand and drop the letters into her palm before closing it and kissing her wrist.

She finally seems capable enough to pull herself together to put her letters on her letter holder. I watch her take a deep breath before dipping her head. "I can't date. It's not that I don't want you. *Clearly* I do. I just can't do relationships. It doesn't work. And I like having you in my space. I'm not a relationship girl." Her voice trembles with apprehension and like it is laced with fear.

"And you think I am a relationship guy." She didn't say it, but I know that is what she was trying to convey.

"You absolutely are. You want a girl you can bring to Sunday dinners with your mom and take on dates. And cheer you on in your corner at your fights." She tries to explain what she thinks she knows about what I want.

"You will be in my corner." I think she forgets that as my trainer, the spot in my corner is hers. If I had to make the choice between her and Eddie, it's her every time.

"That's not what I mean. I can't be your girlfriend, Rory." She starts to play a word that I don't recognize on the board and if we were sitting together under normal circumstances, then I would challenge her on the validity of her play. But I won't dare break the careful stability of this moment.

"I'm not asking you to be my girlfriend. I'm asking for you to play me in a game of scrabble." The frustrated growl that leaves her is definitely not meant to be cute. So I hold in my smile. I also push down the hurt that is trying to wash over me at her decision to vehemently reject me.

"Can you please just make sense for one minute?" She is still a little frazzled by tonight's events but that's okay. I can give her what she needs to quiet that beautifully crazy brain of hers.

I pause from playing my word off of hers and make sure she knows I am taking this seriously. She needs to feel safe and at the moment she feels unsteady. I always want to be her steady. I lace my hand with hers and let my thumb rub a tiny circle on her palm.

"I'm not asking you for anything because I know how much stability means to you. I won't break that. But I want what you give me. I love being in your space. So let's not blow this up. It's a good night for an orgasm and scrabble. Let's keep it that way." The look she gives me lets me know that she is still apprehensive of where we stand with each other. I am not afraid of putting in the work with her though.

Twenty-Two

*"Don't you dare.
You know how mean she gets."*

AJ

"**A**re we going to talk about it before or after the run?" Oliver is helping me stretch out this morning and I knew he would know something happened. I also knew he would bring it up and make me talk about why he is the one with me this morning instead of my new minted workout partner of the past two months.

"Talk about what?" God. I can't even make eye contact with him. He knows. I don't even know how he knows. I can feel his dumb ass smirk from here. A normal person might question their reasoning behind getting off with one guy and then calling another guy the next morning. I didn't question it one bit. Oliver is used to my messy head.

"I know what you look like after you have sex, A." If he wasn't holding onto my hands and pulling me towards him, my back would have met the mats. My eyes immediately find his. And his pretty brown eyes are seeking out any kind of tell that I'm not okay. He's always the first one to check on me and the first to know when something has happened.

"I'm okay." I don't have the energy to refute what he said. He finishes his inventory of me and seems to believe me. Then he brings his hand up to play with the ends of my hair.

"You always wear your hair down to the gym the day after you have sex." His voice is accusing but not jealous. His issues with Rory are his own but he will always be protective of me. I snatch his wrist in my own hand and lean forward, putting pressure on that one spot that I know will make his arm immediately feel weak. His smile just grows bigger. Oliver is a bit of a sad boy most of the time. That's part of what makes us so kindred. But he's also a little shit when he wants to be too.

"I never wear my hair down at the gym." I defend.

"How long has it been since you've had sex?" He asks casually but he already knows the answer to that question. Asshole.

"When's the last time *you* had sex?" I raise an eyebrow at him and this fucker laughs.

"We're not talking about my sex life." His smile falls and his voice goes monotone. He's way too quick to shut that down which I find interesting because he normally tells me about his hookups.

"I think we should all talk about our sex lives." Mia appears out of thin air and plops down between where Oliver and I have our legs stretched out. "I met a guy last night. Super cute. *Really* great kisser. He even texted me a cute little good morning text this morning." She pumps her eyebrows up and down when she looks at me. It's impossible to not be in a good mood when this girl is around.

"Where did you even come from?" I ask her with a smile on my face. She has the unfortunate skillset to always sneak up on people.

"She walked in like five minutes ago." Oliver leans his body to the side to speak around Mia.

"I didn't even hear the door open." I was so in my head over Rory that I wasn't even able to hear the door open. This is going to be a problem.

"Me either, but I smelled cherries the moment she walked in." His words cause both our heads to swivel to where he is staring back at us like what he said wasn't completely out of character for him.

"You know what she smells like?" I call him out.

"You paying attention to me, tough guy?" Mia coos.

Both our voices mix together but Oliver definitely feels the pressure of both of our questions. He points to the other side of the gym and glares at Mia, "go away. We were talking about something important." Mia jerks her whole body around to face Oliver now.

"Make me, you overgrown bear." Her voice is drenched in defiance. Oliver loops his right arm around Mia's stomach and lifts her easily from the mats as he stands.

"What the hell, Oliver!" Mia squeals and I don't even try to hold back my laughter. Mia looked like one of those tube guys flailing her arms and legs around in every direction. Oliver readjusts and throws her over his shoulder to have better control of her body. The loud smack of her open palm landing on his ass reverberates through the whole gym. The only tell that it hurts him is the slight grimace he allows to sneak out but corrects quickly. "Jokes on you. I happen to love this view." Mia's hand swings wide, as if she is going to smack his ass again, but she brings her forefinger and thumb together at the last moment to pinch instead. She's such a menace.

A yelp leaves Oliver's lips and the laughter in the gym grows louder as Eli and Max are now losing it. He carries Mia across the entire gym to the corner where the boys are filming their videos. Oliver drops Mia down on the mats in front of the boys but he does it so gently so she doesn't get hurt at all.

"I hate that you can just do that." I hear Mia huff from across the gym. She stands and flips her hair into a better lying position from where she had been upside down. Her crazy curls don't move much though and her cheeks are flushed a deep pink.

"No you don't." She really doesn't. She has mentioned on multiple occasions how she loves working with strong guys and how it isn't a hardship to watch them every day. Mia had a small crush on Oliver before she ever started working here. I haven't asked her about it since, but I am confident Oliver still works his way under her skin on a regular basis. Only now it seems like she has made it her mission to do the same to him.

Oliver closes the distance back to me quickly with large strides. When he is back down on the ground across from me, he takes his feet, placing them on the inside of my ankles and presses outward to go back to our stretch we were in before Mia interrupted.

"We have maybe fifteen minutes before the boys lose the ability to keep her attention focused on them and she barrels her way back over here." He reaches out and locks his hands over my wrists pulling me forward. "So you and Davis." He prompts me to tell him more.

"Don't call him that. You have literally known him longer than me. Use his name." We change positions. "And there isn't a Rory *and* me. We just hooked up. Kind of." I grimace because I still feel bad about how I handled it all afterwards. I was intentionally riling him up, but then he put his hands on my body and I had no self control.

"Semantics." He throws away my words. I raise my eyebrow at him when he moves just his eyes to look up at me.

"We didn't have sex!" I hiss, dropping his hands and giving his shoulder a shove. "He got me off on the kitchen counter with his fingers and then dipped them in the icing and ate it and then we played scrabble." The words fall quickly from my lips. Oliver sits there staring at me. His face stoic and his eyes full of absolute shock, maybe horror? I can't tell. "What?" I bark.

"You played scrabble?" He's definitely shocked and maybe a little bit concerned by the tone of his voice.

"It was his idea!" Groaning, I face plant into the mat. When he said it like that, I realize how pathetic that sounded. But it kept my head from feeling fuzzy afterwards. I think that was the point. Rory always seems to cultivate the space I need in the form that I need it. And I was absolutely about to spiral after our little kitchen adventure.

"Do you want to do it again?" I can't tell how Oliver is actually feeling about this conversation. He doesn't seem upset. I knew he wouldn't be jealous, he has no reason to be. We know where we stand with each other and it has been a good distance in time from us being together for any complicated emotions to bubble their way up. I think he's just trying to assess how I'm truly feeling. Which is what makes him my closest friend.

"Desperately." I admit easily. I know the answer without having to spend a second contemplating it. Rory has had his hands on my skin on several different occasions and every time it happened it put me into a state of shock because I didn't have the immediate need to pull away. Rory's the type of steady that stopped the chaos in my head without even trying. It's peaceful.

"Okay." Oliver nods his head and then pushes out a breath, "so go after it." My surprise must have been evident because he chuckles, shrugging his shoulders. "My issues with him have nothing to do with the type of guy he is. Him being able to chase after the one thing I lost fucks with me. But I'm trying." His eyes find mine and there is a resonation reflecting back at me. "Rory is one of the best guys I've ever known, A. And he's never gone after anything that isn't worth it. Don't let fear rob you of that." And just like that, I'm reminded that there isn't anything hidden from how Oliver can see right through me. There's also a peace in that.

"His mom is here. He loves this gym. He has shown all the signs of someone who is here to stay." My heart knows that is a good thing. For everyone. Melinda does so much good with her center and Eddie seems to really enjoy having her back around. Having Rory here at the gym brings good publicity and he's getting more passionate with his training. He fits here. How am I supposed to taint that with my mess?

"Talk to him." Oliver encourages me like he can hear the turmoil in my head.

"What do I say, Ol? Tell him that I grew up unloved and abused and now I'm fucked up? Because I feel like that is just not something that you casually drop on to someone. Especially not a guy that is fighting for his career every day and we both know how important mentality is with this sport. I can't trauma dump my shit on him. That's not fair." Because Rory is genuinely all the good parts of life. He is kind and outgoing and pays attention to the tiniest things. He makes sure that the attention is appropriately placed in all situations. He understands the kind of healing the gym can provide.

"You give him the space to show up, A."

"He hasn't asked me to do that. He didn't say anything after it happened. We played a game of scrabble and then he went home. I stayed up until three in the morning with my head just ping ponging thoughts." I also replayed what happened a few times but I wasn't going to admit that to Oliver. We still have some boundaries.

Oliver hangs his head in laughter again. "I'm sorry. The scrabble is still just killing me." This time I kick him but he catches my ankle and pulls me in closer. His hands bracket each side of my neck and he drops his head to be eye level with him. "I want you to get your pretty head out of your ugly thoughts and listen to what I'm about to say. Okay?" I barely give him a nod but he knows he has my attention. "You can't keep running from the things you deserve because you are too afraid of actually obtaining them. It's not fair to the people who belong in your orbit." My ears start to burn a bit and there's a hard lump in my throat.

"I'm not running..." I choke out.

"No. You're just walking in place hoping that all the good passes you up and you have a valid excuse to not allow it to affect you." I feel the pressure of his hands squeeze to keep my attention. "Let him try."

I find the strength to lift my eyes back up to meet his. "Let him try what?"

He gives me his trademark smirk that I know works on every single girl he has ever given it to. "Whatever he wants. Let him try." I fill my entire chest with every ounce of air it can consume and hold it for five seconds before letting it out slowly.

"Okay, Ol." I resign and promise at the same time.

I feel his lips touch my forehead before he releases me. "And also, maybe have sex with him. You need sleep." Gone was the soft Oliver and back was the asshole that is my best friend.

"Oliver!" He tries to pull me into a hug but I slip through his arms and roll out of his reach.

"What? It works. You know it works. I know it works. It works." He starts to come towards me again but I put my hand up to keep him away.

"We are done with this conversation now." I look around to find where Mia is. "Mia! I need you!" I shout across the gym.

"Don't you dare. You know how mean she gets." He slants his head and his eyes are pleading but it's my turn to laugh.

"She is an angel." I come to her defense.

"Her tequila angel!" I feel Mia's arms wrap around my shoulders right before her whole weight now rests on my back. She is leaning fully over me since she's a few inches taller than me.

"My tequila angel."

Mia brings her middle finger up in front of us, directing it right at Oliver's face. "And I'm not mean. You just can't handle me."

"I can handle you just fine, pretty girl." I expect her to come back with something but she just has a wide smile resting on her face, her eyes dancing.

"Why are we standing around?" Eddie's voice booms from the top of the stairs where the office is.

"Hot dad alert." Mia whispers from where her body is still draped over my back.

"Gross." A shudder works up my spine.

Movement from behind Eddie catches my eye. Rory steps out behind him. Even from here I can tell he is looking over my body, checking for something. Then his eyes drift to where Oliver is standing, and then shifts back to where I am standing. My chest feels the heat of his stare and I realize I am holding my breath when I see his lips tilt upward.

"I'm not going to be mad that you talked to Oliver about whatever happened between you and Rory first. But you are absolutely going to tell me why Rory is staring at you like he's seen you naked over margaritas and tacos tonight." Mia keeps her voice intentionally low but I know she is serious. She takes our new Monday ritual with all the seriousness of abiding by a law. Well, let's be honest. She probably breaks laws in her free time. But whatever we talk about over margaritas and tacos is sacred.

"We have three and a half months until Rory's title fight. And I have a smoker scheduled in two weeks to keep him fresh. And Mia's banquet for Changing the Culture was approved by the city board. So I will need you two to get to work on planning that. Melinda has a connection for a venue, I made lunch plans for you two to meet her today to talk it over." Eddie points to where Mia and I are standing. He's completely unaware of the life leaving my body. I can barely wrap my head around wanting to have Rory come back to my apartment and now I am going to have to have lunch with his mom. I'm going to have to look her in the eyes and pretend like her son's fingers weren't just inside me less than twenty four hours ago. *Fuck me.*

Meanwhile, Mia has left my side to run up the stairs and hug Eddie. She has been working hard on her pitch for this banquet since she brought it up the other week at our taco night. For all of Mia's chaotic personality, her heart bleeds for the forgotten and unloved children. She wants this with every fiber of her being and I promised her that we would make it happen. So I will have to suck up my inner panic over this lunch and make it happen. For her.

I turn around to beg Ollie for one of his pep talks but he is on the phone in the corner of the gym, his voice too hushed for me to hear. He's ending the conversation by the time I make it to where he is standing.

"No, I'll be there." His voice is tight and it makes the hairs on the back of my neck stand up.

"You'll be where?" He pockets his phone and gives me the look he gives when he is desperate for me to drop something. "You'll be where, Ol?"

Nothing. No answer, no explanation, no words. We are just standing there, staring at each other, the weight of who would give in first so heavy that the air was thinner. His eyes give it away though. Guilt. Guilt in the thickest depths of those blue eyes. I know what he is struggling with better than most. The incessant need to prove that he can do it. That he can still fight. It has been tied to his identity for longer than I have been in his life. I know that Rory being present every day is a burden on his darkening thoughts. Just like I know Oliver just took a fight.

"What day do you fight?" At least he has the dignity to not hang his head in defeat. His eyes never leave mine, but an apology crosses the distance from where I am standing from him. I don't get to ask him not to fight. This is something he would have to work out himself. The Poolhouse is always clutching for a new fight, even more so when that fight would feature a crowd favorite. I turned down fights at least once a week. And even I would get the itch to say yes. The release your body expels when you are in the ring is a high that is unmatched.

"In one month. The guy asked for me specifically." That means whoever it is knows what Oliver is capable of, where he trains, who trains him. "Please don't be mad at me." This time his words are barely audible with the noise that is quickly approaching behind us.

"How many until you are convinced you aren't broken?"

"I don't know."

Twenty-Three

*"Do what you need to
do to survive it."*

AJ

Watching the sun fill the space in the gym is always one of my favorite parts of the morning. My other favorite moment is when my sleeplessness consumes my time. It's the moment of being able to come into the gym and the glow from the emergency lights are the only visibility allotted. It is when I can be less controlled. It is when I am able to fall apart with the weight of the life I had before this one. If I didn't have that moment, I know that I would eventually just remain fragmented. Broken down into little parts that I held for the few people that have taught me the differing degrees of love. Desiring to find the space that I could be free.

The abandoned gym always gives me the closest opportunity to feel free. I could spend hours running through the fundamental drills we teach all of our beginner classes. Eddie is a stickler for foundation. If you have the foundation, you grow more naturally. That's what I choose to do this morning while my mind runs with all the thoughts that refuse to be quiet. The part of me that kept me shackled to the little girl of the past. The parts of me I fight to break free.

Mia is desperate to bring that part out of me, just like Chloe was. Mia is the definition of unconfined. She walks into every room with the desire to do whatever her heart sought to do with no doubts present to hinder her actions. She just lives. She doesn't worry about losing people closest to her. She doesn't fear her life being ripped away from her and having to start over again. She takes each day as the opportunity it is. Mia just lacks roots.

I don't lack roots. If anything, I am too rooted.

If I focus on cultivating what is already in my grasp, then I don't have to be concerned with anything dying or falling away from my life.

So that's what I do. I wake up each day, work out all my hazy thoughts on a bag or by going for a run. I open the gym up for the stragglers that need a morning workout before work and then set up for classes throughout the day. Then I close down the gym and do the whole process over again. I've been doing this for years. On the weekends, I might go out with the boys. And on Sundays, I eat dinner with Eddie and we watch trashy TV.

I like the predictability of my days. The stability of them. Stability is something I have been chasing for what feels like my whole life. And Eddie is the one who provides it. He and this gym and the triplets have healed something in me that I didn't even know could be repaired.

Now Mia and Rory are in my day to day and they are wreaking havoc on my ability to maintain that stability. Mia is bringing back something that was stolen from me. It's like the world recycled every single piece of genuine goodness and love that resided in Chloe's heart and implanted them into Mia's. And then for whatever reason, the universe dropped that sweet little ray of chaotic sunshine into my life. And I plan on protecting her at all costs. She is a part of our dysfunctional family now.

Rory is harder to accept as a permanent fixture. But I fear he has no plans of moving on from being here. He told Eddie the other day that he finally feels like he is home. His mom is here, she has a career here. And her job facilitates a lot of what Mia and I want to do with this new program for foster kids. He trains at the gym that holds mats that bleed my blood. He makes friends with every old couple we pass on our morning runs. He teaches underprivileged kids art classes, while training every day. That kind of mindset is not for the weak.

The fighting mindset is what ultimately left me in the void, on the brink of succumbing to madness or letting it go. And if it wasn't for Eddie, I wouldn't have chosen to let it go. Being able to have the control to hurt people was a battle for me. I lived for the rush of it. To train so hard to be able to ultimately demoralize someone. It was a type of power that needed balance.

I was never able to control that balance. I was always consumed with the electric pulse of strength it fed me. I would walk into that abandoned pool and everything else would turn into shadows. The only focus was on winning. And that focus quickly transformed into a need to showcase that no one was ever going to cause me damage again. I would always be transported to that old beat down blue house, in the hallway or the bathroom. Kyle never had a preference for where he liked to unleash his anger. But if he did it in the bathroom, he could leave us there to clean up our wounds under the guise that we were taking a shower. Less questions that way.

Eventually every punch I threw landed on his face. Or I would see Chloe as a shell of the girl I met when I was fifteen. I would see her curled up on her own kitchen floor, completely strung out on whatever drug her boyfriend brought home for her. I would sit there for hours holding her like she used to hold me outside our foster home. I wanted to leave no room for her to feel alone.

I wanted to save her like she saved me. Countless times. I wanted to wake her up from the nightmare her mind was trapped in. She got us out. But her mind had stayed locked in that house. In what happened between her and Kyle in his room.

Chloe taught me the truest definition of family. She made me realise that people choose who they love. Because love is an act of sacrifice and hard work. Love is something that you give with your whole heart with the acceptance that it would be worth it if it got broken. Her love filled the cracks of my heart and helped it beat a little better. And I miss her every damn day. But I know she somehow sent me Mia.

I find my way over to the bag. Letting the sound of each hit pair with the music in my headphones as I let the sadness pour from my body with every bead of sweat. This week marks five years since she died. And while the triplets know that this week is the hardest week of each year, they don't try to make it better in any way. They let me do whatever I want and just give me casual glances to try and take inventory of my emotions. Oliver knows more than his brothers but he always just offers to cook for me or play scrabble. Talking about Chloe never makes losing her easier, so I choose to just wait for the onslaught of grief to pass the best it can.

My music cuts out abruptly causing me to whip my head to where I left my phone on the bench. Eddie is sitting there, holding a bottle of water out towards me.

"I always like the gym at this time too." His eyes trace over the emptiness of the gym around us.

I reach over to put my headphones on the bench next to my phone checking the time. It was five in the morning. I have been here for three hours. Time is always lost when I can't escape my mind.

"I couldn't sleep." I don't need to explain, the reason is obvious since he smiles sadly at me.

"I know what week it is, kiddo." He nods to me and I watch his grin shift to a sad and almost choked smile. "Do what you need to do to survive it." Eddie is always able to meet me where I need him to without even trying. I always wonder what he would have been like as a girl dad because I know that raising his three boys was hell.

"Why are you awake so early? We agreed that you would still do light work with the gym." We didn't really agree. I had argued with him relentlessly until he conceded.

"I talked with Rory. Since we will travel to Florida for the smoker, I told him that he could choose who he wanted as his corner." I have put months into training Rory for his title fight and he is ready. We all know it. But putting him through a prep fight is never a bad idea. It's a way to let out any doubt and stress with the upcoming big fight. It doesn't hold the same level of pressure, and the fighters are usually able to work through whatever mental blocks that might have crept in.

I stare at Eddie, waiting for him to tell me that Rory chose him. Why wouldn't he? I would choose Eddie to corner me in any fight. He is one of the best and he's known Rory since he was a kid. He would be able to predict any movement that he would need to recalibrate in the moment and help coach him through adapting to the fighter he was facing.

"He chose you." The pure shock on my face is not mirrored on Eddie's. He seems to be...happy?

"Why?" I mean, I have been training him. But I have never even been to this other gym. Eddie has taken Oliver before. And he has sent a few guys over to do training camps. But I have less than ample experience to coach a fight at that gym. Not to mention that if Rory walks in with a girl as his corner coach, he would immediately lose professional respect.

"Didn't ask." He shrugs.

"I'm not going."

"Yes, you are. I already booked you two conjoining rooms and called Henry to let him know you would be the coach representing our gym." His tone is filled with finality but every atom in my body wants to protest.

Eddie doesn't know what happened between me and Rory last week. If he did, I doubt he would be so willing to send us off together to represent the gym. Eddie has never shown a care about who I choose to spend time with. Given, I don't really spend time with anyone. But one thing that Eddie does always have a big interest in is keeping the gym professional and respected.

"You're going." He stops any argument from exiting my lips before I have a chance to speak the words. "I don't care about whatever is happening between you two. You're both adults. And Rory already promised he would make sure you were taken care of while you're gone." I'm sure he did. "I know this week is your own personal hell, but I think maybe this will be good. Change up what you normally do. Healing is growth and growth means change." I hate when he pulls the dad voice out. It always makes me feel a foot smaller. And I am already a foot shorter than all of them.

"Fine." It isn't fine actually. My insides are screaming. The fight is next Friday. That gives me this weekend and all of next week to figure out how to talk to Rory. To let him know that while what we did was fun, and made my body feel every bit alive, it would not happen again. I like having him in the gym. That is something that still surprises me every time the realization comes to me. He makes me laugh, and he doesn't even try to. He makes me feel safe without having to prove he is a safe person. He gives me the opportunity to just feel like I can breathe without being weighed down. And I don't want to lose that. He is becoming one of my closest friends.

Am I attracted to him? Hell yes. You would have to be blind and deaf, and unable to feel touch to not be attracted to Rory Davis. But that doesn't mean that I need to pursue him. And that doesn't mean I need to let him pursue me. If that is even what he wanted to do. I am still a little confused on that part. He hasn't really talked to me much since that night.

Going to a different state and staying in a hotel with him will be easy.

Twenty-Four

"I wish that you weren't so attractive."

I can still taste her. It's been nearly two weeks and I can still remember what she tastes like. What her lips feel like. How her legs trembled under my hands. I remember how her eyes widened a little when I told how much I like being around her. The way her face twisted up slightly when I told her to not make a big deal out of what happened. I don't regret a single second of it though.

Everyone knows I am attracted to Avery. Hell, even my own mother knows. I don't work too hard at hiding it. But what everyone is missing is how drawn to this girl I am. From the first day I walked into the gym I was immediately locked in on wanting to be close to her. And now I am desperate to know her on a molecular level.

She doesn't make it easy though. Just this week alone she's been all business. The only thing we've talked about is training. And if she was like that with just me, then I would assume it is her still processing what happened. But she's been like that with everyone but Eddie. And when I try to talk to Eddie about it he shuts me down every time.

And now I'm at the gym for our scheduled run. She has added an extra mile to this week to keep my cardio up before the fight. I have no concern for this one. It's nothing but a practice round and it's basically for show. Eddie knows that I'll be able to defeat this guy no problem. I've watched his old fights and he posts on social media nearly every day. He is good. Solid even. But I am better and Eddie knows it.

I knew that Eddie wasn't concerned in the slightest when he brought me to his office to ask who I wanted to take with me to be my corner coach. Without hesitation I chose Avery. Eddie just smiled and told me he would handle the travel details. No questions asked. That was the first thing that made me question why he set this fight up.

Eddie is always so serious, especially about training and his craft. And while this smoker is going to be a real fight, and help hone in my focus for my title fight in three months, he isn't concerned about the outcome. As his fighter, that makes me feel confident. As the guy that is nearly obsessed with his pseudo daughter and about to spend a few days alone with her, I expected him to at least give me a speech about keeping my focus. Eddie was the first to clock my interest in Avery and the only one to tell me to protect myself.

I've been warming up with stretches for nearly thirty minutes before I start to worry. She is never late. Avery is, annoyingly, always early. She made it nearly impossible for me to surprise her. I check my phone from where I texted her this morning to see if she has responded.

Rory

> I'm going to bring you this new protein bar I found. It's strawberry flavored. I think you'll like it.

> You don't have to eat it, it just made me think of you.

> Okay, focus on training. I get the message.

No response. She always responds.

Rory

> Are you okay? You're never late. Not a big deal at all. I'm just a little worried.

I give it five minutes before I start calling her. Straight to voicemail. In the middle of my second time trying to call her Oliver comes barreling through the front door. His hair is still wet and he looks like he is still trying to wake up. Which makes sense since Avery makes me meet her at five every morning now. She said that training hard in the morning allowed for my body to get the proper nutrition and rest to fuel it better. I just show up because she asks me to.

"Hello?" I greet Oliver as he tosses his bag down with a sigh.

"Okay, so we're not running the extra mile. AJ is a psycho and I'm not doing it." Oliver blows out a breath.

"What are you doing here, Ol?" I try again. He's getting dressed down for our run but I need him to focus. "Where is she?"

"Actually can we run like just a warm up mile and then do drills?" He ignores my questions entirely. I'm going to punch him. Why isn't he concerned?

"Where is she?" I ask again. This time with more aggression.

He looks up at me with a face that tells me that I;m being too much in this moment but I don't give a fuck. One thing about Avery that is a fact is that she will be at this gym. Every day.

"She's always off on this day." I watch his face fall slightly before standing and heading to the door. Trying to get our run started and dismissing my worry.

"Hold up. What do you mean? She never takes off." Except a few weeks ago, but that was to prove a point and she had already been here for hours before that.

"She does today." He speaks without looking back at me.

I follow him out of the door and we both start off in a small jog to warm up. "What's today?"

I feel it in my gut before he speaks. Something turns sour in my stomach.

"Chloe's death anniversary." He finally answers me. Fuck.

We round the corner for the big stretch that aligns with the beach shore.

"We don't talk about it. We don't bring it up. She takes today off and she will be quiet all day tomorrow. Then she will be back to normal." He explains. That doesn't sit right with me though. She shouldn't be alone today. I've learned that Avery's mind is not her safe space and it doesn't treat her kindly. There's no way in hell I am going to let her be alone today.

"Where is she?" I demand because I know he knows. And if he doesn't, he has her location and can tell me.

He comes to a stop by one of the piers and turns to face me. "She doesn't need to be coddled today." His eyes narrow slightly but his intimidation misses its mark since he's slightly out of breath and I honestly just don't give a fuck. I'm going to find her.

"She definitely doesn't need to be alone," I argue.

"She does this every year. I tried to be around her for years and she fought me on it. Dad thinks she just needs to work through it on her own and that's okay." I can see the turmoil in his eyes, hear it in his voice but I haven't tried for years.

"I'm going to say this and you're going to hate it." I watch his jaw tick. "I'm not the same as you."

"Don't fuck with her peace, Rory." It's a warning. It doesn't hold much weight behind it because even he thinks she shouldn't be alone today. That much is clear. "Today isn't the day to try and push her boundaries."

"I want to be her peace." And I do. I want to be a safe place for her to just stay without feeling crushed by everything else. I'm not going to explain that much to Oliver though.

I watch as he digests my words and makes a decision. "She was at the bakery ten minutes ago. She usually heads to the liquor store on Mitchell Street and then to the grave yard. She will be there for a few hours." I must have given him a look of absolute confusion because he doesn't even have to check his phone to know her location. "Don't look at me like that. It's creepy, I know! But she's had the same routine each year. I worry about her too." His voice gets a little smaller with that last part.

"Thank you for telling me." I'm not going to train today. It's Wednesday and I have a fight on Friday. I'll be leaving with her tomorrow morning to travel down. I *should* be training today. But I am going to find her instead.

"She's my best friend, Rory." I turn back around to where he is still standing. "I know you care about her. And I know that you're a good guy. But I will absolutely destroy you if you break her." This conversation is going much better than the one we had outside of Eddie's apartment.

"I just want to be there for her today. She deserves that." She stands in everyone's corner every day. She might not think she needs someone to be there for her today because she has been dealing with it every year on her own. But I am willing to push her a little to make sure she knows she isn't alone.

There are three graveyards in this town. And she wasn't at the first two. According to Oliver's timeline, she should be at the graveyard by now. This one has to be the right one.

I get out of my car and grab the bag of snacks and my sketchpad. I find her instantly like I always do. She's sitting on a blanket holding a cup of what looks like donut holes and talking to a tombstone with an angel sitting on top. She looks every degree of sad and for a moment I question whether I should go through with crashing her date with the ghost of her best friend.

"Who was the rat?" I love that she doesn't even have to turn around and see me to know it's me. I hate that she's missing the smirk that I can't hold in. She always fails to hold in her own smile when I do that.

"You didn't show up for our run this morning. And you haven't answered any of my texts." I don't tell her that it was Oliver. Once I'm closer, I realise she is lining up shot glasses with donut holes through toothpicks along the base of the tombstone. I feel like I should be concerned but I'm way too interested in what she is doing to be worried.

"Donut shots?" She shoots me the sweetest glazed look. She's obviously already had a few. In her lap she holds a bottle of Jack Daniels and a bottle of Bailey's Irish Cream. *Please let her have food in her stomach...*

"These were her favorite!" She picks up a shot and hands one to me. "She used to steal Jack Daniels and Bailey's from our foster parents. Everyone else would be asleep and Kyle would be out with his disgusting friends. She would sneak us the alcohol and the shot glasses she lifted once from a gift shop. We would go out into the woods in the back yard and every time we saw a shooting star, we would take a shot and make a wish." She starts giggling. I don't think I've ever heard her giggle. "I don't think she ever really saw a shooting star. She would just say she did so we would take a shot." She lifts one of the shot glasses and tosses it back before picking the donut off the toothpick and eating it in one bite. At least she's eating with the shots. "There was a boy at the bakery who always thought she was cute and would give her a bag of donut holes every week if she asked." Judging by the way she acted the night I picked her and Mia up from their Margarita Monday, she is slightly tipsy but not quite drunk yet.

Drinking is absolutely not a part of my training. I look down at the shot glass that holds matching liquid to hers. "Wait. So what are you drinking to? It's daylight." She scrunches her nose up at me and her eyes are not the storms that they usually were. They are lighter and softer and definitely sadder than I've ever seen them.

She rolls her eyes as she clumsily waives around above her head. "Wow. You're so observant. I completely missed the giant ball of fire in the sky." *There she is.* I love her attitude.

"You didn't answer my question."

"We drink every time a bird lands on her tombstone." That couldn't happen too many times. "And you have to make a wish!" She points the donut hole at me.

"Deal." I wink at her and sit down on the ground next to her.It takes only ten minutes for the first bird to land. We each take our shot, which is much sweeter than I thought it would be.

"I wish that you weren't so attractive." She whines and I nearly choke on the donut hole at her first wish.

"That's rude." I lean forward just enough to be eye level with her."I wish that you would let me kiss you again." My eyes drop to her lips. She reaches out and shoves my shoulder, but her laughter rings through the air around us. I really wish I could keep her laughing right now.

"You can't say things like that." She attempts to whisper but her voice is just at a normal level.

"I'm just playing the game, Avery Jude." I watch her eyes catch on my sketchpad that I brought with me as she holds her hand out for my empty shot glass. Eddie is going to kill me for taking these with her. Or I will get a pass since she seems to be his favorite. Or maybe we just never tell him.

"What are you always drawing in that thing?" She points to where the notepad is laying. I really hope she doesn't ask me to show her because I'm pretty sure that her sad eyes have the power to make me say yes to anything and I am not prepared to explain why half this book is filled with her.

"Whatever I find is worth my time or things I can't get out of my head. So I sketch them out instead." There, that isn't a lie. It's honest without giving her the exact answer.

I watch her face light up as another bird lands. There is no way this is how she normally did these shots. It's only been five minutes, maybe seven. She definitely made that rule up the moment I asked her. She downs her shot and shimmies her shoulders a little as she eats the bite sized pastry.

"I wish that you would stop flirting with me." She narrows her eyes at me but it only causes me to get slightly giddy. I see we are keeping the theme of our wishes being on us. That's fine by me.

I drop back my shot and wipe the left over drop from my lip. "I've been flirting with you since the day we met. I won't be stopping any time soon." I promise her then hand her my empty glass. "I wish you would let me take you on an actual date." I can see her mind already rejecting even the notion of what I said. I expect that though.

"I don't date, Rory. Not that I don't want to. I don't know how to. And I don't like relationships." That isn't a no to dating me in particular though. And I can sense a deeper meaning behind her words. She isn't just against relationships. Something made her closed off to them entirely.

"Make an exception." I nearly beg.

I can hear the lack of breathing from where she is holding her breath. I almost have her. Is this possibly the worst time to be having this conversation? On the anniversary of her best friend's death. Literally on the grave of said best friend. Probably. But just from what she has told me about Chloe, I feel like she would be rooting for me right now. Hell, maybe she is.

"I've never been on a date." Her words barely audible and laced with what sounds like embarrassment.

"Let me be your first." I can't bring myself to back down. My mind is telling me to pull back and calm down, but my mouth is forming words without permission.

My eyes catch hers and I can see her working through all the reasons she can fathom to say no to me. I can also see her fighting the want to say yes. And that is enough to keep me hoping for more. Within a second I can tell what decision she has come to and I know that I will have to accept defeat for the moment.

Another bird lands, we take our shots.

"I wish you would... Tell me all of your favorite things about Chloe." I figure it's best to pivot the conversation. I'm not afraid to keep showing up for her until she knows I am worth facing whatever is holding her back. I know she likes me. She's the type of girl that wouldn't give a guy a second glance if she didn't want to. I know parts of her trust me, but she isn't sure how to handle that revelation. I know that she wants me, probably not as much as I want her, but I can hope.

I pull out my sketch book and rest it on my legs, out of her direct eyesight. I toss the bag of snacks toward her and motion for her to speak. "Go ahead. Tell me everything good about your favorite person, Jude." I encourage her. This will hopefully be something that can make this melancholy day more healing.

Her whole body relaxes as she lets her mind drift to good memories. I watch her eyes dance and her face light up from love and laughter for the next hour as she tells me about Chloe. The birds and shots are forgotten. I watch her face transform with a glow that I've never seen before. And I can't stop myself from wondering if anyone has just let her talk about the girl she lost. It's clear that Chloe changed the course of Avery's life and grief holds no favoritism. It holds you in a chokehold and just when you think you can breathe again, it reminds you it is still there.

We both sat there on that blanket, in a graveyard, eating snacks and laughing until the sunset and she let me take her back to her home.

I noticed when I said goodnight and left her on the other side of the door that she breathed lighter. I want to convince her that she and I could be good together. I want to beg her to give me all of her time. But mostly I just want to be what she needs because if anyone deserves to have someone, it is Avery Jude.

Twenty-Five

"I'm good at a lot of things, Jude."

RORY

Maybe choosing Avery as my corner coach for this fight was a mistake. Not because she isn't fully capable of being the best person for the job, but because I'm about to spend roughly six hours in a car ride alone with her from our little town in South Carolina to the gym in Florida. I'm craving the close space with her, but after her day spent grieving Chloe, I don't want to put pressure on her. I stopped by the coffee shop Mia apparently still works at. She gave me Avery's usual order and I had already stocked up on the random things I know she keeps in the gym for snacks.

Eddie and Avery are already waiting in front of the gym when I pull up. She looks exactly the way I love most. She's standing there with her hair down and wild, drowning in my old favorite hoodie. I watch her race back up the stairs as Eddie makes his way to me. I get out of my car and reach for the bag he is holding, I assume for Avery.

"Don't wreck." He says with a quiet threat in his voice. "And give this to her before she corners you. It'll be her first time at a different gym and actual corner instead of just assisting me." Avery will be just fine. "She will be fine, of course." His words echo my thoughts. "But she always needs a small reminder." He holds a folded piece of blue paper out for me to take. It's one of the blue post-it notes I find all over the office. I noticed a few around Avery's apartment when I was there last. *Don't think about being in her apartment right now, dumbass.*

"I got her." I promise him.

"Does she know that?" There's an edge to his voice and I know this is Eddie's way of trying to get a feel for if anything new has happened since his warning speech about her hurting me if I tried to pursue anything with her.

"Do I know what?" Avery brings our attention to where she is already standing on the passenger side of my car.

"Nothing."

"You get the thing?"

Eddie and I speak at the same time. I know that she's definitely going to make me tell her what we were talking about as soon as I'm closed up in the car with her. I quickly shove the blue note into my back pocket and out of her view.

"I got the thing." She laughs as she comes back around the car to give Eddie a tight hug.

"I'm serious. If anything happens to her... I'm coming for you, Davis." Avery pushes Eddie's shoulder with her hand, wearing a softer smile than I usually see on her.

"Twenty three years of taking care of myself. I don't need you doing it now, Eddie." I watch her nose scrunch. I think that's my new favorite thing.

"Always my kid, remember?" I don't think I've ever seen Eddie so soft. He wraps her in for one more hug and kisses the side of her head. He whispers something to her before releasing her.

"You're not going to wish me luck on the fight?" Avery makes her way into the car and leaves us standing here. Eddie gives a slight shake of his head as he looks up at me.

"You'll beat him in the second round. Don't hit him too hard, take it to the ground and make him tap on the ground. Once you take his back, you have him. He has zero spatial awareness to get out of that situation. You have the quick instincts to go for it and not second guess." He has zero concern for my capability going into this fight, almost like it isn't necessary for me to even go.

"Then why the fuck are you making me go and do this?" Questioning Eddie isn't something I make a habit of doing but I know that there is some other reason he is pushing this smoker fight so hard.

"She needs to be out of this town for a minute to breathe. This is the hardest week of the year for her." He admits quietly.

"Because of Chloe. I know." I can count on one hand how many times I've seen Eddie taken by surprise. He didn't expect me to know about Chloe.

"She's talked to you about Chloe?" I keep my mouth shut. Afraid to answer him at the risk of losing whatever trust Avery has in me. "I changed my mind." He steps just a little bit closer to me. Close enough that there is zero chance for Avery to hear or make out what he is about to say. "She obviously trusts you. She doesn't talk about losing Chloe or her life before the gym. So, if she is telling you, then that means you are closer than I thought she would let you be." He somehow moves a little closer and I feel my stomach drop with the way his eyes seem to hold a dark promise. "If you hurt my girl. I'll break your legs." Funny. I'm pretty sure I said those exact same words to the dickholes thinking they were going to get close to Mia and Avery that night on the beach.

I don't know the right words to say at this moment so I just nod my head. Avery is all fire and bite. But at the graveyard she was drenched in grief and reminiscing on what I imagine was one of the only good things life brought her and then ripped away. She seems to be chasing the security of never losing someone like that again. Which makes for a miserable life. Never loving out of fear of losing it.

I get into the driver's seat while rearranging my thoughts back to our road trip. Avery has her bare feet on the dashboard, already trying to hook her phone up to be a passenger DJ, and the bag of snacks between her legs. The moment I close my door I'm blanketed by wildflowers and spice. My favorite scent now.

I tap the top of the coffee lid before putting the car in reverse. "Mia said to give you a kiss for her, but since I'm not allowed to flirt with you anymore I don't think I can follow through with that demand." I tease.

I catch the glare she sends my direction but also notice that hint of amusement resting on her pretty lips. "I never told you that you aren't *allowed* to flirt with me." I'm about to argue with her but she cuts me off as soon as I open my mouth. "What did Eddie say to you outside the car?"

I really don't want to talk about that. The fear of telling her about Eddie warning me to not hurt her and then ruining this road trip before it even starts makes me keep my mouth shut . I comb over my conversation outside the car to find the small truth I can tell her without showing everything.

"He just was doing the thing he does and making sure I'll take care of you while we are gone." That should pacify her curiosity.

"I don't believe you." She says instantly and then purses her lips, "that's fine, keep your secrets." I plan on it. If she knows he's making a big deal out of her talking to me about Chloe then she will stop. And that isn't an option. Giving her the space to speak about it is the only time she lets the rest of the world fade away and lets me just see her.

"How about I tell you another secret." Why the fuck did I offer that?

"Oh absolutely!" She shifts so she is facing me more now, her perfect legs more on display. She's wearing a smile that in every way lets me know that she isn't going to make this easy. "What's in your top secret little book?" She asks like she's had this question prepped and ready. My sketchbook. That's the only thing she could possibly be talking about.

You know what? "Fuck it." I keep my left hand steady on the wheel and reach into the back seat with my right. I know exactly where it is and

I already tore the most important sketch out, so it's safe for her to see it. Although she will probably freak out. I'm okay with it.

I hand the book over to her, but hold on a little tighter when her small hand wraps around the other end of it. "Are you sure you want to look at this?" I give her a chance to back out.

"Do you draw naked women or something?" She asks under a breathy chuckle she pulls the notebook closer to her.

"Or something." That causes her to pause. I watch her eyes dart back and forth between mine, thankful I am on a straight road for the moment. "Don't you want to find out?" Challenging Avery Jude is quickly becoming a favorite hobby.

She tugs just enough that I let go of the sketch pad. There is a small catch in my chest working its way up the back of my neck. It's taking every ounce of my willpower to keep my eyes on the road. My hands are restless, gripping and ungripping the steering wheel.

I know when she gets to the first of many sketches of her. I hear the catch in her breath. The car is void of any other sound but her fingers lightly brushing over the pages and the flip of the page to the next. The pages are full of mostly her at the gym. Some are just of her eyes or her tattoo.

"This is me and Mia?" I forgot about that one. I glance at the page she's fixated on. It's the girls outside that Mexican restaurant, drunk off margaritas, and newly found salsa fiends. I added color to that one. It was a moment that I was able to capture her just feeling free. The same feeling she is always talking about chasing. "Can I have it?" Her voice is quiet but so full of hope.

"Of course." She can have anything in that book.

"You're kind of obsessed with me aren't you?"

"You're kind of all I think about, Jude."

Note to self– don't make long car rides with Avery a habit. I clearly have no objections to letting every thought run out of my mouth.

"I don't think you're supposed to just say that outloud." She continues fingering through the pages.

"I don't think that you are supposed to be so calm about opening up a book to see it full of drawings of you."

"How am I supposed to feel?" Her voice softly lands in the space between us. She's not even remotely shocked to see what is in my book.

"I don't know. Maybe more concerned?"

"You are constantly telling me that I'm safe with you and I don't have to be concerned."

"Since when do you listen to me, Avery Jude?" She has no response to that.

"Thanks for sitting with me at the graveyard."She asks, still flipping through the book. I'm getting used to her abrupt subject changes. A part of me feels pride that she can't take her eyes off something I created. Each glance I take her way, her eyes are glued to the page in front of her.

"You're welcome."

And just like that, the space is filled with comfortable quiet. It's one of the things I love most about being in the same space with Avery. She makes it feel easy. When she is done going through the entire book and flipping back to a few that she seemed to like most, she grabs her phone to start a playlist. This girl loves her music.

"I will also accept no slander on any of my music choices. You asked to drive, so I get to choose music." I didn't just ask to be the driver. I demanded it. I can't be sitting this close to her and not want to touch her. But we seem to have taken several steps back in the physical department. She assured me she didn't regret what happened. But she also made it clear she isn't interested in dating me. So here I sit in between knowing what I want, and trying to figure out what she wants.

"That's actually not the rule for shotgun, but okay."

"I don't follow rules."

Sugar by Robin Schulz starts playing and I can't stop myself from turning it up. I grab the phone out of her hand and set it in the cubby under the dash so she can't change it. I love this song. I sing every word.

When it ends, she shoots forward and turns down the whole system. "There's no fucking way."

"What's the matter?"

"Your existence is actually unfair to the universe." I turn to face her and her head tilts, her mouth slightly open. Which causes me to stare at her lips a little harder than I intend to.

"Am I not allowed to sing in my own car?"

"You're not allowed to be good at it!" She throws her hands up and I can't help but laugh. "How are you good at so many things..." She complains, reaching over to turn the music back up.

"I'm good at a lot of things, Jude." I wink at her just to watch the pretty blush I love so much creep over her chest and cheeks.

Twenty-Six

"What did you just call me?"

AJ

I need to be sedated.

That is the only explanation for why my brain cannot seem to grasp the concept of forming a complete thought that doesn't end with watching the sweat drip down Rory's body.

Rory in the gym training daily is something that I am intimately educated in. Rory sitting quietly in the corner of the gym with his damn sketchpad is also something I am used to seeing. Rory being a menace any chance he gets while he thinks he's charming is something I'm annoyingly becoming fond of.

Rory locking in all his focus into his pre-fight mode is a different animal. Every inch of his skin gleams with sweat. Which might not have been this suffocating degree of hot if every inch of his skin isn't basically covered in tattoos. Each one shines bright even in the dull gym lights with only sparse sunrays across the gym. I don't even think any of them hold any kind of meaning to him. Rory is the type of guy that if he saw it, and loved it, he probably got it.

"AJ!" The sound of him yelling at me makes me reluctantly take my eyes away from the divet on his hip where some kind of wings are drawn.

"What did you just call me?" I crane my neck to look up at him from where I am sitting on the floor by the bag he's working. Pulling myself out of the daydream that is me sexualizing sweat I realize for the first time he called me back my nickname.

"Your name." He takes the towel in his hand to wipe the sweat off of him. Shame.

"You've literally never called me AJ." I pout as I try not to show how much him not using my full name throws me off.

He drops the towel from his face and gives me a devilish smirk. "Are you mad right now?" Pure amusement is written all over his face.

"No." Maybe a little. Anything but Avery Jude or Jude coming out of his mouth left a bad taste in my mouth.

"You absolutely are!" He drops to the floor and lays back on the mats. "You were zoned out and I couldn't get your attention. Promise to not call you that again, Jude." His voice drops lower when he calls me Jude and it does unwelcome things to my heart rate.

Clearing my throat and mind, I lay back beside him on the mats. It was nice for them to let us use the gym this evening. Even nicer to block it off on the schedule so we could get our workout in alone.

"You nervous for tomorrow?" I ask him but I make the mistake of turning my head to look at him. He's already facing me and I find myself assaulted with the prettiest shade of green in his eyes. He always looks at me like he's trying to hold on to something and I'm not sure what it is.

"Not at all." He lets the words fall from his lips so easily. Of course he isn't. Rory is the definition of confident. Everything he does is with the reassurance that even if it fails, it will be okay. He is so unbothered. He just accepts whatever the universe gives him.

"My prediction is that you make him tap in the third round. He has good stamina and he will use the first round to just gauge. Second round he will go hard but he won't give you the full opening. Third round he will decide to try something but you're way too fast and grounded. There's no way he gains any real ground. He also only has a record of three wins and two losses. Which isn't incredibly terrible, but yours is better." The way his lips spread in the widest and cheekiest smile makes me stop talking. "What?"

"Listening to you talk about my fight is hot as fuck."

I lift my leg to kick him but he is faster. He gets his leg under mine and pivots his hips throwing me over him. I am flat on my back in less than a second. I hate jiu jitsu. Eli is the biggest trainer in our gym for it and he is always trying to get me to roll more with him. He's even pitched for me to teach a women's only class many times. But it's not my thing. I enjoy hitting things more.

I'm able to catch Rory off balance long enough for me to reverse our positions and to put me back in guard. Now he is laying on his back, staring back up at where I am straddling his hips. His hands rest on my thighs and I feel his thumb graze over my tattoo softly.

"Thought you didn't train jiu jitsu?" He could easily overpower me but I know he won't.

"I know enough." I shrug.

My hands rest on his chest and I feel his heartbeat under my palm. My braid falls over my shoulder, dangling in between the small distance that separates us. I watch him wet his lips but he makes no effort to move. His eyes dart between my own.

"Are you going to kiss me, Avery Jude?" I am weak. I want to kiss him. I want to get lost in the way his hands feel on my skin. But I know what his intentions are. He wants to date me. And I don't know what I want, but I know I do not want a relationship. I don't even know how to function in a relationship. I'm far too dysfunctional for that kind of emotional commitment.

My chest rises with the breath I take and I can tell by the way his smile drops slightly he knows I am not going to kiss him. He recovers quickly though.

I pat his chest and swing my leg over, standing up. "We should probably get to the hotel actually."

I won't lie to him. He knows I want him. And I know he wants me. But I also don't want him to be my learning curve for how to function in something new. I like my life. I know where I stand with everyone. I am able to predict all of their reactions to everything, for the most part. I don't have to question their intentions. The guys have had a few short term relationships. But they never panned out. I just know that I watched Chloe try to fix herself with dating Scott. She thought it would heal her and she could forget everything she went through. But she suffocated trying to be everything she couldn't. Trauma doesn't have an expiration date. You don't just wake up one day and everything is sewed up and scarred over. Sometimes you bleed with no wound.

Rory doesn't deserve that.

Twenty-Seven

"The British ones are always so much funnier!"

Thankfully Eddie got us separate rooms. I should get a medal for having her on top of me and not pulling her down so I could kiss her. But she needs to have control right now. She needs to realize that I can handle whatever is going on in her head. I can handle the roughness of her scars. I can hold the weight that seems to always be drowning her. But I can also see the storm that is always raging in her eyes becoming quieter. And whatever is making that happen, it's my new mission to keep that in her life.

I hear her on the other side of the wall. My phone tells me that it is past two in the morning. I should be sleeping. The fight isn't a professionally sanctioned one. I don't have to weigh in or go through a process beforehand. I just have to show up to the gym. I'm sure there will be local supporters and fans to show up. Most of these types of fights aren't advertised but word of mouth still made sure that people would show up. People love to see other people get violent.

The guy is ready though. He has been posting all of his training views extra hard the past two weeks. Mia wanted to do a whole highlight reel for me and it was a fight at least three times a week to keep her and her equipment away from me. She is good at her job though. We have someone come in every day asking about membership and training programs just because of the advertisement that Mia is putting out there.

I spent the past two hours trying to stay quiet so I wouldn't bother her if she finally found the quiet to fall asleep. But all I really did was fight every moment to knock on the door that joins our room. I'm pretty sure that would be overstepping though, in some way. Every few minutes like clock work she moves from the bed to the bathroom. I hear the bed squeak and then the water run. The boys weren't lying when they told me that this girl never slept.

It's time for her to come back to the bed, but instead of the noise of the frame moving, I hear a scream and then laughter. Followed by a very loud thump and what I'm afraid was her possibly falling out of the bed. I'm up and at the door in less than two steps. I don't care that I'm aggressively knocking. That sound of her falling was enough to make the hair on the back of my neck stand up. I have to check on her. "Open the door, Avery Jude." I called out.

I can hear faint whisper-yelling on the other end of the door. She's alive at least.

"Jude." I call, knocking again.

The door creaks open to reveal her in another barely there shirt and pantless. *Fuck.*

I grip the doorframe and groan, "what do you have against pants?" She's holding her phone out from her face and still recovering from her laughing fit. I scan her body for any obvious fresh wounds but all that is there are her faint scars and my favorite pair of legs.

She keeps giggling. "I love living a no pants life. You already know this."

Keep your eyes on her face.

"I heard you fall and just wanted to make sure you were okay." I clear my throat and run my hand through my hair, finally focusing back on her face.

"Mia was telling me about her date and his obsession with cookies and cream, sex edition." She scrunches up her nose with even more laughter.

"I don't even want to know what that is..."

"He dipped oreos in milk and smeared it.. DOWN THERE RORY!" Mia's terrorized voice comes from the phone. What the actual fuck. She can't be serious. I actually don't want to know if she is serious.

"Hi, Mia." I nod to where AJ moved the screen to face me.

"Shirtless is such a good look for you, my guy." She nods approvingly before immediately going back into her outrageous recap. "He said he was *making his own cream...*" Mia starts gagging and that sends Avery into an even bigger fit. She's so tired she is delirious. "I will never look at oreos the same. He ruined oreos for me. That should be a crime!" She keeps rambling and I have to agree. No one should have oreos ruined for them.

I grab the phone from her hand gently and stare down at Mia on the screen. "Goodnight, crazy girl. I'm going to get our girl to bed, okay?"

Mia salutes, blowing kisses at Avery before hanging up. Avery's now wiping tears away from her eyes from all the laughing she's done.

"Want to come hang for a bit?" I invite her to come inside.

"Do I have to put pants on?"

"Not if you promise to keep your hands to yourself, Jude." I walk backwards with my hands up knowing she will follow me.

"No, seriously, why are you still awake?" Avery closes the door behind her and immediately crawls into the side of the bed that isn't messed up. "Are you nervous about tomorrow? We talked about this. You'll be fine." She reassures me kindly.

"That's not why I'm still up." I nod to where she is playing on her phone. "What are you still doing up?"

"Sometimes I don't fall asleep until early morning. Sometimes I take a long nap and then wake up in the middle of the night." She tosses her phone on the bed away from her. Her stormy eyes seek me out and I know I can't get in that bed with her just yet. She wants to hold back from what we can be and I know she has very valid reasons for doing so.

But that doesn't make this long game with her easy. I'm always at her mercy even if she isn't making me be.

"What do you normally do to try and sleep?" I ask her. A sort of exasperated sound escapes her lips. I watch her fall back onto the mountain of pillows. I stacked all the extra pillows on the side. Who needs more than one pillow?

"Nothing helps. I just either fall asleep or I don't. I usually end up surviving off day naps in the office. But don't tell Eddie or he will end up putting a whole ass bed in there." She pats the side of the bed that I clearly vacated to check on her and gives me a sleepy smile. "I promise I won't bite you." She wiggles her fingers up at me and her face scrunches up adorably. "Hands and teeth to myself." *Was I allowed to find her this cute when she was clearly about to pass out from exhaustion?*

"Are you going to judge me for watching British baking shows?" I turn the tv back on from where I had turned it off earlier. My mom and I watched these for hours on days that she just wanted to sit and give her brain a rest. Something about watching strangers bake gives you serotonin.

"The British ones are always so much funnier!" She wiggles around until she gets more comfortable with her body under the cover and one leg wrapped around the outside. Her body is slightly turned toward me and the cover is up enough around her leg that I can see her tattoo and how the tail of the viper rests just above her hip. My hand twitches with the absolute need to trace that tattoo.

"Hey Jude?" I keep my voice soft and low because I desperately do not want her to move.

"Hm?" She doesn't take her eyes off the screen to respond to me. She just hugs one of the extra pillows a little bit tighter.

"Do you trust me?" I already know she does. But I really want her to be able to show that without thinking that I would use it. I know that is important to her.

I hold my breath, watching her eyes go back and forth from mine. She's trying to make a decision. Just when I can't hold my breath any longer, she nods her head so slightly that I almost miss it.

"Lift your head." I place my hand under her cheek that is resting on the pillow and shift it to where it is now in my lap. "Come over here." I have my hand already resting gently on her neck, so I start to massage from the base of her head following her spine and then back up into her scalp.

A small whimper ghosts over her lips. I feel her body get heavy as she starts to fully relax. She tilts her head to give me better access and her eyes flutter closed. My finger tips brush over the hollow of her neck. Goosebumps blanket her arms but she still doesn't open her eyes.

It takes all of ten minutes before I feel her breathing even out and she's asleep. And I don't move a muscle the rest of the night out of fear of waking her up.

Avery's been asleep the whole morning. I got roughly five hours of sleep before I was up and ordering coffee to be delivered to us. I don't have the heart to wake her though. Sometime in the middle of the night we positioned ourselves to more of a cuddling position. Her legs draped over mine and her head on my chest. I watched the sunlight bathe her for over an hour before I managed to slip out from under her. I took extra care to cover her up a little more fully and put a pillow within reach for her to grab like she did when she first got into my bed last night.

I have to get my breakfast in before we go to the gym to meet the guy I'm fighting tonight and get a small workout in. Thankfully Eddie is really good friends with the guy that owns this gym and we don't have to find a different place to workout. Even though the fight is only scheduled to bar my progress, I still have to follow my normal routine before every fight. Not that I'm crazy superstitious but why mess with something that works.

I know she will freak out when she wakes up. Or maybe she'll feel relaxed since she got almost a full eight hours of sleep in. She will for sure want to go for a run. So I grab her running shoes and just her whole bag. Then I grab her bag from the bathroom bringing everything from her room to my room.

A notification comes through on my phone, letting me know that the coffee and breakfast I ordered is outside the door. When I bring it over to the side table, she still isn't awake. She isn't even stirring. I brush her hair back from her face and gently shake her shoulder. The tiny noise leaving her body almost makes me laugh, but I'm able to contain it.

"Wake up, pretty girl. I brought you coffee and bagel bites." One eye peeks open and the other quickly follows as she sits up.

The cover falls to waist level. The bottom part of her tattoo is visible. She looks so sexy right. The sight of Avery Jude in my bed, with messy hair and sleep drunk eyes, is my new favorite thing.

"Why are you looking at me like that?" She's trying to seem annoyed but the way her eyes light up with the coffee in her hand is giving her away.

"I like having you in my mornings, Jude." I say simply.

"Did you bring all of my stuff into your room?" She looks around to where some of her things are around the room

"Is that weird?" I ask, sheepishly realizing that it probably is.

"Well, you're kind of weird. I guess that makes it normal." She shrugs, standing up not letting me forget she is completely pantless.

"Figured we could go for a run. I know it isn't as early as you are used to. I couldn't make myself wake you up since you were sleeping." I warily watch her reaction. Waiting for her to freak out that she slept with me in the bed since she has been so against anything like that happening. I mean nothing sexual happened at all. So she shouldn't freak out. I just don't want us to take a step backward.

"Thanks for that by the way." She motions to the mess of the bed and all the damn pillows that are now somehow all over the bed. "I've never had anyone put me to sleep like that before."

"I can put you to sleep in other ways too. All you have to do is ask." I shoot off with a wink before even thinking.

"I'll remember that." She sends a grin my way as she passes by with her bags and her coffee in her arms. She leaves me there with my mouth slightly open and trying to not make a big deal out of the fact that she made note that she would remember all she had to do was ask for sex with me and she could have it.

God, I hope she asks for it.

Twenty-Eight

"Give them hell today."

AJ

Mia

> **Did you fuck Rory?**

Mia

> **There is a right answer and a wrong answer.
> Don't disappoint me.**

AJ

> We slept together.

Mia

> **MY GIRL.**

AJ

> No. Like I slept and he slept. Clothes on.

I look down at my phone and watch it vibrate from her trying to facetime me. Twice.

AJ

> Stop calling me.

Mia

> **Then answer.**

AJ

I'm still in his room. I'm not answering.

Mia

I have so many questions.

AJ

He literally put me to sleep. Like he massaged my neck and back and my head. And I just blacked out.

Mia

Are you going to fuck him now? How could you not? Be weak. It's okay.

AJ

His hands, Mia. I fear I'm now a slut for his hands.

Mia

** changing your name to hand slut in my phone now

AJ

I actually can't stand you.

Mia

Then maybe go lay down. On your back. Under Rory.

AJ

Go eat some oreos.

Mia

Fuck you.

I choose to ignore her after that and get ready. I have the opportunity to corner Rory for the first time today and in a semi-professional way. I can feel my body vibrating with excitement.

I unzip my bag of clothes and find a blue post-it note resting on top.

Give them hell today

Twenty-Nine

"Want me to end it this round, coach?"

Aj

Walking into a new gym is both exhilarating and misplacing at the same time. The air isn't the same. The mats are a different thickness. The bags are hanging on the wrong side of the gym. And the sun is barely coming through the glass from where they haven't been cleaned in forever. It's not West Haven.

Rory follows my lead as we walk across the gym to where there is a group of guys standing. I recognize the guy that Rory is set to fight tonight instantly. And I assume the guys shouldering him are his coaches. I step front and center before their group, putting on my best professional smile.

"You bring your girlfriend, Davis?" Rory's opponent, Theo Grayson, has the voice you would imagine to come out of his pretentious face. His eyes are a little too close together and his nose crooked, probably because he is nearly incapable of keeping his hands up during fights.

"She's actually…"

"You're just going to assume I'm here because I'm his girlfriend?" I take a pointed look around their gym. It's nearly ten in the morning. We would have already had one all women class and be starting another by this time of day. Eddie and I sat down one day and I asked for the gym to be more intentional about making it a safe and strong place for women. And he put an ad out the next day for classes.

Looking around this gym, there isn't a woman in sight. I bet there is one in the office though, men never want to do paperwork.

I take another step closer to where Theo is standing. I make sure I am wearing my fakest sweet smile before I speak. "He would actually be so lucky if I was his girlfriend. Just to clarify, I'm not."

"She's right though. I would be lucky." My lips twitch as I feel Rory step closer to my back.

"Eddie said he was sending AJ as Davis's coach. So we just expected him to come this morning too. Theo didn't mean anything by what he said." One of the other guys cleared his throat in apology.

"Oh, how thoughtless of me." I let my voice get more animated than normal. "Hi." I stick my hand out to the older guy that had just spoken. "Avery Jude." I introduce myself formally.

"She prefers AJ though." Rory steps beside me now, shoulders fully squared as he stares down Theo. "And she's the best striking trainer I've ever had. So, if you want her to give you some pointers after the fight I'm sure she would love to help you." He throws a wicked grin Theo's way.

Theo snarls. "Not to be disrespectful. But too many women like to think they know what it takes to fight. But men are just stronger and can take a harder hit." He isn't technically wrong but that doesn't stop my body from vibrating with the impulse to punch him. Dick.

I can't help the laugh that escapes my throat. "I wouldn't know much about taking hits. I learned really early to keep my fucking hands up. I would suggest you practice that before the fight tonight. I'd hate for this to be a pointless trip." I turn my back entirely to him and face the other men. "Can we get our light workout in, or do we need to continue standing here making a big deal that I don't have a dick?" Their faces fall in embarrassment.

One of them steps around Theo giving me apologetic eyes. "Theo doesn't know how to shut his mouth. Of course, get your workout in. If you need anything at all I'll be in the office and you can just come and get me." He nods to where I assume the office is and holds his hand out for me to shake. "Tim. The only information we got on you was Eddie saying that AJ was the best he ever trained. I apologize for my son's behavior." He shakes my hand respectively and then glares at Theo. "Move your ass." He barks at him.

Theo hangs his head like a scolded dog and sulks across the gym. He really is a decent fighter though and I anticipate the fight tonight to be a good one. I've been stalking every video he has uploaded online the past few weeks of his training and his footwork is consistent. His ground work is solid but not aggressive. His hands are always dropping though and that is such an easy weakness for Rory to take advantage of.

Rory wraps his hands while I stretch. He keeps checking on me out of the corner of his eye and I have a feeling he is extra ready for this fight tonight. I could feel his annoyance roll off of his body as he stood behind me. But I didn't miss the way he let me handle the entire situation. I am used to guys thinking I am less capable in this industry because of my anatomy but it doesn't deter me. Coaching and training has quickly become one of my favorite things.

"Want to give them a show?" Rory is now standing in front of me.

I have to lift my head to see him. "They already know how good you are. This fight isn't for you. They want to humble Theo." That was obvious the moment I met him. It's not out of the realm for coaches to set up smokers to pivot a fighters mindset and remind them that they can always be training harder and learning more.

"I wasn't talking about me showing off, Jude." His voice is a low hum laced with devilish intention. He is holding the gray wraps that he had given me as an invitation.

I place my wrist in his hand for him to start wrapping. "Fuck yeah."

I know we are supposed to be here to be professional. But fuck it. It is always fun to shatter male egos.

"Does it ever get old?"

"What?"

"People assuming you're a guy because you go by your initials?" He did the same thing when he first entered Eddie's gym. The difference was that he didn't make me feel less than him the second he opened his mouth just because I'm a girl.

"I genuinely love it. Being underestimated gives you the power to stand on a level that they can't even see." He velcroes the last part of my second wrap. "What are you thinking?"

"Circuit combos? Bag and then mitts. I'll call it out as you go." He walks over to pick up mitts from the corner without asking permission to use any extra equipment.

With every contact made with the bag I feel my body get lost to the sound. Everything else fades out and Rory's voice is the only thing breaking through. I love this. This makes me remember what breathing truly feels like. The sting to my skin from the slap of skin to material of the bag failed to register.

Combo after combo for a twenty minute circuit without a break would put most people down. Most people don't have the deafening inner battle that I do. All the weight of every person who broke me or left me to be broken is what drives me to disconnect and just let my body move. Every ounce of anger held and not healed. Every word that scratched the wound of abuse. Every self doubt and failure to see the light. It disappears in moments like this.

The blood rushes to my ears and the smoldering in my lungs is what alerted me that I need to take a break. I bring my leg back down for a roundhouse kick and am met with Rory's face gleaming with pride.

"Atta girl." His voice ghosts over me. The proximity does nothing to help my heart rate slow down. The mix of him being proud of me and giving me the platform to show I am capable and strong is doing things to me. It makes my heart feel like it is trying to claw its way through my throat.

We stand here, staring at each other. His breathing is calm and steady, emanating the very essence of who he is. While I stand a breath away from him and he is unaware of the chokehold his stare alone has me in at the moment. This moment feels like it will be cemented in my memories.

"I take it back. You're a bad ass Avery Jude."

"Don't call her that." Rory breaks our stare in exchange for delivering a death glare at where Theo is standing and holding a bottle of water out towards me. "It's AJ." Rory grabs the bottle of water from Theo's waiting hand and opens it before handing it off to me.

Theo shakes off the ice in Rory's voice and turns more fully towards me. "Would you be down for an apology lunch?" I feel Rory's eyes land on the side of my face instantly.

Theo is standing in front of me with a coy smile and a slightly puffed out chest. Like his fuckboy charisma would convince me to go on a date with him less than an hour after he insulted me.

"I have lunch plans actually." I hand him the water back. He is able to not let his smile drop too much. "You're cute but I don't tend to give my time to guys who intentionally make me want to punch them."

I see Rory's head drop from my peripheral and I just know he has a wicked grin spreading his lips.

I lead the way past Theo as Rory grabs our bags. I pass Tim on the way out and give him a small wave letting him know we would see him tonight. Rory is holding the door open for me.

"You think he's cute?" He asks me as I walk past him.

"You jealous, Rory?" I tease him.

"Would that be a bad thing?" His voice holds a tinge of vulnerability in it.

"I didn't agree to go on the lunch date."

"Thank fuck." Jealous Rory is fun.

The gym is packed from wall to wall. It's maybe only a fourth of the size of the back part of The Poolhouse. But the noise is just as vibrating. Theo looks far more locked in than he did this morning in the gym. Tim is his corner coach tonight.

There is such a difference between Theo and Rory though. Rory stands at six foot three while I would guess Theo is about two inches shorter. Rory's fully clothed in tattoos on both arms and has them scattered over his legs and probably his thighs. If he has thigh tattoos, I would have to sign my death certificate. I'm such a slut for a thigh tattoo. Theo has one tattoo on his ribcage, and it's his last name. Something about that makes me laugh. More than just their physical appearance separate them. Theo looks concentrated. Rory looks deadly. One of the things that makes me so comfortable in Rory's presence is his ability to not reject the seriousness of this sport. He doesn't just come in here hot headed and ready to fight. He is reverent in his way of preparing for even just his training. He sits in the silence of the day to day of training his body to endure the few minutes of intense exposure to violence. He understands the work and healing part of this sport. But it doesn't define him and he is teaching me the same thing.

Rory walks to his corner and I am on the outside of the ropes. I love when gyms have indoor rings.

"When he gets within striking distance his back foot flutters. I would bait him the first round and tire him out the second round and then use that foot flutter to break his base and take him to the ground." I insert his mouth piece into his open mouth as he nods in understanding of my instructions.

The bell rings and Rory walks to the center. They touch gloves and the first round begins. Rory does exactly as I suggested. He lets Theo make any first movement and creates an illusion of open space for Theo to attempt to move into. But he shuts it down quickly. Watching Rory is like watching an artist paint. He knows exactly the direction he wants to move and when to change course. Every movement is fluid.

By the end of the first round, Theo is visibly flustered that he didn't land anything on Rory. And Rory barely even needs water since he didn't worked up.

"That foot flutter is barely noticeable." He comments as I give him a smile. Eddie always says that I can catch the smallest weaknesses. "You're brilliant." He breathes out. I try to not allow that compliment to mean too much.

"Make him work this round." I instruct.

"Yes ma'am."

He swallows some water and gets ready for the next round. I watch them circle around each other for roughly ten seconds. Rory looks over at me from over Theo's shoulder and winks. It is only a second and nobody else probably caught it. But it is my job to stay glued on him.

Rory throws a nasty punch straight down the middle causing blood to immediately pour from Theo's nose. I did warn him to keep his hands up tonight. I could have sworn that Rory looked a little too happy to have drawn blood though.

Rory lands two more solid hits. One cracking Theo's eyebrow only slightly. The bell rings for the break before the third round. Theo has been holding his own decently well but it's clear that if Rory wanted to end it early, he could.

I put the stool in the corner and swing through the ropes to give Rory some water. He doesn't have a mark on him but he doesn't open his mouth for some water.

"Want me to end it this round, coach?" Him calling me coach makes my breath stutter. He's asking in a serious manner though not to flirt. A fighter to his coach. And the way he's showing so much respect for me right now makes him even more attractive.

"Yeah. Take it to the ground and make him tap out." He nods again and stands to get ready for the third round.

I watch Rory make super quick work with this round. He opens up his fighting stance to allow Theo to move in and as soon as he is close enough and that back foot double tapped, Rory takes him to the ground and is able to get the rear naked choke in less than ten seconds. Another five seconds and Theo taps.

It was beautiful.

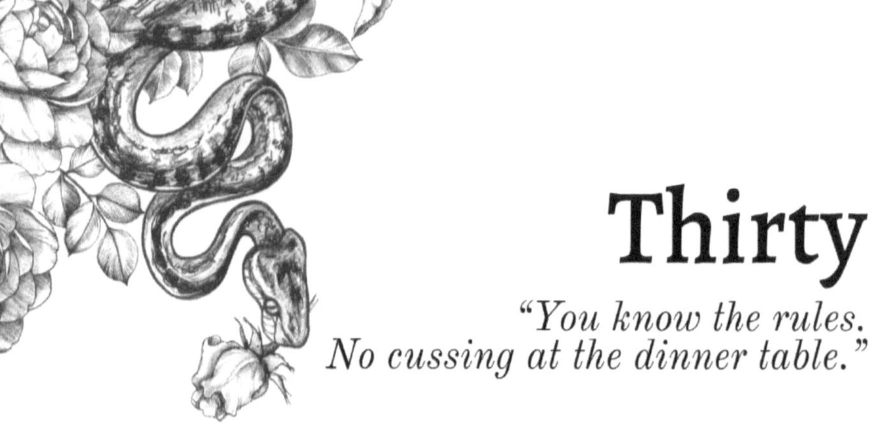

Thirty

"You know the rules.
No cussing at the dinner table."

AJ

West Haven Delinquents

Mia

> Not updating us is just rude. Did you kick his ass? Is there a video? I would like a video, please!

Oliver

> If they wanted to talk to us, they would talk to us. Not everyone has to listen to you.

Mia

> Ol doesn't like to be submissive. I just put that in my notes under the category of things I don't give a fuck about.

AJ

> Of course he won.

Rory

> Henry has a video that he is sending over to Eddie.

Maxwell

> Hell yeah! Go team!

Eli

> Did AJ get to do her thing?

Maxwell

> PLEASE tell me that they assumed she was a guy. They always assume she is a guy. It's my favorite thing.

AJ

> You know they did. Then Theo asked me out after he realized I could throw a better left hook than him.

Eli

> Dumbass.

Maxwell

> Rory, my guy, did you punch Theo?

Rory

> We're going to bed now.

Mia

> Wait! Is Theo cute??

I spent the next night in Rory's bed again. I slept with pants on this time. He downloaded Scrabble on his phone and we played against each other before he put me to sleep again. It's not like I didn't think cuddling would have been a good fix to my insomnia problem. In fact, I've tried it with all three brothers. Thinking that just having a warm body sleeping near me would help initiate a sleep response on my own. It didn't work. Their breathing was always too loud, or the blanket made my skin itch.

But sleeping next to Rory is peaceful. My breathing syncs up with his without me even trying and his hands moving over my neck and back is better than any sleeping pill I've tried. It's like my brain just knows it is safe to go quiet.

It's a problem.

I didn't have any reservations about knocking on his door the second night. I was desperate to sleep again. And he didn't make it a big deal or anything. Rory makes me feel like I've always belonged in the space around him.

And now I'm sitting at Eddie's dinner table with my boys around me, my family. And my eyes keep glancing at the door and my phone. Anticipating Rory randomly showing up or texting. We traveled back yesterday and he was invited to dinner but he said he needed to go and take care of something for his mom. That left me sitting here missing his energy in the room.

I had given a full run down about what went down at Tim's gym. How Theo was an absolute asshole but they missed their favorite thing of someone assuming I was a guy. Whines collectively echoed around the table. Except from Eddie. He wore a soft and proud smile as he looked at me.

Eddie clears his throat as the triplets all settle down. "Tim said that you really did an incredible job in the corner. Talked Rory through it all." I watch as he rubs his chin and smirks. "He also said that you really toyed with his son before sending your boy in to finish it."

"He's not my boy." I correct him. "And Rory made him tap. He really didn't make it an aggressive fight at all. Just really technical rounds. I think he gave Theo a good humbling experience."

"He's absolutely your boy." Maxwell calls from the other end of the table. I look over to see Eli and Oliver hiding their faces from me.

"What? No comment? You all share the same half of a brain." Eli grabs his chest pretending to be offended.

"You're getting a little red on your chest there, A." Oliver points to my chest.

I throw a potato at him and in true guy fashion, he picks it up off the table and eats it.

"Shut the fuck up, Ol." I know he knows something happened between me and Rory. I know he knew the moment he came to pick me up for dinner and he made a comment about how I looked like I had finally gotten some sleep. I probably shouldn't have avoided talking about it. That is my giveaway. And he has been giving me that stupid fucking look all night long. The look that let me know that he is going to give me so much shit when we are alone again.

"Don't be mean." Oliver's voice holds no seriousness.

"You know the rules. No cussing at the dinner table." Eddie breaks through and we all grow quiet. That has always been the rule. Their mom apparently told Eddie before the boys were born that she wanted the dinner table to be the best part of the house and filled with only goodness. And now anytime someone breaks that rule, they get dish duty from Eddie and have to buy a round of drinks for the rest.

"Wait. What are we missing?" Maxwell, for all his goofiness, and chaotic energy, never misses when something is being hidden from him. Very much the youngest of the triplets shining through with not wanting to be left out.

"Nothing."

"Avery got a full night's rest."

"Don't ask."

Oliver, Eli, and myself all speak at the same time. And I shoot Oliver a glare for outing me at the dinner table with Eddie. Who has been suspiciously quiet. And that thought made me turn to face him.

"No comment, Eddie?"

"Do you want me to comment, Avery?"

"Nothing happened. I kept it professional." I feel the need to defend myself.

"Did you or did you not sleep with him?" Max picks up his fork and points it at me.

"Can we not talk about this right now?" I let my eyebrow lift as I stare back at him, silently trying to communicate that I really do not want to have this conversation in front of Eddie.

"That wasn't an answer." Eli pulls my attention to where he is sitting. I am going to get whiplash from each brother taking turns cornering me.

"I hate you all." I grumble into another bite of food.

"You love us." Oliver says smiling. Why is he smiling?

"What's wrong with your face?" He just shrugs.

They all do the creepy triplet thing they do and fix their faces in the same orientation and just stare me down. I meet each set of blue eyes and hold their gazes, trying to make them back down. Not a single one of them does though.

"You are all the worst!" I point to each one of them. I clasp my hands together in my lap and sigh dramatically, for their benefit. "I'm going to say this. We aren't going to make a big deal about it. And we aren't going to have a conversation about it. And then we are going to finish eating because I'm starving."

They all nod in agreement, salute, and motion for me to continue with their right hand waving in my direction.

Fucking triplets.

"He's not my boy." I give a pointed look to Maxwell daring him to say anything. "I did get a good night's rest. Two actually," I say tilting my head at Oliver. "And nothing happened. We just slept *beside* each other." My features soften when I look at Eli, because out of them all, he is the most like a real brother. I turn to face Eddie last. "I kept everything professional inside Tim's gym. And I will keep everything professional in your gym."

"*Our* gym, Avery." Eddie is always so quick to correct me by making sure I am forever a part of what he has built. "And I trust you to make the best decisions for yourself. Always." He stands up and walks to the fridge, bringing back a pie to place on the table.

A pie that looked very familiar. "What is that?"

"A pie." He starts to slice it up and hands me a piece.

"It's a chocolate pie, Eddie." I feel my words get weaker as I speak them but Eddie only smiles reassuringly at me.

"He dropped it off this morning."

Rory baked me a pie. My favorite pie. A chocolate pie that is the perfect consistency and tastes like hot chocolate. I'm fucked.

It's been one week since Rory's fight last Friday. One week of him being the biggest gentleman throughout every day. He always makes sure I have water. He offers to carry my equipment for me when we work out. He always brings me a protein bar in the morning. He doesn't bring up what happened in the hotel room. He is just really kind and always there. I asked him not to flirt with me, and he listened.

Since when do guys listen?

"You look lost." Mia calls out from behind the door in her closet. I'm at her apartment. She had to cancel our Monday margaritas and I haven't seen much of her this week. She still made sure all of her work was done for the gym, but her presence was scarce and missed. Even the guys were asking me where she has been.

"He hasn't even tried to flirt with me, Mia." I sit on the edge of her bed as she digs through her closet. She is literally throwing things around in every direction. Mia's room is a disaster zone. Mainly just like a clothes volcano that exploded.

"You told him not to." Her voice carries from somewhere deep in her closet. Mia has a really nice apartment. Much nicer than mine. Nicer than what I would assume she can afford, even with what we pay her at the gym. Which is a decent salary. And she has all these random jobs she keeps.

"So?"

"So he is obviously a guy that appreciates communication and respects boundaries." Her head tops with her wild hair popped out from behind a pile of clothes she is holding. "And we're complaining about that?"

"Not complaining. It's just weird. We at least always have this back and forth. And this week, nothing." She drops the pile of clothes on top of my stomach and flutters back into her closet.

"I think he's just waiting for you to make the decision. He laid his cards out, told you he wanted you. Told you he wanted to take you on a date. You shot him down. He's here to train and he respects you as his coach and trainer." I don't like this Mia. This Mia speaks too much logic and that's when I pick up on her tone. She seems keyed up and not in a fun way like normal.

"Are you okay?" I ask her gently.

"I'm fine. I just can't find this one top." She sighs in frustration. She doesn't come out from her closet and I can tell she doesn't want me to press. When Mia gets stressed, she over compensates by doing a million things to make her feel like she has control. I recognize and respect that. We all handle it differently.

"Where are we going again?" She texted me this morning to let me know she wouldn't be at the gym, and that she wanted to go out tonight but never said where.

"You can't say no." Her voice has a tilt to it that lets me know I won't like what she is about to say. "The Poolhouse. And before you say no, even though I literally just told you that you couldn't say no, all of the boys will be there."

That is enough to make me sit up straight again. "All of them?"

She comes out from behind the door frame holding a leather jacket that I am instantly in love with and what looks like a black laced bra.

"All of them. And this is what you are wearing."

"No I'm not. That will show my scars." I don't mind Mia seeing them. She never asks about them, not that I wouldn't tell her if she did. And the triplets obviously already know that I got them from my abusive foster home. And Rory knows that they are a part of my past. He just also doesn't ask questions. But everyone else? They will all smile at my face and then let their expression drop and contort from pity to confusion to sometimes disgust. I hate it.

"That's what the jacket is for! It's oversized, so it will cover it. The lighting is so dark, no one will see them. I promise. Oh!" She fumbles through the pile still resting on my lap and pulls out a cute black skirt to go along with the outfit. "And this! You will look hot as hell and super fuckable." She winks at me, clearly proud of herself for putting this outfit together.

"I don't want to look fuckable." Although, I kind of do. It is such a freeing thing to feel confident in your own skin.

"You want Rory to fuck you. Don't even argue with me. I would too. That man is tall and I would lick every inch of him. But that would be weird because he is really only into you. And he's one of the few friends

I have. So let's pretend I didn't say that." She is back to moving around chaotically throughout her room. I assume finding herself an outfit now.

I did want Rory to fuck me. I haven't been able to sleep since last friday when he was next to me. And I also can't stop thinking about how hot he was the whole time I was in his space for those two days. And now he is playing the soft guy but I miss the guy that pushes me. And maybe Mia is right and he is leaving it up to me. That is on brand for him.

"Would it be so bad to want him to fuck me?" My words are soft but I know she heard them even through her disordered thoughts running wild throughout the room.

She pauses, looking at me with her big sweet eyes and grabs both of my cheeks. "You deserve the things that you want. If you want Rory, he is waiting and ready. I promise you." She kisses my cheek and points to the waiting outfit in my lap. "And if you wear that, it will raise his heart rate and make him follow you around like a lost dog. And I personally love seeing a man walked like a dog. So please, for me, make this happen."

It could just be sex. Probably really incredible, mind blowing sex. My whole body is vibrating just anticipating it.

"Okay." I surrender.

Mia screams so high pitched that I feel it travel down my spine. She spends the next two hours dressing me up, fixing my hair, and dancing in front of the mirror. I am convinced that Mia could make anyone feel free in their own skin. I don't know what I did for the universe to bring her to me, but I will make sure to thank it somehow. And when she is finished, she tells me that even she would fuck me.

Thirty-One

"Can I steal your girl?"

Did I have plans on coming to The Poolhouse tonight? No. Because this week has been super intense with training. Eddie has pushed my cardio every day. I haven't even had the chance to really talk to Avery. Which has put me in kind of a bad mood this week. The two days we spent together were enticing to say the very least.

Being around Avery Jude feels like finally being able to breathe.

I came back to this town to feel something when I stepped into the ring again. Avery makes me feel everything. And I don't know how much longer I'm going to be able to easily stay away from her. I've been utilizing all of my strength to keep the power in her hands. Whatever she asks for though, I easily hand it over to her. Even if she doesn't ask for it. If she is there, I'm going to be there. It's that simple.

And that is how I ended up sitting here at the bar at The Poolhouse with the triplets. All it took was one of them telling me that Mia is making Avery come with her tonight for me to be here. Eli and Maxwell definitely know that something happened between us last weekend. They keep looking at me and then raising their eyebrows in sync and then laughing at whatever thoughts they're communicating telepathically.

Meanwhile, I just keep my eyes on the open doorway that leads into the room. I have been sitting here long enough to be tired of people trying to talk to me. I can go out in the general public and not be recognized hardly ever. The first time I had come here with Avery, she moved through the crowd so fast and so much attention was on her that I slipped through without being recognized at all really. This time is different. In this space, where fighting is the main source of entertainment and the common ground between all of the people, staying under the radar is nearly impossible.

Girls have already been coming up to me and offering to buy me drinks. Hell, guys are too.

My focus stays on the open doorway. Every girl that walks through is wrong though. The hair isn't dark enough or it's too dark. They are too tall or too short. They don't have storms in their eyes. Their laughter isn't the kind to wake up a room. Not that Avery laughs often. When she does though, it steals all my attention.

"She will be here." Oliver sits down next to me, nursing a glass of bourbon. Eli and Maxwell are still on my other side but they are both currently taking bets on which girl is going to come up next to ask if I'm really *the* Rory Davis. They probably haven't even watched one of my fights before. Odds are that they heard some of the other girls talk about me tonight and they want to take their shot. I don't really date much anyway. I would take a girl home occasionally if I felt like there was mutual respect for what it would end up being. But dating isn't something in my line of focus.

Training takes all my focus and streamlines my sight on my end goals. I've given up a lot to make them a reality. I've sacrificed a lot. Avery isn't a distraction though. She is one of the forces driving me forward now. She has taken every fiber of this sport that I love and awakened it to a new level. She makes me want to walk into the gym every day with her. And since I now know what it feels like to fall asleep to the sound of her breathing next to me, I want to leave the gym and spend my afternoons with her. I told her that I liked having her in my mornings. I really just love having her near me all together. In every way she allows it.

I move to face Oliver better. "Why are you over here sitting next to me? Aren't you normally in the corner sulking in your loner boy aura?" He tips the glass back before flexing his hand around it.

"I figured you didn't want to be found talking to some random fan batting her eyelashes at you when AJ shows up." He makes a good point and I instantly feel like a jerk. He's really backed off his protective mode with me when it comes to her.

"Thanks man." I let my chest rise and fall, steadying my breath. I pick up the napkin laying down and start to fold and unfold it. "Do you think she is going to give me a real chance?" I can't manage to look up where Oliver is staring a hole into the side of my head. I know there is a good chance he won't even answer me. I wouldn't help me if I were him. Then again, he did come and sit over here to help ward off stray girls.

I keep my focus on the napkin. I feel Oliver move beside me, face forward, and place his empty glass down on the bar. He taps the rim. I glance up to see a thoughtful expression on his face. "I'll never speak for her." He rubs his jaw before making eye contact with me. "She has never given someone her time like she does for you. It took me months just to get her to come down to the gym and workout with me." Oliver takes a breath. "She just lives in this world where she thinks she has to stop herself from infecting others with the sharp edges of whatever is in her past." His voice takes a sharper tone. "If she does decide to give you a chance, you'll have to be patient with her. Don't let her give up believing she is worth it." His voice is a little shaky but his point is delivered clearly. *Don't break her more.*

"I'll take care of her." It's the best promise I can make to him. I know they are closer than she is to the other two.

He opens his mouth to say something more but I watch as his eyes catch over my shoulder. He drops his head back, swallowing hard. "Fuck me." I know instantly the girls are here.

I feel it in the way the air in the room changes. I turn and my eyes find her instantly, like they always do. And, "Fuck everyone in this room." I understand Oliver's reaction now. His eyes aren't on Avery though. They track the walking sunshine explosion next to her. Mia is in this dress that laces up on each side and makes it very clear that she is only in the dress and nothing underneath. She is here dressed to kill and Avery must have the same goal. I've been thinking about the first outfit she wore here for months.

This outfit is sexy and calm. Like her. She has on baggy jeans that she has clearly worn a hundred times, an oversized leather jacket that she allows one shoulder to peep out of, and the sexiest fucking black lace bra that I have ever seen. The two of them together look like the physical representation of yin and yang.

Mia drags Avery behind her by their linked hands straight to the center of the dance floor. Both girls start dancing together without a care in the world. And every guy turns to watch them. Avery holds a certain level of known respect in this building though and no one is approaching them.

"Usually she is here with you, my guy. What happened?" I feel the hair on the back of my neck stand up. The guy behind the bar is speaking to Oliver with a shitty grin resting on his face.

"That was just a moment in time, Ty. Wasn't a thing, hasn't been a thing, and won't be a thing." Oliver double taps his empty glass on the worn out wood. This bar top is probably recycled from some old run down bar. The guy, Ty, fills up Oliver's cup.

"Does that mean I can finally see if she will let me dance with her? Maybe be her new guy?" His voice is light and unserious. But I know there is a part of him that would jump if Oliver told him he was free to do so.

"If she wanted you to be the guy then she would have already asked you to be." I am thankful for Oliver's quick shut down.

I turn to find Oliver's focus shifted back to where Mia is locked with Avery, her hand draped over her shoulder. Thank fuck they are dancing with each other and not random guys. I know I have no ground to stand on to be jealous or want Avery to be untouched by anyone but me tonight but that doesn't stop my body from firing off of every nerve ending to try and make that the reality of this evening.

It's been two songs. Two songs of watching the girls grind on each other, throwing their heads back in laughter, and throwing glances our way. Oliver is stiff as a board beside me and I can't figure out if he wants to fuck Mia or kill her. That seems to be the consensus from anyone who spends time around them. It's not my business though.

Avery walking in here looking like my every daydream is enough to make me fold.

I am done waiting for her to come to the same conclusion I've been at for months. We want each other naked, that is for certain. I want her naked under me, over me, suffocating me. She even wore her hair down the way that I always compliment it. That couldn't be for nothing.

"Hey Tyler!" I shout down the bar top.

He turns towards me with raised eyebrows. "It's just Ty."

"I don't care." I point to the pen on top of a notebook behind him. "Give me that." I know I sound like an asshole but I don't care. I don't mind being an asshole to people I don't care about.

I took my time writing on the wrangled napkin from where I kept folding it earlier. It isn't one of the damn blue post-it notes that her and Eddie seem to be partial to but it would work.

Let me be the guy

I send Eli over with the napkin to where the girls are dancing. I watch as he places the napkin in her hand and kisses her cheek before doing the same to Mia. He leans into Mia's ear, asking her something before heading back our way.

"Mia wants a drink." He announces in Oliver's direction as he gets closer and then turns to me. "AJ told me to tell you that if you had something to say then you can use your words." Of course she did.

I hear Oliver order a cherry margarita before I walk away without giving them another word.

I make my way over to the girls. Mia's whole face lights up with mischief when she sees me approach from over Avery's shoulder. I wrap my hand in hers and spin her around out of Avery's hold before leaning in and speaking just loud enough for both girls to hear me. "Can I steal your girl?"

"I'm always willing to share!" She shouts over the music and her words drown in the laughter that leaves her tiny body. "I have a drink waiting for me anyways." Mia motions to the bar where Oliver has a glass filled with red liquid sitting next to him. She prances her way across to both.

I turn to see Avery already staring at me, standing still while the whole room moves around her. The scene is symbolic of the way I now feel when it's just me and her. Everything always blurs into nonexistent wings of reality when she is in sight.

"Hey Jude." My voice is low as I approach her. She doesn't take a step back though. She doesn't have that weariness in her eyes like she normally does. She looks settled.

"What is this?" She holds the napkin up in between her index and middle finger.

"A proposition. Obviously." Her lips spread into the prettiest smile I've ever seen.

"The guy? You want to be the guy? What does that mean?" The leather jacket is slouching down her bare shoulder and my lips itch to touch there.

I reach my hand to her bare waist and softly turn her around. This isn't a conversation that I want to have with everyone in ear shot, but it's also a conversation that I wasn't going to waste another minute waiting to have.. I pull her back to be flush against me. My hand now resting on her stomach. She instinctively starts to sway to the dirty and gritty rhythm of a song I don't recognize. She is ethereal.

I brush her hair to the side, letting my fingertips barely brush over the sensitive part of her neck. Her head lolls back towards my chest, giving me better access to lean down where my lips were on the shell of her ear.

"Let me be the guy, Avery Jude. Your guy. Whatever that looks like. You want a guy to run with in the mornings? I'll be there. You want a training partner? You got me. You want someone to sit with you and say nothing? I love the quiet. You want someone in your corner? I've already taken up residency there."

I feel her hum. I already am that guy. I've been that guy.

I can feel her thoughts running, and I feel her pulse race when I let my lips drop down to softly kiss the hollow of her neck. I can be patient while she uses her words too.

I trail my lips over to her bare shoulder. The softness of her skin here has been tempting me since I saw her enter tonight. I let the tip of my tongue take the quickest of tastes before kissing a whisper of how much I adore her.

"What if I want a guy to fuck me?"

My hand tenses around her waist and I instinctively pull her closer to me. I know she can feel the reaction I am having to her and I don't care. I'd let her feel every inch of me if she asked.

I take my time letting my lips make their way with tiny kisses and a soft bite to the space behind her ear before making her a promise. "I can be that guy."

Thirty-Two

"I promise to be good."

AJ

I can be that guy.

What. The. Fuck.

I hear him say it, but the way his hands feel on my body right now is drowning out the ability to respond to anything else other than his touch. He brings his lips back to my shoulder and the back of my thighs quiver. I'm somehow simultaneously moving with the music and being held in a vicegrip at the same time. It is in the exhale of my breath I know that I am done fighting him.

"Jude?" His voice is just a whisper at the base of my neck but it touches every inch of my body.

"Hm?" I am still unable to speak full words. His fingertips trace the edges of my scars as if he already knows where each of them is located.

His hands grip slightly tighter as he spins me around to face him. I take a moment to just take in his features. He has a fire in his eyes as he looks at me. I can tell his jaw is clenched with restraint as his hands are still tight around my bare skin at my waist. I lift one of my hands to the back of his neck for stability because he is making me feel weaker by the second. My other hand moves to his waist so my fingers can fit in the belt loop of his pants.

"It's just sex, Rory." I use all my strength to get those words out and I am afraid that they still sound weak.

"Okay." He is quick to answer me.

"I mean it." My words get a little stronger.

He brings his face more to my level which makes my arm relax around his neck. My fingers tangle in his hair causing him to close his eyes and when he starts to pull away to look at me again I grip tighter to his hair.

A whimper leaves him as he makes our bodies collide closer. "I promise to be good." His voice is strangled and it makes me squeeze my legs a little tighter. "I won't ask for more." His lips are touching mine, our breath mixes together, and I can feel his heartbeat in time with the music. "Please can we leave now?" He is kissing my lips with each word.

No woman is immune to a whimpering and begging man covered in tattoos. It does something to our brain chemistry. Gives us a sense of power that pulses through our blood.

I lean up and crush my lips with his. His tongue wastes no time finding my own. The whimper is replaced by a starving groan in his throat. My body is flush with his and I can feel how much I am affecting him, and it only makes me more ready to be alone with him.

"Let's go." The words are still leaving my lips when he grabs my hand and starts leading me through the crowd. His presence is enough to part the way through the bodies. He stops at the bar where Mia is placing her empty margarita glass on the counter behind where Oliver is sitting. She is standing between his legs and I recognize the look on her face. Mia is the queen of trouble in the most endearing way. We watch her hook her finger under the chain necklace Oliver wore and lean in and whisper something. I'm not close enough to make sense of what she says but Oliver is shaking his head. Mia shrugs her shoulders and turns, grabbing a guy that has been watching her entire interaction with Oliver. She is making her way to the dancing crowd again when Rory lightly grabs her wrist to capture her attention.

She swings her head my way and blows me a kiss. "Proud of you! Play dirty." She winks and lets the guy pull her into him as his hand goes through one of the gapes of her dress under her boob. I shoot a glance in

Oliver's direction and a pang hits my chest. His whole body is vibrating with an emotion I'm not familiar with seeing on him.

Rory breaks my line of vision and brings his hands up to cup my cheek. "I'm taking you home now." A smile breaks out across my face. It feels good to just give in to this. I trust Rory.

I open my apartment door, close, and lock it all with one hand. Rory hasn't let go of my other hand since we left The Poolhouse. It's like he is afraid if he lets go, I will change my mind. Small chance of that. I want this man desperately.

He lets go of my hand only to wrap both hands around my waist and lift me up. He spins me around for my back to be supported by my front door. He uses his finger to brush some stray pieces of hair out of my face from the quick movement.

"Before we do this. I appreciate communication. You want something, you can have it, just ask. You need me to stop? Tap out. And use your words. I love a screamer." Why is a guy giving me instructions for sex so hot?

He moves his arms to reposition himself. One arm is now under my ass to hold me steady while the other hand undoes the front clasp of this bra. His teeth latch onto one of my already hard nipples. He sucks hard, making it pebble even more. His mouth leaves that nipple and he makes his way to the other. My hands find dark strands of hair to hold him where he is. I feel his teeth graze before his tongue makes a soft and slow circle before he sucks again. I'm almost fully lost in the sensation when his mouth leaves me and his eyes meet mine.

"One more thing." He trails soft kisses across my jaw until he finds my ear. "Don't forget you promised to leave a mark." My brain short circuits as I recall when he asked if I would eat him alive and I told him I would definitely leave a mark.

"You.. you remember that?" I stutter.

"I remember everything when it comes to you, Avery Jude." He kisses me, giving me no room to speak again. His tongue chasing mine. His hand now spreads across the side of my neck, his thumb reaching over to tilt my head to the side so he can nibble his way down my neck. He sucks on the hollowed out spot above my collar bone, not hard enough to leave a mark but enough to make me want to feel his mouth and tongue everywhere.

I'm still fully dressed even though my bra is undone. And I'm desperate to have all of our layers of clothing gone. I pull on his hair a little as he is still kissing my neck and that same sound he made earlier makes a new appearance. Who knew that a professional fighter would like his hair pulled.

"Clothes off, please." He picks me up fully and I take that as an opportunity to shed my jacket and bra as he carries me down the hallway. "Last door on the left." I know he is making his way to my bedroom.

His lips and tongue find my tits again. Alternating between them as he walks me down the hallway. We make our way through my bedroom door and he finally lets me down. I watch him pull his shirt over easily with one hand, his eyes only leaving me for the half of second it takes for the fabric of the shirt to come over his face. He unbuttons his pants as I do the same. Our shoes come next as we both shimmy out of our clothes. He loses his pants and boxers in one move and I lose all the breath in my lungs when I see all of him. It felt impressive when he was pressed against me on the dance floor earlier. But it is so much more than the bulge I felt.

Rory walks around with the energy so I don't know why I'm even remotely surprised. I hope it fits.

I drop to my knees and he lets me. All I can picture is Rory coming undone. I want to make that happen. I look up from where I'm kneeling and his eyes hold a warning. I don't even try to stop the grin from spreading across my lips as I keep eye contact and open my mouth to take him. He's thick and feels heavy on my tongue. Heat and lust pool between my legs in anticipation of having him there.

I let my tongue trace the vein underneath before circling and sucking his tip into my mouth. Then I relax my throat to take him deeper again. My hands hold onto the back of his thighs to help me keep the pace without choking too hard. Spit is already leaking from the corners of my mouth. Rory's hands wrap up in my hair and tilt my head for him to be able to better pump in and out.

"Fuck. Fuck. Fuck." He mumbles through a groan and I try to smile, but it is hard with my mouth so full. My imagination did no justice to him losing control with me under him. I watch his tattoos across his abs convulse before I'm yanked back abruptly.

"Fuck, Jude." He points behind me. "I need you there." I stand and walk slowly backwards until the back on my knees hit the edge of the bed.

He drops to his knees and roughly grabs my calves causing me to drop my ass on the bed. "I wanted the first taste." He only wastes a moment complaining before he licks right through my center. My head falls back to the bed and my hands fist in the sheets. His hands roam over the tops of my thighs to the inside and he takes his time tasting and sucking. His tongue stops and the lack of connection makes me sit up and stare at him demanding the reason for him pulling away.

"Question of the day, Jude." His voice is raspy as he looks at me. He has traces of me already on his lips. And I can't stop myself from imagining what it will feel like when he is finally inside of me.

"I thought we were past that stage of being friends." His teeth sink into my inner thigh causing me to hiss with the short sting of pain.

"Don't call me a friend when my tongue is inside of you, Avery Jude."

"Your tongue isn't..." His tongue pierces me with clear intention to drive his point home directly to the spot I need him most. His hands bruisingly pry my legs open wider. And he doesn't take his time exploring now. He devours.

His fingers replace where his tongue was. He pumps a few times until his fingers curl and he bites my clit before sucking. His other hand is holding my one leg up higher, giving him better access. My thigh resting in his palm. He keeps the strokes of his tongue and fingers alternating in perfect sync until I can't hold on anymore and the orgasm he is chasing for me makes my body explode.

I make the mistake of glancing down at him between my legs to find him wearing the proudest grin I've ever seen on his face. He slowly withdraws his fingers from where they are still inside me to trace a line down the inside of my thigh. "Trembling." One word. That's all it takes to remind me that Rory is going to ruin me.

He crawls over me as I back up further on the bed. "Condom?"

"Mia put some in that jar." I point to a jar without a lid to my right and he shakes his head. He lifts it out and tears the package open and quickly puts it on.

"If it hurts, let me know." For a man that just ate me out without a care in the world to how much he made my body writhe, his voice is fully tender now.

"I kind of want you to make it fit." His head drops to my chest and a mumbled curse leaves his lips. He said if I wanted something to ask.

He positions above me to grab himself and I feel the pressure as he slowly pushes in. It burns for a few seconds from the pressure and pain of me stretching to fit him. I love it though.

"Fuck, you're tight." His neck is straining as he lets the last few inches sink in. He brings my legs to wrap around his waist.

He runs his eyes over my body and pauses on my face, checking that I'm okay for him to continue.

"Go hard." I command, watching all the air leave his body in a harsh exhale. He trusts me though and doesn't ease me into it. He picks up his pace aggressively.

I bring one of my legs out of his grasp and rest it on his shoulder, which causes him to drive deeper and a rattled groan leaves his lips. A new wave of pleasure starts to ripple through my body but I fight to watch Rory.

He lets me use my leg to flip us so I'm on top, never losing our connection. His hair is sweaty and falling into his face and he has a look of awe as I sit above him now.

"I knew you liked the look of me underneath you." He teases me. *He remembers every fucking thing.* I give him a sweet sex hazed smile before I start rocking hard over him and he sits up to kiss me. Our bodies move together and our kiss is sloppy. I feel his hands on every inch of me. And when the pressure starts to get to the point that I know I was about to come again I push him down to work a little hard to get him there with me.

My finger nails dig into his chest. Leaving little crescent shaped marks. He's close because I can feel his body tighten underneath me, but I'm already there. I cry out as my release runs down my legs.

Rory flips us again so he can drive into me and continue to watch me come undone at the same time. A moment later and he's coming. I feel him pulse inside of me and the room starts to get hazy as I wind down. I feel him pull out and can hear him move around but my eyes are too heavy to try and open them.

The bed dips behind me and I know Rory is back in the bed. He pulls the sheet over us and I feel his hand pull my back to line up with his chest. We are both sweaty and my body is still covered in goosebumps but I don't dare move.

Thirty-Three

"You being mean to me kind of turns me on."

RORY

She fell asleep so fast that I didn't get a chance to even ask her if she wanted me to stay or leave last night. I didn't get the feeling she wanted me to leave though. So, I stayed. I held her through the night. She had a nightmare and she twitched and whimpered. I held her through that too. I woke early and watched the sun wash her entire room in a warm glow.

Her skin is warm and I let my touch lightly caress the outline of her viper tattoo. I knew the tail of the snake had to line up her hip and it is the sexiest thing in the world. She wasn't joking when she said that sex wears her out for her to sleep. This girl hasn't even moved with a twitch of her hand. I sent a text out to Eli to see if he could cover her morning classes today. Saturdays were always more lowkey but she is going to be pissed when she wakes up and realizes she missed them. Eli didn't even ask questions, he just let me know it was taken care of.

I am stunned that last night happened. And I'm already trying to find a way to convince her to let it keep happening. We fit together. Everything about her compliments every aspect of my life and made me want to chase new ones. Desire new things.

Eddie will want me in the gym this afternoon, but I can give her my morning.

I decide to take the risk of making her breakfast. Friends eat breakfast together. I know she is going to be firm on her stance of this not being more than sex. I'm prepared for her whole serious glare and setting of rules. I just don't care. I wasn't lying last night when I told her I would be whatever she needed. She doesn't do relationships because she doubts herself and her ability to give the relationship what it would need. She doesn't shy away because she is scared of commitment or loyalty. She holds both of those things in the very core of who she is. I can be patient while she catches up with the fact that we work together.

A few protein pancakes and some turkey bacon later, I hear her start to shuffle around in the bedroom. She even keeps most of the same food I keep in my apartment minus I now keep a random ass jar of strawberry frosting. I haven't even opened it yet. I saw it on the shelf the last time I went grocery shopping and it was in my cart before I could give myself a reason for it not to be.

Soft steps came from the hallway and I ready myself for whatever version of her would emerge. Will she be guarded and ask why I am still here? Or maybe she will be sleepy and bacon will make her happy. Or maybe she will ask me to just come back to her bed.

She comes around the corner dressed in my shirt. Which makes me immeasurably happy. I left it on the bed with the hopes she would put it on. I also hadn't put my pants back on and opted for just my boxers. Avery hates pants and that is a lifestyle I think I can adopt. Especially if it means seeing her in my clothes.

I can't look away. I've seen this girl in nearly every way now. But her swallowed in my clothes, sex hair, and sleepy eyes is my favorite way to see her.

She doesn't glare. That's a good sign. She looks up at me for just a few passing seconds before she sees the plate of food I am holding.

"You made me breakfast?" Her voice is softer than I've ever heard it and it pulls at something in my chest.

"Well, it's nearly ten in the morning. A late breakfast." Her eyes grow wide and I know she is freaking about her classes. "Eli has them covered for you." She looks relieved but her eyes still hold a tinge of questioning.

"Why did you make me breakfast?" *Because I want to take care of you but you're stubborn.*

"A girl has to eat." I say instead.

She takes the plate from my hands and goes to make herself comfy on the couch by pulling the blanket over her lap. Shame she is going to hide her legs from me this morning.

"Don't you have training?" Of course she would be the girl to ask me about training the morning after we have sex.

I cross the room and sit opposite of her with my own plate of pancakes. "It's this afternoon. Eddie and Eli want to fit in some extra ground work."

"This is actually super good." She says while shoving another bite of pancake in her mouth. Sleep looks good on her. She is more relaxed and her skin looks brighter. The fact that she slept because of me is not lost in my thoughts.

I clear my throat. Maybe if I bring this up while she is eating and still sleep-happy then it will go over better. I place my plate down on her table and her eyes track the movement.

"If you are about to have the whole 'this was fun but we probably shouldn't' conversation... don't." She holds up her hand and sits her plate down next mine, keeping a piece of bacon in her hand. "It was just sex and that's okay." She holds up the bacon and smiles. "Breakfast in the morning was a sweet touch though. But it's boyfriend behavior and I can make my own breakfast."

"If you think that making you breakfast is how I would act as your boyfriend, that's pathetic." Her smile drops and I wink. "I would treat you so much better than just making you pancakes and bacon. And you know it." I let her push me back because that means that she feels me getting closer. And I want to be closer.

"It was great sex, Rory. Doesn't mean it needs to happen again."

"Make no mistake, Jude. We're definitely doing this again. Sex, breakfast, and this." I motion between us. "You being mean to me kind of turns me on." My hand finds her leg under the cover and I pull her into my lap with ease. Her hands grip my chest to try and keep her balance, like I would let her fall.

"You want to keep having sex with me?" She whispers.

I bring her face closer to mine. I can feel her fingertips trace the marks she left with her nails over my chest and I have to fight to keep the focus of the conversation, keep her in the moment. If I let too much silence go by then she will start to get lost in her head.

"I would like to take a shower first and then we can get back to the sex part. I did miss my cardio this morning. Someone decided that they wanted to sleep in." I feel her lips smile against mine as I kiss her just once. I can feel it at this moment. Her starting to let the broken thoughts that she allows keep her caged up start to break free. She won't break others just because she lives in darkness. That is what I need to convince her of.

Thirty-Four

"Slutty bangs! Yes. That's exactly it."

AJ

"Do you think they are hiding something? They always let me in on everything. We're fucking triplets!" Maxwell is sitting between me and Mia nursing his own margarita. I'm honestly surprised she allowed him to crash our Monday Margarita ritual. Mia is very territorial about these dinner dates and always adamant that no guys are allowed. But everyone has a soft spot for Max. He is the sweetest of all of the brothers. It's nearly impossible to be upset with him. So when he called and asked if we would get dinner with him because he needed to talk, Mia didn't hesitate to send our location for him to meet us here.

"They just turned their locations off and left you on read?" The feeling of guilt is making me nauseous. Especially with the tequila swimming in my stomach. Oliver must have told Eli about his fight but not Maxwell. I can't figure out the reasoning behind that other than maybe he didn't want Eddie to find out and out of all of the brothers, Max would be the one to slip. But he knew about the last fight? Or maybe he didn't want to let Max know because I already told him I wouldn't corner him and Max hates when any of us are fighting. He takes it as a personal mission to fix it.

"Yes!" Max let his hand fall and slap the top of his legs. He lifts his eyes to mine and I can see worry in his eyes. "Do you think he took another fight?" I know he did.

"Like fuck he did. His leg isn't even healed yet and he knows better." Mia's tone of voice makes both mine and Max's attention swing to her. "What?" Her blue eyes get bigger as they move between where Max and I are sitting.

"You sounded pissed just now." Max moves forward so he is leaning on the table closer to her. "And worried. Do you have a hard on for my brother?" Mia nearly chokes on her margarita causing some of it to spill out of her mouth and fall on the bottom part of her white shirt.

"Fuck." Her bottom lip juts out into a pout. She loves that shirt. She recovers quickly and smiles brightly at Max. "Give me your phone."

He hands it over without question and she taps away for a second. "There. Location off. And I vote we go out to a bar without them. The pier is littered with a ton of them that we never go to." She points to me and then my phone. "You too." I do as she asks because I know how much she will push if I don't. She is in one of her moods that only results in massive trouble.

"You can let Rory know where we end up. He isn't on the shit list." It takes Maxwell no time at all to join team Mia and her chaotic plans.

"How was that by the way?" Mia's energy is back, full force. She was in the middle of making me give her the recap from Saturday night when Maxwell crashed out date.

"We can talk about it later." I give her a look but she ignores me.

"Oh please, A. Nobody blames you for fucking the tattooed mountain of a man. It's the slutty bangs. Hot as fuck. Bet he let you pull on them too." Max casually drinks his margarita while Mia and I recover from choking on ours. Her shirt is going to be ruined.

"Slutty bangs! Yes. That's exactly it." Mia shoves a taco into her mouth before standing up. She holds the bottom of her shirt out towards Max. "Can you rip this bottom part off?" She is already dressed in the cutest little skirt and boots. Max rips the bottom half of her shirt off effortlessly and Mia sighs before growling. "Why are you all ridiculously hot? That?"

She points to the ripped piece of shirt dangling from his fist. "Was hot. You're all menaces." Max smiles big, showing off his perfect teeth.

He stands, leaving nearly a foot of space for her to look up at. "You totally have a thing for my brother. I'm sure he could rip the rest of your clothes off if you asked him nicely." Mia smacks Max's chest hard which only causes him to explode into a fit of laughter.

"What if I asked you nicely?" Mia purrs as Max shakes his head.

"Absolutely not. I like my hands not broken." Even I know that Mia isn't being serious.

She wraps her arm around his and motions for me to come along as Max drops money on the table to cover our drinks and tacos. That was his rule for being allowed to come, he had to buy our dinners.

"Let's have some fun. They want to leave you out... we can be petty and leave them out." Mia shrugs and we head off walking in the direction of the street of bars. Maxwell's mood is lifted easily. That is Mia's gift though. She takes every situation that feels heavy and lifts the weight for you without even trying.

The night fell fast after we left the restaurant. We have been at this dive bar for nearly two hours. Mia and Maxwell have beat middle aged men at Pool three times now and made them pay for their drinks. I have been drinking nothing but water since we got here. It is still a Monday night and I have classes to teach in the morning. I have been keeping to myself mostly, letting Max and Mia get their energy out. But the same man that has come up twice to ask Mia to dance is making his way to her again. He obviously has been watching her since he waited until Max went to the bathroom to come up to her again. I immediately start making my way up the ramp to where the pool tables are located. I don't want to leave Mia alone with this guy for even a second.

He looks like grease would feel. He is taller and probably thinks that all women are attracted to him. But he has bad tattoos and a creepy ass smile that makes my skin crawl. I watch him lean into her space as she finds herself backed against the pool table. She doesn't let it show how uncomfortable she is though. She simply stands taller and smirks at him.

He put his hand on her hip. She quickly lets the poolstick fall from her hands as she grabs his wrist to pin his arm behind his back and smash his head on the green felt of the pool table. She got the upper hand because he underestimated her. And she didn't falter in her confidence or hesitate. It's not always an effective move, but in this situation, it works beautifully.

He chuckles and moves his eyes around the bar where Mia's little show is gaining attention. "Your boyfriend teach you that move?" His voice is high pitched and he forces another laugh, trying to play off that he just put his hands on her without her consent.

I tap Mia's shoulder to let her know she can let go of him. He shakes his shoulder out and turns to face me. "Hi." I give him a viciously sweet smile. "I actually taught her that move," I say, giving him my best right hook.

"The fuck is wrong with you two?" He is holding his jaw and starts to advance towards me when a hand grips his bicep and stops him mid-step.

"I'd really consider what you're about to do. Because I taught her that right hook and I know how hard she punches, but I hit harder you fucking piece of shit." Sometimes I forget that Maxwell shares the same blood as his brothers and Eddie. They are all hard lines and little communication. Max is usually so full of life and takes nothing seriously. At this moment, he looks lethal.

"Little Avery Davenport." Ice runs down my veins at the voice that is coming from behind me. "You really grew up well these past few years."

I swallow the weight in my throat as I turn to face the boy I used to live with. The one who gave me all my scars. I am suddenly thankful I am in a hoodie and shorts so my scars aren't on display. My fingers twitch as I try to even my racing heart. I feel the panic rise but he won't see it. I refuse to let him know he still has any control over me.

"What are you doing here?" My voice somehow comes out even.

"This is my pal Tray." He slaps the creeps shoulder. "When I saw this little barbie twist his arm I had to come see for myself. Then I walk up to you busting his lip. You definitely learned that from me by the way." I clench my hands into fists. *Fucking breathe Avery.*

"I was just going to wait until the fight for our reunion. But then you threw that punch and I knew I had to come say hi."

"What are you talking about?" My voice breaks a little.

"He probably doesn't even realize that we are connected." His eyes catch on something in the corner of the bar momentarily and then focus back on me. "I have a fight next Saturday with Oliver." If ice was what filled my blood earlier it is now fire that courses through it. *No.*

"Sure hope his leg is all healed up." I make sure my expression stays ice cold as he looks past me to where Mia is.

He holds his hand out to where she is standing a little behind me and I knock his hand out of the way. "Don't fucking touch her." I let the anger build at the same time I will myself to not let the tears fall.

"You know blondes are my type." I am shaking now. I think I hear footsteps behind me but with the blood rushing in my ears and my battle to keep control over the panic I can't be sure. I don't take my eyes off of Kyle as he takes a step closer and drops his voice. "How is Chloe? Oh wait. She..." I lunge for him and I get a good kick straight to his balls. I throw my knee up as he buckles over and I know I make contact. He stands up as I move in to land another hit but I'm pulled backwards and Rory steps in front of me.

Where the fuck did he come from? I claw at the arms holding me back and I don't realize I'm screaming until Oliver's voice breaks through. "It's just me. It's me. *Fuck*. It's just me, A."

"Let me fucking go!" I thrash and kick until he loses his hold and I'm running out of the bar.

I keep running. I run even though the tears no longer hold still in my body. I run even though I can't breathe. I run because I have to get away.

Thirty-Five

"You are not broken."

RORY

I have whoever this fucking guy is pinned against the wall with my hand. All the pool sticks fall off the wall when I slam him against it. When AJ sent me their location, I knew that there was a reason. When Oliver and Eli sent me a text asking if I knew where they were because Max stopped sharing his, I quickly gathered the guys and headed their direction. I didn't expect to find this. The girls and Max are squaring off with some strange guy. The sounds of Avery lashing out manically set every protective atom of my body on fire. His eyes are wild and dark as they stare back at me and I just know that he has something to do with Avery's past. The past that she has only allowed me glimpses into. I squeeze tighter reactively.

"Who the fuck are you?" He doesn't even try to fight me which just pisses me off more.

I want to chase after her. I want to break his neck for even making her freak out like that.

"What the fuck did you do to her?" I slam his head again.

"Rory..." Mia's voice breaks through the haze. "You have to let him go."

"No." I lean in closer to his face. "Why did she react like that? What did you do to her?" I need answers more than I need to protect my career at this moment. She's more important.

"Ask her." He spits out. I ram my elbow into the side of his face, cutting his eyebrow.

"There are phones out Rory." Eli speaks from somewhere behind me. Cameras. Fuck.

I can't be caught fighting outside of a sanctioned fight.

"Better let me go now before you fuck up all your fancy sponsorships." It isn't the sponsorships I am worried about.

I did release him though. Because I don't need it filmed when I beat him so badly that he can't walk straight ever again.

He wipes blood from the side of his head. "Kyle Mitchell." He nods to Oliver. "I'll see you next Saturday." He walks backwards to where a group of guys are waiting for him.

The owner of the bar looks at Oliver. "From what I saw, he was defending himself." That is the one rule. I am only allowed to have an altercation outside of the promotions if it is in self defense. This one time I'm happy I was easily recognized.

I start towards the door. I don't have time to question Oliver about what the fuck that Kyle guy meant. I have to get to my girl. I know exactly where she is running to.

Luckily for me, it is only two blocks over and I am able to make it there fast. I swing the gym door open, that isn't normally unlocked, and find her working her favorite bag.

I don't take my time getting to her. She is still in my hoodie and her favorite mint shorts. She did not however take the time to wrap her hands up. They are bloody from her hitting the bag so hard and she is sobbing uncontrollably. The kind that breaks your heart just hearing it. Her whole body is shaking. I wrap my arms around her and grab her hands to stop her from hitting the bag again. Her knuckles are split and her body is ice cold from the sweat coming off of her.

"I got you." She crumbles in my arms and her body loses all of its fight. I feel all her weight land in my arms and we tumble to the ground. She is screaming and crying at the same time. She isn't breathing for long seconds and then she gasps for air, the sobs aggressively racing down her soaked cheeks.

I try to wipe them away but it's useless. They are coming down faster than I can wipe them away. Her head lolls back on my chest as the rest of her body folds between my legs. She is so shattered that I am just trying to hold the pieces as they fall. Her pain is visceral. I hold her tighter, whispering that I am not letting go. She is so fragile and small. The storms are gone from her eyes and they are void. Her fight is temporarily lost.

We stay like this for an hour. Until her breathing evens out and I think she passes out from all the exertion from crying and screaming. I carry her up to her apartment. Thankfully she had shown me where the spare key was. I carry her to her couch and lay her down gently. I go to find a first aid kit in her bathroom to clean up the cuts on her hands. The blood is already dried and caked around the split skin.

I sit on the floor and get all of it set up. She starts to stir and I get up on my knees to draw closer to her.

"You're okay." I speak as gently as I can while trying to mask the worry from drenching into my voice.

I watch her eyes flutter open as she tries to sit up. "No no... just stay laying down. You had a pretty bad panic attack or episode. I'm not sure what happened but your body is going to feel really bad in a little bit." She ignores me as she slinks to the floor to sit opposite me.

"It was Kyle." Her voice sounds like she swallowed a handful of gravel. I open the water bottle I pulled from her fridge earlier and hand it to her.

"Small sips okay." She tries to hold the bottle but I can see her arms faltering. I grab the bottle before she drops it.

I scoop her legs and gently pull her close to me so her legs are bracketing my own. I lock my ankles behind her back to help keep her supported.

"Let's get your hands cleaned up and I'll carry you to the bed, okay?"

"It was Kyle." I pick the bottle back up and tilt her head back so she can take a small sip of the water.

"Kyle Mitchell. Yeah, he introduced himself." This is not the time to push her for information. Oliver, Maxwell, Eli, and Mia have been blowing up my phone since I found Avery in the gym. I only answered Eddie's text when it came through asking if she was okay. I know he will relay it to the others that I have her and am taking care of her.

I have only seen my mom have episodes like this before and it took her days to fully recover from them. I'm not a doctor. I have no idea how to help her right now but I know that I will do whatever it takes to make sure she never breaks like this again.

"Kyle is the reason I have these scars. He's the reason Chloe is dead. He's the reason I'm broken."

I cup her cheeks and make her look at me. "You are not broken." I grind my teeth together to keep composure. She doesn't deserve any of my anger right now.

I clean, treat, and wrap her hands then move her to the bed. I cover her up and turn to head out of the room to let her rest.

"I need you to stay. Please." Her voice breaks on that last word and my chest concaves with an ache.

"I'm not going anywhere." I crawl into the bed next to her and she rolls to lay face to face with me.

"I need you to just let me get this out. I've only ever told one other person and I've never spoken about it again." I reach over to hold her hand and nod my head. I'm too afraid to speak to ruin her ability to tell me what she wants to tell me.

"Kyle was my foster brother. He was always obsessed with fighting. Thought it was his God given talent. He would come home and have us hold mitts that were so worn down and broken that the padding was non-existent. He would throw with every ounce of strength and call it an accident when his fists would land anywhere but the mitts." Her eyes close as she takes a deep breath. "I was fifteen when I moved in there. And that's how it started. His dad would applaud us for helping him train. His mom was too drugged up on pain pills to notice anything that was happening."

She opens her eyes back up but her hand has a death grip on mine. "It started with just the punches and misplaced kicks to any part of the body he wanted. Then he decided that he wanted to practice with knives." Her voice is rough but she continues. "I volunteered for that. I couldn't handle watching the littles get hit anymore." A lone tear races down her cheek but I catch it. "He would throw them or just flat out see if I could block him with just the mitts. I had no clue how to protect against a knife and he found a sick joy slashing through my shirts because I only had so many and he craved destruction. One time the knife cut so deep I needed stitches. The doctor said I was lucky an organ wasn't pierced. That's when his dad decided that he couldn't have the weapons in the house because doctor's visits were too expensive." A short exhale leaves her lips. I am trying to steady my own breathing because her voice is so small I am afraid if I breathe too loudly then I won't be able to hear her. I am also trying to keep my rage in check. Who the fuck allows this to happen to children?

Then a soft smile crosses her lips. "Then Chloe came to live with us. She would stand in front of me with Kyle and dare him to touch her. She was so full of fight and courage and everything my heart needed to be reminded that it had to keep beating." I watch her chest hiccup with a quiet sob as she takes her time to collect herself again. "It didn't last long though. I watched her light fade slowly and so fast at the same time. She started sneaking pills from Mrs. Mitchell's secret cabinet in the bathroom. Or she would get weed from her boyfriends."

She shifts closer to me. "I didn't realize what was happening at first, Rory. If I did. I would have died fighting him for her. She protected us all." I want to ask her what she is talking about but I am actively trying to keep myself quiet like she asked.

I silently wipe the tears as they fall. It's the only thing I can do at the moment.

"We got the tattoos together, Rory. She protected me for nearly two years before taking me out of that house. And she asked me to get a tattoo with her when we finally broke out of that home. I was seventeen and they no longer cared what I did. So when she moved into her apartment with her boyfriend. I went with her. Slept on the couch and kept the part time job cleaning the gym that Eddie had given me."

She searches my eyes and I know she sees the unspoken questions resting in them.

What did she protect you from?

What happened to her?

I follow Chloe down the street as we make our way to the tattoo shop. She was lit up with so much excitement that her body was practically vibrating. I have tried to research some ideas for what I wanted to get and checked the pain levels for each part of the body. Chloe told me that I can handle whatever pain because pain is just something our brain tells us is real. If we decide it isn't real, then it's not. That's how she lives her life.

We enter the shop and are immediately met with a scent I'm not familiar with. It smells strongly of some kind of cleaning supplies but also faintly of something else that tickles my nose a little.

"We have an appointment." Chloe tells the girl at the desk.

"You're signed up for a medusa?" The girl's voice takes on a level of sadness that catches my attention.

"On my thigh. Yes. And I'm paying for whatever she decides to get." Chloe hooks her thumb in my direction like she didn't just shatter my entire being. I know why girls got Medusa tattoos.

I yank on her hand and pull her to the corner. "Why are you getting that tattoo?" I demand her to answer me.

"You know why. Let's not do this here okay?" Her eyes plead with me.

"Station is prepped. Who is first?" A beautiful girl comes around the corner and stops in front of us. She is edgy and sharp and looks exactly the way I imagine a tattoo artist would.

My own body is flooded with rage and grief and confusion. How could I not have known what happened in that house? We lived under the same roof.

"I promise to tell you everything after." She kisses my cheek and follows the girl to the back of the shop. Apparently Chloe had already given her the design idea she wanted. It is a Medusa but broken up in fractured pieces. The snakes are curling all around. Everyone knows the legend of Medusa. That she was transformed into this creature of terror to replace her beauty because of her act of disrespect to Athena. But Medusa has been weaponized as a victim's strength and show of power, protected by her snakes.

"What kind of snakes are those?" I ask the artist.

"I chose vipers. I know that no one really knows what kind of snakes Medusa was cursed with, just that they are venomous. I personally think a viper is badass. Takes no prisoners, strikes when necessary, and is loyal to their own." She says as she puts the transfer on Chloe's skin.

"I want the same snake, wrapped around my thigh." I circle my finger around my thigh and up my hip to show where I want it.

"I can make that happen."

"She told me that she would sneak out of our room we all shared in the basement to go to Kyle's room. The first few times he made her. He would have his friends hold her down. Then he got possessive and didn't want to share her." Her grief filled eyes lock with mine and tears flow over her lips as she pushes through. "Kyle threatened to take me instead if she didn't go."

Motherfucker. I am going to find a way to kill him.

"She told him that he couldn't touch me. And a few weeks went by that he didn't even hit me, but I think he grew bored. And he started hitting me again. Sometimes just because I was there. But he never touched me any other way. And it was because Chloe took it all so I didn't have to."

She lets go of my hand and wipes her face. "I would find her outside beside those damn trashcans smoking and she would be trying to wipe her own memory of what probably just happened in his bedroom and I had no idea."

She starts sobbing again, not as bad as before but enough to make me wrap her up in my arms and hold her until she stops.

"After we got those tattoos." She starts to speak again and I'm honestly scared for what else there could possibly be. "I came home a few months later and found her on the kitchen floor. She overdosed." My hold on her gets even tighter and I don't think I can let her go even if she asks. She's been through so much.

"I got the viper because I wanted to protect her like she protected me. I wanted to be in her corner, always. She was my family. And I failed her. I couldn't protect her."

I hold her as she cries herself to sleep. I keep holding her throughout the whole night afraid that if I let go, all her fractured pieces will fall through my grasp before I have the chance to glue them back together again. I hold her until I watch the sun come up.

Thirty-Six

"Because words matter to you."

RORY

Avery is still in my arms when I wake up from falling asleep early this morning. I stayed up through the night just to make sure that if she woke up and started to relapse into her panic then I would be awake with her. When the sun had come up, I shot a text off to everyone letting them know that she had slept but wouldn't be coming into the gym today. She can fight me, but I will win.

Holding her while her soul splintered in my arms shattered me. And I haven't figured out how to slow my mind down since I found her last night. Who allows that to happen? How did she survive that? I recall every single piece of information she has given me about Chloe and my heart aches even more.

I've admired her since I met her. I've been drawn to her strength, her fight, her loyalty. And it's because she has had no choice but to be. She's been a fighter her whole life.

"You're still here." She mumbles in a sweet voice.

"I told you last night that I wasn't going anywhere." I promise her.

"You don't have to stay here, Rory. I'll be fine after I take a shower and eat."

"Take a shower. I'll make you something to eat." I kiss her forehead and wait for her to tell me to back off. She sinks into it instead and I close my eyes and take a shaky breath.

Just be the guy.

"Don't pity me." Hearing the bite in her voice makes my heart flutter. I'm desperate to see her fight back.

"I'm not pitying you. I'm starving." It's taking all my own strength to not coddle her right now. That's not what she needs right now. She needs me to be steady. I can be that.

"You have to train."

"Not today."

We have a stare down. I am not going to give in on this one though. I've given her space since I've met her. But I will not allow her to fight the war in her head on her own. Not anymore. Seeing her like that yesterday only confirmed that I want to be around her in a permanent way. I watch as her body deflates and know I won. I wink at her before leaving the room to go make her something to eat.

I have an omelet and coffee waiting for her when she gets out of the shower. She walks into her living room where I have it all set up next to her very worn out scrabble board. I need her to not recede into whatever darkness is trying to call her back and I am already fighting against her reflex to want to be alone. Scrabble will be my saving grace. Well, scrabble and Eddie. It was his suggestion.

"Why are you really here, Rory?" She asks as she gets comfortable on the other side of the board.

"Do you want me to leave?" I raise an eyebrow at her.

"Would you use it against me if I said no?" Vulnerability bleeds through her words and I fight a grin.

"Not at all, Jude." I motion to the board as she sets up her letters.

We play three games back to back. I watch as life comes back into her eyes with each word she plays and it's a sight to behold. This beautiful, resilient, fearless girl sitting in front of me makes grown men take a step back and here she is, finding joy in playing a boardgame.

"Promise?" Her eyebrows pull in confusion. "I know what letters are left and you have a much better word to play. Why play such a low scoring word? This is why you lose, Rory." I have to cover my mouth to hide my smirk.

"You count the letters?"

"You don't?" This girl.

"I wanted to play that word." I stare at her, practically begging her to ask me why.

"Why?"

"Because words matter to you" That earns me her full attention. She looks up at me with the sad eyes that look more like a rainy day instead of a raging storm. " And I made you promise last night but I don't think you actually heard me."

I swallow down the emotion clogging my throat. I'm not confident that I am doing or saying the right things with her right now. I don't know how to help her heal or if she even wants my help. She just keeps all of this burdened on herself and I don't know how she does it. How she breathes with that much pain surging through her daily.

"I won't let him get near you like that again. You don't have to sit in that pain alone. I'm not going anywhere." I make sure my voice holds the promise I mean.

"He fights Oliver next Saturday." She reminds me like that's not something that I already have an internal countdown for in my head.

"Does Oliver know?" I don't have to clarify what I'm asking that he knows.

She shakes her head softly and brings her eyes down to where she is ringing her hands together in her lap. "Only Eddie." It takes me a moment to recognize the tremble in her voice because it's barely there. Fear. She doesn't want the others to know.

"Why did you tell me?" I don't want to question her finally letting me in but I am also so desperate to know why.

"You came to find me." She finally looks back up at me. "I haven't had a friend do that before. The boys all just leave me alone and I haven't had a bad breakdown since Mia has been around."

"You needed me." I inhale deep. "I don't want to be your friend, Jude." I know that now is not the time to bring it back up but I need her to know that my need for her to be okay ran much deeper than friendship.

"Rory..."

"I know. I just need you to know that I don't want to be *just* your friend." I clear my throat. "I'm going to crash on your couch for a few days. I don't want to leave you alone." I change the course of conversation before she can decide to put up a wall thirty feet wide between us.

I'm positive she hears the unease about leaving her in my voice because she just nods.

"I have to leave for a few days to go to some business training thing with my mom on Saturday. I can stay here until then, if that's okay with you." I leave the decision fully in her lap. She glares at me for a few long moments but the glimmer in her eyes lets me know what she decides before she even speaks.

"I sleep better with you next to me anyways. It's fucking frustrating." *There's my girl.*

"Did you just invite me back to your bed?" She pushes my shoulder but a genuine smile lights up her face. She trails her finger tips across my shoulder blade as she walks back towards her room.

"To sleep. That's all."

I follow her easily. I will gladly hold her and sleep every night.

I leave Avery at her apartment to take a bath and spend some time with Mia. I can't keep them all away any longer even though I want to. They have all but banged down her front door to get to her but she just now got her energy back up. She's been asleep for basically two days. I think her body just finally caught up to her constant push to keep going without giving it time to recharge.

I knock on the door hard and aggressively. I've been ready to combust for the past few days and I am desperate to talk about it all.

The door swings open and Eddie lets me inside. "I want to kill him."

"She told you." He is much calmer than I am. How is he so calm?

"I held her screaming and sobbing her lungs out after seeing him, Eddie! Do you know what that feels like?" I feel a burning in my chest start to build. "She was so helpless and I couldn't make it stop."

"How is she now?"

"She's eating and sleeping. Mia is over there now. She's doing okay. She wants back in the gym. I only convinced her to rest for a few days." That isn't what's important though.

"She's going to be okay." He assures me.

"She's not okay! Everything that he did to her? That he did to Chloe?" The pressure is getting tighter. I stand and start rubbing my chest to try and alleviate it.

"She is okay. You are just now processing this, but she already lived it. She survived." He takes steps towards me as he speaks.

"How does that even happen? I want to kill him, Eddie. I want to make him think that his life is nearly ending and hurt him so permanently that he feels pain every day for the rest of his life. He put scars all over her!" I can't stop the pacing.

"You're going to have to take a breath, Rory." He stops me by putting a hand on my chest and pressing down. "Breathe, son." Then I'm in his arms. All I can picture is her curled up like a broken doll in my arms on that gym floor. And I just break.

When I am able to pull myself together, I address the issue again. "We have to make him pay for what he did."

"What do you want to do?" I have a plan. I will need everyone in her life to make it happen though. I can't betray her trust by telling them everything, but I can tell them just enough for them to piece it together to have them all on board.

I spend hours at Eddie's going over the plan and figuring out how to make it actually work. I am running out of time. I have to leave in the morning and won't be back until the day of Oliver's fight. Eddie makes the call to get the triplets to meet us. We are all on the same page to make Kyle realize he fucked up with ever showing back up in her life. He clearly knew who he signed up to fight when he did. And he has every intention of making her life hell. I don't know what he said to her before she attacked him but that's what set her off. We all have a part to play next.

Thirty-Seven

"A piece of me with her."

AJ

I faintly remember Rory kissing me before he left but the sun wasn't up and my eyes wouldn't work to open. I know he had to leave this morning to go with his mom but I'm not prepared for the cold that hits me when I turn over and he isn't in my bed. So much can change in one week.

I move to get out of bed and knock something to the floor. Crawling over the side I'm met with a piece of thick paper on the ground. Rory must have been sketching. I caught him doing that the other night when I woke up. He was just sitting on the floor with his back against my bed and my lamp on the floor so it wasn't too bright. I remember crawling over to see what he was drawing and it was just me. Every day we have gone for a run, sometimes two. He makes sure the gym is empty before training. He just knew that I needed the quiet for a few days but also I needed the place that makes everything quiet. I didn't have to tell him. And that no longer scares me. Seems like falling apart in a guy's arms and spilling all my secrets broke the impenetrable wall I've spent years reinforcing.

I turn the paper over and nearly fall flat on my face as I tumble to the floor losing my balance. My ability to intake air is stripped away as Chloe's face is staring back at me. This is a full blown piece of art. It is vibrant and full of the right color. He has somehow gotten the exact shade of green for her eyes. Her blonde hair is the exact length I remember it being and with the perfect amount of untamed curl. He even added the freckle under her left eye. It is like looking at a real life version of her and he has never even seen her.

A glimpse of blue catches my blurry vision from where I am now sitting on the floor.

You protect her every day by keeping her alive in you.

If I thought that tears were falling before they are now falling hard and fast enough to make puddles on the floor. When did he draw this? She didn't look haunted the way I feel with her memory. She looks alive and happy. She looks like she is about to come off the page and leave chaos in her wake. When I look closer, she has a viper necklace hanging delicately from her neck. A piece of me with her. I know that's what that means.

Thirty-Eight

"Healing isn't peaceful."

AJ

"You're going to have to protect your left side more. He already knows about your injury. And trust me when I say he will try to break you down with it." Oliver is out of breath and already looks defeated.

"I swear I didn't know who he was when I took the fight, A." He has also been apologizing with every breath. I know he didn't know. Kyle is calculated. I knew I would have to face him again in my life at some point. Nightmares always return.

"I know, Ollie." I reassure him. He knows about Chloe. Well, he knows enough about Chloe. He knows my tattoo is for her and that she was my foster sister and that she died. I never went into detail about everything else. I couldn't stomach him looking at me like a sad puppy.

I also can't watch him go into this fight already injured. Oliver gets in his head and he will overcompensate and he will lose. He's a better fighter than Kyle any day of the week. But right now Oliver is blaming himself for me breaking down the past few days. He's never seen it happen. I keep it locked so tight that no one has other than Eddie. And now Rory.

"I think you need to rest. I don't want to put more stress on your leg. Let's run foundational drills, light work, just focus on doing it right. Kyle will be overly aggressive and crowd your space. So let's focus on utilizing that space the best way we can and control his space more."

I motion to the open floor. Classes have been over for a while and it is Monday. Mia already told me she's going to bring margaritas and tacos to my apartment because she doesn't feel like going out. Which I know is a lie. She is just worried about me. They all are.

"I'll run circuits with you." He is pouring sweat from our workout already but still wearing his hoodie.

"It's like a fire in here today, why are you wearing that?" He averts his eyes and shrugs his shoulders. "What are you hiding?"

"Nothing!" His voice gets slightly higher. He can never look at me when he lies.

"Fucking liar." I start to lift his hoodie and he pushes my hands away.

"What is wrong with you? You can't undress me."

"Did some girl sharpen her nails on your skin or something? Why are you acting cagey?" His eyes grow big and I watch his cheeks flush. He lets go of my wrists and shakes out his hair. "Who was it?"

"No one. Don't worry about it." He starts running through the circuits I have laid out for us and I decide to drop it.

We are almost through our final round when Mia comes through the front doors. Her hand is wrapped up. I ran over to her.

"What happened?"

She starts laughing and holds out a half drunk ice coffee. "I burned my hand on the espresso machine while closing up today. Turns out that letting a cute guy flirt with you while making his coffee isn't a smart distraction."

"You are always hurting yourself at that coffee shop, Mia." She has one injury per week by my count.

"If she stopped flirting with the guys that came in, she probably would have a better success rate of leaving a shift without injury." Oliver steps up to join us and I can feel the heat rolling off of Mia from her rage.

"You never complain when you come in and I flirt with you." She squares off with him and he gives her the grin that makes every girl he talks to act dumb.

"I think it's cute you have a crush on me. It's okay, Mia."

"I *used* to think you were cute. Before I knew you. Now I have been educated. On to bigger and better things."

"You want bigger?" Mia flips him off so fast that I nearly die from laughter.

She turns to me and gives me a hug, completely dismissing Oliver's presence. "I have all our stuff ready upstairs. I know you probably want a shower first. But you're mine the rest of the night!" She kisses my cheek, sending daggers Oliver's way. "You should shower too. You smell like a dumpster." Oliver gives her a slow look from top to bottom, his dimples on full display, and Mia shifts on her feet.

"You girls have fun tonight. Call me if you need me." He gives me a hug before leaving to do exactly what Mia told him to do, take a shower.

I turn to face Mia, knowing my mouth is still hanging open. "What was that?"

"Nothing."

"It was definitely something." I follow her as she heads towards my apartment.

"He just likes to run his mouth. All the time. He thinks everyone just loves listening to him." That's not Oliver at all and she knows that. Oliver would probably rather cut his arm off than talk to a lot of people. It's why we are best friends. But I have noticed that he pushes her every chance he gets.

When I get out of my own shower, I find Mia wrapped up in the cherry blanket I bought her. The same blanket she always cuddles up with when she is here. She already has one of her cherry margaritas and is holding something that I thought I had put up somewhere.

"What is this?" She holds the portrait of Chloe up. I found a frame to put it in so no damage would be done to it. "Rory drew this. Who is she?" I'm not even surprised she knows it is a piece from Rory. I know they teach art a lot together at his moms center.

"That's Chloe." I am done keeping it all from everyone. They will probably stop worrying so much if they knew why I reacted the way I did.

"She's the most gorgeous person I've ever seen. Holy hell." She *was*.

"I miss her every day." I sit down next to her and she hands me my own margarita.

"He really cares about you." I know he does. I think about everything that he has done for me the past few days and how big he has shown up for me by just being here. How he's been showing up for months.

"He wouldn't leave." I still don't think I can be what he needs me to be. But it is very clear that I have feelings for him. And I am doing my best to figure out what to do with that. "Is it weird that I miss him?"

"I think it's sweet." I have picked up my phone at least twenty times today to text him. I called him Saturday to thank him for the portrait of Chloe. And he has checked in on me every few hours even though I know he is super busy with his mom. "He wouldn't let any of us near you. I thought the triplets were going to break down the door. Eddie is the only reason they didn't." Thank God for Eddie.

"I'm sorry I scared everyone." I hate knowing that I made them worry at all.

"You scared the shit out of him. Out of all of us, A. Who was that guy?" I try to hide my surprise. I expected Rory to tell them if only so they would stop worrying about me. But he kept his word.

"I think we should be a little more drunk before we have this conversation." Mia's whole face lights up.

"You'll really tell me?" Her voice is so small and I realize she thinks I don't trust her. "I can order tacos and we can get extra drunk since we are already here and don't need to find a ride home. You can tell me all about this goddess in this portrait that Rory drew and the bag of dicks that you attacked at the bar."

"Deal." I drink the rest of my margarita and she takes the empty glasses to the kitchen to make us more.

We are three margaritas in by the time I get her caught up with everything. She hasn't let go of me for probably ten minutes now. She crawled over into my lap and latched on and won't let go. I can feel tears roll down my own arms that come from her silent sobs. It is a lot to process. I know that. But all I can think is what Rory wrote on that blue post-it note. How I am protecting her by keeping her alive. Her story deserves to be told. Her strength deserves to be remembered. And her love deserves to be shared. And I am going to do a better job of doing that.

"I love you." She whispers softly as her tears slow down.

"I think Chloe somehow brought you to me. You two could have been sisters. Same hair, same wild energy, same beautifully big heart." I wipe her tears away and smile.

"Healing isn't peaceful." She wraps my hands in hers the best she can with her one hand still bandaged. "And you have a whole bad ass family behind you now. He will get what he deserves. I promise you." A lot of promises have been made lately. It's overwhelming the type of peace that the freedom of speaking about it all brings.

She stands and gathers all our empty glasses. "I'm going to go get us some water."

I pull my phone out to text Rory.

AJ

I told Mia everything.

Rory

I'm proud of you.

AJ

I miss you.

That is probably too much to just throw at him but I am feeling braver lately.

Rory

You miss all that peaceful sleep you get when I'm there.

I smile down at my phone.

Rory

I miss you so much that I've been daydreaming about just kissing you.

AJ

Stop flirting with me.

Rory

I love flirting with you.

AJ

Will you be back in time for the fight?

I hold my breath as I watch him type. I need him there. I don't even care that he knows that.

Rory

I will be there.

AJ

Goodnight, Rory.

Rory

Sweet dreams, Jude.

Thirty-Nine

"You can't do this."

AJ

T he Poolhouse is packed. Oliver is always a fan favorite for this crowd and Kyle is a newcomer. As far as I know he has never fought here before. After tonight, he won't fight here again. I'll make sure of it. I don't know how, but I refuse to let him back into my life for longer than tonight.

The door to the designated room set for Oliver to get prepared swings open and in comes the boys. All dressed in the same zip up hoodies that they had made for when Oliver tried to make it pro.

"You have forty five minutes until your fight is up. They saved it for last." I inform them.

Oliver comes and sits with me on the bench for me to prep his hands. Eli and Maxwell stay near the corner. It takes me only a few minutes to wrap his hands the way he likes. I grab the pads to warm him up.

"Is Rory here yet?" I ask Eli. Rory promised he would be here and I haven't heard from him nearly all day.

I am not fully confident that Oliver can win this with his leg. I thought it was too soon to take a fight when he took that phone call weeks ago. His leg took a small beating in the last fight. I know he isn't doing his rehab properly either. He is too stubborn.

Eli shakes his head at me at the same time Maxwell walks over to give me a quick hug.

"I'll go check out front, A. I'm sure he is here."

"Thank Maxie. You're my favorite." He puffs up and then points to both his brothers.

"You heard her!" I watch him walk back out of the door and hope he finds Rory. Usually his confidence that everything will work out upsets me. Tonight I am desperate for his steady presence.

"They're ready for him." Eli announces from the doorway.

I turn around to stand in front of Oliver. I lift my head to look up at him. "You can do this."

He doesn't look nervous in the slightest. He looks excited. More than excited. Which raises an alarm inside me. Just a few days ago he was doubtful. He wouldn't tell me that, but I could tell. We know each other's tells by now.

"Kyle Mitchell will pay for what he's done. Tonight." He smiles big at me.

"This isn't going to be a fun time, Oliver. You have a weak leg and Kyle is a psychopath." I try to remind him but his smile only gets bigger.

"What is wrong with you?" He is hiding something.

He leans in and kisses my cheek. "I just can't wait to see this guy bleed."

He walks around me and enters the hallway. Eli and Maxwell already have their hoods up and Oliver pulls his up as he steps in front of them. We make our way down the long hallway with Oliver in front, flanked by his brothers, with me in the back. My heart is beating faster the closer we get. I can hear the crowd get louder. And the walls start to feel a little tighter.

Oliver just has to be faster. He can do this.

I hate not knowing what Kyle is about to bring to this fight. I haven't seen him do anything in years. I assumed he was off doing whatever pieces of shit that wastes of space do. Or maybe he still lives with his parents. I don't fucking care. I just never want to see him again.

We turn the last corner and the crowd consumes us. I search around the best I can to see if I can find Rory anywhere. He's been in my life for nearly six months and not once has he not done something he said he would do. He barely wanted to leave me alone after the night at the bar and now he can't show up?

We hit the edge of the abandoned pool and my heart falls. Oliver might think he is ready for this, but I know Kyle. He is ruthless and sadistic. He has no issue tearing someone apart. He doesn't have a love for the sport like Oliver. He has bloodlust.

I turn to face the boys after setting our corner up and my heart doesn't fall this time, it completely stops. Rory is standing in front of me, unzipping the same fucking hoodie Oliver was just wearing.

He gives me that grin that he's been giving me since the day he met me. "Hey Jude." He closes the distance between us until there is only a breath of space between us.

"What are you doing here?"

"You asked me to come."

I glance down at his hands to notice they are wrapped. I bring my gaze up the rest of his body and notice that he also has a new tattoo. A snake wrapped around his neck. A snake that looks exactly like the one on my thigh.

"What is that?" I can't even point to what I am talking about. My whole body is paralyzed at the moment.

"I don't have a lot of time to explain it all. So I'm going to break it down and I'm going to need you to listen to me. You trust me?"

"You know I do." He cups the back of my neck and brings our noses close together but also gives me no other option but to maintain eye contact.

"I want to protect you too. You got that tattoo for Chloe. I got this for you." He closes his eyes as he lets out a breath. "You own me, Avery Jude. I will always be in your corner." He opens his eyes again and takes a baby step back. "Tonight I need you in my corner."

"Our corner." That voice is the last voice I ever imagined hearing in this building. It is clear and breaks through all the noise.

"What are you doing here, Eddie?" He pulls me into his arms at the same time I practically fall into them.

"Hey, kiddo." He squeezes me and I know I am going to lose the fight to not cry right now.

"This is about to be so hot." Mia's voice is so full of excitement. I pull away from Eddie to see her standing next to the triplets. "Our corner." She blows me a kiss.

"And we are all here to protect you. We're your family and he won't touch you." Eli steps forward. He reaches down and pulls his pants leg up to show a viper wrapped around his leg.

Maxwell unzips his hoodie and shows me his collar bone. He has a smaller viper laced through the skin like it is wrapped around the bone. Oliver unzips his hoodie and gives me his back to show his viper wrapping around and peeking over his shoulder. Mia giggles and lifts up her tiny black shirt to show a dainty little viper curled next to the side of breast.

Eddie steps back in my vision and pulls his shirt sleeve up to show a viper resting on the forearm. "They promised me that this wasn't some weird cult shit."

"You got a tattoo for me?" The tears are coming down without permission.

"I have several, but this one is for you. Yes."

"We got them to remind you that you aren't a victim anymore. And you are the definition of 'fear the creature they created.' You're the strongest and most vicious person I've ever met. And we will protect our corner, our family, until the day we die." Maxwell is the one to speak now. His heart is the most passionate out of all of his brothers and I am so thankful he loves me.

"I love you. All of you." I look at each of them, ending on Rory. Then his words from earlier ring back through my head. Realization hits me. "You can't fight tonight."

"I assure you I am perfectly capable of fighting tonight."

"No, dumbass. You *can't* fight. It'll void your chance in the promotional fight. And you are not doing that. We have worked too fucking hard for you to throw that away."

Mia taps my shoulder to get my attention. "I already handled it. All cellphones have been confiscated at the door. Rory can be very intimidating when he wants to be. Everyone in this room went through another check for devices. And no bets are being made. So as long as there is no physical proof. He is in the clear."

"I'm also not asking permission. It's my risk to take. And you are worth it."

I am speechless.

"When did you all do all of this? You haven't left my side in over a week." My mind is reeling. I've never felt so loved and the weight of everything that they have done is almost suffocating.

"Are we going to fight?" The ref calls over to us. Which means Kyle is ready.

My eyes land on him and his shitty grin. He has a wild look in his eyes and won't stop moving from side to side.

"Break his legs!" Mia whisper-shouts as Oliver helps her back up the ladder and out of the pool.

Eli and Maxwell are already waiting for them up top. Eddie stays. Thankfully. I won't be able to corner this fight without him. My heartrate is still racing.

"You can't do this."

"I'm already doing this." He leans down and kisses me quickly and harshly right before the bell rings and he leaves the corner. He gives no time before his fist collides with Kyle's face.

Forty

"She's worth everything."

My whole body is pulsating with the need to break him. This isn't a fight where I need to show my skillset or earn points to win the round. I can just unleash. The rage that floods every fiber of my being by just laying eyes on the guy that caused her so much pain makes me want to paint this entire pool with his blood. My first punch lands and blood spurts from his nose. The moment I make contact I feel euphoric knowing I will not be holding back. There is so much truth to what Avery said when she spoke about a bloodlust in fighters. Ultimately, in the professional ring, they are my coworkers. In this setting, with no rules, no career depending on your outcome, you are able to just relish in that dark hunger. I am able to bring an elbow in to land to his nose and I feel the cartilage fold and crunch under my skin. I know I broke it that time. I watch him smile as blood falls over his teeth and into his mouth. Good, I want him to think he has a chance in this fight. It will only make putting him down that much better.

"Oliver too much of a pussy to fight me himself?" He spits blood out near my feet. He looks over my shoulder where I know that Oliver and Avery are standing. I step sideways to block his view.

"No rules in the pool. Right?" I switched out for Oliver with the ref, if he can really be called that. He's just a guy that used to fight and can't let it go. He is here to emulate the real thing and to keep it from being a massacre. I think he knows that he won't be able to stop whatever is going to happen to Kyle tonight though.

"Taking out the new local celebrity will be a better win anyway."

"You talk too much." I charge him and throw a great combo with a right hook and a kick to his stomach that slams him into the cement wall. I watch him try to catch the breath that was just knocked out of him but I don't give him the chance. I close the distance and keep him there. I crowd every empty space so he has no opening to get away. Every punch slams his head into the wall a little harder each time. I watch his eyes close and his body start to go limp just as they ring the bell.

I walk back to my corner and let Eddie wipe the blood off my hands with a wet towel. I try to keep my eyes on Avery but she keeps pacing around me.

"How long do you want to play with him?" Eddie asks. He knows my plan to break Kyle so bad that he won't be able to walk out of here. He is also the reason I am able to be the one fighting him instead of Oliver. He helped me come up with this entire plan. Eddie called Mia and got her involved as far as making sure the social media would be a blackout during this fight.

"Until he goes to sleep." Eddie pours water into my mouth to cool me down a little.

I feel Avery's hands carefully patting at the sweat around my neck. The tattoo isn't fully healed but it is scabbed over. I hope she doesn't think I'm crazy for doing that. For getting the tattoo. We all did. I knew I was going to do it as soon as she told me why she got the viper. She needs to know she has her own family behind her and ready to protect her. That's why we are all here now. I reach up to tap her hand to let her know that I got her.

Bell rings again and Avery steps back beside Eddie to make room for me to exit the corner. Kyle walks towards me and is already swaying a little. His pride won't let him show how much he is already hurt though.

He doesn't have the same kind of gritty survival that he made sure Avery would need for the rest of her life.

This time I go straight for his legs. Just for Mia's request. I kick so hard that he stumbles to the right a few steps and grabs his legs. He is barely able to stand, but I'm in his proximity so he lands a solid punch to the left side of my jaw. That's unfortunate. I really wanted to go through this without a single touch from him. He circles around me, thinking that he has some kind of upperhand because he landed one punch even though he is still limping.

I kick his other leg to take away his stability and land a nasty right hook causing more blood to pour from his mouth. He falls to his knees, still smiling.

"I broke her a long time ago. She isn't worth it." Blood drips from his mouth, his teeth red. He tilts his head to where Avery is standing in the corner, her eyes glued on me.

I grab the back of his head and pull so hard that I can feel the hair start to rip from his scalp. Pivoting him so Avery is out of his line of sight. "You don't even deserve to lay your eyes on her. And after tonight, if you ever come near her again. I will end you. I don't give a fuck. You can choke on your own blood right now and the world would be a better place." I grip his throat tight with my other hand. He makes a gurgling noise and I can feel his windpipe bend. "She's worth everything." I squeeze tighter and his body goes limp but I don't want it to end so quickly. I release with just enough time for him to take a breath in and watch his eyes open as he coughs. I take a few steps back as he regains his breathing. As soon as I know he has, I close the distance quickly and grab his head again, kneeing him so hard that I drop him unconscious. I watch him lay in his own splattered blood.

I know he won't ever have another fight here, in this town. Eddie is a scary motherfucker when he wants to be. He threatened to have the entire ring brought down if they allow him to even step foot in the building again. I don't know how Eddie would have brought this place down and I don't want to know.

Eddie also said he would take care of Kyle leaving town. He told me to not ask and to just trust him. And if I'm being honest, Eddie now scares the shit out of me.

I walk over to Avery. I didn't get a good amount of time to gauge how she was feeling about everything we bombarded her with right before the fight started. I go to open my mouth to apologize for dropping this on her the way we did, but she jumps into my arms. I instinctively catch her and her lips are crashing to mine before I can even register what is happening.

This is Avery Jude. My Jude. My stubborn, fierce, self-preserved girl.

Her hands go to my hair and they pull lightly. Something she was quick to figure out I really love. I grip her tightly, not even caring that she probably has blood on her now. I pull away just enough to see that her eyes are a little glassy. Her forehead rests against mine.

"You're going to have to slow down unless you want me to make this a very inappropriate hug in front of all of these people." I feel her smile against my lips.

She slides down my body and her hands lightly touch over my new ink. "A neck tattoo?" I know she is avoiding the bigger issue at hand right now of me taking this fight. I also know that she is probably going to make me run until I puke every day in training to punish for being so reckless. I don't care. I had to.

"You think they're hot." Her hands are softly mapping out the viper that wraps around my neck.

She runs her hand over the small cut on my lip from the one hit he was able to land and her eyes take on a very concerned glare.

"This was impulsive and reckless." The caring tone in her voice is new and it makes my chest tight.

"It was decisive and worth it." I promise her. "You realize you just kissed me like that in front of all of your people?"

"Our people." She corrects me. She looks all around as everyone forgets that Kyle is still laying limp on the ground and starts to make their way to me. Not a cell phone in sight. Thank you, Mia. "And I had to make sure that they knew that they didn't have a chance with you."

"Possessive are we?" I squeeze her hip to pull her closer to me. "No one has had a chance since I walked back into West Haven." I cup the side of her face, ignoring the growing crowd that was still closing in on us.

"It's the neck tattoo. It's doing things to me." She grins.

"What kind of things?" I try to wrap both arms around her but she takes a step back as our friends get closer.

"Things that I definitely will not be talking about while Eddie is still in ear shot." I let out a groan because I have many images flooding my head at the moment.

"I wasn't joking." I pull her back close to me. I know the boys and Mia are steps away from being by our side but she has to hear me. "You own me, Avery Jude. In whatever way you want. I'll be whatever you want." I decide. I want her to be mine. I'm already hers. I know it will take time for her to catch up to me though. I'm okay with that.

She leans up on the tips of her shoes as she captures my lips again for a brief moment. "Just keep being my peace." I can hear the hesitant plea in her voice. I know it's a big deal for her to ask anything of anyone. The fact that she wants me to be her peace is bigger than anything else she could ever say to me.

"I can be that."

Forty-One

"Admit it. My tattoo
is your favorite."

AJ

Maxwell demanded that everyone meet back up at our bonfire spot after the fight. It wasn't a hard decision for me. I was ready to leave that place the second Rory wrapped his arms around me after the fight. I've never had anyone fight for me the way I watched him fight tonight. He didn't even allow Kyle to look at me one time. He controlled every aspect of tonight to keep me protected and that fact continues to overwhelm me.

I'm waiting for him to get out of the shower for us to go and meet up with the rest of them. I told him I could just ride with Mia over to the bonfire but he pleaded with me to just wait for him. With the exception of us being separated by the half wall of the showers, he hasn't let me leave his side since the crowd filled the empty pool. I think he's scared I'm going to break down again. They all are. Oliver and Mia definitely didn't want to leave me alone either. Mia had to convince Oliver that I would be okay. Eli and Max only left because Eddie made them take him home.

They all have a viper tattooed on them now. *For me.* That's a forever kind of thing. They love me enough to do that.

I know that Rory must have told them the story behind my tattoo, and a part of me feels like I should be upset but I'm not. For the first time in so long I feel like breathing isn't a fight. My mind is idle.

"Did I fuck up?" Rory is leaning against the wall in just a towel, water droplets falling to his bare shoulders and chest from his wet hair. His nerves have his whole body pulled tight. And his eye contact isn't steady like it normally is. He really thinks he fucked up?

"You just beat a guy that marked me for life, is the ghost residing in my thoughts, and distorted my ability to love then left him laying in his own blood. I feel like I'm living in a dream right now." Walking over to where the wall is still holding his body up, I lift his head so I can see his eyes. It's crazy how my entire life my favorite color has been green and the guy standing in front of me has green eyes. Chloe always said the universe has a front row seat to everyone's desires. And that she would deliver them when we are ready to take care of them. If Rory needs the reassurance that what he did shattered the casted pieces of my heart, I'll give that to him. "No one has ever been willing to sacrifice what you just put on the line for me. I don't really have an adequate appreciation for you doing it." His hands rest on my hips but he doesn't break eye contact.

"I didn't do it for you to say thank you. I selfishly wanted to be the person to fight that demon for you." I love Rory's honesty the most. He never fails to make sure that I know exactly what his intentions are behind every decision he makes. I watch his throat bob with a hard swallow.

I reach up and brush his wet bangs out from his forehead. "Being able to cause that much destruction and rock slutty bangs is unfair and ridiculously hot." My attempt to break up the worry building in his mind is successful as the empty room erupts with his laughter.

"Did you just call my bangs slutty, Jude?" I'm always thankful for his ability to read when I don't want to keep talking about something. This is why he didn't fuck anything up. His ability to give me what I need without me spelling it out for him is what brings so much stillness to my life now.

"Technically, Maxie did." He squints his eyes before smiling with perfect teeth.

"I knew he thought I was hot." A boyish smirk rests on his face before the somberness returns. He rests his forehead on mine and closes his eyes. "Are you okay?"

"More free than I thought I could ever be." I give him a soft kiss and I feel his lips tilt up in a smile against mine.

"I need to get dressed before Mia kills us for leaving her alone with the guys." He groans out the words.

He kisses me soft and slow, spinning so my back is to the wall and his leg slots between mine. "Rory."

"Hmm." He goes back to kissing me.

"Get dressed." A disgruntled sigh leaves his body but he walks over to his bag to grab his clothes.

Slowly making our way to the oversized flames of the bonfire, Rory's hand in mine, and the sight of all our friends circling up, brings me a sense of home that floods every fiber of my being. This is what I've fought for. What Chloe made sure I knew was worth fighting for. Laughter and love and unwavering support. It's a beautiful thing how the universe recycles the things we lose and the people we mourn, giving them back to us in ways that we don't even understand we need.

When I get closer I notice that there is another girl near Mia. Dark waves falling down her back, piercings dotting both ears, and the caramel glow of her skin dancing with the flames. Eli's watching every movement her body makes while she dances with Mia.

"I didn't know Devyn was in town." Rory is still holding my hand and keeping my steps steady in the sand as we get closer to the fire.

"She's who did all of our tattoos." He comments. That makes sense. I haven't seen Devyn in over two years. Eli has traveled to see her a few times because she couldn't make it back home with her apprenticeship she was doing in L.A. I know he's missed her a lot.

"Care to elaborate how you convinced them all to get that tattooed on them?" I make an effort to keep my voice as light as possible so he knows I'm not upset if he did tell them the full truth about Kyle. I feel his grip tighten around my hand though and know I failed. He halts in front of me and turns around.

"I told them that you got that tattoo because Chloe was your family and it was a symbol that you would always be in her corner to protect her and take care of her. I told them that I wanted to take Oliver's place in the fight and explained that Eddie already made a plan to help and that I was going to get that tattoo. I asked the guys where they get their ink done and Eli informed us that he had the perfect person. It spiraled from there. Mia didn't want to feel left out and demanded that she also get the family snake tattoo. And then of course Oliver wasn't going to let Mia show more loyalty to you than him. And next thing I knew we were all crowding this corner in a tattoo shop that Devyn's friend owns and spending hours together figuring out where we were getting the damn snakes." I love them. All of them.

"Breathe. You're all insane. You know that right?" I see his worry leave as his eyes glimmer and his trademark grin appears.

"Admit it. My tattoo is your favorite." He pulls his collar to the side so I can fully appreciate the viper wrapping around his neck.

"It's actually Eddie's." I tease. He tosses his head back, rolling his eyes.

"Avery!" Devyn realizes that I'm here. Her and Mia doing their best attempt at a run towards me.

Rory reluctantly lets me go when Mia wraps her small arms around my waist and I have to use all my strength to help hold her up. "I love you." Her voice is small but it holds so much strength and she wraps around me tighter.

"I know." I hold her.

"About time that you two show up." Maxwell and Eli appear behind the girls and I notice Oliver off to the side.

"This one had to shower the massacre off his body." I tilt my head to where Rory is now standing behind me with his hand wrapped around my stomach.

"Watching you lose control tonight was the highlight of my year." Maxwell claps before clutching his chest.

"I never lost control." The growling undertone of Rory's voice sends shivers down my spine. He didn't though. He calculated every step he took. I've been watching him train every day for the past few months. I've memorized his movements. He wasn't erratic or random in his decisions tonight. He knew exactly the outcome of every move he made.

"God, you sound like dad." Eli points out followed by manic laughter from Oliver.

"You are basically dating Dad, A. How does that make you feel?" I flip him off which only causes him to laugh harder.

They all make their way back to the bonfire. Rory takes a seat first, pulling me to sit with my back to his chest. He's a little extra assertive with his touch tonight but I know it's because he needs to have me closer after fighting Kyle. I get it. I watch the waves and close my eyes to just sit in the sound of them.

"It's a shame it's gotten colder and we can't swim." I love being in the water.

"If you're referring to that diabolical night when you wore that black bikini, I hope you realize you almost cost a man his legs that night." I swing my head around to question him. "Don't look at me like that, Jude. I was losing my mind that night."

"You did not threaten someone over me."

"I absolutely did." No hesitation or remorse in his voice.

"We weren't even a thing then." Should I be upset that he threatened some poor guy that night? Maybe. Was I? No. I am oddly satisfied that he wanted me so much that he did it.

"We've been a thing since you kicked my ass in Scrabble at Eddies and I made you that pie." That night flashes through my mind. I loved that pie.

"Will you make me another pie?" He kisses my neck as he wraps his arms around me, pulling me as close to him as he can get me.

"I'll make you all the pies."

Epilogue
Three Months Later

AJ

In two minutes I am about to step up and give a speech to over a hundred donors. I have no idea who any of them are, where they came from, and why they care. I have Mia and Melinda to thank for them being here though. When Mia came to me months ago and told me she wanted to start the foundation to give more kids scholarships for the gym to help them find a sense of purpose and routine, I was already willing to do whatever my part would be. Eddie decided that I needed to be the representative for the gym to speak about what we could offer the kids.

I personally think that our newest resident professional fighter should be the one. He will be the biggest cash flow, and we can do a lot with more money. We can maybe even get more equipment and start up a program at Melinda's rec center. Cornering Rory's professional fight was a dream come true. I didn't come down from the high of being involved in his win for nearly a week. He took it all the way to the last round and got a submission in the last thirty seconds. It was a high paced and aggressive fight. It was beautiful and poetic.

"You're up, sweetheart." Melinda extends a hand out to me. "I'm so proud of you." The more I'm around Rory's mom the more I understand why Eddie was so adamant that I was kind to her the first time I met her.

I take a deep breath before walking to the center of the stage. I made note cards. But now that I am looking out at the crowd, I know I won't have the ability to read them. I will just have to wing it.

"A very passionate and beautiful soul told me recently that healing isn't peaceful. And that resonated in my soul. My name is Avery Davenport. I am one of the instructors at West Haven Martial Arts. I also help manage the gym. Eddie West found me on the streets, staring into his gym windows when I was fifteen years old. He gave me a part time job cleaning equipment after hours. When I was seventeen, I showed up on his doorstep running from the devastation of losing the only person that I cared about in the world. The only person that made sure I survived an abusive foster care placement. My sister, Chloe, was the definition of sunshine. She was the one who taught me how to love. She taught me to fight for what made me feel alive. She is the reason I fought to stay here and not give up. That's why we are dedicating this new foundation to her. You are here tonight to open your wallets to help the success of the What's Our Dream Foundation. Because Chloe cultivated dreamers. And that is what we will do with this program. My partner in this foundation is sitting in this very room. Her name is Mia Cassidy and she brings rays of sunshine into every room she steps in. She makes each person she comes in contact with feel like they can win any situation. Mia will carry on that same fighting light with every step of this foundation because she is the reason it exists. Without her, this entire donation dinner wouldn't be happening. The opportunity to bring stability to children's lives that need it wouldn't exist. She is the strongest and most brilliant person I know. We will care for each and every child with the purest form of love and protection. We will make sure that they know that they have a purpose. We will stand in their corner and fight for them every day. And we just want to say thank you for making that happen." Applause echoes throughout the room and I exit the stage.

Rory is standing at the end of the stairs from the side of the stage, his hand waiting for me.

"You are incredible." He presses his lips to the inside of my wrist. He brings me over to the wall that I used to showcase Chloe's portrait. Eddie added a few more details to the wall. Surrounding Chloe were blue post-it notes that his wife had left him. They were all clearly written with the greatest of love. My favorite one read- *i love being in our corner.*

"She accidentally ordered ten thousand of those damn blue post-its." Eddie appears beside me. "She was always running around and handling everything for me, for the gym, for us. She missed an extra zero on the order form." He rubs a hand down his jaw. "The delivery guy carried box after box of them. And she just sat on the floor and laughed hysterically. She was always able to make the best out of anything." He wraps an arm around me. "She would love what you are doing here. The love you bring to her favorite people in the world." He leans in and kisses my head. "I'm so proud of you." His voice breaks on that last part.

I see the emotion wash over him after remembering the woman he loved the most. He clears his throat and excuses himself.

I look around the room full of people that are going to make this foundation become a reality and my heart expands. Eli and Maxwell are talking to a group of older ladies, clearly using their charm to help the cause. I love them for it. I scan for Mia but I haven't seen her since I saw her wiping her face after my speech.

"Have you seen Oliver?" Rory asks from beside me.

"Mia is missing too." I point out. Rory raises his eyebrow. "Not my problem. They are probably murdering each other."

"She is kind of terrifying." I slap him in the chest lightly. He isn't wrong though.

"She just knows what she wants." I correct.

"Follow me." Rory interlaces our hands and pulls me towards the back door. This donor dinner is being held in the building across the street from the gym. And I know that is where he is taking me.

"What are you doing?" A laugh escapes me.

"I'm stealing you away."

Bonus Epilogue

RORY

I quickly pull her through the gym doors. I've been staring at the slit in the mint green dress for approximately two hours now. Since I picked her up to walk over to the banquet. The dress was missing the entire back and was barely being held up by the fabric flowing down her shoulders. It touched the floor but the slit raised high enough to make an educated guess she was wearing nothing underneath it at all.

That thought alone made it hard to focus on anything other than her tonight. I watched her tattoo peep out of that cut in her dress every time she walked and my hands have been itching with the desperation to be on her skin.

"You drug me to the gym, why?' The knowing tone in her voice tells me she knows exactly why I brought her here.

I stare right into her eyes and watch her lips twist in want. "You have access to the cameras, right?"

"Yeah…"

"Turn them off."

"Excuse me?" Her voice falters slightly but she reaches into her clutch to get her phone.

"You heard me, Jude." I love that she still gives me attitude even after spending every day together for the better part of three months now. I never want her to lose her fight.

"Cameras are off." She looks up at me with her pretty gray eyes, still full of storms but not the raging kind. They make me think of a perfect summer storm. I brush her hair over her shoulder and let my finger travel down her arm until the strap of her clutch is resting off of it.

I drop it to the ground and use my other hand to guide her hip and make her walk backwards. It only takes a few steps until the back of her thighs hit the bench. She lowers herself to sit and I kneel before her.

"I need these off." I cup the back of her right calf and start to untie her heel. I bend to kiss the inside of her knee before doing the exact same thing to her left.

"If you want shower sex, we can just go upstairs." I stand up again and open the locker behind her where she keeps her wraps. Hers are always somehow clean.

"We can have shower sex after if you want."

"You know I love a good workout, but I'm not exactly dressed for this right now." She motions down her outfit giving me the opportunity to appreciate it again.

"You're dressed perfectly for this workout." I keep the gray wraps I gave her a while ago in one hand and pull her to stand with the other. I walk her over to her favorite punching bag. I've never been more thankful for this bag being wall mounted. I swing it so it would be braced by the wall and not sway back and forth when I put her on it.

"I've been watching you beat the shit out of this bag for the better half of a year. Like you could beat your demons out of it." I move her to face me with her back to the bag. "Let me see your hands." She lifts her hands to me without question. The fact that she hands me her trust so easily now is still the best feeling in the world. I make sure to wrap her wrists with care so they are supported properly for what I'm about to do. Leaving enough of the end hanging, She knows what's coming next, this isn't our first time doing this. I've never tied her to any of the gym equipment though. And I've never used hand wraps but fuck it. Her eyes shine with anticipation. "Remember when I said that sometimes we have to change the habit?"

I watch her fight a grin as she nods her head. I move in closer to her. Close enough that my legs line up with hers and her chin rests on my chest when she lifts it to look at me. I tap twice on the exposed part of her thigh and she wraps her hands around my neck. I place my hands under her ass and lift her up. I pin her back to the back with her face so close to mine that our noses are touching. "Hands up, baby." I smile as my lips softly touch hers as I speak. She releases her hold from around my neck and does exactly as I ask.

I take the left over ends of each wrapped and tie them around the chain holding the bag off the ground. I lean in to test the stability by kissing her. She nips at my bottom lip and I feel my dick twitch with need. I kiss down her jaw, then neck, across her collar bone, until I hit that one spot on her shoulder that causes a wave of quakes down the back of her thighs. She moans so softly.

I grip the underside of her thighs as I bow down before her on each knees to keep her steady as I rearrange her legs to rest on my shoulders instead.

"I love this dress. You are breathtaking in it." She smiles down at me. "But it's kind of in my way." I move my hands over the top of her legs and grab each end of the dress where it is split by her hip and rip until her center is on full display. Confirming that she was, in fact, bare under this dress all night. "Fuck me, Jude." I swear under my breath but I was positive she still heard it because she left out a breathy giggle.

"I've been waiting for you to figure it out." *Fucking brat.*

I waste no time talking. I need to taste her more than I need to breathe at this moment. I take my time, just the way she likes. Soft strokes until I reach her clit and bite down before sucking the sting away. I look up at her to find her already staring back at me with hooded eyes.

I pull away and bite down on her inner thigh and suck there too. She tightens her legs around my head. I fucking love her legs. And I'd gladly die right here between them. I look back to her as I give her a few soft kisses.

"I want you to think of this moment, right here, with me worshipping your body every time you decide you need to try and beat the demons out of your head by punching this bag. They don't exist in this space anymore." I insert two fingers and revel in the choked gasp that leaves her lips. She pulls on the wraps and I feel her legs pull me in closer too.

"Please, Rory." She whines.

"Please?" I act like I don't know what she wants, but I know exactly what she wants. My girl is impatient.

"Stop talking." I barely let her get the last syllable out before I match the rhythm of my fingers with my tongue. I don't slow the pace or let up on the pressure. I feel her legs start to shake on my shoulders and suck hard on her clit as I curl my fingers inside her.

"Fuck, Rory!" *I love when she screams my name.*

And she comes undone on my tongue. I let her release coat my tongue and swallow thickly. Her body goes limp and I press up a little to give her more slack so her wrist isn't pulled too tightly. I finish cleaning her up with soft swirls of my tongue. Then I stand up and let her legs fall to wrap around my waist. She is a little too weak to hold on tight enough to keep her stable. So, I keep one arm around her as I untie the wraps one handed. She rests her head on my shoulder and sighs before placing the sweetest kiss to my neck. I start walking her with her torn dress barely hanging onto her body towards the back of the gym.

"Where are we going?" Her voice is so sex drunk and addictive.

"I'm not done with you, and you mentioned something about shower sex." I feel her hand tangle in my hair. It's my favorite thing she does when she gets like this. I don't know how our lives just fell in sync with each other. But she is the perfect balance to everything I've been searching for.

And for the first time in forever I can feel something whenever I'm with her. Our desires for each other and our lives are no longer fragmented. We are two halves of a searching soul that found peace with each other.

Oliver &
Mia

"That's a whole house."

The Poolhouse is not my favorite place to go out and get a drink. It's where I fight and let everything else fade out. But Mia decided days ago this was where she wanted everyone to go and asked me to make sure the guys were here, including Rory. Getting him here was less than hard. All we had to do was tell him that AJ was going to be here and he folded. He is now sitting twenty feet away from me trying to avoid all of the girls that recognize him and are trying to take their shot. They don't stand a chance though. The way that Rory orbits around my best friend is sickening. Another girl comes up and I watch his whole body seize up while trying to keep his distance.

Why I feel the need to help the poor fucker, I'm not sure. I make my way over to the space next to him and take a seat, bringing my bourbon with me. If I am going to willingly spend time with our new golden boy then I need the sweet burn to keep my blood going. He is so focused on keeping his attention on the door. He's always looking for AJ. He doesn't even notice me slide into the seat next to him.

"She will be here." I take a sip of my drink letting my eyes fall to the same spot his are solely focused on. He's waiting for AJ to walk through. I'm dreading the girl that she is going to walk in with. My dumbass brothers are a little further down on his other side with a group of girls, all laughing and being lively. Maxwell is always the magnet in every room. Eli is our steady pulse. And I'm always the shadow. Those are our roles and we fulfill them well.

Rory swivels to face me. "Why are you over here sitting next to me? Aren't you normally in the corner sulking in your loner boy aura?" *Fucker.* I let the rest of the whiskey burn down my throat before re-adjusting my grip around the glass.

"I figured you didn't want to be found talking to some random fan batting her eyelashes at you when AJ shows up." Just the simple fact that he had fangirls batting their fake eyelashes at him is enough to make me regret coming over here. AJ has been lighter lately though. And if Rory is the driving force behind that, then I will help cultivate that connection. She deserves only the good things this world has to offer. And if he ends up hurting her, then I'll make my brothers help me dig his grave. In the meantime though, I made a promise to Mia that I would be encouraging to Rory and help him with Avery. That girl seems to live to make my life hell. No matter how much healthy distance I try to keep from her, she somehow seems to soak every part of my life with her brilliant laugh, smart mouth, and her heart that is so full I don't even know how it fits in her chest.

"Thanks man." With me helping block any unwanted attention, he relaxes. "Do you think she is going to give me a real chance?" I feel for him, really I do. He won't look at me right now, but I can see his thoughts being flooded with the fear that AJ won't give him the opportunity to show her how much he cares. I've known AJ for years though, and she already gives him more time than I thought she ever had the capability of doing. She doesn't give people opportunities to get close to her. I had to fight like hell for my place in her life.

"I'll never speak for her." I scratch through the scruff on my jaw. I really need to shave. "She has never given someone her time like she does for you. It took me months just to get her to come down to the gym and workout with me." I have to maintain the balance of not giving too much of AJ away than she is comfortable with. "She just lives in this world where she thinks she has to stop herself from infecting others with the sharp edges of whatever is in her past." I try to level the shake in my voice. "If she does decide to give you a chance, you'll have to be patient with her. Don't let her give up believing she is worth it." Just thinking about AJ letting someone try to heal the parts of her she still hides from me and my brothers makes me emotional. She's a part of us.

"I'll take care of her." I hear the genuine promise in his voice. This conversation is much different from the one we had outside dad's apartment a few months ago. I wanted to punch him then for even thinking he was remotely good enough for her.

I start to say something else when a flash of blonde catches in the doorway that we had both been watching before our annoying little heart to heart. Mia and AJ just entered the room and I immediately know there is a strong possibility that I will start a fight tonight.

"Fuck me." *I need a new drink.* I lean my head back and squeeze my eyes closed. Maybe if I count to three, her outfit will be a hazmat suit instead of the torture device she thinks is that dress. No such luck. I open my eyes to find the girls searching around the room. That fucking dress though. It drapes over every inch of her body like the fabric was made to move when she moves. She turns to the side and I see that it has cutouts all up each side. With this new view of the dress, I feel every inch of my skin start to itch. She isn't wearing a damn thing under that dress and it is obvious to everyone in this room.

She's your best friend's new best friend. Avery needs Mia. Don't fuck that up for her.

That mantra is something I keep repeating to myself when Mia is around. It only helps sometimes.

I'm too caught up in keeping Rory from fighting the bartender over him wanting to ask AJ to dance to notice the girls making their way to the dance floor. Rory is wound tight now that AJ is here. If he really wanted to go after Tyler there is no way I was going to be able to stop him. Luckily we're both busy watching the girls and making sure that no one touches them without their permission. If that happens, blood will be spilled. Mia and I jokingly fuck with each other but I will lose my mind if someone touches her without her permission.

Rory lasts two songs before he is writing something on a napkin and making Eli walk it across the crowd to where the girls are. Their heads snap to where we are standing and I see a wicked grin resting on Mia's lips. Whatever Rory wrote on that napkin earned her approval. She's been rooting for them to get together since day one though. Eli cuts his way back through the crowd.

He stops in front us but he looks at me expectantly with raised eyebrows. "Mia wants a drink." Of course she fucking does. He doesn't even have to tell me what she wants. She knows I know her favorite drink. He turns to Rory and laughs. "AJ told me to tell you that if you had something to say then you can use your words." That's our girl. I hope she never stops giving him a hard time. Watching her be so much more alive with the self preservation aspect is the best thing.

I slap the top of the counter to get Tyler's attention and order a fucking cherry margarita, extra cherries. I watch the whole exchange between Rory and the girls. He spins Mia around and she giggles, I can almost hear her across the crammed space. He leans his mouth to her ear and she beams before looking back directly at me. Like she's known where I've been the whole time. I nod to the margarita sitting on the counter next to me.

She's so intentional with the way she moves and makes her way over to me.

"You ordered me a drink?" She wraps her dainty hands around the stem of the glass and her perfectly polished nails shine under the dim lights. She keeps them long enough to leave a mark, something I've thought about too many times to count.

"You wanted a drink." I watch her lips rest on the rim of the glass as she takes a sip before she does a small shimmy which causes the dress to move. She turns around to look for something and gives me a moment to freely appreciate the dress more without her calling me out for it. It's also backless, meaning I can smell the cherry body wash mixed with the sweat from where she's been dancing and I have to swallow and dig my fingers into the wood of the bar counter to stop myself from reaching out to her.

She spins back around with her nose all scrunched up and irritation clearly visible. "I asked Eli for a drink. Where did he go?"

Without taking my eyes off of her, I nod my head to my right in the opposite direction of the dance floor where quieter sections are. My brothers took their little party over there about fifteen minutes ago.

"Extra cherries?" She's fighting a smile at my doing something nice for her.

"You've been working hard out there. Figured you could use a snack." Her pretty lips smirk and I'm flooded with the need to messy them up. *No. Don't be a weak bitch. She's just a girl.*

I watch her tip the glass back and finish the drink in one gulp. She takes a step closer to me and uses her hips to press the inside of my knee to move it to the side so she can step between my legs. She is fitted perfectly in the space. I'm actively fighting the impulse to squeeze my legs tighter around her. She leans down with eyes never leaving mine. She sticks her tongue out just enough to get the drop of cherry juice from the last cherry she ate and then smiles reaching over my shoulder to put the empty glass behind me on the counter. She doesn't lean back though. She keeps invading my space further. She uses the same hand and trails her finger over my shoulder and across my neck, hooking it in the chain that I always wear. I have to lean my head back to keep eye contact with her. This is the game we play. We push, hoping the other breaks. And when neither of us do, we play again another day. She pulls me closer with her finger still looped around my necklace. "Dance with me." She isn't asking, she's daring. I smell the tequila on her breath mixed with the cherries and I have to steady my breathing. She can feel my resolve crumbling. I hesitate too long though. I give the slightest shake of my head and she takes two steps back. I have to grip my knees to have something to hold on to so I don't pull her back to me. She lifts a shoulder and shifts her focus to the idiot that has been watching her since she first came over to me. She places her hand in his and he makes the decision I couldn't. He follows her onto the dance floor. *Fucking menace.*

I keep my eyes on her for the next two hours. She has danced with more guys than I can keep up with. I nearly come undone when she starts making out with one of them. But she gave me the option for that to be me and I declined. Trying to be a good friend is exhausting. I also have no plans to leave while she is still here. AJ texted me as she and Rory went back to her place and asked if I would make sure Mia got home safe. I already planned on it.

Mia breaks away from her current dance partner and wobbles over next to me and looks around dramatically before pouting. "Where's my drink?"

"You drank it." I actually drank it half an hour ago. I push the ginger ale I ordered for her. She takes the glass and holds it above her head and squints at the bottom. "I put cherries in it. Just drink it." She smiles at me like she knows a secret before drinking the drink. She loses her balance and nearly falls forward but I'm close enough to wrap an arm around her to steady her. "I think it's time to take you home. Have you had enough fun tonight?" I wouldn't make her leave if she isn't ready but if she chooses to stay, she will have to drink more water and she hates water.

"You can take me home." She nods her head before resting it on my arm. Mia seems to always be sweeter when she drinks. I grab her phone and small bag she's kept around her wrist and support her through the building and to the parking lot. She stops walking as soon as we hit the black top though.

"What?" I take a deep breath as she huffs and crosses her arms.

"Carry me." She demands.

My eyebrows lift and she grins.

"You refused to dance with me and I look too hot for you to do that. So make it up to me." She holds her arms out. "Carry me." She wiggles her fingers to summon me closer.

I take her hand and wrap it around my neck, still holding her stuff in my other hand. I motion with my free hand for her to jump. She smiles excitedly before giving the smallest jump. I scoop her up with my one arm, lifting and cradling her to me. I take her all the way to my truck and buckle her up.

"This is hot. You're hot, Oliver West." Like I said, she's sweeter when she's drunk.

It's a short drive to her apartment and she stays quiet the whole time which isn't normal. My chest rattles with unease. She sits up slowly as I park. "Thanks for looking out for me tonight." I nod my head at her as she moves to try and get out.

"I got you, Mia. Hold on." She is too tipsy to walk herself up the stairs. I open her door and hold out my arm. "Want me to carry you again?"

She knocks my arms out of the way, grumbling something. The cold air must have sobered her up a little bit. Moody girl. I walk behind her and just casually hold my arms out around her to make sure if she stumbles she is caught. We reach the top of the stairs to her front door. She is shaking her small bag and threatening to throw it away if it doesn't cooperate. I bring my hand to my lips to smother the laughter trying to bubble out of my throat.

"It's not funny, Oliver." Glaring at me, she shoves her bag into my chest. "I can't find my keys." I take her bag and rifle through it, looking for her keys to appear. All I can see is three different lipglosses, cherry lifesavers, and bandaids.

"Did you leave your keys at AJ's?"

Mia throws her hands up and lets out a harsh breath. "Well I obviously don't know that, Oliver. I thought that they were in there. Now I'm homeless!"

"You're dramatic." I correct her as I zip up her bag after putting her phone in it. "You're not homeless. We will look for your keys tomorrow. I'm sure they are at AJ's." She reaches for the bag but I hold it out of reach. "And you're coming home with me. I have a spare bedroom you can sleep in."

"You want to take me home?" All agitation forgotten and her playful smile was back.

"Get in the truck, Mia."

"Yes sir." Her words roll down my body, causing tingles to travel down my spine.

"Don't do that." Her laughter lets me know she got the exact reaction she wants. *Brat.*

When we reach my long driveway, she launches her body forward so fast she nearly hits the dashboard.

"That's a whole house." She announces like I don't know what is sitting right in front of me.

"Great observation skills." She swats my arm and moves fast to get out of my truck when I put it in park. "Slow your ass down, Mia. You're going to get hurt."

She unlocks the door and steps out of the truck. She's still a little wobbly, but sturdier than she was. She turns around, her mouth still wide open. "Oliver."

"Yes, pretty girl?"

"You own a whole ass house!" I'm not sure why she is freaking out the way she is but it's the cutest thing I've ever seen.

"I'm aware." I lace my hand with hers and help guide her to the door. "Let's get you to bed."

Oliver and Mia

Coming Soon

Acknowledgements

I put off writing these for the longest time because I knew without a doubt that I would cry. This book was written literally off my blood, sweat, tears, sleepless nights, anxiety, and tireless efforts to hold everything together and never give up. I started writing this story in early April of 2025 and finished the first draft at the end of July of the same year. During that time, my husband had a massive car accident that reshaped our entire reality. And I genuinely believe this book is a testament to what someone can accomplish if they truly believe in it. Writing a book has proven to be the hardest thing I've ever done. It broke me countless times and it reminded me of the grit that rests deep in the marrow of my bones to never give up. And these people deserve all the love for standing with me and by me and holding me when I needed it and yelling at me when I needed it. They are the reason this book exists.

So, with that, my biggest thank you and acknowledgement will always go out to my husband. For always standing by me. For supplying me with redbull and snacks to keep me going. For letting me cry my heart out and fearing I will never be good enough to put this out here and then kindly pushing me to make it happen. You have always believed in my capability to do whatever I want to do. And you have been begging me to write a book for the entirety of us being together. This wouldn't exist without you. You never fail to tell everyone we meet that I wrote a book. Your pride in me for accomplishing this is so precious and heartfelt. You are the steady beat for which I wrote these words. And I love you for all that you do and all that you give. This book was written because you changed my life all those years ago when we met in that frozen yogurt shop. This book is truly the healing journey of a broken girl who was so afraid of breaking others and you taught me the truest definition of love and how to love others. My heart is so big because you never try to limit the way I use it to love.

Aubrey, you are my biggest cheerleader and we made a deal that 2025 would be our year. We just didn't know that I would randomly decide to write a whole book. I believe with my whole heart that our souls were always intertwined and designed to come together at the exact time that they did. Our grandmothers knew we would need each other to fill that gap. You are my best friend and I don't even know what a day looks like without you in it now. Thank you for literally every piece of support you give me. For loving every stage of this book. Thank you for screaming so loudly for me that I don't even hear the negativity. Thank you for reminding me that love should be unconditional. Thank you for understanding me to my deepest core. Thank you for being my favorite sad girl with a bite. I will always stand in "our" corner with you. Mia was written for you. For the girl that feels everything and loves loudly and full of so much talent and brilliance. Love you endlessly, your Killer.

Mik, you sweet angel, thank you for your endless love and support for this book. Thank you for editing it time after time. For being there for me to randomly message and keeping a running log of my chaotic thoughts. Thank you for loving these characters as much as I love them. Thank you for truly understanding the depth of what I wanted to show with this book and the love I wanted to give the readers through every character. God gave me you. I never doubt that. You are my sister in every sense of the word. I love you.

B. I love you forever, my sweet wild favorite redhead. You are the biggest source of family I have. You're more like my little sister than a niece. And I can't thank you enough for consistently telling me to write this book. You inspire me every day with how much you are always willing to take on and how much you are intentional about always growing and giving it your all. If you look closely, you are found in this book too. I love you with my whole heart, and will always be thankful for marrying into your family and having one of my closest friends for life because of it.

My editors, Mik and Jess. You sat with me in the trenches and helped meet deadlines and get this book into the beautiful version that it is now. Thank you for seeing the potential in the mess. I will forever be indebted to you both for all the work you put into this book.

My alphas, Jes, Delaney, Jasmin, and JJ. You all were the reassurance I desperately needed to keep my voice strong when writing. Thank you for handling my chaotic writing process and helping to make this book happen. For always being available for my questions to try and make each character and moment the best it can be. You are incredible and I love you all so much.

My betas, there are so many of you. Jasmin and JJ, thank you both for doubling up and being an alpha and a beta. Ailsin, for being the first beta to make me cry. Sophia, B, Courtney, Jillian, Bree, Jessi, Lizzy, Netty, Cyenna, Kristina, and Janelle. Thank you for giving your time and energy into this book. I am so grateful for your willingness to be a part of this.

To my West Haven Delinquints, you all jumped on this burning ship without hesitation and just made sure I had the support from day one. I love you for that. You loved my characters fiercely before you even got to meet them and that is wild. You are the best street team a girl could ever dream of having.

To the Luna team, you are all such inspiring and strong women. Knowing that my book was in your hands and that my readers were treated with the utmost respect and love was such a relief throughout this entire process. Lemmy, you are an angel on this earth and we do not deserve you. Thank you for making this entire thing happen in a much bigger way than I could have imagined.

To my readers, if you are still here, it was long. I will not apologize because I am a firm believer in everyone getting recognized for the support that they show and I love screaming about the people that are in my corner. I hope that AJ and Rory spoke to you on a personal level. I hope you are ready for Mia and Oliver's story next. And I hope that every single one of you has an Eddie who is always ready to protect you in a heartbeat.

M.K. Jensen is a lover girl at heart, a wife, and writer. She thrives off of organized chaos, redbulls, and pizza. She's obsessed with going on random adventures and therapy car rides with her dog. Playlists are her favorite form of showing love. She adores all the small details of everything. She is known to binge tv shows and stay up all night devouring a good book.

Feel free to say hi:
Instagram: @mkjensenauthor
Email: mkjensenauthor@gmail.com